A Question of Realities

A QUESTION of REALITIES

Book Three of The Grid Saga

J. J. Overton

ISBN: 9798779591324

For Sandra, David and Chris, and this time, for the other people who have made my life significant. This includes Doug and Mary Horton, David and Violet Davies, Stephen Horton and especially, Connor Horton for his encouragement just when it was needed.

Acknowledgments

Grateful thanks to the following: Sandra Horton, Mike Williams, Heather Harper and Pauline Weston for their Beta reading. Grateful thanks to David and Chris Horton. Brenden Hindhaugh and Andy Docking provided original thinking and some wild laughter during my writing of the books in The Grid Saga. Thank you, Brenden and Andy. Also, a big thank you to Toby Knight for admitting that he reads the Grid Saga books more than once.

Glossary.

Wasiri-Poya. The world where all things began. Home of the Wasiri-Chanchiya.

Wasiri-Chanchiya. The people from the beginning of time.

Thar-Thellin Spiral. The home Galaxy of the Wasiri Chanchiyans.

Stessar Tharon. The double star system containing Wasiri-Poya.

Stessar Tharon 7. Wasiri-Poya in the Stessar Tharon system.

Wasari. More than a single person of the Wasiri-Chanchiya.

Wasaru. A single person of the Wasiri-Chanchiya.

Wasar. The universal language of Planet Wasiri-Poya.

The Second One. The name the Wasiri-Chanchiyans call the Earth.

The Hnioss. The Great Council of Worlds who oversee the administration of the known and the emerging worlds.

Hnion. An individual member of the Hnioss.

Ahra-Than. One of the lands on Wasiri-Poya. Hnions reside in Ahra-Than.

Krel-Rahn. Preceptor of the Hnioss.

Lan-Si-Nu. Grid Commander. He is a Wasaru.

Fen-Nu. She is also a Wasaru and is Lan-Si-Nu's second in command.

Thal-Nar. A Wasaru and Temporal Engineer in Lan-Si-Nu's crew of three.

Sar-Theit-Nos. One of the ancient Grid Travellers.

The Great Annals. The entire body of knowledge and exploration attained by the Travellers of the Grid.

∿ The Onnoth symbol, standing for The First One, Wasiri-Poya, in Wasiri-Chanchiyan.

Phaelon 23057C. Wasiri-Chanchiyan for the Milky Way galaxy.

Hnirath of Science. A Mastership of learning on Wasiri-Poya.

Comash. The couch on which the Wasiri-Chanchiya empty their minds and rest.

Chakrakan. A rogue planet. One-time sister to the Earth. Moved in ancient times from its twin planet position for the safety of Earth's inhabitants. Chakrakan is known as Nibiru to the people of Earth.

Chak. An inhabitant of Chakrakan.

Specier. A Chakrakan measure of distance

1

Magnetism fascinated young Charlie Villiers. The unseen forces involved as the nine-year-old moved two bar magnets close to each other, like pole to like, held an air of mystery that he felt compelled to investigate.

The bar magnets were painted an exciting bright red, apart from a quarter-inch of shiny metal at the north ends, which were stamped with a capital N. The red was a hot colour, not a dull nondescript red, but a brilliant flame-red, appropriate for the hidden forces pushing the magnets apart. *Like poles repel, unlike poles attrac*t, he read in the Encyclopaedia Britannica.

He turned the bars around and offered them up to each other. It surprised him how difficult it was to keep them apart. It was almost as if there was something physically intervening. Some invisible alien fingers pulling the magnets together. As he tested the way the magnets behaved, the young boy's mind fastened onto an interest that in his teenage years would develop into an obsession to understand the nature of matter.

Over the next years there was intense study and at night, to save electricity, a candle shed its feeble flickering light over the textbooks which were beyond Charlie's years but which he understood.

University followed and during a period of intense research, he wrote a thesis about an object that was being talked about in obscure circles. The theorists were convinced that a rogue planet that some called Planet X, and others called Nibiru, was approaching the Earth from the obscure reaches of the solar system. Villiers, as he worked on mathematics, viewed himself as a potential saviour. The young man reasoned on a powerful way to address the threat. In short order came a doctorate and slender years later a professorship and research at the Cavendish Laboratory in Cambridge, alongside Ernest Rutherford.

Villiers' mind yearned for more space than the enclosed walls of the Old Cavendish. He was unusual in this regard because most young scientists would have given their eye teeth for a chance to work with Rutherford. But not Villiers. In 1943, he shipped to the States from Liverpool on the ship, Tyndareus in Convoy ON181, to work at Los Alamos with Oppenheimer on the Manhattan Project.

Almost immediately there was intense disagreement between the two men with the way the project was developing on a war footing. After an argument during which they had to be separated by other members of the team, Villiers returned to England and was given space and money to set up a laboratory in a disused, out-of-the-way part of Warwickshire's MoD Kineton.

In Kineton's obscurity, he worked, on the face of things, on research for the protection of the public from radiation in the event of nuclear war. In reality, his government money allowed him to spend half his time on the protection of the public and the other half of his time on the theme of his thesis, how to address the threat Nibiru posed to the Earth.

1959

It was after the End Time weapon, his solution to the Nibiru problem, was cased up and ready, that Professor Charles Villiers had a chance meeting over a beer in a local public house with Josiah Dearden. A close friendship developed and Villiers made regular excursions to Dearden Hall Farm. With Josiah, he spent some time in Leofwin's Hundred, the nearby forest, a place that he soon realised was associated with ancient legend and mystery.

This was also the time when Villiers and his team began to research sub-atomic particles in a way tangential to the accepted hierarchy of physics, and one morning, when Villiers entered his laboratory in R1, a mainly disused building in MoD Kineton, that he noticed something weird going on in the hollow core of a large high-frequency induction coil.

The eight-foot diameter coil was part of a state-of-the-art circuit that involved electro-magnetism. It had been placed, for convenience while it was on test, some three feet away from a lead-lined cupboard where a small amount of antimatter was stored. Not that the team fully understood the nature of antimatter, which they stumbled upon by chance; but the combination of antimatter, magnetism and another newly found component produced the side effect of a vortex in the hollow centre of the coil. When they peered into the vortex and saw what looked like a landscape, Villiers and his assistants failed to realise that they had glimpsed the landscape of an alien world.

"Do you notice anything odd about that?" Villiers said to his assistant, Professor Robbie Cranford.

"Do you mean how the movement taking place in the

landscape is in slow motion?"

"Yes . . . unnaturally so, don't you think?"

There was a sight of the other world once more during the months that followed. It fascinated them. And then they found out how to amplify the core.

Sheet metal fabricators constructed a door frame to house components Villiers came across on one of his expeditions into Leofwin's Hundred with Josiah Dearden. When it was finished the team called the completed device the *Switch*. The importance of its function determined that the first letter of its name should be capitalised.

They fitted the fabricated frame around the doorway into a room at the far end of the laboratory. The room itself appeared to serve no purpose. It was a nondescript room. The walls were built with an unusual looking material, sandwiched in layers. It was interesting, historically, however. It smelt ancient, and of earth, and it had a mosaic floor that Villiers and Cranford, both of whose forte was science, not history, assumed was Romano-Celtic. There were wall paintings too, of tall, slender figures with the remnants of a light green colour on their faces, and the figures had oddly shaped hands. History aside, Villiers decided to experiment with the Switch device.

After dark one evening, Villiers took his close friend, Richard Martell, the Keeper of the Knight's Templars' Sanctuary in Temple Balsall, to his laboratory. He took Martell along because Villiers craved support for his ideas and needed praise for the unique device he had been working on. It began as an innocent excursion, but an hour later the two men bitterly regretted meeting up that evening.

*　*　*

Earlier in the day Villiers' team had completed the internal circuitry and fitted the last of the panels onto the face of the fabricated door frame. Switch-on was planned for the following morning. Villiers was usually meticulous with procedures, particularly when working close to the boundaries of current knowledge. Every system was usually triple-checked to ensure that its function was fail-safe. However, a moment of foolhardiness overtook him and he overlooked the vital decision he had stipulated, that the newly constructed device should only be used for observation.

With Martell at his side, Villiers switched on the high-tension supply and above the slight buzz of the electronics within the door frame, he heard what he initially thought was music. He opened the door and was captivated by the vision.

"Where on earth is that?" Martell asked in a hushed voice. He and Villiers peered at the land they could see clearly through the doorway. Without thinking, they walked forward.

It only took half a dozen paces past the doorway for them to realise that the place they walked into bore no resemblance to anything they had experienced before. Even the blowing breeze was strange. There was a cloying feel to it as it touched their skin, as if the moving air had more viscosity to it than there should have been. Villiers looked around, saw small colourless masses that made no sense to his vision. He was trying to analyse the strange sight when the wind gusted and the door slammed shut behind them. Villiers, in a moment of panic, rushed back to the door and tugged it open. The panic turned to terror because all he could see through the doorway was blackness, interspersed with countless stars.

Before that fearful day, Professor Robert Styles Cranford, Villiers assistant in MoD Kineton, had been the last person to leave the laboratory. He was the first in next day. All the lights were on, but Cranford knew for certain that he had switched off the lights before he left the previous evening. At first, he suspected a break-in. The lab was full of data and the End Time Weapon, crated up and under wraps, was a prize any rogue government would like to get their hands on. The weapon was on the Diamond T Low-loader trailer, ready for despatch to whenever it could be used.

At the far end of the laboratory, a light above the door they called the Switch was illuminated, which indicated that the equipment had been switched on. Commencement of the trial was scheduled for ten a.m., so the light should not yet be on. Ted Roper, the foreman machinist, startled Cranford when he came into the lab from the workshop and asked about a machining tolerance.

Cranford ignored him. "Ted, come to the Switch with me, will you?" he said, "That warning light over the door shouldn't be on."

When they got close to the door frame, ambient heat was radiating from it and they could hear the distinctive buzz of HT current. Cranford carefully opened the metallic door, saw the blackness and the stars and slammed the door shut. He gasped and stepped back quickly.

"What the hell was that?" Roper asked.

"It appears to be a star-field," Cranford said.

"But how can it be?"

"I have no real answer to that . . . I wish I had."

Roper looked at Cranford, who was illuminated by the dim light some distance away in the lab. "What is that . . .

thing?" He pointed to the door, set in its frame, and his hand was shaking.

"It's a type of switch . . . we think it goes to other places."

"You can say that again."

"The point is, Villiers stipulated that we should make observations through the Switch, and now I think the damn fools stepped through it. See here," Cranford pointed to the floor and picked up Villiers' notebook which was lying on the threshold of the doorway. "He never usually goes anywhere without this notebook. It contains all of his ideas."

In the ensuing months, the technology to produce mapping of the places that the Switch accessed was impossible to devise. Professor Robbie Styles Cranford did his best with further research. But it was highly theoretical and technical beyond the brightest flame of intellect of the nineteen fifties.

Cranford gave his effort to find Villiers a further six months. Once a week, always with two or three of the team present as witnesses, he opened the door, but the team obtained no result that would help them rescue Villiers. There was nothing beyond the door when they opened it but a black void and an infinite number of stars. Very occasionally there was a brief glimpse of worlds that defied reason.

"We've done all we can here. Villiers has had it," Cranford announced to the team gathered around him one day in August 1960. Money Villiers had siphoned off from government sources to pay for the End Time Weapon only had a month and a few days to run.

"Before we leave we must seal up the Switch," Cranford said. There were objections to this because the men said Villiers was still some place beyond the doorway, but as the senior man, Cranford's word was law. He ordered lead sheet, a quantity of dressed Hornton Ironstone blocks, cement and sand for mortar, and they sealed up the opening against outside meddling. To finish the job, one of the machinists, who was also a carpenter, disguised the Switch by installing another door in a wooden frame, directly in front of it.

2

2010

There was anger and confusion after Harry and Esma walked through the door. Villiers had been trying for years to figure out a construct of information and technology to get him and Martell back home.

Villiers, to his complete frustration, could not make the equipment to get them back home. He had plausible theories about where they were and had been able to make some tools, which were primitive, but sufficient to help him and Martell build a shelter. It had two separate living quarters because there were times when they got sick of each other and argued violently.

Apart from the occasional exploratory journey which would last for a few days when the adventurous spirit took over, Villiers and Martell never moved far away from the door in the odd-looking wall partially hidden by weird vegetation. The door was their link to home, although, as time passed, home became a distant memory. When they opened the door, which they did quite regularly, they saw a different place each time, usually it was a view of the cosmos. There were occasions, although they were seldom, when the door opened onto another new world, always an unfamiliar place. Never Earth.

And then, two people, a man and woman, he, maybe in his early twenties and she, could be slightly older, burst through the door. Villiers had yelled at them urgently not to shut the door, but they shut it before what he had shouted registered with them and the way back home was lost again.

Charles Villiers had an edgy temperament. People had said that it went with his creative nature. Sometimes his sheer brilliance of invention was subsumed by periods of rage over the slightest challenge.

"Oh, you stupid young fools, that's torn it," he shouted, as he ran up to them. And then he broke into a chain of expletives, some of which the Anglo-Saxon girl, Esma, recognised. Esma retreated behind Harry and peeped over his shoulder at the man who was purple with rage.

Harry's first reaction at seeing the apparition of someone he thought was dead, was to step back and gasp,

"Professor Villiers . . . but you disappeared."

"Good observation; I did disappear, along with my colleague." He started ranting again and then the other man arrived, short of breath after running.

"Shut your damn mouth or I'll shut it for you," the other man shouted, at which Villiers shut his mouth, simmered down, and looked embarrassed.

"I am sorry. Dick has to keep me in check," he said. "Sometimes things get out of hand . . . up here," he tapped his head. "This is my colleague, Richard Martell. Dick was the Keeper of the Knight's Sanctuary back in Temple Balsall. My apologies, young man. I ought to have been pleased to see you; and you too, young lady." Villiers' voice sounded cultured, like the BBC English of the nineteen-forties.

"You have added your problem to ours," Villiers said.

"What problem—"

"The damn doorway. The doorway you just came through is shut again. The link is variable and we can't get back home. We could have done if you had kept the door open."

Out of habit Harry looked at his watch. It was a quartz watch, with hands. It had developed a fault. The hands were moving far quicker than they ought to be. He unstrapped it and put it in his pocket. He would see to it later. He didn't intend being phased by Villiers' attitude.

"Professor Villiers, I would suggest that, if we are going to get through *our problem*, we should get together and work on it in a constructive way. What do you think about that idea?" The professor looked him in the eye. After a second, he nodded.

"Point taken, young man . . . shall we talk things through?"

They went to the place Villiers and Martell had built. There was a communal area separating their living quarters, which were built one each end of the ramshackle shelter. The tools in Harry's tote-bag rattled when he put it down and sat on the ground. Esma sat by his side and tried to understand what Harry was saying when he asked probing questions about their surroundings. Villiers felt he was under interrogation by the young man and he became prickly, prompting Martell to become impatient with him again. He stomped off to a container, came back with drinks and after a while the atmosphere lightened. The liquid was surprisingly good, definitely alcoholic, served in purple earthenware vessels, which Harry thought marred the effect.

"There's a preponderance of manganese in the rocks and soil here. That's what has given these cups a purple hue,"

Harry studied his vessel. Rough-made, still with thumb and finger marks, but rock-hard. He placed his own thumb and fingers into the marks. "It's not bad as a colour," he said. "I'd prefer a glass to drink from, but the drink's good, whatever the colour of the container."

They got to talking about their situation. Villiers spoke

about the planet they had ended up on. They had taken to calling it Earth 2. Harry told them about Earth 1 and its encounter with Nibiru. Villiers was fascinated by what Harry recounted.

"So, a delivery system for my End Time Weapon was developed in time?"

"It was, and it was on track to preventing Nibiru colliding with the Earth." Harry told them how, at almost the last minute, it was discovered that Nibiru was inhabited, and because of that the End Time weapon was diverted.

When the trauma of the entry into the alien world had cooled, Harry's incisive mind began to analyse the observations he had been storing up mentally. Vegetation was radically different to all the species of Earth vegetation he was familiar with. Not that he was a botanist, but he had a photographic memory and his retention of information gave him a prolific amount of data at his disposal, and he had the ability to reason on it in a refined way.

*   *   *

The weeks went by, much of it spent in the exchange of ideas with Villiers and Martell. Harry was upbeat most of the time. One time, when they were sitting in the communal area of the hut, Harry launched into an explanation of what he understood about the world on which they were marooned. He spoke about the huge life-forms, and the odd physical attributes of the surroundings.

"What I can detect about the vegetation, if that's what it is, reminds me of some research I did after one of the Controversial TV programs."

"Controversial TV?"

"Yeah. It was a television channel that always broadcasted challenging information. Things the establishment didn't want in the public domain. Anyway, one of the programs was about Mycelial life and its connectivity."

Villiers was controversial at heart, challenging by nature, which is why his inventions breached the frontiers of science. "Tell me more," he waited expectantly.

Harry pointed, "See there, how the vegetation bunches up in groups, and the foliage of each separate tree, or whatever they are, move in an identical way. And then a distant group responds. It reminds me of the murmuration of a flock of starlings, how they appear to instantly communicate when they're in flight. That's what I'm seeing with these lifeforms, mass communication." Villiers scanned the emerald green foliage and saw how the movement was being replicated. Group compared to group the movement was identical.

"Where will knowing that about the Brobs get us?"

"Brobs?"

"Brobdignag, the land of giants Gulliver went to. Jonathan Swift . . . Gulliver's Travels, remember? We call those things the Brobs. Seems appropriate because they are Brobdignagian in size. Dick thought of it."

Martell smirked.

"OK, Brobs it is." Harry humoured Martell. "Anyway, there's something else. See what's happening now?" The others looked at the vegetation. Villiers shook his head and said, "The foliage is pointing toward us. All of it. Even those in the distance."

"Trees know we are here," Esma suggested.

"Exactly," Harry agreed. "That is my conclusion, take it or leave it. Do you think what we're seeing is communication between those lifeforms?"

"Maybe we are seeing that. I reserve judgment," Villiers said.

"That's OK. Do you want to hear more?" Villiers and Martell nodded. Esma looked puzzled.

"I think that this vegetation is fungal, even the big stuff. I also think that it could be a higher form of life that is vegetable but also possesses intelligence."

"I have wondered why we see no sign of animal life, as we know it," Martell interjected. He was astute in his comments. He said little but thought a lot. Only when there was a real need did he comment. "The life here is different to anything we know," he said.

Harry was surprised at Martell's comment. It should have come from the scientist. "There is something else," Harry then seemed at a loss for words, embarrassed, which was unusual for him these days.

When they had been on their own, out of earshot of the other two, he and Esma had talked about time, the passage of years. "They have been here nearly fifty years, why don't they show their age?" Harry had said.

"How old they are?" Esma's modern English had been slightly wrong again.

"Counting in Earth-years I think Villiers should be more than a hundred years old."

"He is no looking sixty years."

"I have an interesting idea about ageing in this place," Harry said to the two men. Villiers looked attentive.

Harry took his watch from his pocket and held it up for Villiers and Martell to see. The hands were moving too quickly.

"I think the ageing process here is slowed right down. My

watch is still showing Earth-time. I don't know why that is happening yet, but I have ideas about it."

Villiers nodded knowingly.

Esma liked Harry's ideas. She liked to hear his voice when he explained them. Often, she didn't understand the things he said, but she trusted him. Trusted his eyes. She knew when he told her his ideas that they were true. So, when Harry was embarrassed to speak about the age of the two men, Esma took over. With her upbringing she didn't give a damn about what other people thought of her.

"How old are you?" Her gaze was direct. First at Villiers, then at Martell. This time she got the English right.

3

Jem Dearden concluded that Harry and Esma were dead. It had been eight days since they disappeared and Dearden felt the empty space where Harry should have been. The disappearance was way out of character for Harry because he was usually meticulous with his communication. It was part of the deal allowing him his own rooms at Dearden Hall, that he had to communicate.

"As long as you don't do anything that would blow the place up or set it on fire you can stay here," Dearden said when he was setting out the deal. "The only thing I will stipulate is that you keep me up to date with the science you are doing in your lab."

That arrangement had been agreed nearly three years ago and now Harry and Esma were seriously missing. If Dearden could have predicted the future from Harry's conversation before he disappeared he would have ensured that the strange events that followed wouldn't have happened.

Before the disappearance Harry and Dearden had gone to the Green Man pub in nearby Hampton in Arden. They found a corner Ken Tillman had restored to its former condition after the cyclone had destroyed half of the public house. Out of the way in the corner's quietness, they could speak their minds.

"Villiers was working on a divergent branch of physics, Jem," Harry had confided. It was a thought that had been bugging him from the time he had been in Charles Villiers' lab three hundred feet below the Castle Inn at Edge Hill village. He had to share his thoughts.

Dearden was silent, but curious as he waited for Harry to

explain what he had found in the old laboratory. He surveyed Ken Tillman's substitute for Abbot Ale, how it sparkled in the glass and retained its head, and said, "Tell me more."

"There is an anomaly I discovered in the lab and I'm not comfortable with it."

"What anomaly?"

Harry leant forward, thinking, considering his words. He spoke quietly.

"I have noticed that Villiers put aside the research into the End Time weapon. It was as if he divorced himself from the Nibiru threat and moved on to something else."

"What did he move on to?" Dearden asked.

"That's a bit vague. One of the formulaic expressions I found in his notes implied that he had found an entry to an alternative reality."

Dearden laughed. He took another swig of the substitute Abbot and considered the young man sitting the other side the table. Harry was usually very rational.

"You don't really believe that rubbish, do you?"

"Without a doubt I do, I've seen the math," Harry said.

A few days after Harry and Esma had gone missing, Dearden, against his better judgment, told Lan-Si-Nu about his conversation with Harry in The Green Man. It prompted the alien to mention layered universes, and that sometimes, by the smallest touch, the universes merged.

Dearden laughed.

"You may find humour in what I say," the alien said, "But don't you think that what you have experienced with the Grid in recent years tests your perception of reality? Reality and our experiences sometimes do not make easy bedfellows. Occasionally we have to accept as real what is different, and difficult to understand."

"Why do you say that?" Dearden asked Lan-Si-Nu, who dwarfed him as they sat side by side on the sofa. Rowan made up a threesome, sitting the other side of Dearden. The others were sitting opposite, hanging on every word. Occasionally the alien did become philosophical.

"Think about it, Jem. What is reality?"

Dearden thought he would humour the alien, so he went along with the question. "Communication, experience marking the passage of time. Thoughts and ideas . . . feelings, occurrences."

"That is correct. These things you mention are events. Take events away, particularly the ones exterior to ourselves, and time and reality would be unmeasurable . . . because time and reality are defined by events. Here's another thought." Sometimes the alien taught the people of Earth by illustrations.

"Please accept what I say, that there are different universes, realities that exist in dimensions parallel to ours. If one of you Earth people were to experience the universe layer where physical laws are lightly bound together, events would flow in hyper-mode. In the universe at the opposite end of the scale, where physical laws are very restrictive and tight, the time taken to experience the blooming of a flower would be epic."

Dearden thought how epic was the knowledge they had learnt of late. The alien continued his explanation.

"In between these two extremes of physical laws lie many universe layers in different dimensions of existence. Each one of them is its own Reality. Near the centre of those layers the universe exists containing the planet Earth and in a distant galaxy, my home planet, Wasiri-Poya, the World Where All

Things Began. Ours is the Prime Reality."

"You said that sometimes the universes merge," Jules said. "We experience times when irrational events occur . . . when we feel and see inexplicable things. Maybe that is when the overlapping of Realities occurs, do you think?"

"Yes, it could well be. You need to open your minds to all manner of possibilities. If you have an open mind you will be able to accept the great difference of realities that do exist."

"I'm not sure about all this," Dearden said, trying to distance himself from the speculation. Although having experienced some surreal stuff in the past few years he thought alternative realities too near the realms of imagination.

Lan-Si-Nu took a long swig of the Pinot Grigio he had in a pint glass. He drank with no effect from the alcohol.

Now there's a different reality, Dearden thought, as the alien drained the glass and asked for another.

4

Five months had passed since the near passage of Nibiru. The changes brought about on the Earth had started to be accepted by the majority of people but a comfort zone was what folks really needed after the stresses of recent months. Nibiru had altered comfort radically.

With the day-to-day affairs of the SHaFT organisation, Dearden led a busy life and this helped him forget the weird idea of alternative realities. It was too much to cope with. He didn't want to face-up to the possibility of Harry and Esma, by some freak accident of science, having been transported to an alternative reality. Dearden pushed the conversation about reality that he had with Lan-Si-Nu to the back of his mind. Trouble was, the conversation sometimes snuck back in.

Tension was still present months after the cyclones stopped. It would take years for the near obliteration events to be forgotten. There were still raw edges amongst the reduced population, although how much it was reduced was still unknown. If incoming statistics proved to be correct, the world population could be half the size it had been.

Life for most people was a relief after Nibiru had been re-positioned by the Wasiri-Chanchiyans. After the planet's passage there was a social levelling when finance suffered its worst ever crash because of the Great Internet Outage. The levelling was welcomed with relish by the poorest in society.

* * *

Sir Willoughby Pierpoint had a source of petrol and he spent a good many miles on the road with his driver, Harvey

Proctor, attempting to contact the SHaFT operatives. Pierpoint's thought about the SHaFT organisation was that its modus operandi would change, but just how it would change could only become apparent over the course of time. An avaricious element was still present on Earth, and because of that, SHaFT would still have work to do.

Bill Templestone had come to see Dearden to borrow some wood-chisels for a job at Keeper's Cottage, where he lived, in Temple Balsall. He stayed the evening for a meal with Jem and Rowan. He missed Harry. The young man's readiness to smile had endeared him to Templestone, who although he loved his daughter, Becky, dearly, had wanted a son too, but his wife died, and there was no son.

Harry Stanway was the nearest Templestone got to having a son and most days since Harry's disappearance he thought of the times they had together. Despite the disparity of their ages they had common interests and their sense of humour was similar. On some occasions they would laugh riotously over an obscure thing that would leave a bystander wondering about the laughter. When Templestone had been kidnapped a while back, and Harry thought he was dead, it left the young man bereft.

They were sitting around the fire after the meal at Dearden Hall, chatting as they used to when Templestone was living with Dearden and Rowan above the stained glass studio across the courtyard. The conversation turned to Harry.

"There's still no clue about what happened to them?" Templestone asked.

"Not yet. We won't give up hope, but I think the chances

are that we won't see them again."

"Sometimes we think of things, where they might be. We go and search, but we are always disappointed," Rowan said.

Later that evening the three of them went to the Green Man. Tillman was grateful that Mitch Doughty and Matt Roberts had repaired the roof.

"Drinks are free tonight," he said to Dearden when he ordered at the bar. Rowan and Templestone had gone to the corner where Dearden had sat with Harry when the young man told him about Villiers' alternative line of research.

Dearden nearly spilled the drinks when he put them down on the table. He was frowning and sat down heavily. Rowan asked if he was OK.

"I've remembered something Harry told me. We sat here before he disappeared. Harry sat where you are, Bill" Dearden felt uncomfortable about what he was going to say. "It could be what happened to Harry and Esma, although I've got a lot of doubt about it." He went quiet as he tried to recall what Harry said, and then what Lan-Si-Nu told him about reality on that occasion he'd been trying to forget. He couldn't get his head around alternative realities. Maybe he'd had enough of the weird stuff going on around Leofwin's Hundred.

"Come on, then . . . tell us." Templestone put his glass down and waited expectantly.

"I think this is impossible but here goes."

"With what's happened around here anything's possible. Just tell us what's on your mind."

Dearden checked to see if anyone was within earshot. He leant forward, indicated for them to get closer, Spoke quietly.

"It was what Harry said when we came here before he and

Esma vanished." Dearden told them what Harry said about Villiers working on a divergent branch of physics.

"Divergent? What means this . . . divergent?" Rowan asked. Dearden explained what divergent was, and then,

"Harry told me that Professor Villiers was working on something new. It was radical. He said Villiers had found an entry to an alternate reality—"

"Ah, I see, and then Villiers disappeared mysteriously." Templestone smiled.

"And being in this place again made me remember." Dearden was deadly serious. He signalled for them to get closer still. Looked around to make sure no-one was in earshot. Spoke quietly. "Harry and Esma may have gone some place Villiers knew about as a result of his experiments."

"And Harry did ask you to help him get into the R1 at MoD Kineton." Rowan said.

"He did. Harry desperately wanted to get into Villiers' laboratory."

"Have you been there since we took the End Time weapon out?" Templestone asked. Dearden avoided his gaze.

"Well?"

"Briefly."

"Why briefly?"

"There wasn't much to see."

"Maybe there wasn't . . . on the surface. You should have taken Jules with you; her thinking is forensic."

Dearden considered this. "You may be right," he said.

"I am."

Rowan stood, "We must get Jules to help us," she said.

"OK . . . let's do it." Dearden finished his pint. "Drink up," he said to Templestone, then he keyed his mobile. The signal was weak but usable and he rang Julia Linden-Barthorpe.

At Moat Field Cottage, in Kenilworth, Julia's mobile rang. It was unusual for Dearden to ring at this time of night.

"We think we may have discovered where Harry and Esma disappeared from. We need your help."

"What, now?"

"Sooner than now if you can do it."

"I'll try. But give me a reason."

"We need your forensic skill in Repository One. We think R1 is where they disappeared from."

"Really?"

"It's to do with Villiers."

"Ah," she said, as if that explained everything. "Do you want me now?" and then, "Sorry, I'll re-phrase that. Do you want me to come over now?"

"We do. We need to get onto this straight away." Dearden heard Clive Fraser's voice muttering in the background. He and Jules were close now. Where she went, he went.

Jules and Clive met Jem and the others at Dump Four in Kineton within the hour. Mitch Doughty was there too, after a call from Dearden. Security was still tight but, at the gatehouse, the SHaFT team were instantly recognised. They were through the main gate in a few seconds.

Dearden had also invited Will Pierpoint along. Pierpoint felt valued, but he also felt it was time to hand over the reins to Dearden. It had been on his mind for a while so the meeting came at the right time. Sir Willoughby Pierpoint felt tired; things locally were getting rather out of this world and with that, very technical. Apart from that, he had begun to forget things that mattered. A younger, more connected mind would be better at the top.

Will Pierpoint suggested they meet outside his office in

Dump Four before they went to R1. He didn't have far to go from Ireton Grange, in Radway, to get to MoD Kineton's Dump Four, the headquarters of SHaFT.

Pierpoint was waiting for the others with a screwdriver in his hand. He came straight to the point.

"It's over to you now, Jem." Pierpoint unscrewed his brass nameplate from his office door. He passed it to Dearden and carefully, screw by screw, attached the new nameplate that was engraved for him by an artisan in Warwick.

Jeremiah Dearden, C.E.O., was incised deeply into the brass and the letters were picked out with black enamel infill.

"There it is. It's all yours now. I'm tired. I'll be on hand of course. Anything you need, Jem, just give me a call, but not too late at night or too early in the day." Pierpoint checked his watch. It was nearly midnight. "I understand there's a lead about our missing youngsters," he said to Dearden.

"We think they may have gone missing from Villiers' laboratory," Dearden said. He extended his hand and took Pierpoint's; they shook, looked each other in the eye. Both knew SHaFT would be OK.

"So, lead on," Pierpoint said. "There's still life remaining in the old dog, and adventure is the spice of life."

5

Lieutenant Colonel Mike Ramsay had developed into somewhat of a maverick. The Passage of Nibiru had altered his frame of mind and no longer did he need a stream of bureaucracy to back up his decisions in the management of MoD Kineton. And neither was there as much bureaucracy to get in the way now.

Ramsey had become very much like Matt Roberts, ex Royal Navy Commander, who left the navy quickly after he got sick of his captain and punched him on the jaw. Roberts and Ramsay now got along famously.

Ramsay had taken to wearing a bandana, the same as Roberts. He was still station commander of MoD Kineton, and due to his unilateral decision to release the End Time weapon, as it turned out, at the right time, his value was recognised by those high up in the chain of command and in government. His change of demeanour was tolerated.

Dearden, Pierpoint and the others walked from Dump Four and met Ramsay at his headquarters in the nineteen-thirties building with steel-framed windows. Armed guards were less in evidence at MoD Kineton after the directive to dismantle nuclear weapons came from Lars Knudsen, broadcasting to the Second Renaissance world from his UN residence in Sutton Place, Manhattan.

"People of Earth, the threat of destruction by Nibiru is in the past. We are now on the threshold of an amazing and fulfilling future . . ." and Knudsen then laid out the essentials leading along the pathway to peace. But because of its history to do with storing high-powered weaponry, security was still tighter at MoD Kineton than anywhere else on Earth.

*   *   *

The massive door at the entrance to R1 stood before them. Jules looked up at their height, where they were hung on a cross-rail below the curved, grass-covered roof of the repository. The stars of the Milky Way shone brightly above, illuminating the outline of the building. Now, whenever she saw the stars Jules felt optimism. She grasped Clive's hand. Ramsay found the large old key on the antiquated ring, opened the personnel door and led the way through. He locked the door behind them. The familiar smell of protective oil and grease was strong in the air. As they walked down the length of R1 Mitch Doughty recalled entering the storage place the first time. He had burned through a chain which secured the iron gates barring entry to the tunnel leading to Villiers' laboratory underneath Edge Hill.

The gates were still partly ajar and the darkness of the tunnel was partially illuminated by dim light from the bulbs running on MoD Kineton's emergency generators.

"What are you expecting to find?" Jules asked Dearden.

"I have no idea, but when Harry and I talked in the Green Man, he said about Villiers working on a divergent branch of science. A couple of days before he disappeared Harry asked me to help him get into R1 so he could search Villiers' lab."

"And you've examined the lab?"

"We have . . . I thought we'd covered it well, but now I'm not so sure. That's why you're here."

They walked on, the lights every forty feet or so picking out a pool of detail below them. They came to where the tunnel widened into a cavernous workshop where there were lathes and milling machines. "Good old machinery, this," Templestone said. "Solid stuff, no plastic here." Templestone recognised an Alfred Herbert 4D capstan lathe, and a bulky looking Cincinnati vertical miller. Close by was a Grey and Rushton height gauge on a surface plate. "This stuff comes from the forties and fifties," he said. "I used to use all this sort of gear."

"Villiers' laboratory is up there," Dearden pointed to a door that could be seen vaguely in the darkness at the head of a short flight of stone steps. "Harry's description of the lab was exactly what I found when I went into it after he disappeared. Laboratory stuff. No odd-looking equipment. Then I ran out of time because I had to meet up with Premier Stephen Marston. It's been a very busy time."

"Don't we know it," Pierpoint said.

"So, we look again; maybe one of us will catch something you missed," Jules said. Switching on her Maglite she headed for the door to the laboratory.

*   *   *

The spiral stairs the other side of the door looked old, with indentations worn in the Hornton Ironstone by the passage of feet over the years.

"Why do we always get ourselves into these places?" Templestone quipped as he got to the top of the stairs and shone his torch around the room at the top.

"Don't know, old chap but I'd prefer it this way than vegetating at home in Ireton Grange," Pierpoint said.

Dearden switched on the light.

"Gather round, people," Jules said. "This is what we'll do in our search. Take a look at the surroundings. "What you see is a room in context." She indicated the laboratory with a sweep of her hand. "The stuff in here is in the context of a laboratory. Look for out-of-context equipment; things that don't appear to belong. Shout up if you spot anything out of context." Each of them searched in silence, concentrating, hoping they would find evidence of the whereabouts of Harry and Esma. The only sounds were their feet moving over the stone floor, and the furniture they shifted.

It was Clive Fraser who spotted the out-of-context object and it was Templestone who made the connection. Clive had come to the far end of the lab and concluded that his part of the search had been useless. He looked up, and there, in the darkness illuminated by his torch, was another short, upward flight of stone steps. He climbed up them to a door set into a Gothic arch. On a flat area at the side of the top step was a neatly stacked pile of dressed stone. On the top of the heap of stone was a lump hammer.

"This is out of context," Clive called. The striking face of the lump hammer was shining in the light from his torch.

"That's my hammer," Templestone said, as he came to the top of the steps. His initials, WHT, was stamped into its side. He picked up the hammer. "Harry borrowed this and my bolster and coursing chisels," he explained. "I sharpened them for him . . . sorry Jules, we don't need forensics to sort this one out. Lump hammer, heap of stones, door."

6

"Asking our age is rather forward, young lady," Villiers said to Esma. The lack of ageing had been a topic for discussion between Villiers and Martell. It had been a challenge too far. Too much of a stretch of the imagination even for Villiers, the scientist at the cutting edge of physics. Nevertheless, he had strong suspicions about the different nature of time where they were marooned, compared to what they were used to back on Earth.

Villiers' watch had stopped a long while ago when the battery became exhausted. He wasn't surprised, because the first time he checked his watch after they came through the door from Repository One he noticed the timepiece had developed what he thought was a fault. The hour hand was moving at a rate of twelve minutes for a mental count of sixty seconds. One thousand, two thousand, three thousand, four thousand, five thousand . . . he counted to sixty seconds and twelve minutes had gone by on the watch. He couldn't understand it. It was as if the natural pulsation of the quartz crystal in the watch's electronics had quickened . . .

"But it's impossible, Dick," Villiers had reasoned with Martell when he looked at the watch. "The pulsation rate of quartz when voltage is applied to it is written into the crystal's structure. That physical law doesn't change, and it is the reason why digital timepieces are so accurate." But as he said the words he could see the hour hand steadily moving, and the evidence of his eyes defied his reasoning.

Nothing seemed to be occurring but the rising and setting of the sun. The origin of the sound that occurred every so often was a mystery. There were no other humans about. No animal lifeforms. Just the vegetation-like things, some of them colossal and none of which they recognised.

During one of their forays into the nearby interior, a long while after they arrived, Villiers and Martell came across rocky outcrops and cliffs that sparkled diamond-like in the rising sun. The two men traversed the steep incline of the cliffs and then descended into a valley. They soon entered outcrops of towering vegetation whose canopy far above moved as they walked past the mighty trunks. It became obvious that the vegetation was the source of the sounds that were occurring.

The multitudinous sounds rose and fell around them in a cacophony of tones, sometimes harmonic, sometimes dissonant. Villiers got close to one of the giant lifeforms, felt it and caught hold of Martell's sleeve. He pulled him to the organism and told Martell to touch it. As the noise occurred they felt vibration in the trunk, and underfoot.

They walked on. Further into the forest there was a clearing, through which ran a river. It was very clear and they could see into its depths. The scarlet sunlight caught the surface. It was beautiful, but distinctly odd.

"This liquid isn't flowing like water," Villiers said. Martell had noticed the unusual flow of the substance too. It had been the first time they had encountered a large body of liquid such as the river. Near to where they had built their shelter, Base Camp, they called it, there was a stream. They found that it was OK to wash in and drink from. At first it was risky to try it but as they needed to drink and to wash they tried it. The liquid had a pleasant taste, although to wash in it was slightly syrupy in texture, sluggish in its movement, slimy in its feel.

The surface of the river was not the same as a river's surface back on Earth. Maybe the difference had something to do with the depth of the watercourse, or the viscosity of the element when there was a large amount of it.

On the bank of the river, gazing across to the further bank, Martell recalled the time long ago when he was on holiday in France, in a cottage near the southern bank of the Loire. The river had passed all expectations for the holiday, with its peaceful progression through the fields near Angers. But although the Loire was a slow and peaceful river, the surface lazily rippled, and the ripples caught the light of the Sun, giving the river life and character. There was no such surface movement on the river here. In the light of the alien sun the surface of the river was as still as a sheet of ice.

Martell wondered whether he should dip his hand into it, to see what it felt like. He prepared his mind like he did before visiting a dentist. He looked into the depths and saw, in his reflection, the face of a man who hadn't aged. It was as if time had slowed right down. It was uncanny because both he and Villiers agreed, when they talked about it, that they had been marooned a good many years, exactly how long was difficult to tell, but they thought at least thirty five years had passed. He should have aged, and he hadn't. He passed his hand over his face. It was slightly sore after his recent shave with a sharp-edged grass-like leaf, but there were no age-lines. He plunged his hand into the river.

The temperature was pleasant, but the movement and the sensation were like it might be to dip his hand into a bowl of jelly that hadn't quite set. The substance plucked at his hand, teased it in an unfamiliar way.

Martell withdrew his hand and looked at it. His skin was undamaged and there was no pain. In fact, it was quite the opposite, it was sensuous and desirable. The substance that clung to his skin was most persistent in its contact. Martell scraped the semi-liquid off his right arm with his left hand and, as he would do before drying his hands on a towel, he tried to shake the remnants of the liquid off. Left, right, left, right, flick, flick, flick and he ended up wiping his hands on his trousers to get the last of the stuff off.

* * *

Villiers took Harry's watch from him. Studied it for a minute. "Mine was the same when we came through. I put it down to a fault."

"So did I, originally," Harry took his watch back. "But I had second thoughts. It would have to be a weird fault. There were no stress factors involved . . . no mismatched battery to force a change into the electronics. No alteration to the mechanics of the watch. Because of what was going on around us . . . rather, what was *not* going on around us . . . I looked in an alternative direction for the answer."

Harry put his chin on his hand, working out how to explain. Then, "What's your opinion about events here being in slow motion?"

"It is rather off-putting at first, but you'll get used to it," Martell chipped in. But he didn't sound convinced.

Harry analysed the material of the wall which housed the door they came through. It looked familiar, built out of a shining, hard-looking material that had been formed into close fitting blocks. Two slightly different colours of material had been used for each alternate course, repeated up to a height of about three metres.

The appearance of the structure was much the same as the

Hub in Leofwin's Hundred. Semi-circular in aspect, with the door at the centre, and each end of the wall disappearing into an escarpment. A major difference was that the roof of this structure was topped with vegetation. Long streamers of oversize lichen-like growths moving in slow-motion, unnaturally, as if in a cloying breeze. Harry could feel pressure as the breeze teased his skin but there was hardly any motion of the air. It was different to anything he had experienced before; the air felt more solid. He analysed his breathing. He had done this before, on Earth, and it was a bad thing to do. The analysis back then made him more conscious of each breath, and that was a problem best avoided. In this isolated place his breathing was slightly laboured, another evidence of the atmosphere being different to that of the Earth.

*   *   *

Some time after their marooning a pattern began to develop in Harry and Esma's life. The mornings were spent doing essential work. And then the four people would sit on the ground near the door they arrived through. They took it in turns to open the door, hoping it would open up to their own world, just a short, but paradoxically, an immense journey through the portal.

Afternoon was determined by judging the position of the scarlet sun in the sky. Its size suggested it was an old sun and, although it was huge, the energy it was radiating made the atmosphere feel like a temperate day in England. Harry tried to assess the time. He was surprised to see that, even though it felt on his body clock as though only an hour had gone by, the hands on his watch had rotated twelve hours and ten minutes. It was difficult to measure the time accurately because of the increased rotational speed of the minute and hour hands. He concluded that comparing Earth-time relatively to wherever they were now, with its quirky physical laws, was pointless. He just had to get used to the difference.

*   *   *

One particular evening they talked about Villiers' research. Flames from dead vegetable matter were slowly writhing upon themselves and giving forth smoke which arose in slow eddies. Harry spoke again about Villiers' End Time Weapon. Went into more detail than before. "There was a great deal of difficulty getting the mission under way, it nearly failed."

Villiers looked perturbed.

"Don't worry, it wasn't your fault. It was discovered that the target, Nibiru, was inhabited, so we had to re-direct the weapon during the final minutes of the mission." Villiers' countenance first showed surprise and then relief.

"What happened . . . how was the problem dealt with?" he asked, which was when Harry revealed how he had been involved with the mission using Evan Blake's Condor Heavy Lift spacecraft. And then he revealed that, just a few years before Nibiru's near-collision with Earth, there had been first-contact with an alien race.

"Nibiru was near-tragedy for Earth. But those aliens rescued us. They are thousands of years ahead of us in scientific progress. They re-orbited the planet Nibiru. It is now in safe orbit." There was silence as the gravity of the recent threat to the Earth sunk in.

Esma broke the silence, and she didn't beat about the bush.

"Are you men going to talk about we getting home?" As usual her modern English wasn't quite right. The occasional

Anglo-Saxon word crept into her part of the conversation too, but they got the drift of what she said.

Harry was silent for a while, thinking things through as night descended. *If vegetation is the only life-form on this planet how come the stone of the wall is dressed? Another agency must have been involved.*

"Who built the wall?" he asked, startling the other three out of their silence.

"I have asked that same question many times," said Martell. "And why is there a corresponding wall at the far end of your laboratory, Charlie? It's an odd coincidence you chose to put your Switch where there was an old door with a room behind it built out of this identical stonework."

Villiers was exasperated. "And I have told you many times that I agree with you Dick. There does appear to have been collusion somewhere along the timeline of history. It's as if there was preparation for our experiment. As though we were prompted to produce the Switch, and place it where it would be paired with the freakish transfer system. How and why there is that similarity I do not know."

"But you designed the bloody device," Martell muttered.

"Maybe so. But I will say yet again . . . there must have been collusion. Looking back with the benefit of hindsight we couldn't have done it by ourselves. The whole course of events to do with the experimentation and build of the Switch was beyond our capabilities. Without a push in the right direction we wouldn't have achieved the transfer."

"Are you suggesting that events were steered in order to lead you to your invention and what it accomplishes?" Harry asked.

"Exactly. Nothing else makes sense. The research and the build of the Switch was straightforward. It was highly complex work at the frontier of science, but everything dropped into place. It was as if we were meant to open up the way to this world; or at least to open up the transfer method."

"Why didn't you query that, Charlie. Didn't you think the whole setup was suspicious?" Martell challenged.

Harry pondered Villiers' explanation. He disregarded Martell's challenge, and said, "The event that the four of us have experienced has happened within the generation of a group of humans who have experienced spatial and temporal transfer across the Grid. Prof, think of the Grid as a three dimensional network of lines of force built into the universe. I've been involved with the Grid and, believe me, it is fascinating. It's broadened our horizons so that we can experience the immensity of the Cosmos."

"All that aside," said Villiers, "How do we get back to the Earth? With the Grid you are on about, it's as if we've been shown the railway track, but now we need to set the points in the right direction."

"I don't think we ever will," Martell said. "Anyway, what the hell do I care about the Grid you're on about." Without waiting for an answer Martell stood and walked over to the door in the wall and kicked it, foot-bruisingly hard.

Villiers shook his head. "He gets like this sometimes when he's down, poor chap," he said, in a voice low enough for Martell not to hear.

Esma understood some of what was being discussed. She didn't like the undercurrent of anger from Martell. She went to get a drink from the barrel-shaped container they used. She scooped some of the liquid into one of the nearby vessels which were a similar shape to a coconut shell, but with a flat bottom. She drank and brought some over to the others.

37

"Water, it is good," she licked her lips.

"We boil the liquid from the stream. The boiling tends to thin it down," Martell said, taking his container from Esma. "Took a chance with it at first . . . hoped it wouldn't poison us. But that was a long while ago. There have been no ill effects. And the food we have on hand is pleasant . . . vegetarian of course. We took a chance on that as well, didn't we, Charlie?"

"Had to," Villiers shrugged.

"We had no choice. It prevented us starving. But it's nothing like a full English breakfast. Talking of which, who's for eats?"

The food was similar to onion bhaji. "They are seeds of a type of vegetation that grows on the edge of a swampy area about half a mile away," Villiers said.

Harry considered how events had worked out.

"Everything's laid on, isn't it?" he said.

"What do you mean," Martell asked.

"You have food, and drink. You have . . . should I say, we have, comparative peace, other than wondering where we are and worrying about how to get back home."

"There's no-one here to steal what we own," Martell added.

Villiers nodded. He said, "We sometimes look up into the night sky, trying to find a familiar constellation. At least that would give us reassurance, a sense of being on our own turf."

"You could look for all eternity into the night sky where we are and not see anything familiar," Harry said.

"Yes. I've spent many sleepless nights thinking about what has happened to us, studying what I see. I don't really want to accept it."

"Probably you don't . . . but let me ask you a question. Have your eyes developed a fault?"

"Yes, why?"

Harry ignored that. "And yours too, Dick?" he asked. Martell nodded.

"Ours have as well," Harry said. He stood and looked around. "What do you put that . . . so called fault down to, Professor Villiers? The greyed-out areas we can all see . . . over there, and over there, amongst the vegetation." He pointed. "What do you put that down to?"

"The different environment has damaged our eyes . . . I think."

"No more than that?"

"Not that I can readily bring to mind." Villiers avoided Harry's direct gaze.

"OK. Let me say that since you went missing there has been great advancement in physics. The nature of matter is being investigated thoroughly. Fascinating things relating to the universe and our place in it are being revealed. But the more we find out, the more we realise how complex is the nature of life and the material universe; and how little we know about it. But we are making progress."

"Harry . . . I am intrigued. But will you get to the point?"

Harry sat again. "I believe we are seeing colours here beyond those which our eyes and brain are designed to perceive."

Villiers and Harry observed each other. Each waiting for a response.

"What we saw, in our original experiment with the Switch, which was an accident, I must add, was an alien world. One beyond our comprehension." Villiers said. "The math I built upon was inconclusive but we could be in an—"

"—Alternative reality. Prof, I found your notes in R1 and completed the equations. What I have studied back home and here informs me that you were correct in your reasoning."

Harry vividly recalled Lan-Si-Nu saying that the subterranean levels of the Hub contained a process enabling inter-dimensional travel. *You are not ready for that;* the alien had warned when Harry pressed him for information.

"You will have to accept it, sir." Harry added the note of respect. You were correct in your reasoning, but slightly out with your math. We *are* in a reality different to that of our birth. The most immediate physical laws that I can detect without instrumentation, reveal that they are different to the physical laws we experience back home . . . Professor Villiers, ever heard of wormholes?"

7

Lars Knudsen the UN secretary general, who had represented planet Earth before the meeting of the Hnioss on Wasiri-Poya, had great moral courage. Now he was heading-up the thrust of Earth government toward universal peace. Nibiru had forced a turnaround into the reasoning of Humankind. Instead of war between countries if there was an intransigent disagreement about land, religion or political belief, the age-old solution of blowing men, women and children up into dismembered body parts had to be considered despicable. The principle of *mutual consideration* had to be adopted . . . no choices. Treat the other person as you would like to be treated yourself.

The post-Nibiru beginnings were not easy. To push out the ingrained psychosis of *harm thy neighbour* took great moral courage. The world was used to the ways of war to sort out its problems. To make progress on a cosmic scale, a stand had to be made that grasped an enlightened approach to ironing out differences.

Knudsen's speech to the United Nations Assembly was masterly, his powers of oration, superb. The majority of Earth people took note of what he said when they heard the translation into their own particular language, and they remembered his words. Some wrote them down because they considered his words were pivotal and that he spoke for each one of them individually. He reached out on their behalf to the other races of the cosmos. What they did not know was that the Alien, Lan-Si-Nu and Knudsen had spent hours together phrasing and re-phrasing the broadcast. It had to set the groundwork from which true progress could be made.

After the broadcast, Lan-Si-Nu and his two colleagues backed off from helping. They retreated into the Hub, to the sealed area at the rear of the room of the exhibits. Earth people had to get on with things. But the Wasiri-Chanchiya remained on-hand, in case they were needed.

Earth people have an ingrained curiosity, as do all intelligent species. Before the near-extinction incident with Nibiru, the Conspiracy TV program attracted a lot of people who loved a mystery. Some people still loved a mystery, a conspiracy. It excited the curiosity, even after the near tragedy of Nibiru.

Information was circulating about an increase in UFO activity and the Nibiru incident had fed the intrigue some folks feel about a mystery. The inquisitive geeks amongst the human race sucked up to what *might be* happening. Of course, they were also interested in *what is* happening, but the mystery of what *might be* . . . that was the golden nugget.

The internet, in an eighty percent weakened state, survived after Nibiru; people began to say *after Nibiru* like they used to say *after the war*. After Nibiru the geeks and the amateur astronomers picked up a lot of UFO stuff. There was no denying UFO's now. *Now you've got to believe us*, the geeks were saying. Sometimes smirking, they said, *we've been telling you for years that there are UFO's and aliens, and the Wasiri-Poya Aliens have even helped us out of deep shit.*

UFO's had been spotted on all continents. Major activity was in the skies above Somerset in the UK. That followed the usual pattern because Somerset had been a target for years. Why that place had been a target was obscure, but for a long while people had gathered on Cley Hill near Warminster to see what was happening at night. It had become a tradition amongst the Ufologists, to go up Cley Hill. There had been noises of thunder, lights that lit up the sky, cars that did not behave as they should, and dead birds on the ground in the morning.

Cley Hill became more interesting for the UFO geeks to visit after Nibiru. Through media channels there had been a gradual disclosure of information about *Our Aliens*, as the Wasiri Chanchiyans were now called and the geeks were very interested in keeping their eyes on what was happening in the skies above Warminster.

A shape, maybe very dark grey or black, often flitted across the night sky over Cley Hill. The geeks conjectured upon what those occurrences might be. Some, but not all people of a scientific bent said the occurrences were not UFO's at all, they were atmospheric abnormalities created after Nibiru's second pass. *What is happening could be a new form of Aurora. The magnetic field of the Earth has been changed*, they pontificated. But the geeks believed in UFO's come what may. Damn science, *UFO's are here in force over Warminster. Against that fact you have no argument!*

What really ended the speculation was when one landed on the summit of Cley Hill. The sleek black vehicle from the stars didn't stay long.

"I think it stayed long enough to take photographs of us," said Rob Greenaway, whose account was reported in the infant Warminster Echo, fifth edition, published monthly. "It was huge," he added.

Photographs be damned. *The intent is far more sinister,* said the geeks. "if those aliens are on the level they should be contacting us through the Lan-Si-Nu guy, not just appearing. Something bad is going on."

* * *

Deep under Edge Hill, amongst the group standing around the door in the oddly familiar looking wall at the far end of Villiers' long-deserted laboratory, a decision was made.

"Let's open the door, Bill," Clive Fraser said. Bill Templestone stood to one side to make room for Clive to stand on the top step. Clive reached for the handle, just an iron affair, old and clunky, with a lot of weight. There was a surface mounted lock in a black iron case below the handle.

Jules put her hand on Clive's arm, and he looked at her to see why. Jules had made him ballsy. She had brought out hidden depths he previously didn't know he had.

"Are we all agreed on this?" she asked.

"We have got to do it," Rowan said, "For Esma and Harry." There was quick agreement that they should open the door.

Clive turned the handle, but the door was locked.

"Let me try," Dearden said. He'd had plenty of practice with doors that opened onto unusual things, and his nerve was steely. "We need the damn key." He got to Villiers' desk to ransack the drawers for the key. But before he did that—

"—You think you need a key to get Harry back? Give me the hammer and move aside," Pierpoint said. Doughty grabbed the lump hammer from the floor, passed it to Pierpoint, who raised it high, sighted on the lock and swung the two and a half pounds of iron in an arc with all his might. Sir Will Pierpoint intended to get through the door to find Harry and Esma. Nothing was going to stop him, just the same as, over the years, nothing had stopped him from fighting on the side of the oppressed with another type of hammer, SHaFT, the Shock and Force Team for justice.

8

The lock mechanism swung on the surface of the door, held by one bent screw, which Pierpoint put paid to with another swipe of the hammer. The lock clattered to the floor.

"Your hammer, Bill," Pierpoint passed Templestone his hammer.

The door was slightly ajar, swinging slightly. This time Jules put her hand on Pierpoint's arm.

"Listen," she said, quietly, so as not to mask what she could hear. There was a sound coming from the other side the door.

"I hear music," Rowan said, tilting her head to hear better.

Doughty got closer to the door. "What is it?"

"Get the door open and we'll find out." Dearden was impatient. Doughty nodded, edged his fingers into the gap between the door and the frame. Incongruously, for the door was in the Gothic style, the frame had a shining metallic surface. Doughty inched the door open and they all stepped back. For beyond the door was utter blackness, interspersed with countless stars.

They left the door swinging on its hinges and got out of the lab quickly. What was on the other side of the door gave Clive Fraser the creeps. It did not make sense.

Back at Dearden Hall, they were gathered around Leofwin's table. The mood was pensive. The way to proceed uncertain. "Harry said Villiers was onto a new field of research in R1. At least we've found what Harry was interested in," Dearden said.

"And my lump hammer Harry borrowed and the heap of stones shows that he made some progress. The young fools have gone through the door," said Templestone.

"I don't like their choice of destination," Clive Fraser shivered as he recalled the scene of blackness and stars through the Gothic door.

"There was a lead sheet folded behind the stones," Jules said. "Lead is a protection against radiation. Have you still got a Geiger counter here, Jem? We'd better make sure we check out OK." With a sense of urgency, Dearden fetched a Geiger counter left over from the Manhattan mission from the basement stores. He quickly swept them for rads.

"We can breathe easy, there's just background rads. But where do we go from here, people? What we found beneath Edge Hill has got me puzzled," Dearden said.

Doughty shrugged. "I guess this is where we would have asked Harry to help us sort out the difficult stuff." No-one else commented. Every time original thinking was needed Harry had been there with solutions. His absence was painfully obvious.

"Harry has got an older brother," Templestone suggested. "And he's as cute as Harry with electronics. They're out of the same gene-pool. If he's still about after Nibiru's destruction he may be able help us."

"He's with the experimental division at Ranstad Nanotech," Jules said, remembering Harry's dealings with his brother.

"He directs it, Templestone said. "Name of Oscar. Their father was a good friend of mine." Templestone flicked on his mobile and scrolled the contacts list. No Oscar Stanway, no Ranstad Nanotech. He recalled that Ranstad Nanotech was in Southampton. "Last I heard, they worked out of the old moulding loft of the Supermarine factory," he said.

"Then let's hope he's survived. I've heard that much of the south coast was wiped out after the tsunami hit," Doughty said.

"We'll go and look for him," Dearden suggested. He opened his laptop and it came out of sleep. He typed the search string, *Detail, English Southern Coast into* Google Two. The search resolved slowly. It took two minutes. Various suggestions, including a recently launched Evan Blake satellite-network image of the English southern coastline were returned.

Dearden surveyed the map. Much of the Somerset Levels were now under water, and the coastline of Hampshire, Dorset and Devon had altered. The White Cliffs of Dover had been eaten away to a quarter-mile from where they had been before Nibiru.

"It doesn't look very optimistic," Clive said, as he studied the image.

Templestone stabbed a finger on the image of the coast of Hampshire. "Despite what the area looks like there could be quite a few survivors. Oscar Stanway is a resourceful guy. If anyone could find a way of surviving he would. Right now, with the technicalities involved, he's our best shot at locating Harry and Esma."

"Who's up for a trip to the Southampton?" Dearden asked.

* * *

Sat-nav was patchy so Jules rummaged around in her father's books at Moat Field Cottage, where she remembered seeing a 2008 Michelin road atlas. It served her and Clive well on the way to the south coast and they encountered little traffic. There were scenes of devastation, skeletal towers where there had been high-rise developments and in places great swathes of fallen trees facing north-west littered the landscape. It was a chilling scene and they were silent for long sections of the journey.

"Looks as though we fared better in the Midlands," Jules said to Clive, who had taken a turn driving. A group of wind turbines had fallen and lay at grotesque angles. One of them had come to rest with the large turbine head resting on the road. Two ruined blades were on the tarmac and the third, undamaged, was poking at right angles, skywards.

"There's a lot of clearing up to do," Clive commented, as he negotiated the turbine.

"There is, but there's a lot of gear that can be re-used. I heard that the remnants of South West Power are restoring wind turbines and bringing them on-stream to reinforce the national grid."

"It'll take years to sort this mess out, and it's not just us, it's world-wide." There was silence again, until eventually they came to a road-sign which stated that Southampton was five and a half miles away.

When they came to the outskirts of the town, signs of the tsunami became obvious with silt covering the level areas. In places the silt was caked and dry, partially broken up, and there were tyre marks impressed into it. Some of it was piled against walls that had survived the onslaught. A few cars and four by fours were about. There were some vehicles parked near a small supermarket on higher ground. Clive headed over to get food and he parked outside.

Inside the shop five men were confronting the man and woman behind the counter and their voices were raised. One of them had a baseball bat held threateningly, head-high, close to the shopkeeper's head. Two of them turned to face

Jules and Clive as they came through the door.

"Oh, shit," were Clive's first words. Jules felt exhilarated. She stepped in front of Clive, said nothing, put her hands on her hips and spaced her feet apart.

The taller of the two men, the one with long greasy black hair, turned and grinned, said, "Who's this sassy bitch just come through the door?" The others, apart from the one with the baseball bat, looked to see what was going on, but baseball bat man pushed the bat under the shopkeeper's chin and held it there.

"Don't hurt him . . . please don't." The shopkeeper's wife pleaded.

It was then that Jules spoke.

"Hurt either of them and it'll be the last people you do hurt." Her voice was deceptive. She had come from a refined background, worked easily through the university system and was a professor of forensic archaeology. She spoke with authority and dignity. And she loathed injustice.

The guy with the bat lowered it and turned away from the counter, grinning as he flipped the weapon from hand to hand.

What Clive and the five thugs didn't realise was just how lethal was the woman in front of them. Jules felt her inner strength coiling inside. It happened just as she wanted. The coiling-up. Her mainspring. The thug with the bat. He was the immediate threat and he had left the man behind the counter alone to deal with Jules. He had designs on her and now he stood four feet in front of her and he grinned again a wide, leering grin. All five thugs grinned. Wide lascivious grins. They had done this sort of thing before. Enjoyed it. Clive looked serious, and he looked pale.

Jules was tall for a woman and she had a good figure, quite

alluring when she was ready for action. What happened next was explosive, the knuckles that smashed the bat-thug's arm at the elbow, the fingers that penetrated the second thug's eyes, the foot that ruined the third thug's balls. The fourth and fifth were not grinning now. One of them sank to the floor with his hands over his head, whimpering. Number five tried to run out the door but Clive tripped him up and instinctively smashed his foot on the thug's ankle. He heard it crunch.

Jules looked at Clive and as she was about to say *Well done*, he beat her to it and said, "Where did you learn to do that?"

"Ah, that's another story. I'll tell you when we've got a spare moment." She faced the shopkeeper. "Is there such a thing as a police-force around here?" she asked. The thugs were rolling in agony on the floor.

"Will you lot just shut the hell up," Jules shouted. They quietened down quickly, sufficient for Jules to have a reasonable conversation with the police on the phone.

The police arrived in a police-car that had seen action on the front nearside wing. It had a siren that sounded marginally off-key. But they arrived, all four of them looking smart and police-like with the stuff they needed, like handcuffs and Tasers.

The mess on the floor surprised them, but what surprised them even more was the cute woman with her foot on the back of a well-known gangster who was moaning and holding his smashed arm. A second, and then a third police vehicle arrived that was big enough to take the five thugs away in. Statements were taken from the shopkeeper, Ranjit Singh and his wife, Muni. It had been the second time that they had been attacked by the gang, who called themselves The Famous Five, in the past month.

Jules gave her statement and not far into it, after she explained what she and Clive saw going on when they went into the shop, she explained what she did about it.

"I am a black belt Godan, a fifth Dan Shotokan Karateka."

"You can look after yourself," the police sergeant suggested.

"Sort of."

"You can look after everyone else too," Clive was impressed by what his girl could do. He would ask Jules to teach him some moves, it would help with his self-confidence. Then he remembered why they had come to Southampton.

"Maybe you can help us," he said to the elderly sergeant. "We're looking for someone who works at Ranstad Nanotech. They operate out of the old moulding loft of the Supermarine factory."

"My dad worked there years ago," the sergeant said, looking slightly vacant. "Dad said that every time he walked by the gate of that place, even years after they stopped production, he imagined he could hear the sound of the Merlins. Sometimes, before Nibiru, we used to get a Spitfire pass over the town, doing homage, I guess. Beautiful sound, a Rolls Royce Merlin."

Clive too loved the sound of a powerful engine. He was on the right wavelength with the sergeant to get his help.

"Problem is that Ranstad Nanotech got destroyed in the tsunami, along with all the other seafront places," the sergeant said.

"It's really important we find a guy who worked there," Jules said. "Do you know if there are any survivors?"

"There are. There was plenty of warning. A lot of us got to higher ground; apart from the diehards who were too stubborn. There were camps on the Isle of Wight and along the coast towards Weymouth. What was your man's name?"

"Oscar Stanway."

"Doesn't ring a bell . . . but along with the salvation army we're building a list of survivors. Come to the station, we'll take a look."

The police station had suffered damage which was in the process of being rectified. Bulldozers were busy in the yard behind an impressive looking Art Deco stone-clad building.

"Most of the infrastructure has gone around here," the sergeant said, as they walked toward the headquarters. "We're doing our best to keep things together. Clock tower fell in the cyclone; killed three officers and crushed five cars, including ours. We parked it five minutes before; lucky, or what?"

A Chief Inspector was in the foyer waiting for them. He had been radioed a report about the incident at Ranjit's Supermarket and was keen to meet the woman who bested Danny Cripps and his gang of four. He held out his hand in welcome but Jules ignored it. She didn't want any publicity that might get close to SHaFT. She didn't intend getting cosy with the officer.

"Tea?" Chief Inspector Wells asked.

Jules said, "I would rather take a look at your list of survivors. We have to find a guy named Oscar Stanway. Time's pressing."

"OK, come with me." Wells adapted to Jules urgency and led them to some stairs at the end of a long passage with water damage. It still smelt damp even after the months since the tsunami hit. Portable heaters were blowing out hot air.

"What's the electricity supply like here?" Clive asked, as they climbed the stairs.

"We get regular outages, but they are happening less

frequently now."

The room where the computers were situated were up yet another flight of stairs and down a long corridor. Inside the room there was no smell of damp. Four female police officers were each sitting in front of a computer transcribing details from lined A4 pads. One of the officers wore sergeant's stripes and she stood as the CI came in the room.

"We need some information, sergeant," she tilted her head quizzically. "Do you have any record of an Oscar Stanway amongst the survivors?" Wells asked.

"I'll take a look, sir." She sat in front of a screen and searched for Stanway in the master file. "Standon . . . Stanford. We have a Stanley, three of them. Father, mother and a son named Stuart. Doesn't appear there's a Stanway. But the list is still being compiled. It's far from complete," She said, glancing at Jules. "What we *do* know is that Wight was really stretched before the event, and people were motoring along the Jurassic Coast, finding the best protection they could on the high ground behind the cliffs around St. Aldhelm's Head. Lulworth, Durdle-Door and Kimmeridge were popular too."

"The problem is that those places offered height as protection against the tsunami, but not much protection when the cyclone came," Wells said.

"Where does your information relate to?" Jules asked.

"The lists of survivors? They're in Wight and the areas nearest to us, maybe fifty miles of the coast each side of Southampton. The general public are being very helpful."

"How complete would you say the list is?"

The female sergeant thought the question through, "Working from the latest census returns minus those known to have died, eighty percent, roughly."

"Where would someone go during Nibiru's passage who had a good knowledge of survival techniques?"

The sergeant tapped her biro on the A4 pad as she thought it through. Then, "When the Isle of Wight became overcrowded folks headed along the coast toward Weymouth. I would suggest your person would have gone to the Isle of Portland. It has extensive tunnelling *and* height. We've heard nothing from there yet, but information about survivors is coming in all the time. There's a lot of work to do."

"You can say that again, sergeant." The CI took out a cigarette and offered the young woman sergeant one. She smiled at him in a way that was more than familiar and they lit up. "Carry on sergeant. If you find anything about Mister Stanway let me know."

They went down to CI Wells' office on the ground floor. "I'm afraid we haven't been much help," he said.

"You've given us a lead. We'll follow it up on Portland." Jules gave Wells a phone number and names she made up. This time, when the CI held out his hand, Jules gave it a firm shake and Wells winced. Clive's shake was less painful.

Jules and Clive walked out the door, leaving the chief wishing all citizens were as publicly spirited as Kathy Smith and John Simms.

They got into the Grand Cherokee. Jules was driving.

"So, we're heading for Portland," Clive said.

"Seems that's where anyone sensible would've gone."

Clive looked at the map. "OK. Take a right out of the car park and then third left. It should take us toward Weymouth, avoiding the coast road."

"Thanks, Mister Simms," Jules chuckled.

"That's quite alright, Miss Smith," Clive said, as he turned to the map on the next page.

9

"The theory of an Einstein-Rosen Bridge . . . of course I've heard of wormholes," Villiers said. "I have also reasoned on an Einstein-Rosen bridge being the cause of our predicament, but that's impossible. An Einstein-Rosen Bridge is theoretically unstable. But what do *you* have in mind?"

"An Einstein-Rosen bridge definitely is unstable."

"Are there alternatives?"

"There are. Since your disappearance in the early sixties there has been research into what are known as Lorentzian traversable wormholes."

"Is that so?" Villiers sat back. Folded his arms, and mentally appraised the young man. He was impressed. A tad jealous. And he hung onto every word.

"In 1973 a guy named Homer Ellis wrote a paper in which he demonstrated the possibility of a stable wormhole, traversable in both directions. Research was intense. In '73 another guy, named K. A. Bronnikov, came to the same conclusion as Ellis."

"Were they working in the same institute?"

"No, they were independent. Ellis was in Colorado, Bronnikov was in Moscow."

"Which makes the concept plausible, I guess."

"Yeah but get this. In '74, a Cambridge team led by a Professor O'Hare was working on the same subject, but with a slightly tweaked formulaic expression . . . called—"

"O'Hare, you said . . . what was his first name?"

"Vernon."

"Bless my soul, Vernon made it to professor. He was one of my students in the Old Cavendish."

"Was he? It was in the Old Cav that O'Hare's discovery was made."

"What was his discovery?"

"In simple terms, he proposed that induced magnetism, on a very large scale, could be used as a contributing factor in the production of what is called a Lorentzian wormhole. Additional influences needed to be introduced for the proposition to work."

Villiers stood up and began pacing. "Shortly before I left the Cavendish to set up the lab in Repository One we were working on induced magnetism, combined with extremely high amperage. The effect the combination of those influences had on particle acceleration interested us. So, good old Vernon followed it through."

"He did. He must have picked up where you left off. O'Hare's project was very much under the radar, ahead of its time, like most of your research was. Trouble is, the timing was all wrong. These days there's a massive device called the Large Hadron Collider that uses the same principle, but O'Hare's research came to nothing because the Old Cav was about to be moved."

"They didn't knock it down?"

"No. It's a museum now. But here's the rub . . . Cambridge getting a new building for the Cavendish in the seventies depended on government funding. Getting the funding depended on government directed work. O'Hare's project didn't line up with what the government thought was relevant, so it was dropped. When it was dropped, it is said that the team destroyed every part of the research. A new team took over in the new building and they pursued research into radio astronomy and semi-conductor physics."

"How do you know all this?"

"Let's just say that I have an interest in the subject. I've made it my business to find out. All of this information can be found if you know where to look . . . even the top-secret stuff."

"Your knowledge is extensive."

"It is. I like to get things done. To get things done I need to make sure I am well-informed. What I will add is that I think you introduced another factor into the wormhole mix that was a result of the production of the End Time Weapon, anti-matter."

"We did."

"And you were a few years ahead of Vernon O'Hare. You created a Lorentzian Wormhole which connects to the Grid and you tucked the procedure into a door-frame. Trouble is, the wormhole you created takes the traveller to unplanned places."

"Maybe you're right. The whole thing was a big mistake." Villiers sounded contrite. But twice I have opened the door onto places I recognise . . . never Earth, but the target varies so we do have a chance of getting back to the Earth at some time."

"One chance in how many?"

"It's a high figure. I have opened the door onto many different scenes, more often than not onto views of the stars. But your entry into this place proves that the link to Earth can occur once in a while." Villiers thought about that for a beat, and then, "Harry, will your scientific studies help us?"

"Not directly. There is new stuff I'm learning which may be useful. But I know some people back on Earth who won't give up on us. They'll pull out all the stops to get us back, no matter how long it takes."

"Who are they?"

"I can't tell you that. But what I can say is that there are a number of very sincere people involved." Harry didn't identify SHaFT. "Between them they've got a lot of influence."

"Where?"

"You'd be surprised. If we get back you might find out. There's about fifty men and women, all-told. But Esma and me are very close to eight or nine of them, plus some who are . . . different."

"Different?"

"There's Tomahawk—"

"Toma who?"

"Tomahawk . . . he's a Black Alaskan Wolf."

"He's real big, and if you don't watch out he'll go for your throat." Esma parodied what she'd heard said about the wolf from Possum Chaser. She mimicked her Lakota Sioux accent.

Villiers chuckled. "And who else in in this bunch?"

"On the outside there's Lan-Si-Nu and his two crew members."

"Who are they, Chinese?"

"Hardly. They're the aliens we told you about. The first-contact aliens . . . from the planet Wasiri-Poya."

*   *   *

The conversation that day opened things up between them. There were some home truths, some ordinary things, and some extraordinary things talked about. All of which helped them get to know each other better. On that day it became obvious the four of them had to pull together. Villiers and Martell buried their differences. They realised that if they didn't, the hope of getting home would be more distant.

Harry Stanway's intellect was recognised by Charles

Villiers. Villiers was an old-school academician who gracefully accepted Harry as his equal. Harry's forthright manner, and a simple thing, his readiness to smile, made him an easily accepted companion to the two men. To Esma, Harry was the person she wanted in her life for keeps, and she was the same for him.

The four of them planned their time so that it would be put to best use. With the combined drive of Harry and Villiers they became cautiously optimistic about a successful outcome to their marooning.

Thoughts of Dearden and the others back home, particularly Bill Templestone, to whom he felt particularly close, was often at the forefront of Harry's mind. Thoughts occasionally returned about how he had helped the alien, Lan-Si-Nu, and his two companions. It had been a full-on test of his ability but he had succeeded. He had restored the Hub in Leofwin's Hundred to its full functionality, which enabled the three aliens to return to their home galaxy. The alien race rewarded Harry by honouring him with the accolade of Hnirath of Science, the Mastership of learning, on the planet Wasiri-Poya. The challenge up ahead was more difficult . . . there was less to go on. No hard evidence of familiar science to work with.

The hours of day in the light of the scarlet sun seemed strung out to the Earth people. In the current season, it took a long while from sunrise to sunset.

"The seasons do vary. You'll be OK with the length of daylight in time," Martell reassured Harry and Esma. Martell had vacated his room and gone in with Villiers, so Harry and Esma could have his room. They knocked up two frameworks for Harry and Esma to sleep on at Esma's insistence that they slept separately. Harry acquiesced. But for someone who always liked every light switched off to get to sleep, Harry found the extraordinarily long hours of daylight difficult. Near the window in their room he rigged an arrangement of large, thick leaves which he could pull across the window space to blank out some of the light.

Esma had thought long and hard about where they were. She reasoned that the way home could lie further afield from where they were, maybe beyond some distant hills that she pointed to. Time was their own to do with as they pleased, so Esma proposed that the four of them explore their surroundings. She put the idea forward when they were all on a high. This was when Villiers had introduced Harry and Esma to a drink that he and Martell had concocted. It was definitely alcoholic, and it produced pleasant results. Villiers called it Fumble, from the effects too much of it produced.

Within two hours of beginning to drink they had made what plans they thought necessary and tried to put serious thought into what kit would be essential to take with them into the interior. Laughter came loose and free, but they got the kit together and, while still feeling very pleasant, they negotiated where they would go. Villiers referred to the south, saying he remembered seeing interesting things in that direction. Harry asked how he knew it was south.

"It was the oldest navigational trick in the world . . . our world, that is. When we came through I was wearing a tie. It was clipped to my shirt with a tie-pin. I looked quite smart. I took it apart."

"You took your shirt apart?"

Villiers thought for a moment. "No, of course not. What use would a shirt be in navigation?"

"Good a shirt would be," Esma said. "You wear . . . it takes you in best direction."

"Yes . . . that's a good idea," Martell's voice was slurred.

"I'm telling you, the process wasn't easy. It was back to stone-age technology. I found a flint-like rock, hard stuff. It wasn't flint because it sparkled like diamond—"

"He said he thought it was diamond," Martell interjected. "I've got a pocket full of the stuff, j-just in case."

"Yes . . . anyway, I got a lump of this material. I've still got it, look." He pulled the sparkling stuff out of his jacket pocket. It was a wonder it stayed in because the jacket was torn to shreds in places. "Anyway, see this sharp edge?" he put the lump close to Harry's face. His hand waved unsteadily and the crystal glistened brilliantly as it caught the light.

Harry nodded at the sharp edge.

"Obviously, I knew that the tie pin was a cheap bit of kitsch, s-steel plated gold, or something like that," he chuckled. "Gold plated steel, rather, because I only paid two pound one and three for it on the high street, I forget where, now. Anyway, with this sharp edge, I rubbed away at the pin part near its pivot until I separated it. I realised that with the rubbing I gave it when I was cutting it off, I would have induced magnetism into it. So, I took some liquid." He laughed. "Fumble, as it happens, because F-Fumble has a high viscosity. I placed the pin onto its surface." Villiers demonstrated how he placed the sharp bit of the tie-pin onto the surface of the liquid. His fingers held nothing, and he placed the imaginary pin onto the imaginary liquid. "Fumble has a high surface tension, and the pin floated on the m-m-meniscus."

"And it wung snorth," Martell said.

"You mean swung north," Villiers corrected. He laughed

at Martell. The sort of belly-laugh that came from deep down when alcohol was involved. He shook his head in an attempt to clear it and wiped tears of mirth from his cheeks. "At least for once in our bloody favour this planet provided some help. It has magnetic polarity north and south. It doesn't have much else apart from food and drink, but it has a magnetic n-north . . . so, there we are. There we have it." Villiers hand waved vaguely in the air, and then he pointed vaguely to a valley separating the distant hills Esma pointed to earlier. "That valley lies due south; let's do it. But . . . maybe a bit later." He sat down rather quickly.

They slept for a while to get over the Fumble and then they set out. They made steady progress. But when they were about a quarter mile away from a megalithic outcrop of vegetation, Harry saw again the movement in the top section of the elongated succulent-like canopy of the outcrop. It slowly moved en masse, until it was pointing in their direction. It was as if it were aware of their approach.

"Did you see that? Harry asked, with sudden urgency.

"See what?" Villiers asked.

"I saw. Trees moved at top," Esma said.

"Like I said before, I think they know we're here." Harry stopped and sat down. Esma sat beside him. And the other two joined them. They gazed ahead, trying to assess the threat level. Now there was no movement in the foliage. It appeared to be focussed on them. All of the branch and leaf-like appendages were pointing in their direction.

Harry thought the interaction between themselves and what was up ahead was similar to when Tomahawk Shahn of Offchurch, the Black Alaskan wolf, fixed his eyes on him. Tomahawk had a penetrating stare. As if he wanted to get inside his head and dominate. With the wilderness dominant in Tomahawk's genes it was best to let him think he was the boss, otherwise it could lead to bad trouble. Harry felt he needed to have the same regard for the outcrop of immense vegetation up ahead as he had for Tomahawk. Apart from the thought that they should proceed cautiously, there was something . . . elemental about the place.

The closer they got to them the taller they realised the trees, for want of a better description, were. They towered above them, taller than the Giant Sequoia trees Martell once visited on the western slopes of the Sierra Nevada Mountains, where the Sequoias thrived. It was when he was a kid, and he had a photo taken when he stood by the General Sherman Sequoia. What lay up ahead was bigger.

"What do you think, Harry?" Martell asked.

"I think we should proceed, but with caution."

Esma grasped Harry's hand, and she pulled him onward.

10

The route to Weymouth was not easy. Jules and Clive had to take numerous detours where temporary signs implied obstructions not yet cleared. A journey that would have taken one and a half hours on a bad day, took over four hours.

In Weymouth, the Georgian esplanade had fared badly. Hotels, shops and amusement arcades were lying in ruins. A swing bridge over the once picturesque harbour, instead of carrying a road, had collapsed on its pivots after the raising mechanism had been destroyed. The two leaves of the bridge were lying centre-down in seawater. The sea had reclaimed buildings and land, and now lapped at the landward side of what had been Radipole Lake, half a mile inland.

Clive was at the wheel and he negotiated the way to the two-mile-long isthmus connecting Weymouth to the Isle of Portland. Jules' Jeep Grand Cherokee bucked in four-wheel drive over the heaps of scattered stones from Chesil Beach, which lay to the right. They came to where the road widened out into a square, where there was a village called Chiswell. Here, the road divided, one branch leading around the coast and the other route led up the four hundred and ninety feet rise to the heights of Portland.

They parked up and walked toward the sound of the surf, and when they topped a rise they looked out over the sea. It was a wild sea, with the breakers thrashing the stones of Chesil Beach and there was the sucking sound of a fierce undertow. The English Channel wind whipped at their clothes and took their breath away.

"We need information," Jules shouted, as she wiped tears from her wind-blown eyes.

"There's the place we'll get information," Clive said, close to her ear. He pointed to a solid, stone building which lay to the right.

"What is it?" she shouted back.

"The Cove House Inn. I remember it from way back."

A granite porch stood side-on and resolute to the gale. To be sure about defence against flooding, the owners had added stainless steel tracks to the extremity of the porch, into which they could slot heavy gauge interlocking steel plates sealed with rubber to keep the sea and hurricane force winds out. They'd had plenty of practice, and that was what enabled the occupants to survive the Nibiru Cyclone and storm-surge.

The Cove House Inn door was shut solid. Clive looked at his watch, 2.30 and the sky was full of black, storm-cloud. There was a note on the door; *Open at six*. Clive attacked a suitably gale proof iron knocker. They couldn't hear the movement inside but seconds later a long-haired artistic type with bleary eyes opened the door. He said nothing.

"Can we come in?" Clive asked.

"We're shut," the artistic type mouthed.

"We're on official business," Jules shouted. She dragged her SHaFT ID from a pocket. It looked convincing, *was* very convincing in fact, with the well-known hand-written signature on it. She put it away quick so that the guy wouldn't get too much detail. He stood aside and let them in.

The artistic type shut the door behind them and the gale outside softened to a dull moan. There was a fire. A proper fire with logs and bright flame, and the smell of burning wood permeated the inside of the inn.

"What do you want?" The guy looked fidgety, as if he had something to hide.

"We're looking for someone named Oscar Stanway . . . it's very important . . . have you heard of him?" Jules asked.

He shook his head. "With what's happened recently do you expect me to remember everyone?" He sounded stressed.

Clive softened the situation. "Any chance of a drink?"

The guy, who might have been an older student making cash to pay for his course, which was probably defunct now, brightened up. He was on home ground, what he was familiar with, beer pumps and glasses. He got two glasses off a shelf, pint ones, and asked, "What is it?"

"Whatever you've got that isn't too bitter but has depth," Jules said.

"Try this." The guy got a small glass from below the bar, pulled some into it and gave it to her.

"Do you want to try it?" he asked Clive, who nodded yes. The artistic type pumped some into another small glass and handed it to Clive. He tried it.

"Two pints of that." Clive got out some change, which was becoming rarer as a means of payment. There had to be a re-think about finance and paying for what you bought off people.

"What have things been like here?" Jules asked, as the guy finished pulling the beer.

He sauntered out from behind the bar, pulled a stool near to Jules and Clive, and sat. "A lot of people stopped here before Nibiru as they trailed up to the heights. We are brewing our own now, trying to make ends meet."

"What was it like for you, when it was at its worst?

"Bad. Jim Connolly cleared off . . . left me to it, me and Brad Hutchings from Brandy Lane. He's due in soon. When the cyclone came we slid the storm guards in and got into the cellar. That place would survive an A-bomb blast."

"Who was Jim Connolly?"

"The owner. We heard he died. Sea took him."

"And you . . . what did you do here?"

"Bar staff. Before he left he said I was due for promotion. I ran the shift . . . sometimes worked on me tod. The old sod always promised things and never stumped-up. I'm the one who brewed what you're drinking." He looked proud. "Looks as though I've got the whole place now." He looked around and grinned. Looked prouder still.

"The people who passed through, where did they go?"

"There's storage caverns. Ex-military stuff. Tunnels. Things people generally don't know about are up there."

"How do you know about them then?"

The bar guy replied that he was a Conspiracy TV type Geek. Interested in mysteries. "I knew this Nibiru thing would happen," he said. "I watched all the broadcasts. Knew it would happen beforehand."

"Are there many people still up there?"

"Underground? Yeah . . . hundreds of them. They've formed some sort of community. The locals here call them the Trogs."

"The what?" Clive asked.

"The Trogs . . . Troglodytes, cave dwellers. We get some of them in here for meetings once a week."

"Where should we go to enquire about Oscar Stanway?"

"Here, tomorrow. One o'clock. They organise things here. Make lists of folks who've joined them."

It was a one-sided, short sort of conversation. As if he was pissed off about things. The guy went off into another room. Rattled some glasses.

"We need somewhere to stay, how about here?" Jules suggested to Clive.

"Should be good."

The guy came back in with the glasses and arranged them below the bar.

"What's your name?" Clive asked. The guy looked embarrassed. They waited.

"Nail."

"What sort of a name's that?"

"A mistake."

"What do you mean, a mistake?"

"Damn registrar wrote it out wrong. Should have been Nial. Been stuck with Nail ever since."

"I guess you're getting used to it now," Jules offered.

"I had to live with it through school and uni."

Jules and Clive nodded their sympathy.

"Have you got somewhere we can stay overnight?" Jules changed the subject rather than talk about names.

"Got four rooms upstairs, now Connolly's gone."

"One'll do." Clive said. Jules glanced at him.

* * *

While it was still light they took the opportunity to drive up the steep road through Fortuneswell and onward, up to the heights. There was flat land on top, and quarries each side of the road, and there was dust everywhere from working the stone. Other than that, until they reached Easton village, there was nothing, only grass, rock, road and dust. But they were high, and there was limestone below them in its various states of calcification. Somewhere there were tunnels and caverns and people.

It was the same topography until they reached Weston, and then Southwell. One or two people were about. In Southwell, a man with a bag came out of a shop that had a sign outside that should have been lit up but wasn't. Driving further on toward Portland Bill it was the same, although now there was no dust, just grass filling empty space, and rock and the road in front of them, and there was fog, which was thickening.

The English Channel swell was pounding against Portland Bill, sending spray up high. From a distance away, Clive said that the lighthouse looked different from how he remembered it. But as they got closer it became obvious the light part was missing.

Amidst large blocks of stone, glass prism segments were glinting where they had fallen, refracting the light penetrating the storm-cloud into the colours of the spectrum. Nothing remained of the public house at Portland Bill that Clive remembered from when he was a kid with his parents. There was just a pile of rubble.

"Must have been bad here," Jules said. The mournful tone of the foghorn blasted out. It wasn't how he remembered it. It was more piercing than it had been all those years ago.

Clive said nothing, he just remembered a different time. The difference was stark. How good things had been that summer with his mum and dad and his brother. Now the place was ruined. The foghorn sent its warning again, out over the wild sea.

"Let's go back," Clive said. "I don't like this place now."

11

They were back at the Cove House Inn, sitting close to a roaring fire, talking. "Where are they?" Jules asked Nail.

"The entrances? Up on the top. Disguised. Difficult to find. They're in the Victorian forts and gun battery emplacements. The entrance to the storage caverns is in a fort overlooking Weymouth Bay—"

The door rattled and a mid-twenties man with a dark ginger beard and hair all over the place from the wind came in. He shut the door quickly and the fire flared, giving out very welcome heat.

"This is Brad Hutchings," Nail said, introducing the guy. Hutchings nodded and disappeared into the gents. When he came out his hair was tidier.

"Glad to be in here," he said, as he dragged a chair up to the fire. "It's wild out there."

Nail nodded. He could hear the wind moaning around the granite eaves of the building. "It's limestone around here," he said. "Some's ground up and used for cement. The harder varieties have been used for buildings. It's been quarried and mined for hundreds of years. During Nibiru, people sheltered wherever they could. The underground places were a good idea." The wind picked up outside and shrieked around the entrance porch.

"There are places near sea level, Hutchings added. Most are blocked off now where there's been rock falls. Those you can get into easily get flooded, So when the tsunami came anyone in the lower levels wouldn't have stood a chance." There was silence for a few moments.

"Want drink and food?" Nail asked.

"What have you got?"

"If you want food quick there's sandwiches. A local baker does the bread. Local caught fish, and double-fried chips'll take twenty minutes. There's not much else yet. Other than sometimes we have chicken, or rabbit, courtesy of Brad." Nail gave a sly smile.

Brad shrugged, "Got to get organised for the classy stuff," he said.

During the evening a few local folks came in. Shook off the rain when they closed the door on the howling wind and the surf-noise, and they got close to the fire

At a quarter-to-one next day people began to arrive through the storm. Men and women were in clothing that had got off-white rub marks from the limestone they had got too close to. Shoes had off-white caked-on mud that they tried to get rid of on the scraper before they came through the door. They came in and sat and at first, they chatted inconsequential stuff. Introductions took place. Clive and Jules told them how things were in the Midlands. The folks told how things were along the south coast. And then Jules asked them about Oscar Stanway.

"Stanway . . . that name rings a bell."

"He's a research scientist," Jules said. "Anything that needs sorting out would attract him. He's that sort of guy. He thrives on challenges."

"Has he got a limp?"

"Yes, he has. His brother Harry said Oscar had a motor bike accident and his leg was pinned back together."

"I remember the man. Stopped with us in the Victorian Tunnels. Helped us sort out lighting. Oscar was full of enthusiasm. But he moved on when they needed help in the

71

old fuel storage depot where a few hundred folks were sheltering."

"He went there about three weeks back," another man with an unkempt beard and bad teeth said.

The others sitting around were listening to a man who was talking about the tunnels. He seemed to be in overall charge. His attitude was considerate, and decisive, and he listened to the others' point of view. His name was Delavan Henry and he came from St. Kitts. His skin was moderately dark and there was a smudge of white on his forehead just below the hairline. It was cut too, and there was a trickle of dried blood where he had hit his head on some low limestone.

A woman spoke up, who said she represented the Victorian Tunnels. Her name was Mel Perry.

"Oscar was with us for about a week. We had a communication problem with one of the comms sets. Turned out to be the damp. All he did was dry it out near a Camping Gaz stove, then it worked."

"Is he still with you?" Clive asked.

"Moved on again."

"Any idea where to?"

"We'd heard that when Portland Light was destroyed in the tsunami Oscar was worried that seaborne vessels would be in danger in the waters off the Bill, so he went to investigate. The currents of Portland Race are treacherous. Come from two different directions"

"He couldn't do much about that, could he?" Jules asked.

"Not for the light, or the Race, obviously. But he thought he could do something about the foghorn. After the tsunami destroyed the light, the foghorn wasn't working either. Oscar thought he could fix it. That's where he went after he left us."

"Clive and I were at the Bill yesterday; the foghorn was

working," Jules said.

"So he did some good there," Mel Perry said. "He's an all-round guy, is Oscar, Good-looking too."

Clive shoved his chair back and stood. Stretched.

"Portland Bill, Jules?"

"Looks like it."

"Then let's go . . . but first, where's Nail?"

"He's stirring the mash tun in the cellar," Brad Hutchings called. "Over there, the black door and down the steps."

In the cellar Clive pressed three twenties into Nails hand. Nail nodded his thanks. "We're trying to get a barter system going," he said, "Seems the fairest way to do business these days. He looked at the twenties and wondered how valuable they would be.

"A barter system would be a good start," Clive said. "But there's nothing else I can give you."

"Keep it. You can owe me. If you find this Oscar guy, get him to stop by and help us improve temperature control in the cellar."

* * *

Up on the heights the dust had been washed away by torrential rain. The rain had stopped now, but the wind was buffeting the car about as Jules drove slowly through the open land between villages to Portland Bill. She pulled up as near as she could get to the lighthouse. Some of it looked precarious. The fog was thicker now than yesterday. Maybe someone standing ten yards away would be disappearing.

They left the Cherokee in the public house car park and walked to the lighthouse. The foghorn sounded again. They felt in their chests. It remained in their ears after it ceased.

Jules thrashed the knocker on the door of the lighthouse-keeper's cottage. A few seconds later it opened and a man stood there with a pistol aimed straight and level at Clive's head.

Jules realised it was Oscar because of his resemblance to Harry. The set of the jaw and the shape of the mouth were similar, and the smile was there too. He seemed more volatile than Harry. Probably his recent experiences convinced him to have the pistol ready.

"We're friends, Oscar. We need you to help us find Harry."

He showed interest. "Who are you?"

"Friends. Has Harry mentioned Jem Dearden?"

"He has." Oscar lowered the gun slowly. "You can't be too careful these days, it's not very populated around here, and things have changed."

"You bet they have. That's one of the reasons we need your help."

"How come?"

"Harry and his girl have gone missing."

"Hell no . . . I thought this would happen at some point."

Jules added, "We aren't talking about them being local-missing. This is serious. Can we come in?" The cold had started to penetrate. Jules shivered as she showed Oscar her SHaFT pass.

He held the door wide and they followed him in.

It was a welcoming place. But maybe a trifle austere, as befitting a small team of men fulfilling an uncomfortable duty on the boundary of dangerous rocks and the wild sea. Two leather sofas were there, with seat cushions sunk through use. A television was switched on. *Next broadcast in 1 hour 16 minutes*, a countdown message said.

A dining table had six chairs, and a twelve by eighteen framed photograph of the Queen was on the wall. The place was warm from a Calor gas heater, the sort that had three ceramic burners in a chromed surround.

"You still manage to get gas cylinders?" Clive asked. Oscar's Pistol came up again. Jules could see Oscar knew how to use it.

"Why do you want to know about the gas cylinders?" Oscar asked.

"Natural thing to ask, isn't it, how you keep the fire going?"

"Maybe it's a normal thing to ask, but we didn't plan the cylinders. They're an afterthought. Didn't fit into the scenario. We found them and the heater in a wrecked garage in Wyke Regis. Anything else you need to know?"

"I want to know why you need the gun when we're around and we're doing our best to be friendly," Jules said.

"Can't be too careful," Oscar repeated what he said before. As he spoke the warning two men came in from another room. There was the faint sound of a generator in the background. Another two came in and they shut the door. The sound of the generator faded. One of the men had a tray with steaming mugs on it. It was coffee, and it smelt good. He put the tray on the table.

"Who're our guests Oscar?" The first one through asked. He had a pullover with flashes indicating he was in charge. Oscar put the pistol away.

"They say they're friends of my brother."

"We *are* friends of Harry," Clive said.

"You helped him out with the Co-Orditrax . . . remember?" Jules reminded Oscar about the instrument he and Harry had invented during the Manhattan crisis.

Oscar's look changed from suspicious to curious and then to friendly.

"Are you happy with the horn?" he asked the crew. He knew what their answer would be. They ought to be happy with it. As there was no light now the horn's piercing noise still warned ships passing by they were near dangerous rocks.

"The horn is better than it's been for a long while," the guy with the rank flashes said. 'We'll keep it going permanently until the light's repaired."

"If we manage to get it repaired," another guy added.

Oscar stood quickly. "Then my job's done. I'll beg a lift off these folks. You are going back to the Midlands, aren't you?"

"Via the Cove House Inn. We need you to help us return a favour. They need help with temperature control in the cellar."

12

Other than the wind turbine lying across the northbound lane, which caused a sixteen-mile detour, the drive back to Dearden Hall was straightforward. That is, if seeing no more than one hundred cars on the way to the Midlands from the south coast of England was straightforward. Before Nibiru there would be a continual stream of traffic. The journey gave Jules and Clive ample time to explain Harry and Esma's disappearance to Oscar.

After they finished telling him the detail he was silent for a while, until he saw a sign for a motorway stop-off.

"I need a strong coffee," he said.

"I'm not surprised, me too," Clive, who was driving, said. His tiredness needed killing with caffeine.

There wasn't much left in the motorway service station. All the gifts had been emptied out. It was doubtful they had been sold. Most of it had been trivia, and people were not into trivia these days. The lights were low and flickering, on emergency generation.

There were not many customers, but the staff on duty were trying to be cheerful and keep things going. Trying to get normality back. So the staff came back and did the shifts. Pay was from the stock of food, the long-dated stuff. Food was what really counted. How pay would come when the stock ran out was a problem for when it happened.

The three sat at a side table with their coffees. Whereas at one time the incessant roar of traffic would accompany a break at a motorway service station, now it was eerily silent.

"Harry is unique," Oscar said. His eyes looked moist. "He

always has been. And he's difficult to keep up with sometimes, with how his mind works."

"We've noticed that. We all love him, one way or another," Jules said. She felt the tears too, and tried to hide them. Clive touched her hand, held it. He touched her shoulder and she drew closer. Clive hardly knew Harry Stanway. Even less did he know Esma. Anglo-Saxon? It was difficult to believe, but he *had* experienced a temporal shift demonstration in the Hub, so he had to believe.

"Why don't the aliens help?" Oscar asked Clive.

"I wish they would, but they've gone to ground. Lan-Si-Nu said they were leaving us to our own devices for a while. The only way we would learn, he said."

"Like a mother hawk kicking the chicks out the nest and saying get your own mice?"

"Something like that." Jules unwrapped a serviette that was around a knife and fork. Wiped her eyes with it.

"From your own observations, what do you think has happened to my brother and his girl?" Oscar had asked this question before, when they were on the road. Now it was different. They'd had time to think and the motion had stopped.

"All the evidence is there that they went through the doorway, but what's on the other side is impossible to tell—"

"There was just blackness when we opened the door. Blackness and stars." Jules said. "We got out quick . . . didn't want to open up something we couldn't control."

"I don't blame you for that. But don't forget, it is a physical thing beyond the door. We just need to understand it."

"What do you suggest?"

"What I suggest, Jules, is that we have another coffee, and

then that we kip for a while in a room in the motel."

"*If* there's a room available."

"Got to be . . . there's no traffic to speak of. No traffic is no people."

"I'll sort it," Clive said. He went across and spoke to the guy behind the counter about rooms. Passed over two redundant two-pound coins and came back with three more steaming caffeine shots, black ones, in large mugs on a tray.

"We've got rooms as well as coffee. 211, 212 and 213."

"Three rooms?" Jules asked.

"Yep."

"How much was that?"

"They said we could sort it out in the morning. One of the guys went and got these plastic key cards, didn't even take our names."

* * *

Next morning there was still no-one at reception. The two guys in the café tried to make three full English breakfasts. They were mediocre but smelt good and sauce put them right. Clive waved a twenty-pound note at one of the guys. He rang up the sale and tilled the money. Gave a receipt but no change.

"When do the management arrive?" Jules, wondering how long the place would survive, asked one of the guys.

"Sometimes they come in around ten. They're trying to get things up and running again. Co-ordinating with other motels in the group and trying to re-organise the supply chain."

"What do we owe you for the rooms?"

"Thirty a night for each room'll do. Cash or card?" Jules had a credit card for a SHaFT account. The card machine was typically slow, but it worked.

There were two women at the fuel kiosk. The pumps had a note attached, *limit ten gallons*. The well-known signature on the identity-card worked again and with the tank full to the neck they took the exit to the Midlands and the north.

Around mid-day they pulled into the courtyard at Dearden Hall. Tomahawk was in his run and came to the wire sniffing Oscar Stanway. Jules gave him the warnings about not looking the wolf in the eye. The warnings were first given when Jem Dearden picked up the Black Alaskan wolf as a pup. *Don't look him in the eye*, Red Cloud had said. *If you do he may go for your throat.* Tomahawk Shahn of Offchurch was, in Red's words, *Real big*.

Oscar sidled up to the wire, stood two feet away looking sideways at the wolf, who looked full-on at Oscar.

"Slowly offer him your hand," Jules said. "He'll get your scent and remember it. He thinks he's the boss. When Jem has him out of the run he is the boss."

"He lets him out?"

"Oh yes. He's often in the great hall with us."

Just then the studded oak door to the manor house opened and a man in his mid-forties emerged. He was well-muscled, at least six feet tall. He had auburn hair, blue eyes and a rugged, handsome face with a scar on his forehead, above his left eye. A tall woman who had everything in the right places came to the door and stood at his side.

Oscar recognised Jem Dearden and Rowan of Maldon from Harry's description. Rowan was a beautiful woman, tall, with clear cut, refined features. Her hair caught the sunlight, which added to her presence. Her coming from Anglo-Saxon England was believable by her looks, but it did stretch the imagination rather too much. Oscar Stanway was intrigued by

Dearden and Rowan. He longed to talk to them one-to-one, to ask how it all happened. To get the fine detail. Oscar glanced behind him and saw the ancient forest where it all happened. He could see native oak, elm and ash, some of the trees fallen and lying at grotesque angles after the cyclone, but the remaining forest of Leofwin's Hundred was huge, crowded, dark and thick. And, according to what Harry had said, amongst the trees, deep in the forest, there was a place called The House of the West Wind, which was a gateway to space-time.

13

The noise grew more insistent and widespread the closer Harry and the others came to the giant outcrop, which lay as far as they could see to their right and their left.

"Any idea what lies beyond that?" Harry asked.

"No; it's the first time we've been this far away from Base Camp. It's risky being away because the way back home could open up again."

"OK. But maybe we'll learn a lot from where we're going now. There's something significant about those things," Harry said . . . "They are more than vegetation."

"What are you getting at?" Martell asked.

"I think I know what he means," Villiers said. "All the time we've been here I've felt we're being watched." Martell had thought this too but it had been too radical for him to talk about, now it was all out in the open.

"We're being watched by those things up front, the Brobs," Harry cut in. "How about you, Esma, what do you think?"

She looked in the direction they were going, sniffed the air, lifted her hand to shield her eyes against the sun. "It is like Arden Forest, where sometimes wolves' eyes watch from behind trees . . . and the eagle with golden eyes sees us through leaves, from sky."

"What are you saying, young lady? Don't talk in riddles."

"Eyes . . . but not eyes, see us here. Look." She pointed to the growths. "They see us. Hear us when we walk near."

"How do you know that?" Martell was sceptical.

"I see, and hear . . . eyes are good, my ears big," she laughed.

"You have lovely ears. Not big. But they are attuned to sounds we don't hear," Harry said.

They reached the outer fringes of the forest. At first, the silence was uncanny, and then Harry picked up a low pulsating noise. He glanced at Villiers and Martell. They had heard it and Martell looked nervous.

"Sounds like Calculus," Harry said to Esma, tilting his head to hear better. She smiled in response.

"What do you mean, sounds like calculus," Villiers couldn't work it out. "Have you got a special affinity with math . . . you *hear* calculus?"

"Calculus is my cat. He purrs, similar to the noise we can hear now."

"This sound is structured at times," Villiers said. He was picking up some repeated tones, and other tones that grew in complexity. From some distance away, another set of vibrations commenced and then to their left there was a more musical sound. They traced the sound to a smaller, but still a giant growth, by Earth standards.

"They talking," Esma said.

She placed her ear to a trunk they came to. It was soft to her skin, and the sound came through gently, like a melody that touched her, deep inside. "Once I hear like this in Leofwin's Hundred. Music from oak tree we call Scop Ac . . . what you say . . . Scop is man who comes to us and sings."

Villiers and Martell became attentive. "Where exactly do you come from, Esma?" Villiers asked. He hadn't been able to place her accent. Or understand the complexity of her presence. He was normally good with accents. Esma's was . . . out of place.

"My home was Maldon. My father put straw on roof."

"He was a thatcher," Harry said. Esma's background was familiar to him. "There is far more to Esma's presence with us than you think, Prof." Harry had taken to calling Villiers Prof. The Prof didn't mind.

"I may as well tell you exactly what happened. You need to know. Come and sit here for a while."

And Harry told them what had happened in Leofwin's Hundred. How the Hub, the House of the West Wind, had introduced them to the phenomenon of temporal shift. Elaborated on how the Grid was a spatial and temporal transfer system. And then the punch-line, when he told them Esma was Anglo-Saxon . . . that she had come to modern times through the Grid.

They both stared at her. Villiers, with his scientific mind, trying to assess whether Harry was telling the truth. But then, over an hour or two, details that both Harry and Esma told them, and the sincerity of their explanation, won out, and the two men cautiously accepted what they had been told. What made it easier to understand was their present predicament, being some place with physical laws that were different to those of Mother-Earth.

"Look, I know it's difficult to believe," Harry said, "But so is what's happened to the four of us, Being some place with physical laws that were different to those of Mother-Earth is very questionable." The two men agreed to that and fell silent. Thinking.

And then, "Tell us what happened when you were at Scop Ac," Martell said to Esma. Esma's reaction to the gentle sound coming from the distant alien life-form was unusual.

"Before Jem, Mitch and Jules come through House of West Wind, me and Rowan go on horses into forest—"

"The House of the West Wind is what the Anglo-Saxons

called the Hub," Harry interrupted.

Esma disregarded the interruption. "In forest is Scop Ac. Ac is oak. Scop like I say, is man who sing and tell story with words that sing."

"And rhyme; Scops were minstrels," Harry said.

Esma nodded. "Scop Ac in Leofwin's Hundred make sound like is coming from there," she pointed to the origin of the more distant sound. "Scop Ac now have name you call Uberatu Oak. He has thunder hit him, make hole, right through."

Harry explained. "You are familiar with Leofwin's Hundred, yeah?"

They both said they were. "What Esma is saying is that there is a tree in the forest that we call Uberatu's Oak that she heard the identical sounds coming from way back in Leofwin's time. That's a thousand years ago"

"Yes, and I hear him two week before Nibiru come."

"Did it sound exactly like what we are hearing from that thing, over there?" Villiers indicated the direction of the source of the sound.

Esma said nothing, just nodded.

They reached the base of the life-form, *It's one of the Brobs*, Martell reaffirmed. It was emitting the sound Esma associated with Uberatu's Oak. "We've walked a mile and a third from the other tree," He had counted 2,358 paces from the life-form making a similar sound.

"That's useful to know." Martell's voice had a hard edge. to it. He didn't bother to ask Harry why he had done the counting.

Harry was a gatherer of information. Ever since he could remember he had been fascinated with facts. He hoovered them up. The ability to rationalise facts, manipulate complex figures and bring to order the most abstract of ideas. made Harry a superb scientist.

Harry had, as near as he could regulate his 2,358 paces made each one of them thirty-six inches, a standard imperial yard. He had done a swift mental calculation and converted paces to distance travelled. Unbeknown to the others on the walk he set the pace to two miles per hour, and when they arrived at their destination he worked out the time taken. He glanced at his watch, as he had done when they started, and from this, he compared Earth 2 time to Earth 1 time. His previous ratio of 12:1 held true.

He looked upward from the base of the Brob. The size of the growth was gargantuan, larger than anything else that they could see. As they had approached the outcrop, there was movement amongst the topmost leafage, which adjusted its orientation so that it faced them. The pulsating tones continued as they drew near the object. This time the sound was more complex. It rapidly cascaded across a number of octaves. There were gaps and re-commencements in the stream of sound.

Standing close to the growth, Harry mentally worked through what Esma said about Uberatu's Oak. He brought the Mycorrhizal Network to mind again, and the other network, the internet, with which he had great affinity. *What if* . . . he thought . . . *no, that surely couldn't be possible . . . but there again.*

"Have you heard of the internet?" he asked Villiers.

"The inter what?"

"The internet. I'll explain it in detail later. Let me just say that Mycorrhizal life resembles the internet, which is a worldwide provision of information that can be accessed by anyone at any time. The internet is accessed by the end user using a computer."

"Harry. You are telling us things we have no clue about."

"So, listen and learn. Mycelial fungal life is conjectured to provide widespread communication between tree species. It is a network that exists below ground level and its presence is most often shown by fungus growing above ground. Sometimes the network spreads for miles underground. There has been some research into this in the Malheur National Forest in Oregon, and it is there that the world's largest organism exists. The network has over two thousand acres of spread, and those doing the research have calculated that it could be up to eight and a half thousand years old. They call it the Humongous Fungus."

"What is this . . . internet you are speaking of?"

"It's a wireless network that is a major means of communication and data exchange. I think what we see demonstrated here is a network that gives a similar result to the internet. It allows transmission of data; hence, what we observe is the obvious interest in us because, as you say, we feel we are being watched. And we see that the interest is coordinated because the Brobs follow our movement collectively. I think these growths may be intelligent."

Martell had the trace of a smile on his face, while, on the contrary, Villiers looked intrigued. His mind was full of questions.

"Before I start further explanation let's build a shelter," Harry suggested. "Doesn't have to be complicated, but it'll provide security. You never know what may turn up here"

14

"I need to see the Hub and Villiers' lab," Oscar Stanway said to Dearden after introductions, explanations, cold drinks and food. On the journey from Portland, Jules and Clive Fraser had prepared Oscar for what to expect at Dearden Hall. The people he would meet. Their names, what they did. He met Mitch Doughty and Lee Wynter. There had been no mention of SHaFT.

"We'll go to the Hub later," Dearden said. Repository 1 and the lab may be tomorrow." There are formalities we need to go through before you can go there."

"Such as?"

"R1 is at the heart of a controlled access establishment. It has to be a joint decision to allow you in. You have my OK, but it has to be verified by Mike Ramsay, the officer commanding MoD Kineton."

"Set this up quickly, will you? I'm hoping Harry hasn't overstepped the mark this time."

*   *   *

Matt Roberts had been hands-on during the transfer of Lars Knudsen, Pierpoint and those representing the Earth when they went before the Hnioss on the planet of Wasiri-Poya. His was the finger that pressed the Onnoth button that propelled them on their way over the nodes of the Grid. Roberts had acquainted himself well with the Control Room of the Hub and Dearden wanted him back at Dearden Hall for what he had in mind.

Matt and Storm Petrel were currently on the loose up north in the Lake District. They were going on a scrambling

break around Broadcrag Tarn, near Scafell Pike, so they said,
"If you need us just give us a call, we'll be straight back,"
Roberts reassured Dearden.

When Matt got a text from Dearden. There was no mistaking its urgency.

Roberts' Land Rover, in desert camo, pulled up and when he saw Dearden he apologised for being late and put the delay down to a collapsed bridge on the M6, which caused a long detour. After Dearden's text saying he needed his finger on the Onnoth button again, Matt and Storm covered the two hundred miles to Dearden Hall with burnt rubber on tarmac.

Dearden led the way into the primeval forest to give Oscar a demonstration of the Hub. It was always the same when a stranger saw the Hub for the first time, and Oscar was no different, A demonstration of the Hub was the *real* test. It usually provoked fear and curiosity in different measure according to the mental stamina of the individual. A small number had freaked out, two had passed out and one had a heart attack and died. Some, although not many, had taken it in their stride. Oscar was one of these.

Roberts led Oscar Stanway and the others to the spiral stairway on the far side of the room of the exhibits; the bizarre space where the Wasiri-Chanchiyan travellers left a record of the worlds they had discovered.

They continued up the spiral stairs and Roberts stopped off at the Control Room to set up the Hub for a local timeshift. Sometimes Roberts and Storm Petrel did this for kicks. They called them Curiosity Trips. They would set up the Hub, press the button and let the Hub run. They would stop the regression to see what was going on outside; what changes there had been in the preceding years. To see how primitive things were. But Roberts and Storm Petrel never let the Hub run for more than fifteen seconds.

Oscar wanted to stay for a while in the Control Room to analyse the layout. "It's alien, but accessible," he said, settling down on one of the oversize seats. He didn't give a damn that his feet were swinging in the air like they used to when he was a kid sitting on a seat made for adults.

"There's no time for this," Roberts cut in. "I want to show you the workings of this place, and then we're going on a trip," so they continued up to the next level. There were storage cabinets around the perimeter wall and projecting through the ceiling in the centre of the room was an immense crystal. It stopped Oscar in his tracks. Sometimes even those used to it were overawed. He rubbed his leg; the one that had the titanium pins and screws in it. Occasionally the injury was useful. This time it gained him a couple of minutes. He winced and cursed under his breath for added effect and took the opportunity to study the interior of the room.

"This damn leg." He rubbed it violently, avoiding the surfaces that were tender, and looked at the crystal. Its base was resting in a cradle. Oscar saw where it disappeared into the ceiling and gauged the height . . . *all of nine feet high, plus what's above, if it does continue through the ceiling. It must weigh tons.*

Storm Petrel pushed him toward the stairs and they climbed onward, to the top level.

"Are you ready?" Matt asked. He looked at them to check them out. They said they were ready. "We won't select any particular date, we'll just press the button and go backward." Matt pressed the remote, which connected to the control room, two floors below. There was the heavy clunk of a relay and then the outer wall and ceiling gradually became transparent. The surrounding forest changed, as if it were a mirage. The trees that had fallen during the Nibiru cyclone were suddenly upright and the forest became stately and in full leaf. The season changed rapidly and the leaf canopy began to rain leaves the colours of Autumn. The change sped up and the outside became a blur. Black cumulus split by jagged lightning twisted in the sky above. Ten seconds of local time passed on the left-hand Carruthers Chrono and Roberts pressed stop. The scene settled on a forest of tall deciduous trees, some with trunks of immense diameter. The scene was full of movement as leafage and lianas hanging from branches many feet above were disturbed by a breeze.

"I'll be damned. That's ancient forest," Oscar mumbled, as he walked to the transparent wall and gazed outside. The others approached the wall too, and gathered close. It was as if there was a need for reassurance, the normality of company. A timeshift was intriguing. Laden with potential. But there was always the uncertainty.

There was cloud cover in the time they had come to and through speakers on the inside of the Portal a cacophony of sound came from the wilderness outside. Deep guttural sounds close by. Distant roaring. A flapping of great wings.

"We ought to pass on going outside," Dearden said. There was no disagreement.

"When is this time, do you know?" Oscar asked. Roberts scanned the central Carruthers Chrono of the three on the wall. It showed the amount of displaced time.

"9,252 years 81 days into the past," Roberts said.

"If what we have experienced and see outside is true, that takes us into the Palaeolithic twilight."

"Believe you me, Oscar, this is true," Jules confirmed.

At that moment the clouds above parted and revealed, at about double the size of a full-moon, a planet clouded with white cirrus. It had the blue of oceans and the green of forests. Oscar reacted with complete surprise. The rest of the team less so. They were used to surreal events. Their surprise level had been muted.

"That's Nibiru. Lan-Si-Nu told us that at one time it was part of a double planet system with the Earth," Doughty exclaimed.

"We could do an action replay of when the Wasiri did the first planetary shift," Wynter suggested. "Like how you see the best shots in a game of soccer."

"We'll pass on that, as well as on going out the door," Dearden said. Then he said, "Oscar, we have broadened your experience. Now we have to talk things over and get organised. Let's go forward to our own time and get back to the hall, ready for Ramsay to give us access to R1."

*   *   *

There had recently been unexplained aerial activity above Kineton Base. And when night fell, the same day Dearden rang Ramsay to get permission to enter R1, an event occurred that caused some panic. Paul Gilbert, one of the night security guards, had stopped for a leak by a hedge on his random patrol about the MoD site. He heard a distant humming noise, looked up and saw some rotating lights. As he later explained, he saw a redness and the heat radiating from some sort of power-plant on a UFO whose black silhouette had blocked out some of the stars.

The craft drifted to the centre of the triangle formed by the three runways of MoD Kineton, and hovered.

Gilbert radioed his sergeant and told him to look outside, above the airfield, *'Bloody quick, while the thing's there.'* The sergeant saw it too. He shouted to the other guards in the security blockhouse. For five minutes they witnessed the craft hovering and then it ascended vertically at a crazy speed before it angled away heavenwards.

Ramsay rang Dearden. Ramsay's respect for SHaFT, whose HQ was in Dump 4 on the Kineton site, had grown enormously and access to R1 was granted with no argument.

2130 hours, ten minutes after the UFO event at MoD Kineton, the telephone rang in Dearden Hall. Lee Wynter was nearest. "It's for you, Jem my man. *Mike Ramsay.*"

"You're in to R1, Jem," Ramsay said. "Unconditional. Whenever you want, as long as you want." And then he told him briefly about the UFO sighting. There was a momentary gap in the conversation, and then . . . "Jem can I ask a big favour?"

"Depends what it is."

"Include me in, will you? All this interesting stuff . . . I want in on it."

"You may get way out of your depth."

"I get bored here, in this damn office."

"I guarantee you wouldn't get bored with what we're up against."

"Can we meet up . . . when you come to R1?"

Dearden thought for a minute. Ramsay was a good man now he had lightened up. He had proved his character with his unofficial release of the End Time weapon. As he was in overall command of MoD Kineton, it would be constructive for him to be acquainted with developments in the search for Harry and Esma as they evolved.

"OK, join us," Dearden told him. "I'll buzz you when we're leaving."

15

Not surprisingly, with his experiences around Leofwin's Hundred, Matt Roberts had begun to view life as being full of uncertainties. But he liked that. Uncertainties gave him an adrenaline rush, which suited his temperament. He was a man of the wilderness and he wanted things no other way. That suited Storm Petrel's temperament too. She was a one-off, like Roberts. As soon as she saw him in the States she was attracted, although it was against her game-play to show it immediately.

* * *

When Matt and Storm went into Charles Villiers' old laboratory again with Dearden and Oscar Stanway the pile of stones was still there, neatly stacked. The lump hammer had gone. It was back in one of Bill Templestone's toolboxes at Keeper's Cottage in Temple Balsall.

Dearden had prepared Oscar for what was on the other side the door. They were at the top of the steps at the back of the laboratory. The door was open and through the space there was blackness and the uncountable pinpricks of light of stars and galaxies. Ramsay squeezed closer to get a good look through the door-frame. He got quite close to Storm Petrel, so Roberts moved between them.

Oscar could see constellations. Groupings of heavenly objects, all of which were unfamiliar. No Orion . . . no Great Bear. No planets near the ecliptic. No ecliptic. He edged into the door-frame, which was deep. It was metallic and warm, signifying electronic activity. He looked down into the void and felt he was falling into it. He held onto the door frame with one hand, stretched his other hand forward, touched a transparent barrier. When they were in the Hub they had stepped forward to look at the primeval forest, separated from the outside by a layer of see-through material. But this was no Earthbound view, and to look out and downwards into the immensity of the Cosmos was deeply unsettling.

He backed away. Closed the oak door and latched it. Stood back and rubbed his temples. He tried to recall something Harry said to him when they met up a while back. Harry's mind was quick and operated on a different level to most people. Oscar was much the same. Their combined intellect was formidable, coming from the same gene-pool. But what was it Harry had said?

"Jem, you said Harry was talking about other realities . . . other dimensions, and you think Villiers was onto that as well?"

"That's what Harry thought."

"What convinced him of that?"

"The aliens mentioned other dimensions in vague terms and Harry found complex research components here in the lab. He said Villiers' notes implied alternative dimensions."

"I must meet those alien friends of yours . . . where are Villiers' notes now?"

"Should be somewhere in Harry's room back at the Hall."

"We have to find them. If I could examine Villiers' work I would probably come to the same conclusion as Harry. Hopefully that would lead us to where he is."

"Where he *and Esma* are," Rowan corrected.

"Yes, of course . . . where Harry *and* Esma are."

"And if *they* walked through that door, why can't we?" Storm asked.

"I'm wondering that myself." Oscar had seen enough, so

they locked R1 and went back to Dearden Hall.

* * *

"I think we should get Bill Templestone along again," Dearden said to Oscar. The two of them were on the threshold of Harry's pad. Dearden unlocked the door and they went in.

"Templestone and Harry were close," Dearden told Oscar. "Harry might have confided things to Bill that he wouldn't speak about to anyone else. He may remember things Harry confided to him."

Dearden phoned Templestone on his mobile but his elderly colleague didn't pick up. He left a text; *Come as soon as you can. It's about Harry.*

Dearden always felt he was intruding when he went inside Harry's room. He never usually went into the room without invitation. It was a very personal area. A representation of a DNA string hung from the ceiling. A photo of Harry's mother and father, and a separate photograph of Oscar and Harry together hung on the wall; the older and the younger brother, each in the cap and gown of academia.

There was a large television, a sound system, a settee and two easy chairs. A kitchen area, which was tidy. A table was laid for two but had chairs for four. Stuck to the wall with blue-tack was a two-feet by four-feet picture of a 4.7 S Maserati Granturisimo. On the opposite wall was a print of the Saturn V launch that paved the way to the Moon. Next to that, stuck with blue-tack, were some sheets of A4, numbered 1 to 6 with the heading on sheet one stating, *Quantum Entanglement of Superior Mass.* Oscar could speed read. He stood in front of the information and scanned it. He nodded and moved further into the room, taking things in, analysing

97

information and objects. Ordering them in his mind.

"I presume his lab's through there?" Oscar pointed to one of two doors, the one with the Greek alpha and omega, A and Ω painted on it. The door was locked. Harry didn't want intruders. Dearden unlocked the lab door, went in, switched on the light. There was a desk, a light oak one with three drawers each side and a knee-hole, into which was nested a chair on castors. There was an Apple iMac and keyboard. An A4 notepad, biro pens, pencils. A twelve-inch rule and a rubber lay on the A4 pad, which was open. The topmost page was busy with sketches and the symbolic expressions of higher math. "This might be useful," Dearden said.

Oscar went to where Dearden stood and looked at the information on the pad, taking it in, working through it. He touched the page, moved his finger down it, tenderly tracing his brother's calculations. He nodded his head in agreement as he came to Harry's conclusion.

Shelves were fixed to one of the walls. Plastic containers, the small red ones that stack together, occupied half the shelf-space. They were labelled, and each one contained electronic components. Resistors in one container, capacitors, condensers in others. There were containers of transistors, each container labelled for a different function. Transformers were lined up to the left of one of the shelves. On another shelf were spools of fine wire; red, yellow, white, black and the rest of the colours used for identification in circuitry. A separate table hosted test equipment, meters, oscilloscopes, a Megger. A soldering iron rested in a stand. By it was solder, and flux in a black plastic tub with white writing and a red lid. Oscar picked up the solder. Although it was only solder he held it gently, as if it was part of his kid brother.

"Harry never used Multicore solder," Oscar said, quietly.

"Quirky thing really. He didn't like the flux, he said it was too resinous, so he always used thin sticks of 50/50 solder and this flux." Oscar lifted up the tub. "It's a non-toxic flux paste, messier to use than Multicore solder but it's good. I use it myself." He put the tub of flux down. Touched other things his brother had touched. There was a movement nearby. Dearden glanced down and saw Harry's cat, who had sneaked in through the door.

"Harry's cat . . . he called it Calculus," Dearden said.

"He would . . . he was always innovative." Oscar sighed, remembering. The cat rubbed his leg. He picked it up and went over to the desk, pulled out the chair and sat, cuddling the cat. Calculus was warm and soft and he began to purr. It was a sound of contentment that was musical in an offbeat sort of way. Oscar put the cat down and opened each desk drawer in turn.

There was nothing of significance until he came to the bottom right drawer where there was a wad of handwritten and printed notes. He recognised Harry's handwriting, bold and incisive, with a slight leftward slope to the ascenders and a slight rightward slope to the descenders. Clipped to Harry's A4 pages were some larger sheets, the old Foolscap size. They were discoloured, and the writing was in faded black ink but it was still readable.

"Bingo." Oscar spotted Charles Villiers' signature on one of the old documents. There were sketches within the documents, done with a fine-nibbed pen, maybe a mapper, main detail in black, secondary detail in red. Straight ruled lines led to appended explanatory notes written in green ink.

Oscar flipped through the pages quickly on his initial read, searching for relevant detail. The fifth page of information in Villiers' notes was on unruled paper, folded to foolscap size.

He opened it up. It was an isometric drawing of a door-frame with sizes attached. It was a copy, one of the old purple ink duplications. A manufacturing drawing because it had tolerances attached and notes for the manufacturer. The material to be used was stainless steel sheet. Its qualities were tightly specified. It would be ductile. It was to be austenitic, containing 20% chromium and 14% nickel. Before it was finally assembled into a box-like structure, the fabrication was to be annealed, so that its crystalline structure would be rendered non-magnetic.

"Why did Villiers specify in so much detail that the door frame was to be austenitic . . . *and* non-magnetic?"

"You're the scientist, you tell me," Dearden said.

"I would suggest that Villiers didn't want any form of *uncontrolled* magnetism to affect the process going on within the door frame."

"What process would that be?"

"I need time to sift through this information and then I'll let you know. It does seem interesting that Harry stuck the information about Quantum Entanglement of Superior Mass on his wall. I need to look at that. I will bear in mind that the door frame, behind which is a technology that I have yet to examine, has been specified to be made of non-magnetic material. I will therefore assume that, in some way, magnetism is involved with whatever process is going on. If the door frame were magnetic could it interfere with a controlled process?

"It looks as though you're suggesting we go back into R1 to examine the interior of the door frame?"

Oscar nodded. "Oh yes . . . we'll have to do that." He pushed the chair back. Got up from Harry's desk and yawned. "Let's relax for a while, sleep on things for tonight. It's been a long day. Tomorrow we'll go back into R1 with some instruments."

But events occurred that scuppered that idea.

* * *

Templestone arrived an hour after picking up Dearden's message. The outer door of Dearden Hall was locked so Templestone hit the iron knocker double-hard to make himself heard. The heavy noise echoed within. A few seconds later the lock grated and Gil Heskin let him in.

Rowan was with Dearden in the great hall, sitting on a two-seater sofa. There was a man Templestone thought he had seen before sitting at the oak table Rowan said was Leofwin's. The stranger looked similar to Harry. Mitch Doughty was there. Matt Roberts and his girl, the American, Storm Petrel were on the other sofa, a three-seater with cloth styled Art Deco.

Leon Wynter, the guy everyone said could think in three dimensions, was sitting in one of the two winged armchairs. The other one was vacant. It was always vacant, waiting for Templestone to come to Dearden Hall because it was his chair. He headed to it and sat. Pulled it round to face the others.

Dearden stood and offered him a drink, expecting him to ask for Glenmorangie.

"Coffee, black and sweet."

Dearden went to a side table where a cafetière was being kept hot on a burner. He added another scoop of coffee into the cafetière. Poured in more water to the right level. Stirred. Let it brew for another minute then squeezed the plunger and poured some of the coffee into a big mug, Templestone's personal one. He handed the drink over.

Templestone grimaced. "More sugar."

Dearden spooned another sugar in. Stirred it. "It's good to see you, Priest." He used Templestone's SHaFT nick-name. "We're thinking you might be able to help us get to Harry and Esma." Templestone looked subdued. Didn't say anything.

"Did Harry tell you his plans?" Dearden asked.

Templestone stayed silent for a short while and Dearden was getting impatient. He was about to unsilence Templestone, and then—

"I told you before, when we were in R1. Listen . . . I lent Harry some masonry chisels. Sharpened them for him; and he was taking a lump hammer back into R1 to do some investigating. I know Harry wanted to see Lan-Si-Nu before he went back into Villiers' laboratory. There were things he wanted to ask the alien. Things he wanted to clear up. Problem was that Lan-Si-Nu and his buddies had gone to ground again so Harry went ahead into R1 without getting the information he wanted."

16

In recent months Storm Petrel and Matt Roberts had taken to spending a lot of time in Leofwin's Hundred. They were particularly attracted to Uberatu's Oak for two reasons. The first, that they could store wine in the hollow trunk of the ancient tree. The second reason was far less ordinary.

"There's something special about that oak," Storm said after she saw it the first time.

Matt sort of understood what she meant. Whenever he was inside it he felt peaceful.

He had fitted a door in place of the hessian plug Uberatu used to disguise the entrance to the cavernous space in the trunk. From the outside it looked like the home of an esoteric forest dweller who floated around on the fringes of humanity.

Some months before the Manhattan incident Uberatu had installed shelving, and Camping Gaz lanterns which hung from hooks screwed into the wooden heart of the ancient oak. Uberatu didn't appreciate the age of the oak tree, or its structure as a statement of arboreal grandeur. To him, it was simply a convenient structure with leaves from where he could spy on excavation work going on at the Hub. Inside, on one of the shelves, he had a Camping Gaz cooker with a hood which was vented to the outside to take away carbon monoxide. Uberatu had thought of everything to make the inside of the tree comfortable and safe to live in for an extended period of time.

Roberts unlocked the door to the oak and before she went in Storm sniffed the forest air.

"There it is again," she said. "That smell of high tension

current. The Hub's active again."

"I wonder who's traversing the Grid this time?" Roberts said. He was intrigued with the surroundings and the high technology of the place deep in the forest. He looked at the Hub through the spyhole in the trunk of the oak. He could see the exposed part on the top of the escarpment. It had dense forest encroaching upon it from behind. The building never changed, never weathered, only had undergrowth encroaching upon it, which Dearden sometimes organised a group of SHaFT guys to cut back. Occasionally there was intense activity inside the place, evidenced by the HT ozone smell and the rapidly gathering storm clouds and forked lightning a few hundred feet above.

Inside the hollow oak Matt and Storm were protected from the fierce wind they knew would follow. Storm shut the door. By the light of a torch held by Roberts, she struck a match and lit the lanterns as the wind arose and moaned through the slight gap around the door. Roberts pressed the igniter button to light the Calor gas heater and the fire soon began to dispel the chill and the damp.

When the wind had abated and the sharp smell of ozone dissipated, Storm became aware of a soft background noise she categorised as a sort of pulsating music. She couldn't put into words what she heard, so she said nothing about it until later, when they were back at Dearden Hall, alone.

"You don't hear music inside a lightning damaged oak when there's no radio there," was Roberts' first comment.

"You do. If you don't believe me we'll go back and you can listen."

"OK, if you really want me to, I'll come. Who was doing the singing, Nat King Cole?"

It was dusk when Roberts went back to the oak tree with Storm to listen to what she had heard. His ears were not as sensitive as Storm's. They had been subjected to small and large calibre gunfire, so they were damaged. He hated admitting it to anyone, but he sometimes wore hearing aids. They were discrete, hidden, expensive ones. Just to be sure about picking up the noise, if there was any, he wore the hearing aids and put them on their most sensitive setting.

They lit the lanterns and closed the door on the creatures of the night and once the fire was lit they cosied up into a night vigil.

When the activity started Roberts was into his second glass of vintage red he'd lifted from Dearden's wine cellar.

"Matt, listen," Storm's voice startled Roberts from the border of sleep and he was immediately awake. A few years of life in the military and then in SHaFT had attuned him to be immediately awake. It was there . . . a rapid pulsation in random bursts, rising to high tones at times and then lowering.

"You call that music?" he asked, remembering, although he didn't really want to acknowledge the memory.

"Well, maybe not exactly music, but whatever it is, it shouldn't be here."

Her words took him back to another time he thought had been a trick of his poor hearing. He had been inside the oak with Bill Templestone, when Dearden and the others were excavating the lower entrance to the Hub. That was when they discovered that Uberatu was using the hollow oak as a base from where he could spy on them.

Roberts heard the complex pulsation back then. Must have been two and a half years back. At the time he thought it odd but passed it off as a spell of tinnitus. An odd sound, admittedly but being the rational guy he was, he assumed the sound was his ears playing up. This time he was with Storm in the oak he was hearing the same sound. He remembered the first time looking at Templestone to see if he was reacting, but he wasn't. The older man's ears were in a worse state than Roberts'. Shortly afterwards they closed the oak up, set a trap for Uberatu by planting a Giant Hogweed by the entrance, and the odd event of the sounds coming from the oak was forgotten.

Initially, when Storm Petrel mentioned hearing noises inside the tree, Roberts kept quiet about his own experience because he was uncertain about how to broach the subject with her. Apart from that, he needed to believe that the sounds were caused by his tinnitus, not the damn tree.

He had grown very attached to Storm Petrel. More than just attached, in fact. When she first mentioned the noises, he thought that if he told her he had heard noises inside the oak tree as well she might do a bunk and take the next flight back to the States to get away from creepy old England.

Back in the present, it crossed his mind that it may be best to call the men in white coats. Oak trees were usually silent apart from when the wind buffeted them about. He wondered whether he and Storm might be suffering from some form of folie à deux, sharing an aural delusion for some, as yet, obscure reason. After all, Leofwin's Hundred was indeed a strange place, and sometimes irrational.

It was time to come clean, but when he was preparing to begin his explanation to Storm she began speaking, and then the noise grew more insistent. Roberts held a finger to his lips for silence. He analysed the sounds more thoroughly than he had when he was in the oak that first time with Templestone.

"I've heard this before," he said. Storm thought he was

going to ridicule her, so she was surprised when he told her about the previous incident.

"It's louder now, more obvious than when I was here with Templestone." He sat still, listening, and a thread of memory formed in his mind. It consolidated into a scene when he had been shore-based for a while.

"And there's something else. When I was in the Navy a few years back I was involved with decryption. It was a special assignment. I was seconded to a team who were intercepting information from terrorist cells. The bad guys were using various methods to communicate, including fast streaming of data."

"What are you suggesting?"

He blew back some strands of hair that had come out of his bandana. "We're hearing a coded message," he said. And then he recorded five minutes of it on his mobile.

*　*　*

Lan-Si-Nu was at Dearden Hall. The alien hadn't been seen for weeks, but he showed up, somehow intuitively aware of the need. He joined Dearden, Mitch Doughty and Lee Wynter, who were in discussion with Sir Willoughby Pierpoint and Mike Ramsay.

Ramsay had called them together to discuss a strategy to deal with the appearance, once again, of the black unidentified flying object over MoD Kineton. It had been in broad daylight this time, and it had hovered for ten minutes. Ramsay felt threatened. He was concerned that the UFO was interested in the radioactive weapon components remaining at Kineton. Weaponry, including nuclear, at MoD Kineton, was being dismantled under the terms of the Prime Directive.

Ramsay showed Lan-Si-Nu a photograph of the UFO. It

was not a grainy photograph that could be a composite image of something similar to a round lampshade photographed out of focus against a bright sky. The craft Lan-Si-Nu looked at in Mike Ramsay's photograph was in sharp detail. It was exactly the same shape as the image of the Chakrakan star ship he had uploaded on Wasiri-Poya. The deeper dimensions of knowledge in the Q-Gate revealed the destructive influence of the Chakrakans upon the Earth in times past. And here they were again.

Chakrakan, Nibiru, the Earths called it, had been a problem to the harmonic balance of the cosmos because of the inhabitants' twisted mentality, hell-bent, as they were, upon ways of violence. Way back in time, Chakrakan had affected the peace of the Prime Dimension. A clear threat was again present. Lan-Si-Nu felt a chill of uncertainty. It was an unusual emotion because it ran counter to the usual steadiness of the Prime Galaxy and the inbuilt calm of the Wasiri-Chanchiyans.

The alien handed back the photograph to Ramsay.

He loped over to a sofa and sat. His visage was so different to the features of the Earth people. At times it was difficult to interpret his facial expressions. This time, when Dearden glanced at him he saw a definite change. The alien's brow was pulled into tight dips and furrows. His eyes, normally quite round, were reduced to vertical slits. His lips were narrow, tight and wide.

Dearden and Pierpoint followed Lan-Si-Nu to the sofa, stood before him waiting for an explanation. Ramsay could see there was a problem and put the photo away. It was then that Matt Roberts and Storm Petrel came into the great hall.

"Ever heard a singing tree?" Roberts asked. He was met with stony silence and blank stares.

"Come on guys, there's a tree in the forest that's making weird noises, and you're not interested?"

"Shut it," Dearden said.

Roberts' eyes narrowed. "Did I hear you right?"

"You did."

17

Lan-Si-Nu, returned to the Hub. The space the aliens inhabited at the back of the room of the exhibits went way back into the escarpment. Those in transit, the many races who used the grid, and the Earths, too, had no idea what it was like beyond the wall. The entrance was camouflaged. No-one, without specialised knowledge, could gain access to that area.

After each phase of the Earths' renouncing of violence was completed, Lan-Si-Nu consolidated its detail in his mind. This time, he sat and entered the neural network by donning the helmet and then he entered his personal code. He allowed his mind to go quiet and prepared himself for communication with the quantum processors at the heart of the system. He shed the worry about Chakrakan and reached the silent part of his mind. After joining the Q-Gate he thought down the latest Earth progress into the library of the Great Annals.

After the recording of detail was complete Lan-Si-Nu lay on his comash and allowed himself to become mind-quiet now he was away from the neural network. He stayed that way for three and a half Earth hours and then arose refreshed. Into his mind, which had emptied whilst on the comash, came thoughts of the intrusion of the Chakrakan into the affairs of the Earths once again.

He remembered learning about how a similar situation had occurred prior to the previous rebellion of the Chakrakan. The Earth, in its young innocence, had been a vulnerable target, taken advantage of by a race whose biomolecular structure was bent away from the normality of peace. How that had occurred originally was difficult to determine. Maybe an external source had bent them. Whether it had been biological or non-biological could not be determined, but they were bent and that was a fact.

The Chakrakans had been contained by their first orbital-shift and subsequent cocooning. Their freedom of will had not been curtailed, so there was always a danger that, at some point, it could be possible that they would break free from the cocoon. From the Ramsay Earth's photograph, it looked as though a crew of Chakrakans had achieved a breakout.

Lan-Si-Nu called his crew together and asked for their thoughts on the matter.

"How has this situation happened?" Thal-Nar, the Temporal Engineer asked.

"It must have been when we lifted the cocoon recently to get positive traction on the planet for the latest orbital-shift."

"The cocoon-lifting took a very short space of time," Thal-Nar said. Whenever a question about time needed addressing he was the most knowledgeable, and he was always the first to respond. "The cocoon locked the population to their planet, so whoever has brought the Starship to the vicinity of Earth must have been ready to act whenever a chance occurred."

"This situation is a challenge to the state of equilibrium throughout the Cosmos," said Fen-Nu, Lan-Si-Nu's second in command. "It seems they have unfinished business with the Earth."

"And this new challenge that faces planet Earth is going to be difficult to deal with. We must refer it to the Hnioss to get a collective decision from the Council of the Interface of Worlds about what should be done," said Lan-Si-Nu.

* * *

After Lan-Si-Nu had left Dearden Hall, Roberts was able to get a word in and they listened to what he said about Uberatu's Oak.

"Man, it's getting weirder than ever round here." Lee Wynter interrupted, remembering the events he had been involved with in Leofwin's Hundred over the past few years. "First, we had the timeshift, and then Jem, Jules and Mitch brought Rowan, Esma and Beggsy back from a thousand years ago. We had Jules and Tomahawk rescuing Jem and Mitch from Manhattan through the Spatial Grid and now you're telling us about a singing tree. Come on, man, that's real creepy."

Roberts wasn't fazed by Lee's response. He relished the challenge because it enabled him to assert the truth of his experience. He sensed that what he had heard was not simply a random tinnitus sound. or the cry of a forest creature but, counter to all of his well-controlled military attitude, he acknowledged that the sound *had* emanated from the ancient oak itself.

"We were in the tree . . . right inside it, Jem . . . I swear, we were in the heart of the old oak, and the tree shared noises with us."

"What sort of noises?" Jules asked.

"There was a pattern of sounds that I thought I recognised from when I had a spell in cryptography."

"You're seriously telling us you heard the tree making noises?" Doughty challenged, trying to suppress laughter.

"You've got it." Roberts took out his mobile. "Give this a listen." He found the WAV file, selected it and played all five minutes of it. The quality was good. The sounds intriguing.

There was no interruption during the whole five minutes, just rapt attention, and then Roberts said, "I've been around

Uberatu's Oak no end of times and heard noises, but it's only since Harry disappeared that there has been this overlay—"

"Since Harry *and* Esma disappeared," Rowan corrected.

"Okay . . . okay. Since Harry *and* Esma disappeared the sounds inside the oak have got me worried. I heard them before, a while back when I was with Bill. What I'm hearing now is different to what it was before. As if the previous sound was a carrier wave and now we're hearing a modulated message borne along on the carrier, like some sort of language."

Jules was more prepared to accept what Matt Roberts was saying now than she would have been two and a half years ago, before the phenomenon of Leofwin's Hundred came to light. "Describe how the sounds are different," she said.

"There's a quick knocking noise, a quickening," Roberts said. "You can discern it in the background—"

"What are you suggesting, Matt?"

"It's just a feeling I've got," Roberts grew silent. Dearden could see he was uneasy.

"Whatever it is, just say it." Dearden faced Roberts. There was a change in his demeanour. A cold look in his eyes that came once in a while when those he was close to were threatened. Dearden wanted answers.

Roberts looked uncertainly at Dearden.

"Spill it, my man," Wynter suggested.

"OK, don't laugh . . . I'm wondering if Harry is trying to get in touch with us. It's just a feeling I've got."

Ramsay sniggered, "You've got a feeling?" then he quietened down when Pierpoint told him to watch his mouth and let Roberts continue.

*   *   *

"We need Trent Jackson in on this. He's the language guy and he's into coding in a big way," Jules said.

"Ring him Jules . . . let's hope he's still about. I haven't heard anything about him since Nibiru," Dearden said. He had contacted most of the SHaFT operatives and those close to the organisation since the passage of the rogue planet. Almost all of them were accounted for, but he had overlooked Trent, the suave founder of GOELD, the Guild Of Extinct Language Decryption.

Jules dialled Jackson's number. There was the usual wait because of the degraded network of geostationary satellites, but then, "Jackson, GOELD," his voice didn't sound quite right.

"Thank goodness you're OK, Trent, it's Jules."

"Jules, it's so good to hear from you. What mysteries do you have for me this time of calling?"

"We have something that will test your expertise. Please listen and do take this seriously. There is an oak tree in Leofwin's Hundred that is emitting what Matt Roberts thinks is code."

Jules thought she heard a sigh. She wasn't sure whether it was a stifled laugh.

"Have you been on the pop, Trent?"

There was a moment's silence at Jackson's end. Then, "I might ask whether you have, Jules," and then, "Damn." Another sigh. Deeper this time. "Most of the work I was involved with has gone Jules. I'm rather at a loose end down here in Bletchley . . . banging about in this large old house close to where dear old Turing did most of his major work. In answer to your question, Jules, I would say that the pop has rather been on me."

"Come here, Trent. We need your brain up at Dearden

114

Hall . . . you dear old fool."

"Do you want me there, Jules . . . really?"

"I'll pick you up. There are virtually no trains now."

"That would be good. When will you come?"

"Tomorrow, I'll start early." She calculated the journey time. Allowed an hour and a half for the unexpected, en route. "I'll be at yours around ten thirty."

"I'll look forward to it my dear. Very much so." Trent's voice was unsteady. Jules couldn't tell whether it was emotion, or drink. Maybe it was both. They rang off.

Down in Bletchley, Jackson topped up his glass. It was a single malt; Glenfiddich. It was good. Not adulterated by any sort of mixer. Something in Julia Linden-Barthorpe's telephone call whetted Jackson's appetite. Hell, he so needed his intellectual appetite whetting. Bloody Nibiru. The culmination of his life's work in Beauchamp Mews had been inundated by the failure of the Thames Barrier, because of Nibiru. All of the equipment was under a thick layer of silt. The priceless records, much of them on paper, ruined.

Jackson needed a project like he never previously needed one, and Jules, in a timely fashion because he was on a real downer, had rung with an offer. Jackson, usually so suave, so immaculate, swayed to the sink. There was a shaving mirror on the window sill and he saw his reflection, the gravy stain on his shirt . . . the three-day stubble, which was grey, the heavy eyebrows. He was showing his age and he didn't like it one bit. He looked at the glass of Glenfiddich, the glass itself engraved with the name of the whisky, Glenfiddich. He sniffed the liquor. By all the saints it was good. He put his lips to the glass and took a draught. It was then that the conversation with Jules jerked him into focus. He spat the whisky into the sink, emptied the glass into the same place.

He did the same with the bottle and watched the amber liquid drain away.

*   *   *

They were fifteen miles away from Dearden Hall.

"It's peculiar, to say the least," Jules said, after relating recent events to Jackson.

"You can say that again." He had woken up twenty miles back and Jules told him what Matt Roberts and Storm Petrel had heard in Uberatu's Oak, that Roberts had the impression it was some sort of communication.

"I don't know what to make of it, Trent. The signal seems in some way . . . organised." Jackson had listened to what she said. He had come out of his drunken stupor a few hours back and afterwards he needed sleep. Now he was awake and he was looking forward to this new challenge. He focussed on languages again. Latched onto where their root streamed through his mind. They were in his DNA, which was yet another intelligent language that interested him. Maybe it was due to a peculiarity in his genes but languages were easy for him, even the extinct ones he had to work on, like Jean-François Champollion did with the Rosetta Stone an age ago.

Transmitted information was a bit different but related. His hero was Alan Turing. How Turing, with his code-breaking expertise had influenced the outcome of things out of Bletchley Park was the driving force behind Jackson's start with languages. That was why he moved to Bletchley when he was young, to get near the place where so much was achieved by the young men and women in the wooden huts when the British Isles had its back to the wall.

There was minimal disruption to the journey. In fact,

there was less disruption on this journey, even after the cataclysm caused by Nibiru, than there used to be before its second pass. Fallen trees and strewn debris maybe, but not the twenty mile traffic jams of old.

Trent Jackson's mind had gone AWOL after his sojourn in the Bakerloo Line tunnel during Nibiru's closest approach. During that time and afterwards Glenfiddich had given him some solace. But now what Jules had on offer was a way back to the mind-trips of language. His normality. The codified ideas of mind, even if transmitted by obscure means, was on hand again and the old intellect he thought lost, was returning into focus.

* * *

They were all there at Dearden Hall, the core crew, efficient in a tight military way, but relaxed, like a bunch of friends. They were seated around the great hall at a loose end, chatting amongst themselves. The television was on, showing a news channel that broke up occasionally due to a weak signal. The mains electricity had cut out again three hours back, so Mitch Doughty had started the Lycoming electro-generator to power-up the essentials in the house.

The heavy front door knocker rattled and a minute later Gil Heskin led a tired looking Jules and Trent Jackson, into the house.

"Are we pleased to see you, Trent," Dearden stood and welcomed Jackson in. They shook hands. Held on in friendship.

They got straight down to serious stuff. Matt Roberts, with Storm Petrel close and listening, played the five minutes of information recorded on Roberts' mobile phone. Trent tried to make sense of what he was hearing.

"Slow it down, Matt. Can you do that?" he asked.

Roberts looked vague. Oscar Stanway came up behind Roberts and grabbed the phone. It was like a high-up Rugby tackle, quick and accurate but Stanway got the phone and fiddled with the settings. Took out his own mobile and copied the WAV file. "I need to go up to Harry's lab . . . need somewhere quiet, and I need his electronic gear." Oscar said no more, just disappeared up the stairs at the side of the great hall and made his way to Harry's pad, where he was staying.

"Where is this going, Jem, do you know?" Pierpoint asked. He spoke loud from where he was sitting opposite Templestone so that Dearden, further away in the room, could hear him.

"Anyone's guess. Best evidence is that they've gone through that doorway in Villiers' lab. Tenuous, but it's our only lead."

"Why not ask our alien friends for some serious help? They're interested in our well-being."

"Problem with that is that they've gone to ground again. I think it's our time of testing before they move us on to greater things."

"I understand that, but two of our own are missing. If we don't ask, we won't get."

Oscar Stanway came back into the great hall and shouted, as he came through the door. He was exuberant. "It's done, I've slowed it down," He waved an iPad in the air. Dragged out a chair and sat at Leofwin's massive old table. "Listen to this." He touched an app on the screen. First of all, a series of chords came from the speakers. Although vaguely musical, they were unlike music familiar to the Earth people gathered around the table. "Here's the interesting bit. But it isn't very audible." Oscar said. He turned up the volume.

There was the noise of the carrier wave, the music, and then a harsh zipping noise that reminded Doughty of the sound of a machine gun. This lasted a couple of seconds, repeated another nine times and then it stopped.

Jackson sat back in his chair, "Interesting that it's repeating."

"The weirdest conundrum is that it's coming from Uberatu's Oak," Oscar responded. "But since it's happening in a rational universe, there has to be a logical explanation."

No-one heard the outer door open. It was a heavy door, ancient, clunky when it opened. Gil Heskin had oiled the hinges and replaced the hinge-pin on the massive iron knocker because it had grown loose and it had rattled in the wind. The noise had been getting on Heskin's nerves, so a few days back he had repaired the knocker and squirted oil onto the grating door hinges, so now no one heard the big door open. The entrant hadn't knocked. Just came straight in. No-one heard the door into the great hall open, or saw the tall, slender figure duck as he stooped under the top of the door frame.

Then his voice boomed from the back of the room. Storm Petrel screamed, Rowan clung to Dearden's arm and Oscar Stanway went very pale, as the alien strode rapidly across the room toward them.

18

Jules whirled around to face the intruder. Her reactions were immediate, strong as ever to protect, with Shotokan fury, those close to her. She realised who the entrant was and cooled the attack mode. She smiled.

"You are welcome here. Long time, no see," she said.

Lan-Si-Nu ignored the comment and stood the other side the table. "I am sorry for coming unannounced, but what I have to say cannot wait on niceties. Some of the Chakrakan have escaped the cocoon we enshrouded their planet with many years ago. This presents a major threat to your planet because the Chakrakan are motivated by anger, which is why we had to cocoon their planet in the first place."

Dearden could see Oscar was shaken by the sudden appearance of the alien. He wasn't used to this sort of thing.

"Don't worry," Dearden reassured Oscar. "This is Lan-Si-Nu, he's a great friend of ours," Dearden attempted to ease Oscar's nerves.

"How do you suggest we deal with the Chakrakan?" Dearden asked the alien, assuming it would be the SHaFT organisation which would deal with the situation.

"Wait, Jem." Lan-Si-Nu raised his hand for silence. "There is more."

"Then tell us, sir, and be quick about it," Will Pierpoint said, unable to resist the urge to take command. He looked at Dearden, shrugged a gesture of apology.

"We have left you alone recently," the alien said. "It was intentional because we needed to observe you individuals who have become our friends. We have also been observing how your Earth people in high places deal with the affairs of government since the passage of Nibiru. The way you deal with the prime directive of peace throughout the cosmos must be analysed to make sure you are doing things right. We are here to help, don't forget."

"How have you obser—" Templestone began, but Lan-Si-Nu raised his hand and Templestone shut his mouth.

"How we have observed you will be known in the course of time." The alien's next words brought an element of hope, and surprised them. "We are very aware that one of the Earth people for whom we have more than the usual respect, the one we raised to Hnirath of Science, Harry Stanway, and his colleague, Esma, are missing."

Rowan answered. "Our friends went missing from R1."

"That is so. They have used the entry at the far end of the place where your Villiers Professor was conducting his trials. It is unfortunate that it happened. It has created a serious situation."

"Really . . . what exactly has happened?" Oscar asked. He sounded nervous talking to the alien.

"They went through an Event Horizon portal, but where it happened *to* is a different question. Do you remember the time Harry Stanway asked me what lies below the ground floor of the portal, the building you call the Hub?"

"I remember. We are all very curious about that," Templestone said.

"Indeed. Harry has a mind that is in advance of humanity's general level of learning, and he has courage."

"We know that my man; but come on, how does what lies below the Hub link to Harry and that door at the back of Villiers' lab?" Some time back Wynter had tried to go below ground level in the Hub. The door to the way down was securely locked. The fact it was locked teased his mind. He had pulled the door first and then pushed it hard, then shouldered it . . . to no avail.

"Differences you could not conceive lie down there," Lan-Si-Nu said.

"C'mon man, what differences?" Wynter couldn't let it go.

"If I were to tell you, you would find it difficult to believe."

"We can take it," Dearden said.

Again, the silence. They waited.

"If I tell you, you must accept what I say. You may not be able to understand it. You are not really ready for this, but be assured that what I say is fact."

"So, surprise us," Storm Petrel said.

"Yeah, surprise us," Matt Roberts echoed.

The alien dragged out a chair from where he stood. It was an ordinary chair. Not an oversized chair suitable for Lan-Si-Nu. When he sat, his knees were on the same level as his chin. The scene was disproportionate, but the seriousness of the situation took away the humour.

"When you enter the levels below ground all semblance of rationality changes. You see, as you go down, each Level represents a different Reality. On the way down, you proceed according to the timeline of the discoveries we have made. Sometimes the laws of physics seem obscure down below, even absurd, from the standpoint of we inhabitants of the Prime Dimension."

"How many levels are there?" Oscar asked

"No-one knows." The alien turned to face Jules, "When you examined the manual you found in the Hub, you may have seen that there are five levels below ground."

Jules shook her head. She had only managed a cursory read-through of Trent Jackson's translation.

"Well that information is over one million of your years out of date."

"What do you mean, no-one knows the amount of levels?" Clive Fraser's curiosity was tweaked. Jules thought he had been asleep, but he had been deep in thought.

"From within each Level on the downward transit, a different Reality is accessed, and the exploration of many of them is continuing."

"Are you pulling my leg, my tall man?" Lee Wynter challenged.

"Far from it, Mister Wynter. In very recent years all of you have had your minds opened to the Grid. With the Grid's introduction into your lives you have become acquainted with just how complex creation is. You Earths have a saying, *The more we learn, the more we realise what we don't know.* Although we have made scientific advancement beyond your imagining because we are an ancient race of people compared to your Earth civilisation, your saying applies to us just as much as it does to you."

"You are still learning?" Mitch Doughty asked.

"Very much so, and we delight in it. But I have digressed. We have two problems. The first, the Chakrakan's emergence from the cocoon and their intent to interfere with the Earth. The second problem is your missing colleagues."

"Will you help us?" Roberts was always direct.

"We will. The Chakrakan will be the easier problem to deal with. Their interference with the Earth is in this dimension, called the Prime Dimension because it was created first. That does make the Chakrakan problem easier to deal with than that of your missing young friends."

"Why are you telling us about the lower levels of the Hub and different realities?" Will Pierpoint asked. He stood up from the winged arm-chair opposite Templestone, stretched and came over to the table. He stood in front of Lan-Si-Nu. Was dwarfed by him although he was over six foot tall.

"Your Professor Villiers was a clever man . . . he thought beyond his time. Sometimes his judgment was off-centre, and that created his brilliance. This has been the case with you Earths throughout much of your history. There have been flashes of brilliance, perceptions that have shown promise beyond even our capabilities, and in their isolation each of those brilliant Earths lifted your race slightly further out of darkness. Unfortunately, you have often resorted to violence as an answer to some of your problems. That was the case with Villiers. His science was innovative to address the approach of Chakrakan, the planet Nibiru, as you call it. But Villiers stumbled upon a branch of physics that was wide in scope. He was unaware of its full potential. His End Time weapon was the result.

"This is the point. By pure coincidence, Professor Villiers experimentation in R1 linked to a gateway into the alternative realities below Edge Hill. It was built by an exploratory party of we Wasiri eons ago. The problem was that the gateway proved to be erratic in its performance and Harry Stanway, being very curious, stepped through the unstable gateway."

"Are you really telling us that our friends Harry and Esma have stepped into an alternative reality?" Wynter asked.

"The evidence points that way. Now we have to find out which layer of reality they have entered. If you are right and

Harry is trying to communicate with you his attempts could give us a lead."

"Tell us straight, have you heard those sounds we've heard coming from Uberatu's Oak?" Trent Jackson asked. He had been quiet up to that point, and felt ill-prepared to talk to the alien. He was nervous.

"We have heard the noise emanating from the tree," said Lan-Si-Nu. "And we know how odd is Uberatu's Oak. For many years, sensors in the outer wall of the Portal have picked up data that is intelligence based emanating from the tree. The transmission of data from a tree is highly unusual and this has interested us."

"So, will you help us?" Dearden asked again.

"We will, but as the Realities are involved the process will be far from easy, and the route, I have to say, will be torturous. I must go now, Jem Dearden. There is much work to do. It will be difficult, but please have patience."

19

Dearden, Doughty and the rest of Cell 1 had arrived at Kineton Base. Dump 4, the headquarters of SHaFT, was the place where they thrashed out problems. SHaFT had a broad spectrum of technology in Dump 4 to address problems they faced. These issues were talked through every two weeks on a Monday to set up schedules for the coming fortnight.

With so many changes wrought by Nibiru's passage, fundamental systems and the infrastructure of public services were sometimes not dependable. They needed re-structuring on a sound foundation earth wide so that governance became effective, but that would take time, maybe years to bring to normality.

What UK Premier Stephen Marston and SHaFT were working on, along with Lars Knudsen of the UN and other world leaders who flew in if they had the aircraft and the fuel available, was a far cry from what had existed before Nibiru. It was basic but had as its core target the pursuance of universal peace, in line with the Universal Prime Directive, under the guidance of the Wasiri-Chanchiyans. Much of this was accomplished in Dump 4, Kineton Base.

Jem Dearden always took the lead fronting the meetings in the large operations room. His mind encompassed the recent events in their totality. He was always ahead of the game planning the way ahead. Sometimes Sir Will Pierpoint attended. Dearden generally gave Sir Will the opportunity to lead off, but more often than not these days, he declined.

On one of those Mondays when the team met at Kineton Base, Jules remained at Dearden Hall with Clive Fraser. His work at the library had come to an end, as had much of the other work at Cambridge University.

Jules' father, Alex Linden, wanted to see his daughter, who was staying at Dearden Hall. Rowan was there, so was Storm Petrel and Lee Wynter, who remained at the Hall as a security backup. The Heskins were close-by. Talk amongst the group was about the outcome of the meeting at Kineton Base when Alex Linden arrived.

Heskin came through the door with Alex and called to the others that, "Something's going on over the forest, you better come and see." He didn't sound his usual self.

They went outside and Heskin pointed to the forest in the direction of the Hub. A sleek matt-black shape was hovering some way up in the sky under low cloud. It was long, cylindrical in shape, with structures projecting from its surface. As Clive said later, *It was utterly black.* It was the blackest black he had ever seen. Almost a non-existence.

The craft rotated until those standing outside watching were looking along its length, and then it moved toward them. When it reached the open ground between the edge of the forest and Dearden Hall it hovered, and then it descended. Dust arose from the reaction of a propulsion system.

"I don't like the look of that," Alex Linden said.

"Nor do I." Jules stepped back, flung the front door open wide. "Get inside, now," she commanded. In four seconds, they were inside and the door was shut and locked.

"Down to the cellar?" Clive suggested.

"No," Jules countered. "There's a better idea." She never ran. Instead, she waited.

There was hammering on the front door. Not the knocking of a known caller, someone known and respected. It was a challenging knock. Heavy stuff. Bang, bang, bang. Angry. And then there was a crash that reverberated through the building.

"Get on that settee," Jules commanded, and then to Storm, "You alright with this?"

"You bet. As much as you." They had talked about this sort of thing. Theorised about it, because after Nibiru there were uncertainties. They were prepared.

Alex took the lead. He knew his daughter's outlook . . . that it was tough . . . at times uncompromising. He sat on the settee, like she said. Clive and Storm followed suit. Storm looked the most comfortable of those seated on the settee facing the door. Her countenance had taken on a hard edge. Jules waited on the hinge side the door so she was hidden when the intruder came through, while Wynter stood at the side of the settee.

The person, if that's what it could be called, that stooped through the door was big. It had a visage that exuded cruelty, and looked like an oversize human, beset with gigantism. But this was not a gentle giant. Deep-set eyes flicked from person to person as it advanced into the great hall, followed by four others of its kind. Alex Linden shivered. After the event he described the intruders as fitting a description he had heard of way back. That they were like *the giants of old* the Nephilim. As they moved further into the room they communicated by making hissing, sibilant noises.

"What the hell chutzpah language is that, my man," Lee Wynter shouted at the intruders, as Storm Petrel got up from the settee. She nodded imperceptibly, and as Jules slammed the door shut all hell broke loose.

* * *

At Kineton Base, Dearden had stepped up to the challenge as the new head of SHaFT. "Where do we go now?" he wanted opinions. He had the respect of the team, much as Sir Will Pierpoint had in his time as head of the organisation. Dearden always listened to what the men and women of SHaFT had to say.

"As I see this situation we have two problems." Trent Jackson said. "The first problem has to do with communication, the other has to do with Harry's location."

"OK. Let's home in on that. Regarding communication, if it is Harry who is trying to get in touch with us how can we respond to him? Oscar, Jules, you scientists . . . or anyone else," he looked around the room, "This is new, any ideas?" Dearden moved over to the flip-board and wrote headings in two columns, *Communication*, and *Location*. "Methods at our disposal; what do we have?" Dearden said, inviting feedback. Oscar took this forward.

"With communication coming via Uberatu's Oak, something, although its nature eludes us at present, is going on that is very high tech. I'm sure there's a carrier wave involved, which appears to be modulating another element. Listen to this," Oscar slipped his mobile phone into a dock connected to speakers and played Matt Roberts' recording. And then, "There is no electronic communication equipment in the Oak so an alternative means of communication is being used. We cannot deny the fact that there is communication."

Matt Roberts was the guy who was clued up on the forest. Could be said he was in tune with its more elemental things. He said, "I've seen and heard things around the oak that I haven't seen or heard anywhere else." He stopped his explanation. It was a bit of a wind-up. Sometimes Roberts played folks along like this to get attention.

"Stop the game, Matt," Doughty said.

"It's no game. This is serious. there is stuff going on out there you wouldn't believe." He was too embarrassed to elaborate.

"What stuff?" Pierpoint challenged.

"Unusual stuff," Roberts was still elusive.

"Matt, just tell us what you've seen and heard," Dearden was getting short on patience.

"Fungus and a sort of music," Roberts said.

"Fungus?" Dearden wondered what was coming next.

"And I heard Uberatu's Oak singing. And the toadstools that are growing around the tree . . . they appeared overnight."

There was a snigger from the back of the room and Doughty's comment, "See any fairies," nudged Roberts' sensitivities. Roberts knew they wouldn't take what he said seriously, which was why he hadn't said anything before. He blew back some strands of hair that had escaped from his bandana, and then, "Do you want to make something of it, Doughty?"

"Just making a point."

"I don't like the way you're making your point."

"OK . . . OK cool it." Dearden stepped in to stop things getting out of hand.

Oscar Stanway was seated at the back of the room. The way he worked when he was onto a lead was to go quiet with his head in his hands. Mentally working things through. And sometimes while he was working things through his mouth moved. Not that he said much under his breath this time. He had been overawed with the vast semi-underground space of SHaFT's HQ as he walked through to Dearden's office, so he had been quiet most of the time he was in Dump 4.

All of SHaFT were seated quiet during the discussion, until Roberts mentioned the emergence of fungus around Uberatu's Oak. Oscar stood suddenly, and this startled Trent Jackson, who was sitting next to him. What Roberts said spurred Trent's mind into action.

"How widespread was the growth, did you notice?" Oscar pumped Roberts for information, unwilling just yet to bring up the subject of hearing things in the tree.

Suddenly Roberts extended his hand to Oscar and they shook. Oscar didn't understand why until Roberts explained, "At least someone takes me seriously. How widespread were the growths? Started off roughly circular around Uberatu's Oak, maybe about ten feet diameter, or so. The growth trailed off into the forest in a straight line which connected to Old Jack and circled around that tree too. But it continued deeper into the forest way past Uberatu's Oak. No idea where it went after that, but it seemed to follow a trail. It was extensive."

Apart from the emergence of the fungus, another possibility occurred to Oscar. Harry and Oscar had talked about this in the past. How siblings sometimes had an altogether different level of communication to what was considered normal. It was non-verbal, non-visual. More . . . subliminal. There was one time Oscar was on his way to see Harry. It hadn't been by arrangement . . . no email, no phone call, but Harry knew Oscar was on his way. Harry had a prior arrangement and he cancelled it. He knew for sure Oscar would arrive within the hour, and he did.

So when, shortly after his arrival at Dearden Hall, and he was inside Uberatu's Oak. Oscar had been startled when he heard *Help us, Oscar*. It was Harry's voice. He dismissed the thought as wishful thinking, but when Roberts spoke about the fungal growth and hearing sounds emanating from the oak, Oscar took the voice he had heard more seriously. The words, *Help us, Oscar* sounded convincing.

"We need to get to Uberatu's Oak, Oscar said to the assembled team. I want to investigate the growths and the sounds coming from the tree," he explained. "But we need to remind your alien friend that he said he'd help us. We might be out of our depth here and I think Lan-Si-Nu may know a lot more about what's happening than he's letting on."

* * *

Returning with Cell 1 from Kineton Base, Dearden saw the alien craft as they were motoring along the winding drive to Dearden Hall. The black shape was sleek and menacing, nestling close to the open ground between the forest and the mansion. Dearden, in the lead vehicle, floored the throttle and Doughty, following, kept up with him, taking the winding drive at seventy-plus.

They heard a commotion inside the house after they skidded to a halt and switched off. The very solid front door made in Anglo-Saxon times was off its hinges, lying askew, half in, half out the entrance. In a beat, Dearden, Doughty and Roberts were into the great hall, where there was action.

Jules was in mid-flight with a drop-kick targeting the midriff of a giant semi-human figure. Others were scattered about. Storm Petrel and Lee Wynter were engaged with another giant form. With fingers extended, Storm had penetrated the eyes of her attacker at least two feet taller than her. Rowan had a poker in her hand that she had grabbed from the side of the Norman fireplace. Frieda Heskin was at her side with a wicked carving knife. Alex Linden, Clive

Fraser and Gill Heskin, who had a butcher's cleaver, were confronting the rest of the attackers. They were an abnormal looking lot, the attackers. Oversized versions of humanity, all of them snarling and squeaking their aggression at those Dearden was close to. He went on the attack which threw the raiders into further disarray.

Jules landed the drop-kick and Storm's fingers had penetrated to the optic nerve of her assailant. Will Pierpoint saw Storm's action, knew from past experience she had done some military training but he had no idea it had so much class. He saw the fingers come out covered in a mess of vitreous humor. Storm Petrel's action was accompanied by an unearthly high pitched scream from her opponent, which was when the Nibiruans backed off.

At that point another character joined the fight. Tomahawk Shahn of Offchurch, the Black Alaskan Wolf who thought he owned Dearden Hall, the forest and everything else around about. He had aroused himself from a deep eyes-moving, paws-moving sleep, dreaming of raw meat, and now he was hungry and interlopers were in his territory.

The Nibiruans had never heard the call of a wolf. Come to think of it, not many of the Earth people had heard the call of a wolf as Tomahawk rendered it. The call from the wilderness, meant to be heard for miles around was meant to strike fear into the heart of his prey, and it did just that. It was the final straw that caused the aliens to flee back out the door they had unhinged, and they were followed by the wolf.

Within a couple of minutes, the alien craft lifted quickly heavenwards. Tomahawk eyed up the alien craft. Followed its upward track. Licked his reddened wolf-lips. He had got a chunk of one of the alien's legs, and it was real tasty.

20

The invasion had been a call to action and the core team were around Earl Leofwin's table in the great hall.

"Time we got all of the crew together here, Jem?" Will Pierpoint asked. "I'm thinking we may have our hands full."

"Already done. Contact's been made and most of them who aren't local are on their way. Vin Rodick's coming in from Germany. He'll probably be the last to arrive."

"Dump four?"

"Yeah, 1500 hours the day after tomorrow. Transport could be an issue for some, so I've allowed the extra day for travel. Will . . . none of the crew have lost the fight."

Rodick arrived on a 2003 Triumph Thunderbird 900, wearing flash leathers and an American GI tin hat for a crash helmet. The meeting in the ops room had started fifteen minutes before, but Dave Beecham, Rodick's bomb-disposal boss, welcomed him with a slap on the back and brief good-to-see-you talk. They disturbed the meeting, but bomb-disposal banished inhibitions and had given a what-the-hell turn of mind to the pair.

All sixty-three in the room quietened down, Dearden, at the front, explained what had gone on three days before at Dearden Hall. How the alien vehicle descended and the occupants, who were unusually tall and muscular, invaded the great hall and were taken on by Jules, Storm Petrel, Tomahawk Shahn of Offchurch and the others. There was laughter when Dearden told how the wolf evened the balance in favour of Earth.

Jules and Storm were at the front of the ops room. Seated.

There were a number of other female operatives seated randomly. It was a good mix. Useful in the field. Efficient and *very* resourceful. Tomahawk, all black and *real big* was seated by Dearden's side at the front wearing a heavy-duty studded collar, and an equally heavy-duty leash that Dearden was holding in his left hand. The pair of them had become a powerful icon in the annals of SHaFT . . . the man and the wolf, defiant against all the odds.

Dearden briefly explained what had happened to Harry and Esma. Told about their disappearance, avoiding the complexities. Quiet reigned in the room. Harry's expertise had become well known amongst SHaFT operatives. He had helped in difficult situations. He was respected, well-liked and missed by all who knew him.

Questions followed. From the left side, near the front, someone asked, "How does SHaFT figure in the threat from the alien spacecraft?"

"We are taking on a defensive role. The occupants are aggressive. We do not know what their methods are, or how they think, so we must be intuitive with our responses."

"One way to deal with them is Shotokan." Jules said.

"And wolf-teeth," someone else added, from the middle of the room.

"We must understand that they will be a difficult opponent to gauge," Pierpoint said. "If we can get to understand their modus operandi, we will avoid undue violence. We have to remember that there is a need for us to harmonise with the Prime Directive."

Dearden was the next to speak. He paced the front of the room. "It has become obvious that the Nibiruans are interested in Leofwin's Hundred, particularly in the Hub and its potential for time-shift and intergalactic travel. All of their activity is centred on the Hub. What we are planning to do is to split into our usual cells and dig-in around the forest. We must not let any outsider get their hands on the Hub. Its power, in the wrong hands, could be disastrous. That is why we are limiting this operation to SHaFT. No outside agency is aware of the Hub's existence and its role in the events of recent years. It has to stay that way."

Dearden indicated to lower the lights. A map of Leofwin's Hundred was projected onto the front wall. It was subdivided into the same amount of sections as there were operational cells of SHaFT. "We have to handle this situation with kid-gloves," he said. "It may be difficult if the aliens from Nibiru turn nasty. There are high expectations in line with the Prime Directive that we will be peaceful in our responses. Remember, we people of Earth are being watched. We have to work along with the Prime Directive, in that we maintain peace at all costs." Dearden paused, asked if there were more questions. There were none.

"As usual, I will command Cell 1. This time it will be made up of Mitch Doughty, Matt Roberts, Lee Wynter, Jules Linden-Barthorpe, Storm Petrel, Bill Templestone, Clive Fraser, Trent Jackson and Oscar Stanway. And, of course, Tomahawk. Lol Penrose, you will command Cell 2 . . .

Cell 1, was passing the ancient oak known as Old Jack. Tomahawk Shahn of Offchurch was anchored to Dearden by the heavy leash. No free roaming this time. In his predatory brain, Tomahawk had worked out that the food who had screamed, had vanished into a thing that arose into the bright region above him. The wolf looked up into the brightness to see if there was more food hanging about, but there wasn't any. The good stench of raw meat had gone and it had been replaced by the good stench of undergrowth and forest-rot. He tried to move forward quickly. Wanted to get to the place where the food that made a noise had got to before it vanished into the brightness, but he felt restrained, held back.

Something else probed his mind and reached deep inside. The image took him to his mother, which was unusual. He had never felt this before because he and his mother were parted and that was how it should be. He had no need for his mother now, nor she for him, but her image had come to him as if out of a dream.

He smelled the place he was familiar with. It was one of the places he marked, and he did so again to refresh his territory. He was pulled by the ring of animal-skin at the back of his head. The good beast that fed him called the sound that was Him, *"Tomahawk,"* and then came noises he didn't understand. "Come on, boy. Old Jack's been watered enough." The food-beast tugged the animal-skin, causing him to follow even though he wanted to stay at the mark. And then came the familiar scent of the trail to the next mark, which was a great towering structure, all of it moving by the life that controlled all things.

Out of the great mark-place-structure came the deep-inside sound that he recognised. And there was something else, a companion-noise he recognised, but it was inside him. It was the other beast who had gone away, who he missed because it sometimes slipped him food secretively off the place where all of them had food. Tomahawk couldn't understand what was happening to the Harry thing; but his thoughts were like the brightness of dawn, after the long, long darkness of night.

* * *

137

Tomahawk was acting strangely. Dearden saw that the wolf didn't want to leave Old Jack. The ancient oak always attracted the wolf and Dearden had to tug hard on the leash. Tomahawk followed reluctantly after spraying the tree again. Just a small squeeze this time.

"Tomahawk, come on, boy. Old Jack's been watered enough," Dearden commanded, and the wolf reluctantly obeyed. They followed the others. Caught up with them as they arrived at Uberatu's Oak. Again, the wolf behaved in an odd fashion. Tomahawk looked at Dearden, directly in the eye and Dearden felt a connection with the wolf, as he had once before, a connection across the boundary of species. Dearden shook his head, rubbed his temples. This shouldn't be happening, but . . . Doughty came to his side and his question was quiet, close to his ear, "Are you OK, Jem?"

"Ask me later." Dearden pushed from his mind that the wolf *had something to say.* He mentally went over the events of the last hour. He was hardened to life's weird changes after the events of the last short span of years. Now, Dearden sensed that Tomahawk had changed fundamentally, maybe on a communicative level. As they approached Uberatu's Oak the creature was eager to get to it. Usually, when Tomahawk was on the leash, and people were about, he behaved cautiously. This time there was no caution. Just the opposite. All the training was forgotten. The wolf led the team.

They gathered at the entrance to the interior of Uberatu's oak. Tomahawk was at the door Roberts had installed. Dearden wished he could read the wolf's mind because there was an urgency about his actions.

Roberts undid the padlock and swung the door open. The wolf rushed in, followed by Trent Jackson, in the forest with the team for his language skills. And then the rest of Cell 1 entered the cavernous space. What they heard was difficult to comprehend.

* * *

Back in the great hall, Cell 1 was analysing what they had heard in the tree.

"When I was a kid I remember my dad telling me to put my ear to a telephone post," Templestone said. "We were on holiday on the coast in Wales, place called Aberdyfi. There was a gale blowing. The wind was howling through the telephone wires. It was an elemental sound, and it was transmitted down the post to my ear. It was as if there was some sort of life I was hearing. What we heard in the forest was similar; like . . . how can I put it? As if we are hearing a radically different sort of life."

"Come on, man. Are you trying to spook me?" Wynter challenged.

"Not at all. I'm saying that we are hearing something physical . . . just different to what we've experienced before. Come on, Lee; recent events should be telling you not to take what's around us in the physical world for granted, life is strange at times."

"I'm with you on that, my man. But don't get *too* way-out."

Then Trent Jackson, the language guy spoke. Put forward the thought that the stream of sound was definitely modulated in structure. "Think of hearing the sound of talking when you're a distance from it. When the volume is too low to accurately hear what's being said you can't identify the words but you know people are talking because of the modulated structure of the sounds. You know for definite that what you are hearing is conversation and taking that a stage further, that what you are hearing is intelligence-based."

"Are you saying there's conversation going on?" Templestone asked.

"Not as we know conversation, but I detected a conversational inflection in the stream of data. It was more apparent when we heard Matt's slowed-down recording." Roberts nodded in response.

"I've schooled myself in picking-up such aspects of speech," Jackson said. "It is rather esoteric, but sometimes the method is useful when deciphering a little-known spoken language. There is a common basis to all of Earth's languages. Same applies with this. We need to get to the *root* of what we are hearing." Jackson had a way of explaining things that made even the way-out sound plausible. After hearing Jackson's analysis, every member of Cell 1 shed inhibitions they previously held about sounding way-out, and each described what they had heard in the tree.

"I think it sounded similar to static," Sir Will Pierpoint said, remembering from his youth hearing between-station noise as he trawled through short-wave radio. Doughty said he remembered his father, Art Doughty, saying something similar and adding that the contention years ago amongst short-wave radio enthusiasts was that the static between stations was the music of the stars. Mitch Doughty went on to say that he was sceptical with what *his* father told him when he was a kid, but what he heard in the oak tree had changed all that.

"How about you, Oscar. What do you make of all this stuff?" Dearden asked. He knew Oscar Stanway would be up to the mark with his analysis. He hadn't known him long but Dearden knew he could trust Oscar's reasoning.

"I've heard nothing like it before. But I thought there was urgency about it."

"What gives you that idea?"

"The tempo of the sounds, particularly when we hear them slowed down. Like when someone has a problem and they ring you about it. You pick up the tension in how they speak."

The room went quiet for a beat. Then Roberts asked, "Has anyone else picked up what me and Storm heard in the tree?" There was silence again. But if any of those in the great hall had hearing as acute as Tomahawk Shahn of Offchurch, they would have heard urgent movement. As it was, there was silence, until . . .

"So, where do we go now, with all this?" Pierpoint asked.

Rowan had been quiet for a while. The invasion of her home by the giants from the sky-craft had unsettled her mind and she rounded on Will Pierpoint with a fury he hadn't seen before.

"Sir Willoughby, here is what we do next. Lan-Si-Nu has more knowledge than we. He knows about *unusual* things. Uberatu Oak unusual. Lan-Si-Nu says there are unusual underground rooms in Hub where help may lie. You contact him about underground places, now."

21

"Tell me more, Harry." Villiers voice had assumed a youthful enthusiasm, a far cry from his previous remote attitude. Harry warmed to the professor.

"The internet is an amazing invention," Harry continued his explanation to Villiers and Martell as the four sat in the shade of the shelter they constructed. "It has taken the world by storm in recent years. Without it, much of the world's infrastructure would break down, finance, defence, the health service; things like that. The problem for the Earth is that, since Nibiru, the internet is operating in a weakened state. Much of the infrastructure we depended on has degraded."

Villiers was silent, absorbing what Harry said. Then, "Young man, you are comparing an electronic network with a biological one. Tell me, how can there be a comparison?"

"OK . . . In recent years there has been a gradual merging of technology with biological systems. Often, it is found that incorporating biological systems as best we can into technological advances gives the most efficient result. The natural order of things has a vastly superior inbuilt wisdom to what we can devise, so we borrow from it."

"I understand that, but how does what you are saying about a network relate to our predicament?"

"There are complex things just out of our reach that we don't understand, but intuitively we know they are present. Take that premise a stage further and bring the intuition into reality."

"Do you think I am stupid . . . I am well aware of that process. In part, that is how I developed the damn Switch that got us into this outlandish place. Harry, explain to us, from your vast fund of superior knowledge, in simple terms if you will, how you are comparing the Mycorrhizal network that connects the organisms on this planet, with your internet."

"Yes, and tell how it'll help us," Martell challenged.

"OK, it's simple really. They are both intelligence-based."

Harry took a minute to frame the rest of his answer. In a flight of fancy a few days back he had brought the Grid to mind. The Hub was the gateway to the Grid, but it was the Grid itself that made intergalactic travel possible. The Hub was also the gateway to travel through the stream of time via the Grid. The Grid seemed central to the structure of the universe. *What if . . .* Harry had taken his premise a stage further. *What if the Mycorrhizal network connects with the Grid too. Could it be used for communication with the guys back home? If so, how can we achieve communication?* He was deep in thought and the silence got to Martell.

"Harry, I asked you a question. How will your network idea help us?"

A few seconds went by and then Harry suddenly stood. "I think the Mycorrhizal network connecting the organisms on this planet may be linked to the grid and I'm going to put it to the test." Villiers shook his head, and Martell grinned that stupid lopsided grin of his.

Harry collected his tote-bag and after reassuring Esma that he needed to be by himself so he could work out a way to get them home, he set out. He needed a quiet mind to work things out on the basis of what he felt and observed.

Almost immediately he missed having Esma with him. The thought of her beauty and her personality filled his mind, but he stepped out briskly and resorted to his habit of counting his steps. It helped. Gradually his mind began to clear and the purpose of the mission took over.

That a network connected the gigantic organisms was obvious when, almost as one, their great succulent-like appendages had turned to face the four of them when they approached the area where they encamped. The Brobs seemed *interested* in them. Harry had a hunch, no more than that at present, a hunch, that the Brobs were intelligent.

After a few hours energetic walking he found a soft place on the ground where he could rest up for a while. It was an area shaded from the sunlight by a boulder. Harry sat down and leant on the boulder, which felt forgiving to his shoulders and head. It was odd, how soft it was to his tired muscles, and when he turned to look at it he saw the faint impression of the shape of his shoulders and head. He was tired, so he settled back again, and was soon asleep.

Harry awoke, stretched and looked at the sky. The alien sun showed a slight change in its intensity of light. He must have been asleep for a long while. He opened his tote-bag. Apart from the stuff Harry thought would be useful, Esma had packed some thick meaty-looking leaves that Martell said were tasty and would remain fresh for a long while. Harry had tried them before and found they had a pleasing savoury taste. He was hungry so he took a bite. It was good and when he had finished the leaf his hunger was satisfied. He stretched again, stood and resumed his trek.

Eventually the mist of distance cleared and Harry saw the clear detail of the giant organisms that lay ahead. He wondered what their response would be when he drew near to them. Would there be a change in the response now he was on his own, which made him think of his utter isolation. He thought of the strange reality he was in, its uncertainties. He squinted and as he tried to focus on the distant Brobs his visual cortex once again failed to respond to the alien nature of some of the colour, which he perceived as a neutral patchwork of grey. He felt his stomach knotting up as the physical laws of this place, so different to those he was used too, hit home.

When Harry was about hundred paces away from the giant outcrop, which extended in a ragged line as far as he could see to his left and his right, he stopped. He sat on the ground, studying the formation. The ground felt soft. Its softness eased his mind from the chorus of information that he was trying to set in order in his mind.

From these hundred paces away, the nearest of the Brobs towered above him. Its structure reached into the sky as tall as the ten-storey flats he remembered from the town where he was brought up. Sure enough, the heavy fronds had twisted upon themselves and were pointing toward him. Slowly, majestically, the rest of the colony were following suit and he knew he had become the focus of attention. He stood and walked forward uncertainly.

He remembered one of his early experiences in Leofwin's Hundred. It had been a very odd experience, and he was determined to tell no-one about it. It was shortly after the time Jules had led the dig on the Hub, to expose its lower entrance. Bill Templestone and he had been talking about seeing the lines of bluish light ascending from the Hub, the House of the West Wind, as the Anglo-Saxons called the structure deep in the forest.

"There's something very different about that place," Bill had said. "I can't define it. But you should go into the hollow oak, the one where Matt Roberts and I planted the Giant

Hogweed. Sometimes there's a sound I can hear inside the tree. It resonates inside the inner ear, not unlike tinnitus; but I know it's not that. I sometimes have tinnitus in my left ear, but what I heard is different to the tinnitus."

"How is it different?" Harry had asked Templestone. "Can you describe it?"

"No, not really. The best thing is that you go and hear it yourself." So, they went, and Harry heard it. "Don't tell anyone about this," Bill had said as they stood inside the tree and listened. "If you do they'll think we're bloody crazy." They stepped outside and made a pact never to speak about it to anyone else. And they never did.

Harry tried to avoid stepping on the fungus that had grown in a trail which culminated at the tree, which later became known as Uberatu's Oak. Templestone didn't care, the prettiest fungus Harry had ever seen was crushed underfoot. Harry had told Bill to try to avoid it. But his older colleague took no notice and down it went, squashed, wherever he walked.

Harry had pondered the nature of the fungus. Considering that the Grid, with all its wonders had been revealed to a few denizens of Earth, that other wonders could yet be revealed was an exciting thought. But, and this was the critical issue that mattered at the moment; could it be possible that there was a link via the Grid, between the alien forest in front of him, and the primeval forest back on Earth called Leofwin's Hundred?

Harry had for a while sensed deep inside that there were definite similarities. Now he saw the proof of similarity. Growing around one of the Brobs was a formation of fungus, the fruiting body of a subterranean Mycorrhizal network, that looked similar, only much larger in size, to the fungus he had seen in Leofwin's Hundred. And the sound inside Uberatu's Oak was the same as the sound coming from the giant growth in front of him It was a challenging thought. If there is a communicative network throughout all of the realities in creation, how could he use it to get them back home?

22

Harry hit the soft bole of the giant growth three times in quick succession, and then three times spaced out, followed by three times quickly again. Dit-dit-dit, dah-dah-dah, dit-dit-dit. He was convinced it would work. Gut feeling, intuition, communication using an abstruse network, call it what you will, but Harry was convinced, deep inside, about the communication.

He hit the thing again. Hard, confidently, with the same succession of Morse symbols. SOS, save our souls, save our ship. It was a nautical distress signal originally. First used in 1909 from the Cunarder, SS Slavonia, when it was wrecked off the Azores.

He wracked his brain to remember the other symbols. At one time he used to send messages to Oscar, when they were kids. A = dit-dah, B = dah-dit-dit-dit . . .

H = dit-dit-dit-dit, **A** = dit-dah, **R** = dit-dah-dit, **R** = dit-dah-dit, **Y** = dah-dit-dah-dah.

* * *

The old manor house near Leofwin's Hundred was quiet, apart from Tomahawk, who was restless. The cat, Calculus was restless too, as were the creatures of the nearby forest. It was as if the creatures perceived some sensory activity that the Heskins couldn't pick up. Weird, but so was much of what went on around Dearden Hall and in the surrounding forest.

It was unusual for Gil and Frieda Heskin to go into Leofwin's Hundred, but they wanted wild mushrooms to add to a four-cheese pizza. They took the route Dearden had once shown them . . . over Shadow Brook and past the oak called Old Jack, and onward toward the Hub. They had seen the Hub previously on one of their foraging walks in the forest and Dearden warned them to ignore it. Never were they to divulge its presence to anyone, and they never did, but they did go foraging, regardless of what was in the forest

They were the most beautiful puffballs and they were growing profusely. At first, the Heskins had been very cautious about eating them. Gil cooked one, as one does, sliced like bread, and fried with bacon, the smoked sort, with the bacon draped around it. He tried a tiny bit and waited a few hours to see if there were any bad effects on his digestion. Risky, but there wasn't any reaction, at least not a bad reaction. He had never before tasted anything so delicious, so he and Frieda fried some more. After they ate it a feeling of euphoria followed.

Their thoughts were incisive, the senses heightened; more vital than they had been since childhood, and something decidedly strange occurred. It was when Frieda had gone to the local shop in Hampton-in-Arden to get supplies. The stock in the shop was run-down after Nibiru but it was improving due to provisions being supplied by local folks for a small profit. Frieda bartered some Welsh-cakes she had made for the goods she needed and then she made her way back to Dearden Hall, walking the half-mile at a steady pace. Gil *knew* she was on her way back. Maybe intuition, he thought at first, but the sense of exactly *when* she was going to open the door into the entrance-hall was strong. It was the same with her. She *knew* he was going to open the door exactly when she reached it, and he did so. Such things that were beyond coincidence happened after eating the puffballs, small occurrences, powerfully felt.

Gil and Frieda went into the forest for puffballs again . . .

this time, they were going to try pickling them. They always seemed to be fresh near the great, hollow oak that Dearden said was Uberatu's, so that's where they headed. Frieda held the bag open while Gil stooped down with the kitchen knife to cut the first puffball, close to the soil.

It was when he sliced the stalk with the knife that he heard the noise again. It was louder this time than it had been before. He took no notice on the previous occasion. There was a different, unusual sound in the background this time. A spaced-out, but rapid tapping that was vaguely familiar.

"Can you hear that, Frie?" She heard a background musical humming that rose and fell like wind around the eaves above their rooms at Dearden Hall. Gil had sourced that sound in the eaves. There was a projection from the stonework; a fourteenth century gargoyle with a hole right through it to allow water to drain through its mouth from a gable intersection. When the wind came from a certain direction it moaned as it blew across the mouth and made it seem as though the gargoyle was alive.

"There's no wind blowing," Frieda said.

"I know. But the noise is coming from the tree, and there's a knocking-sound too. Come on, let's see what's happening."

They walked around the oak, homing-in on where the sound was coming from. There was a door of sorts with hinges and a latch; a modern, galvanised latch that worked by pressing a lever and then by pulling the door open by means of a handle hooped over the latch.

It was dark inside, apart from a hole that, when Gil looked through it, was dead in line with the Hub. The whole of the strange-looking building on top of its escarpment was observable through the hole. Gil put the bag of puffballs down on a chair, the folding camping type, blue, with a comfortable nylon seat and back. Frieda, as best she could in the meagre light, looked at the surroundings inside the tree. There were two lamps hanging from hooks screwed into the roughly hewn surface of the ceiling. They were gas lamps, the blue cannister type used for camping. Frieda knew about these from when she and Gil used to go camping. She pushed open the door to let in light from outside, turned the on/off knob fully and then the piezo ignited the gas. The mantle quickly glowed white-hot and they could see into the farthest parts of the cavity. The noise coming from the tree was loud, like surround-sound, and the knocking was persistent. Gil frowned as he thought back the years to navy-times. The knocking, discernible over the other noise, triggered the memory of times in Plymouth at the appropriately named *Anchor Arms*, over fish and chips and beer.

Gil Heskin, like Matt Roberts, had been in the Royal Navy. Gil hadn't risen through the ranks like Roberts. Heskin, the rating, had a colleague, John Partington, who aspired to be a radio technician. To be accepted for the post John had to attend an electronics course. Part of the course was to do with Morse-code, aiming for a speed of forty words per minute using standard words, like *Paris*, or *Codex*. Gil had helped his colleague bone up for the test. He got to use Morse himself and was gifted with it because he achieved an incredible sixty words per minute.

Gil was with his colleague on the day for John's Morse test, so, as they ate and drank, they talked Morse.

"**P**." Gil shot across John's bows.

"Dit-dah-dah-dit," came the sure reply.

"**Y**."

"Dah-dit-dah-dah," was Partington's certain answer.

*   *   *

The knocking came again from the tree, persistently, like surround sound.

"Hear that knocking, Frie?" She cocked her head on one side and heard it. "That's some sort of code. Don't tell anyone else about this, especially Jem Dearden, because they'll think we're bloody crazy."

23

The Luminant gradually awoke. It was a long, long process for vitality to return to its entire body. As always in a new awakening it cared not whether it was male nor female, progenitor or progenitrix, it just *Was*. But then, as the life-force returned in this awakening, its first thought was of the missing one. She had made its life complete.

The Luminant slowly formulated a plan to investigate the Realities systematically, starting with the Prime Dimension, where all things began. His lost one was missing here, somewhere in the dense forest of Leofwin's Hundred and he would search and search and search.

When he was fully awake the Luminant lay awhile in the cool of the sanctuary to allow his limbs to loosen up. The glow of the surroundings exuded warmth and familiarity and made him feel like rising, to flit unhindered through the forest greenery before, if he desired, leaping at unhindered speed through the multitude of Realities; in line with the Prime Directive, putting right whatever wrongs he could.

The Luminant felt the cells of his deep being had undergone regeneration. The familiar pulsation of vital energy coursed through his nervous system and he stood, shakily at first, and then he felt himself solidify to the loosely-bound structure of Prime-Dimension invisibility.

He sauntered inwards from the Sanctuary, stopped in front of the Portal set in the wall and gazed into it. So much lay through the Portal for those who used it for dimensional transfer. But the Luminant did not need the Portal, for his metabolism was mycorrhizal and thus related to the Grid.

First must come a test of the new awakening. Out the Luminant went, past the statue of his ancient forebear made visible in stone. Then fast through the drenching waterfall, up the hillside, racing fast into the forest, the side-effects of the awakening seeding the ground as it ran.

There were humans ahead, talking softly. The Luminant edged forward through the undergrowth to where he could see, sitting in a small clearing, a group of five males, one with brown skin, and one female, each of them with a weapon.

The Female's beautiful countenance brought back sharp memories, of his lost love, the gentle female, and the Luminant wept large and bitter tears. He raised his eyes to the sky and gathered grim determination to find his soulmate once again.

*   *   *

Vin Roddick raised an arm and Cell Four, creeping in single file down a narrow trail, stopped. They were used to no-noise jungle transit. In Leofwin's Hundred they could hear the sound of wildlife. Birds in the tree canopy far above them. Occasional noise in the undergrowth close by as something moved stealthily, but occasionally there was another, distant keening sort of noise that Roddick couldn't identify.

"We're being watched," he whispered to the operative behind him. She slipped the safety off the M16 A2, turned and whispered the message down the line of six. Quickly, at the end, Six indicated that he heard and understood. He looked around . . . looked up into the dark canopy. And then Six noticed the ground, the fungal growths, and he heard a sound that was unlike anything he had heard before. He tried to rationalise it, so he could write it up in his mission report when they got back to Dump Four.

"Hear that?" he whispered to Five, who nodded and felt the uncertainty.

"What is it?" Six asked Five, he spoke quietly in his ear.

Five passed Six's question up the line to Four. "What is it? Hell, I don't know." Five breeched a round while Four looked at the leaf canopy, which he thought was dark and menacing. He slipped the safety off his M16. Slipped his mind into attack mode. He didn't like what he heard because he had heard nothing like it before. He felt safe with the M16 in his hands, cold and deadly, and he grasped it tight. He knew he shouldn't be reacting like this with a weapon because of the Prime Directive, but what choice was there? There was a newly arrived tussle of conscience created by fear of the unknown.

Vin Roddick signalled for them to draw up to him. They were in a small clearing and Cell 4 formed a semi-circle facing him.

"What is it, boss?" Dave Beecham asked. Roddick shrugged, looked about. Took in the fungal growths scattered along the trail back where they walked from and forward to where they were going. He got on the comms, signalled the other cells, who reported a similar phenomenon they had come across.

Roddick signalled for them to relax. He sat. Pulled out the map of Leofwin's Hundred. Signalled for the others to sit. He zipped up his pocket. He was usually extrovert, Beecham was like that too. Bomb disposal had made him and his colleague next in line, Chuck Catesby, like that. They usually had a *what the hell* attitude, worked hard and dangerous sometimes and made up for it with playing and laughing hard.

Roddick was out-of-character quiet. Beecham sat next to

him, looked around, checking. Always checking. "Any ideas?" Beecham asked. It was then that Six, Balvinder Singh, Bal for short, felt something brush by him, touching his calf hard enough to bruise, and he saw depressions forming quickly in the leaf mold covering the track going out of the clearing in the direction they were to follow. Undergrowth was whipping aside as if caused by someone's rapid passage

Bal leaped up, trained his M16 on the track. Roddick had seen the urgent trail of footprints too, forming as something rushed by.

"Hold," Roddick shouted, "Don't shoot."

Bal lowered his weapon, bent down, rubbed his leg. "What the hell was that?" he said, looking along the trail. He saw undergrowth and saplings shifting as the thing rushed along in its frenzied passage.

"You OK?" Roddick's voice was urgent. Bal nodded OK.

"Then let's go." Roddick led off, fast.

As he rushed along the trail following the intruder Roddick got on the horn to the other cells to tell them what was going on. He learned that the other cells had similar experiences. Lol Penrose, heading up Cell 2, spoke of something tearing past them after they had camped for the night. "It was curious," he said. "Not threatening . . . more like surprising."

It was as if they were being played with. Like some young brat was taunting them. Nothing tangible could be seen other than, occasionally, the outline of a figure, partially visible after it disturbed moisture on the leafage it passed through.

*   *   *

The fungus was most peculiar. Within an hour of its passage, wherever the rushing presence had travelled, the stuff began to grow. All the cells reported similar activity and Lol Penrose conjectured that the creature, or being, whatever it was that passed by, seeded the ground wherever it went.

"Fungus doesn't have a seed cycle like vegetables or flowers do, nor should it grow so quick," Ffion Ingram said.

"What should fungus do?"

"It usually propagates by releasing spores when the Mycelium fragments."

"And what is the Mycelium?"

"A complex filament that expands radially."

"And it shouldn't do it this quick?"

"Shouldn't do. That's what makes this so intriguing," she said, as she pointed to one of the growths. When Ffion was studying agriculture, she didn't come across this specie of organism that was growing in Leofwin's Hundred. It was unique, a challenge to identify it. And there was that inexplicable background noise present.

Cell 4 lost the trail. It was at a point where the footprints in the leaf mold were all over the place. Direction became indistinct, so Roddick called a halt to the search. There appeared to be no logic to the movement, no reason for the footprint-effect to be present and the evidence Roddick could see was confusing.

"Think it's done it on purpose?" Beecham asked.

"Led us on a false trail you mean, to tease us?"

"Something like that."

"It does seem to be enjoying itself."

The cells reported to Dearden and the information was the same in every case; that an indefinable rushing presence was contacting them in an indistinct way. There was no conclusion about what it was, or what its motives were.

"Uncertainties are happening here again so be careful," he commented over the horn, "We're trying to work out how to deal with the presence . . . whatever it is." Dearden commanded the cells to stand down when he heard Bal Singh almost opened fire on the presence, "The last thing we want is to get a response we can't handle. So, get back here"

* * *

After a half hour mission report the cells drove away from Dearden Hall in the outwardly civilian vehicles, which were heavily military with Kevlar under the toughened steel bodywork. Dearden looked around the great hall and wondered where things were going. The Leofwin's Hundred area was behaving according to type. Reality was becoming vague and Dearden felt that he needed grounding. He went to the sideboard, poured a Glenmorangie. Maybe it was a triple but he didn't give a damn. It was always good for grounding, was Glenmorangie. He splashed in some dry ginger from the cooler. Sat down on one of the sofas where Rowan was reading. She had learned to read. Liked historical novels. Dearden put his arm around her shoulder and she snuggled-up close, looked into his eyes. "I want whisky and dry ginger too," she said.

* * *

Dearden and Mitch Doughty had some discussion time. "Why don't we get Red Cloud along?" Doughty suggested. "He's useful when things get vague."

"That crossed my mind too. We've gone through some weird stuff here but, alternative realities, I don't know. Maybe Red's Lakota Sioux genes would get him closer to what's going on than we can get."

"What's going on is connected to events that are beyond our comprehension, and the Uberatu's Oak noise stuff certainly comes into that category. Rowan's suggestion makes sense Jem. We need Lan-Si-Nu and his pals on board ASAP." Doughty was trying to understand recent events that were difficult to rationalise.

"OK, we've got to try to make progress on this." Dearden felt the frustration. The alien, Lan-Si-Nu and his two buddies had gone to ground again. They always seemed to be doing that, as if they had an agenda. But the alien commander did say that there was a lot of work to do. So Dearden thumbed the keypad on his mobile. A few seconds later Red answered. What he said sounded something like, *Toníktuka hwo*. He always used the same Lakota Sioux greeting on the phone.

"HI Red, Jem Dearden."

"Jem, how are you?"

"Troubled, if you want the truth."

"Why is that, my friend?"

"Things are going on here in Leofwin's Hundred that we don't understand."

"You are full of surprises," which was an unusual touch of sarcasm from Red Cloud. "Why call me?"

"Because you can help us."

"OK . . . but you must tell me more."

"It would be better if it was face-to-face."

"Uh-uh . . . from you, that means something *very* unusual is going on."

"You can say that again."

*   *   *

Chief Red Cloud and Possum Chaser, his wife, arrived two days later. He apologised for the delay getting to Dearden

Hall. They had things going on they couldn't leave.

Tomahawk Shahn of Offchurch recognised Red Cloud's voice. A sound that reminded him of another home, way back. The wolf stood and bounded across the room to the two who arrived. Red looked the wolf in the eye, which could be dangerous, but there was a *new* understanding now. An alteration. Tomahawk sat in front of the Sioux chieftain. Different species on equal terms.

Dearden unhooked the wolf's heavy leash from its place on the wall near the fire and along with Red and Possum Chaser, they went on foot into the forest, making their way to Uberatu's Oak. Dearden told them about Harry and Esma's disappearance and that he wanted their opinion about the phenomenon occurring inside Uberatu's Oak. He briefly explained.

"*'Curiouser and curiouser,'* as Alice said in her wonderland." Possum Chaser said, as she looked up into the dark overhanging canopy of leaves. She shivered. Red looked at Jem and frowned.

"You are a master of mystery at times Jem, my friend. And this forest of yours gets more mysterious as time passes by. I am concerned about Harry and Esma, and I am intrigued about how you think an oak tree fits in."

They had walked past Old Jack and were crossing the bridge over Shadow Brook when the wolf stopped dead. His hackles arose. He growled. The growl, as dark as the tree canopy above, told them that threat lay ahead. The three people took the clue from Tomahawk and stopped. Red gently touched the wolf's head. Said *Shhhh*, quietly, at which the growl quietened and Tomahawk inched forward around a bend in the forest track. He cautiously went forward ears upright and attentive, twitching, listening for what lay ahead.

They came to the escarpment on top of which lay the above-ground part of the Hub. To the right was a clearing and, on its edge, the great broadleaf tree, Uberatu's Oak.

"Look at that, Jem," Red Cloud said, pointing at the ground ahead around the oak tree.

"Yeah we know about that."

"It is *c ˇhaŋna ´kpa*. You say tree-fungus; mushrooms that grow from rotting wood. But it is not like any *c ˇhaŋna ´kpa* I recognise."

"Looks like Puffball, only bigger," Possum Chaser said. She remembered picking a giant puffball in a place where their sheep sometimes roamed behind one of the outbuildings at their place in Offchurch. One of her elderly neighbours had suggested she could slice the fungus to quarter inch thick and cook it with bacon and fried bread. *It is delicious*, he had told her, and it was.

"Strangest puffballs I've ever seen," Red Cloud said. "They are not that light creamy colour they should be."

"I'll look it up in the fungus book when we get home," Possum Chaser suggested.

They reached the ancient oak associated with Theodore Uberatu, and given his name. The tree's girth surprised folks who hadn't seen it before. Some privileged folks who saw Uberatu's Oak had seen the Rufus oak in the New Forest, where William Rufus had met his end on a hunting ride in a time when kings held all power in England. All who had seen both mighty trees said Uberatu's Oak won hands down for size.

Dearden looked up as a shadow came between the meagre sunlight and the green darkness of the forest canopy. Red and Possum Chaser saw it, so did Tomahawk. There was a hollow pulsating sound coming from far above.

"Ho, you Earths . . . be quick." The shout came from outside the tunnel leading to the Hub's ground-level entrance. Lan-Si-Nu, seven and a half foot tall, was calling. Fen-Nu and Thal-Nar were there too, waving their arms, urgently. Dearden and the others broke into a fast run, as if they were being chased by a predator with big teeth.

"In, quick." Lan-Si-Nu didn't waste words when they reached the tunnel entrance. They were in and he slammed the door behind them, locked it and led the way in a sort of loping trot through the ground-level room to the stairs going up. It was the first time Dearden had seen such fast activity from the large alien. He thought, for a fraction of a second, how comical it looked, but realised how serious things must be by the out-of-character action of the alien.

They arrived in the control-room and Lan-Si-Nu hurled himself into the commander's seat in the middle front. Fen-Nu and Thal-Nar sat just as fast, one each side of him. Thal-Nar said some words, rapidly, in Wasiri-Chanchiyan, Lan-Si-Nu nodded and pressed a button. A screen illuminated right of the centre-screen in front of them. Displayed in high-definition close-up was the black silhouette of the Nibiruan star-ship.

24

"They're back for more punishment," Jules said to Storm, who stood and grinned. Storm said something quiet Matt Roberts thought sounded like, *come and get it*. He looked at her and thought how she looked like the Amazon he had seen in a modern take of Midsummer Night's Dream. In jeans and sweat-shirt she was impressive and ready for action. He put his arm around her shoulders but she shook him off. It wasn't the time for sentiment. He shrugged in response, blew some hair escaped from his bandana away from his face. He forced his way to the front of the group at Dearden Hall's ancient front door and gazed in the direction of the forest.

The vessel in the sky was hovering maybe a couple of thousand feet above the high point of the forest which, although its detail was shrouded with broadleaf trees, was the place where Roberts was well aware the Hub was situated. The craft descended quickly to half the height and a deep, hollow pulsating sound came to his ears. He glanced at Doughty, who caught the look and pursed his lips, which was when Sir Will Pierpoint and Trent Jackson arrived in Pierpoint's Bentley Mulsanne, tyres spitting gravel. Pierpoint didn't wait for his driver, Harvey Proctor to open the door. He thrust the rear door open himself and strode out. Jackson was out just as quick from the other side and they rushed to where the others were standing. Lee Wynter and Jules joined them from the basement with arms and ammunition.

"Where's Jem?" Pierpoint asked. He looked into the sky over the forest. He, Jackson and Proctor had seen the craft in the sky as they approached Dearden Hall, and Pierpoint told Proctor to step on the gas. For the final mile Proctor tooled the Bentley through country lanes using all the road.

"He's gone into the forest, with Red Cloud and Possum Chaser . . . and Tomahawk," Rowan said, as Wynter and Jules handed out guns and ammo. There was the metallic snick and chack sounds of cartridges being loaded. Templestone declined the over and under shotgun. He pulled out his Smith and Wesson 38. A business-like weapon he kept in his pocket all the time these days for good measure even though he was well aware of the Prime Directive of Universal Peace. Problem was that he had spent years combatting those who dealt out pain and suffering and it was difficult to shake that off. He cracked open the cylinder, loaded it with rounds from his pocket and slipped on the safety.

"OK, let's go." Pierpoint led the action. He had been yearning for just such an opportunity since his retirement and the hand-over to Dearden as head of SHaFT. Trouble was, this opportunity was rather a stretch from the usual. Wisely, Mitch Doughty deferred to Pierpoint's long experience.

"We'll go on foot," Pierpoint said. "We don't want to announce ourselves."

"Too right," Wynter said. "Not with those woojies around."

So, they set out, all ten of them, armed to the teeth and two of them, Jules and Storm Petrel Karateka-ready.

Trent Jackson walked quick to catch up with Doughty.

"Remember when I told you about the separate coded note I found in the manual relating to the Hub?"

"I remember you saying about it way back. You were saying the translation was difficult . . . why, has something changed?"

"I've translated the note. It's a strong warning. It names the Nibiruans. They are not to be trusted, not one little bit.

That was the thrust of the message."

"You know, I sort of understand that now," Doughty said. He took his eyes off the track in front and looked at Jackson, then back at the alien craft. It suddenly descended and hovered mid-way between cloud level and the ground, directly over the Hub. Projections began to morph from below the hull of the vehicle which now, instead of being intense black, shifted gradually from the base upwards into a dull cherry-red colour.

*   *   *

"What's happening?" Dearden, safe inside the Hub, asked Lan-Si-Nu.

"They are in attack mode. Their vehicle is equipped with powerful weapons, different to those you Earths have devised. But be quiet and watch what happens next." Lan-Si-Nu spoke Wasiri-Chanchiyan again. Short, clipped phrases. His attention was on the screen up front.

Lan-Si-Nu's large hand hovered above a button on a panel that had risen from a blank area above the temporal controls. He turned to face Dearden. "We are now engaging our defensive mode." On the screen they saw ports open in the hull of the Starship and as they did so the vehicle began to morph from black to a red colour that grew in brightness.

Lan-Si-Nu stabbed the button and the Hub became active. From its depths the familiar sound of an engaging relay punched the quietness, and the Chakrakan craft, visible on the screen right of centre appeared to be wavering, as if in a mirage.

"We have now engaged our defences." The large alien seemed unruffled. "We are now within a compacted neutron-shield, through which nothing can penetrate. Observe the activity that is about to start on the Chakrakan ship."

A second later pulsating beams of purple light exploded from the projections around the hull of the space-craft . . . the ceiling of the Hub became transparent, like it did in temporal-shift mode, and the action outside became visible to those within the portal. The alien craft was above them, close and massive, a scarlet colour now, its weaponry in fiery action with bolts of intense energy like lightning splashing the surface of the Hub's neutron-shield.

"They have based their weapons on laser technology. It is in advance of your laser research but it is easily contained. With our cocooning of their world, and its shift to an extremely eccentric orbit, we have limited their capacity to make much progress."

"They still have a starship to use . . . that is not old technology," Red Cloud said.

"Admittedly. Although in certain aspects, their technology is old-fashioned in relation to yours. There are similarities but their science diverged. The Chakrakans took a tangential course to that of Earth-science and arrived at alternative conclusions. They are very different to you people, and to us, and evil is ingrained in their psyche."

All the time Lan-Si-Nu was talking the alien space-craft was attacking the Hub. Stream after stream of energy pounding the neutron-shield had no effect.

"They are like naughty children who do not intend to learn by experience. Now, see how we deal with them. They will not be harmed. Their situation will be . . . altered."

*   *   *

Doughty sped up, setting a pace too fast for Pierpoint and Templestone, but the others kept up. They got to where the

166

great oak, Old Jack was growing at the side of the path. Suddenly, with the alien craft now a bright fiery red, the projections around the base of the craft exploded into energy that violently thrashed the Hub, a few hundred yards ahead.

"Jem's in there," Doughty's voice was a mixture of anger and desperation. He stopped dead. They all stopped, crowded together. They could feel the heat from what was going on ahead. A hot wind tugged at Doughty's face, blew his hair, and his open jacket streamed out behind him. Rowan was desperate for Jem's safety. She forced her way to Doughty past the others, grabbing at the undergrowth to help her get to him. She grabbed his arm, shouted close to his ear so he could hear her above the noise of the alien craft.

"Will Jem be OK?" she shouted, as Templestone and Pierpoint caught up, out of breath.

Doughty looked at her. Her golden blond hair was streaming out behind in the fierce wind from the attack on the Hub. Doughty was unsure how best to answer. So he shouted, "Jem knows how to survive." Dearden had tenacity. Demonstrated many times in the past that he was a survivor. Doughty took Rowan's hand. Squeezed it. "He'll be OK, he always is," he said, hoping. She returned the squeeze.

And then an extraordinary thing happened.

* * *

Inside the Hub Possum Chaser was terrified when the alien vessel opened fire. She calmed down when it became obvious they were safe behind the neutron-shield. A while back she and Red had been on a boat, the Hornblower, looking upwards at the deluge of water as the Niagara thundered downwards ahead of them. "It is like being under Niagara." The noise of the attack was similar to the falls and even inside the Hub she had to shout to be heard.

The Alien shouted, his voice was deep and mellow, "If you were outside you would not enjoy the experience like you did at Niagara. What you see is concentrated radiant energy."

Dearden, looking through the transparent wall, could see the trees at the edge of the clearing and the surrounding undergrowth being scorched by the heat unleashed by the attack. He stood close to Lan-Si-Nu so as to be heard. "They must not destroy Uberatu's Oak," he pointed to the stately form of the ancient tree. "Communication is occurring there, it could be Harry." Lan-Si-Nu nodded and turned to Fen-Nu. He spoke again in their melodic native tongue and Fen-Nu shifted her hand to a series of buttons in front of her seat. She asked her commander a question which, if the Earth people could understand it, would be, *How far shall we move them?* And Lan-Si-Nu's answer, *Send the Starship into forced orbit around Chakrakan. Do it, now!*

* * *

As Doughty and the rest stopped their headlong flight toward the Hub the alien craft careered heavenward. The branches of the ancient oak, Old Jack, partially obscured the craft's ascent so Doughty walked forward a few yards so he had a clear view. The alien craft was just a speck in the sky.

He began to run again, as thoughts of the fate of Jem in the fiery onslaught got to him. Red Cloud and Possum Chaser were there too, and Tomahawk. Doughty set a blistering pace and left the others, even those younger than him behind. He reached the clearing at the foot of the hill with the Hub built into it. It was a mess of blackened earth and scorched trees.

Doughty glanced desperately around the site as the others,

apart from Templestone and Pierpoint, caught up with him. It was then he realised the visible part of the Hub on top of the escarpment, was unaffected.

"Did you see that?" Dearden called to them from the top of the hill. Rowan pushed by Doughty and scrambled up the hill and into Dearden's arms where he was waiting by the door into the Hub. They went inside and the others followed up the hill and into the alien building. Pierpoint and Templestone, both out of breath, came last.

Doughty waited outside the Hub with his back to the wall, which was cool to the touch despite the fiery onslaught a few minutes back. As he surveyed the scorched trees, anger welled up inside because of the wanton destruction. His gaze settled on Uberatu's Oak, standing undamaged beyond the scorched trees as if, in some way as yet obscure, it had been protected. The sun was glinting on its leaves, which were moving in a moderate breeze. Doughty heard an unnatural sound coming from the tree. It was carried on the breeze, which ruffled his hair. It was a moment of truth and he remembered laughing when Matt Roberts mentioned hearing sounds issuing from the oak tree. He forced himself to turn and he stepped through the door into the alien building, the Hub, that the Anglo-Saxons had named The House of the West Wind.

*　*　*

It was Max Dearden, Jem's father, who originally called the alien building the Hub. His son, Jem and the others were in the topmost room where temporal and spatial transportation occurred. Lan-Si-Nu and his two companions were there too, studying the forest through the transparent wall.

"The Chakrakans are foolish," Commander Lan-Si-Nu said. "They are set in their violent ways so much that they are unable to learn from their past mistakes. It stops them from moving on to a constructive way of life."

"Until lately it was the same for some here on Earth. People were desperately afraid with Nibiru's second pass," Pierpoint said. "It's altered the mind-set of the majority." Pierpoint had experienced trouble first-hand over the years he headed-up SHaFT. Lovers of trouble had dogged his life and he had fought it in many theatres of action trying to combat trouble.

"Yet again we have contained the Chakrakans to prevent their wayward course. Remember how we did it, and learn," Lan-Si-Nu said.

Red Cloud nodded. "We people of the Sioux Nation have learned how to work peacefully with the Great Spirit who has all things in his domain. It is a pity the people of Nibiru have not considered the Great Spirit, and worked with him, like the Sioux and some others on Earth have done."

"You speak truth, Chief Red Cloud. Now, since the Chakrakan rebels have once again been put in their place, we have time we can devote to finding your colleagues, the esteemed Hnirath, Harry Stanway, and his Esma. We will go Down. The lower levels of the Hub are beckoning. The underground levels, in conjunction with Uberatu's Oak and the growths that are appearing in Leofwin's Hundred may help us locate your two friends."

The tall alien led the group to the locked door leading down from the ground floor of the Hub. The doorway was well-known to the people of Earth involved with the Hub. Harry Stanway, in particular, had tried feverishly to go down. With Esma one night, he arrived at the door with tools to help him to break through. A twenty-four inch forged steel crow-bar was favourite but after considerable force on the edge of the door, which left no damage whatsoever, he gave up the attempt.

Harry had spoken to Dearden about his effort. "I don't know how or why they've secured the lower levels. There has to be something down there they want to hide. It's impossible to get through the door to the lower levels."

"Let it go, Harry," Dearden had advised. "It could lead to things we can't handle."

And now the door was open and they were standing on the threshold of the lower levels. On a balcony at the head of the spiral stairs leading underground. Dearden saw that the room at the bottom of the first set of stairs followed the same profile as the building above-ground. It was circular and about ten feet from floor to ceiling. The diameter was the same as the rooms above-ground, apart from the room of the exhibits, which was ovoid.

There was a large, complex object in the centre of the room which was similar to the apparatus in the two highest above-ground levels of the Hub. This device also had a crystal at its heart, but it was more massive than the one above-ground. As did the crystal at the top of the Hub, the subterranean one disappeared through the floor into the level below. The great crystal was active, its interior glinting and flashing as if it was reacting to an external energy. Other than the device, from which immensely thick cables arched like flying buttresses to the outer wall, the first room underground was empty.

Lan-Si-Nu and his two crew members led the way down the stairs. "I'll need a damn walking-stick for this sort of thing before long," Pierpoint said to Templestone quietly, as he negotiated the steps. The risers were identical in height to those of the stairs above-ground, made for the Wasiri-Chanchiyans, who were a third taller than the average human.

The three aliens reached the foot of the stairs and turned to face the SHaFT contingency. Matt Roberts, at the rear with Storm Petrel, raised a question before the alien commander spoke.

"How far down are you letting us go?"

"We will go all the way down, to the Level of Latest Defining."

"That sure sounds like something out of mythology m'tall man," Wynter quipped.

"Far from being mythological, that level is where you will observe some of our latest Reality exploration. Follow me. Be prepared for a long, but brief journey and surprises beyond your furthest imagining. I must warn you," Lan-Si-Nu looked at Wynter, "Do not be tempted to touch anything." He walked over to a large transparent cubicle set fully into the wall of the room on the opposite side to the stairway. He spoke three words in Wasiri-Chanchiyan and after a door raised vertically, they stepped into a large elevator.

Below them, seen through a transparent floor, was a great dark tube, into which light from the progressive levels downward penetrated the dark to where light overcame the darkness at a vanishing point an unknown distance below. The door slid shut and the elevator began to take them downwards at a slow pace. As it did so, Fen-Nu began an explanation in a voice richer and more eloquent than the commander.

"The First Level below ground, which we have just left, is the oldest of all levels. Every subterranean level going downwards is dedicated to interdimensional travel, other than the first two levels, which contain the motive power of the

Virtuality. Each successive level downwards houses the data and access point to a specific dimension, or Reality, which has its own set of physical laws. Each level is fixed on a timeline of discovery and exploration. The deeper the level, the nearer to the present day did the exploration begin. Due to the complexities of accessing dimensions throughout the Virtuality, it has taken varying amounts of time, sometimes hundreds of your years, to open up each level's Dimensional Gateway."

"What is the Virtuality?" Oscar asked.

Jules, a fellow scientist, opened her eyes and waited for the answer. She hated heights, they unnerved her and she had divorced herself from the scene through the transparent floor of the elevator by closing her eyes. She fixed her gaze on Fen-Nu. The enormity of Oscar's question, *what is the Virtuality*, in such surreal surroundings, won out and the fear of heights became less of a problem.

Lan-Si-Nu's other crew member, Thal-Nar, answered Oscar's question about the Virtuality.

"Imagine realities, or dimensions, as layers. In simple terms, you could liken the situation to layered geological strata. The Virtuality is the sum total of all the strata, or realities that have been created and subsequently experienced by us and many other races. The total amount of levels is being added to as exploration continues. The Virtuality is expansive. We believe that the number of realities is likely to be infinite."

"What—"

"Please listen . . . all will be explained as we descend and you assimilate what you behold. Before that, more historical information will help your understanding.

"The first two levels of the Hub below ground where the

motive power of dimensional-shift is situated took a long while to become operative after the building of the Hub commenced. We had to learn and apply many new scientific principles. It was an age of originality such as we had never before experienced, nor are we likely to experience in the future. Back then, our ancestors had good evidence that there are dimensions beyond the Prime, which is the dimensional reality in which we are now present.

"It took our Hniraths of Science almost a thousand Earth years to discern how to manipulate the new and sometimes vague physical laws to allow us to enter the Virtuality and begin the process of interdimensional travel. The first two subterranean levels are what can be understood as the engine which drives interdimensional access."

Lan-Si-Nu carried on the explanation. "People of Earth, we *were* not going to allow you to access the lower levels of the Portal because of their abstruse nature. We have changed our minds due to the present circumstances to do with the Harry and Esma people. You will understand, better than we can, how Harry Stanway's mind works. Clues to his whereabouts that we may miss might be evident in the levels below ground. Chief Red Cloud, your perception may also prove valuable."

Red nodded his understanding. "Your ways are different to ours, my friend. I can understand that each of these realities you speak of may be very different to each other, so some slight Earth-event within a non-Earth reality will stand out amongst the other data like an eagle stands out against the bright sky of morning."

"Exactly what we thought," said Fen-Nu.

"Tell me, Lan-Si-Nu, do you have sensors that pick up the ethos of life energy on each level of reality?"

Lan-Si-Nu stepped back a pace. He was surprised by Red's question. "You are perceptive, Chief Red Cloud. What you say is close to what happens. Analysis of each dimensional reality takes place via bio-sensors. It is their analysis that will carry a lot of weight in the mission to find your friends."

"Nos Successio Procul Totus Sumptus," Sir Will Pierpoint said, loud and clear.

"Yes, that is so true with your SHaFT organisation, Sir Willoughby. It has accomplished much,"

"We Succeed At All Costs," Jackson, the language guy, said.

"Indeed, you do. So, please," the tall alien continued, "All of you, try to view what you will experience without pre-conceived notions as we go downward. In that way, we may, through a process of elimination, reasoning and science, start to follow the trail into whichever reality your Harry Stanway and Esma of Maldon have become marooned. Let us hope they are in a reality we have already discovered."

"Why is that?" Red Cloud asked.

"Because if it is a new Reality, there will be a whole new hierarchy of physics to learn before we dare venture into it."

25

Fen-Nu slowed the elevator briefly as it passed by the transparent door into each level going downwards. The travellers were able to briefly view the interior of the levels as they descended and then they reached level seven. The elevator stopped. The door opened, the three aliens strode out and Lan-Si-Nu told the others to follow. Two other beings were there. Odd looking creatures with a mop of hair that looked as if it had been blow-dried to stand two foot in the air vertically.

As they drew near to the creatures, Clive Fraser nudged Jules' arm. He could see that the appendages were not hair but were tentacles, which were constantly active. They looked to be intensely busy. More vegetation-looking matter projected from the front of the creatures. These extremities laboured upon the buttons of a complex panel which was sub-divided into squares of brilliant colours, having complex symbols written on them.

"Those life-forms are Vastrons," Fen-Nu said. "They are members of a race of bio-mechanical sensory life-forms whose metabolism requires data to survive. That process is useful for us because, not only do they consume data and convert it into life-giving energy for their survival, but they also dispense it, which is essential for cross-reality understanding.

"Each of the Vastrons is an encyclopaedia of knowledge. We have known their race many years and we work closely with them. Two of them are present on each level. They remain in position constantly to assimilate, record and analyse data, which benefit. the whole Virtuality," Fen-Nu explained,

"They are a life-form from one of the planets in the Prime Galaxy of the Reality accessed from Level Seven . . . do you see over there?" The visitors shifted so they could see where Fen-Nu pointed. There was an arched framework set in the wall some ninety degrees to the right of the elevator shaft.

"That is the entrance to the Seventh Reality."

Lan-Si-Nu spoke up. "Come, let us go now. We must not disturb the Vastrons at their work. We have much to see."

As they walked to the elevator Thal-Nar explained what would happen next.

"The Seventh Level is the oldest Reality Level that we discovered where exploration is still ongoing. Occasionally the oldest levels need further investigation when we receive new information from the Vastrons."

"Do you discover new Realities often?" Jules asked.

"There is no predictability about when a new level will be found. The tuning-in is a slow procedure and from Level Seven downwards every Level of the Virtuality has some form of action going on at our side of its Gate. Could be minimal activity to maintain connectivity, but that depends upon the Entry-Planet's complexity of physical laws. Activity could be intense or minimal."

"So, there is an Entry-Planet for every reality? Oscar asked Thal-Nar.

"There is'"

"Why have you set all this up?" Templestone asked.

"For the same reason your mountaineers say, *Because it's there*," Thal-Nar responded. "They climb mountains because they are challenged by them. We are inquisitive too and we *do* like a challenge; much like yourselves."

"Too right you do m' tall man," Lee Wynter muttered.

*   *   *

The transparent door slid shut and they began going down again. The rate of progression sped up to such a degree that the levels they passed became a blur, and then they gradually slowed down and stopped.

Lan-Si-Nu spoke again.

"This is Level Forty-two."

On this level they could see intense activity. And at their panel, consuming energy and data, were the two Vastrons assigned to Forty-two. "There is much work going on here. It is an older-age level, but the Vastrons here have detected deep unrest. We are going to send a diplomatic mission to investigate."

"Were you concerned about unrest on Planet Earth before you came in contact with us?" Will Pierpoint asked.

"We have been interested in your race from the time of its creation. It is your intensity of feeling, your similarity to ourselves, and your world itself that has attracted us to you. And yes, because of your propensity to embrace violence there has been a great deal of concern."

"It seems as though the Great Spirit has created a diversity across many, many worlds," Red Cloud observed, "But freedom of will shines clearly through it all."

Down, down, down they went. All was quiet as the travellers took in what had been said. They tried to view the levels they rushed by but the speed of the elevator made that impossible.

"Why is this contraption on our world and not on your own?" Lee Wynter challenged Lan-Si-Nu.

"There *is* a Virtuality Gateway on Wasiri-Poya. It is progressing forward with discoveries at much the same rate as the contraption on this world of yours because there is an automatic transfer of information between worlds about the Virtuality Column. There is an equal amount of levels at each location. More to the point, just as there is a Portal on the many worlds throughout the cosmos that connect to the Grid, in every location where there is connectivity to the Grid, there is also a Virtuality Column."

"It must take an awful lot of logistics to maintain all that exploration in a cohesive way," Trent Jackson said.

"True. But like I said, we have many galaxies which are connected by the Grid. They are united in providing the resources and the intelligence to make progress. The majority of members of the Council of Worlds have the desire to continue exploring."

The elevator began to slow down. The occupants felt their bodyweight grow considerably heavier and then grow light again as the transporter stopped.

"This is the Four Hundred and Seventieth level," said Thal-Nar. "At present it is the deepest level and until another Reality is discovered, it is known as the *Level of Latest Defining*. The definition of the Levels, each of which leads to a unique reality is in a constant state of flux because of the discovery of new Realities. We will disembark here for a while and observe the research and exploration that is taking place on this Level."

From a compartment behind a concealed cover in the elevator, Fen-Nu lifted a device which she said translated the neural stream of information assimilated by the Vastrons into a universal language.

"Does that happen to be English?" Wynter asked. Fen-Nu disregarded the comment. Just looked at Wynter briefly, sort of smirked. Trent Jackson awaited the response eagerly, and then Fen-Nu carried on explaining.

"With this equipment," she moved it slowly past each of the travellers, "We are able to connect with the memory bank of the Vastron Cohort. The information is laid down in logical form by subject index. The data can be translated into *any* of the languages of the Cosmos, Mister Wynter." The Wasiri-Chanchiyan sort of smirked again. "Languages emerging from newly-located realities are dissembled and analysed and then uploaded to the language library."

"Let me see." Trent Jackson stretched out his hand for the device. He expected it to be heavier than it was. "How do you work it?"

"You will see shortly," Fen-nu told him.

The door to the elevator slid upwards and Lan-Si-Nu made his way to where the two Vastrons assigned to the Level of Latest Defining were seated; although seated was a loose term for how they were positioned. They were slouched in an untidy fashion, with their upper appendages moving chaotically, whilst the frontal appendages moved precisely over the controls in front of them. Wynter thought they vaguely resembled sea anemone, but with more tentacles than the sea creature he was familiar with.

Jackson reluctantly relinquished the device when Fen-Nu indicated she wanted it. Jackson was holding it tightly and Fen-Nu snatched it back. She grimaced, spoke quietly, close to Jackson's ear. "I know you are a language professor, Trent Jackson, but you must have patience. There is much that you will learn and it will be a delightful experience. Please cooperate."

Lan-Si-Nu spoke so that all the Earths could hear. "We are on this level to help you understand the complexities involved with locating your two friends. Your saying, about finding a needle in a haystack, becomes a problem as simple as one plus one equals two, compared to finding Harry and Esma in the Virtuality."

26

Lan-Si-Nu touched the body of one of the Vastrons. Its somewhat frenetic motion stopped and it rotated in its seated position to face the Wasiri-Poyan. All of the motion of its topmost and frontal appendages ceased as the connection with its task was broken. Lan-Si-Nu spoke to it in a language the Earths failed to recognise.

Trent Jackson stepped forward, being most interested in the language, and he listened to Lan-Si-Nu's translation, trying to record in his mind the sounds he heard the Vastron speak so that he could relate them to the translation.

"I have asked this Vastron, Chka, who is in charge of this level, if it has heard any signals of distress. In this Level of Latest Defining the Vastrons receive a summary of information from the Vastron cohort inhabiting all of the other Realities in the Virtuality Column. You could also describe this level as the newest revealed Reality. It is a shifting platform because newer Levels may be discovered at any time and then we have to construct the next Level down in the Column to accommodate its access Gate. It then becomes the new Level of Latest Defining."

Oscar looked at the gate. He didn't see the puzzled look on Lan-Si-Nu's face. There was mud on the floor near the gate. "So, has Chka heard or seen anything unusual recently?" Oscar asked the obvious question considering there was mud on the floor.

Lan-Si-Nu was slow to answer; then, "The Vastron says that there is a great source of distress coming out of this Four Hundred and Seventieth Reality but the origin of the distress within the Reality's cosmos is indeterminate. It is likely that your friends are within that Reality, but which planet, within what galaxy the signal is originating from is the puzzle we have to solve. The Vastron, Chka says that the signal is peculiar to the psyche of the people of Earth. I must tell you that there is a powerful communicative force at work, and it is new to us."

"OK, you are the guys with all the technology. The Vastron has heard a disturbing signal from within this Reality. How can we home in on the source?" asked Will Pierpoint.

"Understand this, Sir Willoughby; on any particular Level of Reality what we are receiving from the Vastron Cohort is a summation of information from the Reality's life-energy. It's collective dominant raison d'etre, as we can best understand it, is what we receive. Its technological prowess, its degree of principle compared to the Prime Directive of Universal Peace is also perceived. There are many other statistical features received and examined. As best we can, we order this colossal amount of information into a constructive understanding and lay it down into the Great Annals for future use and for the benefit of the Virtuality. Sir Willoughby, can you comprehend how complex this process is?"

"I think so . . . marginally. You are telling us that you receive a great body of information, so, amongst all of the chatter, you are saying that it is almost impossible to distinguish an individual call for help."

"That sums it up."

"Where does that leave our lost friends?"

"At present they are in a hopeless situation . . . but we do have an added asset in our resources."

"And what is that asset, may I ask?"

"Oscar Stanway." Oscar looked up sharply.

*　*　*

Gil Heskin and Frieda were in the forest again. They couldn't really explain why. Rationality was not involved. They simply *had* to go into the forest to observe the fungus and collect some of it. They still had a big one in the fridge. It hadn't deteriorated like mushrooms do after a while when they go limp and mushy and begin to smell like the earth out of which they grew. This one was as fresh as when it was cut from the forest soil. Gil and Frieda didn't discuss the matter. They just *knew* that they had to go back into the forest to where the fungus was growing.

With Jem and the others away at the Hub, Tomahawk was restless. He seemed to need the company of humans now, but particularly the company of Dearden and Rowan. The wolf was aware of the Heskin's getting prepared to leave the house. He aroused himself from near-sleep and mooched to the entrance-hall. Gil lifted the thick leash off a hook screwed into a beam and attached it to the wolf's studded collar. Tomahawk waited, big, black and expectant, very close to Heskin's right leg. Frieda joined them and Gill led the way out the ancient front door and they headed for the forest.

Once past the boundary they followed the usual route, past Old Jack, then over the bridge spanning Shadow Brook, and a while later they reached Uberatu's oak, where the puffballs always seemed to grow at their best. Tomahawk was distracted when they got near the oak tree. He dug in. All four legs opposed to moving from where he stood. Gill Heskin tried the dragging technique, Frieda tried persuasive talk, but the result was no-go. Tomahawk was not going to be budged. Gil knew better than to try to apply any more leverage because it was the wolf who was the boss and the wolf was going nowhere.

The Heskins were exasperated. The puffballs were eight feet away, but the wolf wasn't cooperating. Of course, the Heskins didn't see what Tomahawk saw and heard, the tracks compressing the fallen leaves covering the ground.

* * *

At that particular point in time, in the Virtuality, way below the forest floor, Oscar Stanway did the typical *What me?* Stuff. The pointing to the chest, the open mouth, the sheepish grin and then self-belief when he rose to the occasion and nodded. "You think *I'm* an asset; in what way?"

"You and Harry are very similar. You come out of the same gene-pool and you both think original thoughts . . . more than most of the people of Earth. More so than we Wasiri-Chanchiyans. We may have advanced scientifically many thousands of years beyond your present capabilities, but we are less able to think beyond a strictly defined hierarchical range of principles than you can do. Some of you Earths are free thinkers in realms far beyond our capabilities. That is why you are an asset, Oscar. Your original thinking will help us in our hunt for your brother and his friend and, I might add, when they are returned to Earth, you and Harry will probably be able to help us progress into the Realities far beyond our present imaginings."

All was quiet in the group . . . the people of Earth and the three aliens. It was Oscar who continued. "Then we will work together. I want to help, obviously. I appreciate your frankness, but with what we have experienced in the Virtuality, we have a lot of catching-up to do."

Jules asked, "How do you think Oscar can help . . . more to the point, how we can all help in the search?"

"First, take some time to think about what you have seen and experienced. Talk about it amongst yourselves. And think about this; the Portal, the device you people call the Hub, had become almost useless to us not long ago. Me, Fen-Nu and Thal-Nar had become marooned. The Virtuality, on this planet had shut down. Harry, in a demonstration of the free-thinking ingenuity some of you possess, got the Hub working again. The Earth Portal became fully connected to the Grid once more. We could return to our home, Wasiri-Poya. The Virtuality became active again. For this, with our grateful thanks, Harry Stanway was awarded the highest accolade of science our planet could offer, Hnirath. Harry Stanway's name is now written in the Great Annals."

"You mentioned that there is a disturbance to the equilibrium of the Virtuality accessed from Level Four Hundred and Seventy," said Trent Jackson. "This is only a hunch but the disturbance suggests that Level Four Hundred and Seventy is in need of further analysis. The problem could relate to Harry and Esma's disappearance. Are you able to give us recordings of the latest information the Vastrons have downloaded from that level?"

"Hold on . . . not so fast," Oscar interrupted. "Lan-Si-Nu, how often do these incompatibility situations occur?"

"They are almost unheard of. I looked into the Great Annals and a major incompatibility occurred some thousands of your years ago. It was in our Reality, the prime dimension, at the time the Nibiruans first invaded planet Earth."

"And that was a safety-critical situation for the Earth?"

"It certainly was and the problem could have had far-reaching consequences for our Reality."

"How is the latest incompatibility safety-critical?"

Lan-Si-Nu wondered how to best frame his answer.

"Think of the temporal travel paradox situation where—"

"—Where you go back and kill your grand-daddy. What happens to you if you kill him before he and your grand-mother conceive your father or mother?"

"Exactly, Mister Wynter. In that case a Reality-paradox might be created. Harmony is critical across the stream of Realities. Entry into a Reality's physicality must be in a strictly controlled way. The laws that define the Realities must harmonise. The physical laws of the traveller's Reality and the physical laws of his destination Reality need to work in harmony. This is achieved by balancing the traveller's metabolism to harmonise with both Realities of his journey."

"How is this achieved?" Jules asked.

"There exists another Portal in a place that is secret because of its consequential nature. It is a Portal where the Reality Harmonics are equalised for all dimensional travellers. However, that will be a new learning curve and a new experience for you all. You SHaFT people certainly have to step up to the mark sometimes, don't you?

"Trent Jackson, you asked for a recording of the Vastron's analysis of the phenomena occurring on Level Four Hundred and Seventy. I will try to get that arranged. but I must warn you; getting the detail of specific occurrences in any Reality is very difficult. The complexities are extreme because of the quantity of information. I will approach the Vastrons to see if I can obtain their findings at the time of Harry and Esma's disappearance. I will also ask them if they can be more specific about the cause of the imbalance on Level Four Hundred and Seventy, and then, it is over to you."

"Do that." Dearden said. "Between us we will locate Harry and Esma. I think your language skills will be needed, Trent.

When we have the recording of the Vastrons' information, you and Oscar and Jules work on it . . . Lan-Si-Nu, get us back up top."

27

Dearden went to the Jacobean sideboard where drinks were kept. He poured a good measure of Glenmorangie and a splash of Canada Dry. He needed it after the recent activity below the Hub.

"Are you well?" Rowan asked. He nodded he was and handed Rowan her Pinot Grigio. "What is next . . . to get back Harry and Esma?"

"There is so much information. It is complicated beyond belief. I think we'll have to get the team on board. The guys in Cell One have a lot of talent and they're original thinkers, so I'll arrange a meet-up."

*   *   *

Oscar poured over Harry's notes about the Hub for three days and nights, snatching brief hours of sleep when exhaustion overtook him. He was living in his kid-brother's space, reading through Harry's assessment of Professor Villiers' research.

Oscar began to home in again on thoughts about the Virtuality. Its complexities and how those complexities were handled. Lan-Si-Nu had an enormous team working on research throughout the structure below the Hub.

Oscar was impressed about how all of the information was gathered and stored in the Great Annals, but . . . *but*

He dropped his mug of coffee. "What the—"

—*Of course* . . . he thought. *The little guys with the tendrils who suck up all of the information . . .*

"Jem . . . Jem." Oscar rushed out of Harry's pad, down the stairs into the great hall.

*　*　*

It was quite like old times when Cell One gathered in the great hall. There was chat at first. Catch-up stuff and easy music quiet in the background, and soft lighting. Dearden was speaking quietly with Sir Will Pierpoint.

"What progress has been made to get our two young friends back?" Sir Will asked.

"It's good Lan-Si-Nu and his crew are on board but there's still nothing really positive," Dearden said.

"Leofwin's Hundred has given us a lot of surprises Jem." Pierpoint was quiet for a beat and then, "I wonder what other surprises it has in store for us."

Dearden had a faraway look in his eyes. His mind took him to another place in time a thousand years back when he met Rowan of Maldon. *Yes, Leofwin's Hundred really is full of surprises*, he thought.

"Jem . . ." Pierpoint was frowning . . . "Are you OK?"

"Yeah—"

—Which was when Oscar burst into the great hall shouting *Vastron*. He was wildly excited. It was his Eureka moment. He stumbled over his words and Pierpoint told him to slow down

"OK, sorry." He took a deep breath and began again. "Each of the Vastrons assimilate and record every scrap of information concerning the workings of the Reality they are overseeing. So, if Harry and Esma did shift to Reality Four Hundred and Seventy the little guys will have recorded that information. We need a recording of that information so we can analyse it. All the support math should be there."

"If you're right we need a serious talk with the Vastron who oversees that level, Chka, I think Lan-Si-Nu called it," Dearden said.

"Yeah . . . and once we have the math available and we've analysed it we'll fully understand the physics behind Harry's Reality-Shift."

"What then?" Templestone asked.

"What then?" Oscar looked at Templestone as if he ought to know the answer. "Think this through. The Vastrons assimilate and record every scrap of information concerning the workings of whatever Reality they are overseeing. So the math will definitely be recorded at the time Harry and Esma shifted to Reality Four Hundred and Seventy. If we get hold of that deep level of information and analyse it we'll be in a better position to get them back."

"As long as the information proves Four-Seventy is where they've gone," Jules added.

"Yes of course," said Oscar.

There was Silence. People thinking of the task ahead. Doughty said, "With what you suggested we'd be in a better position to get them back than we are now . . . there's another thing that could be worth looking into. We know nothing about the process Villiers used to energise the door Harry and Esma went through; you haven't analysed that yet, Oscar."

"Haven't had time to do it."

"So let's do it now guys." Storm said,

"No. It has to be the Vastron's guidance first," Trent Jackson said. "The information Chka can give us describing the physics used in the process will be more valuable than playing around with the equipment Villiers used."

To those of SHaFT's Cell One gathered around Leofwin's table in the great hall, it seemed as though the enigma about how to get Harry and Esma back to Earth had been, in part, resolved. Now they were eager to get started.

"Nos Successio Procul Totus Sumptus," Pierpoint said.

"Indeed we do, Sir Will," Julia Linden-Barthorpe said. "We Succeed At All Costs."

"With a certainty," Pierpoint said, thinking back.

"OK. We'll go to the Hub and contact Lan-Si-Nu," Dearden said. "Hopefully he'll take us down the Virtuality Column again to meet Vastron Chka. Oscar, Trent and Jules, you're with me . . . Let's go."

After Oscar's manic entry into the great hall, Dearden, Oscar, Jules and Trent Jackson were very quickly on their way to the Hub in Jules' Grand Cherokee.

"Lan-Si-Nu said that information is the Vastrons food" said Oscar. "Their physiology is sustained by information just as our bodies are sustained by a slap-up meal. The Vastrons hoover-up facts and record them, but what they don't do is understand all they assimilate. We eat all sorts of food but we don't deeply analyse everything we eat."

"What's your conclusion?" Trent Jackson asked Oscar.

"That within the information the Vastron has assimilated about level Four Hundred and Seventy, there will be some clue that will help our understanding about what exactly went on at the time of Harry and Esma's Reality transfer from R1. If we analyse that information it may acquaint us with how to get them back. It's a hunch I've got, Jem."

"Well done Oscar," Dearden said, as they pulled into the space in front of the Hub. The ground-level entry door was unlocked and Dearden led the way into the Hub to where he remembered that the disguised entry was to the Wasiri-Chanchiyan's private quarters. He hit the wall a few times and within seconds Lan-Si-Nu opened the door.

*　*　*

After they talked for a while Lan-Si-Nu came up with a suggestion. "The data downloaded via the Vastron Cohort into the Great Annals is downloaded in a raw state, It is refined over the passage of time. We can open the data bank to the required date and time for further investigation. Vastron Chka heads-up the Vastron crew on Level Four Hundred and Seventy, it will help unravel the math involved."

"Sounds good," Oscar said.

"A Poly-linguistic Translator will be used so that we will be able to understand the exchange of information and math in great depth. Please wait one moment." Lan-Si-Nu went to the back of the room where he communicated with Level Four Hundred and Seventy.

He returned and nodded to the others. "It is set up. Chka will meet us tomorrow."

*　*　*

A short while after Cell One had left for Dearden Hall, Lan-Si-Nu again messaged Chka, saying he needed to talk. The Wasiri-Chanchiyan Commander stressed the urgency of the situation and hurried down for a meeting.

The Vastron was waiting for him, its tentacles moving in an agitated way. Generally, the Vastrons were stable even under duress. Not that duress or from happened to them very often. They were normally seated, which vaguely described their attitude working in front of a screen, They had no legs or posterior. When moving they slithered along. Chka was away from his screen, really worked up.

When La-Si-Nu questioned him through the Poly-linguistic Translator, a bio-mechanical device, the Vastron's answer surprised him.

"I hope this investigation will succeed, the balance in Reality Four Hundred-Seventy is highly disturbed," Chka said. Its tentacles ceased waving and, instead, they were grouped and aimed at Lan-Si-Nu, which indicated that the conversation was serious.

"The current imbalance has been caused by two extra Earth people's random penetration of the Buffer between our Prime Reality and Reality Four Hundred and Seventy. The random penetration *must* be corrected or there could be catastrophic consequences," said the Vastron. It had slithered up close to Lan-Si-Nu and was staring at him with its multicellular eyes.

Lan-Si-Nu was a veteran of communication with alien races from multitudinous sources and never had he experienced such a passionately delivered request. "Do you have any suggestions," he asked.

"Yes. In this situation it is imperative that the Earth people are removed from Reality Four Hundred-Seventy. Their presence is slowly eroding the stability of that Reality, it could implode and take Toraddon with it. There could be consequences for all life if Toraddon is destroyed. I recommend that one of the Luminant helps us because of their ease of Reality transfer, their speed of transfer and their knowledge. Lan, we must move quickly with this situation, otherwise there could be total annihilation."

"I think we should contact one of the Luminant quickly. One of them is engaging with us on our periphery at present. He is very elusive, as if he's playing a game."

"On a new awakening he does tend to be juvenile for a while but he soon matures. There is a way to get him interacting more seriously with us," the Vastron said. His eyes diminished marginally in their piercing gaze.

"What do you suggest?" Lan-Si-Nu asked.

"The involvement of the wolf creature named Tomahawk Shahn of Offchurch in a rescue mission. You see, the Luminant is very close to a female of his kind who has gone missing. By his actions and the way he calls out at times I think the Luminant believes she might not be dead. Now, I have detected the energy of a female life-form of the same race as the Luminant. She is somewhere deep in Leofwin's Hundred, but exactly where is impossible to determine.

"I suspect the Piper knows the wolf is a superb hunter and he is trying to work out how to get Tomahawk to locate the one he has lost. If we can help the Luminant find her, his life will be complete again. When his mind is not in turmoil he will automatically detect the Reality imbalance and feel compelled to put it right."

"Chka, one of the Earth people you will meet tomorrow is Oscar Stanway. He is the brother of one of the missing Earth people, Harry Stanway, Their combined intellect reaches dazzling heights at times," concluded Lan-Si-Nu.

28

Next day, 9-30 am and Lan-Si-Nu was waiting outside the ground level door into the Hub. They walked past the familiar objects in the room of the exhibits, toward the doorway leading down into the Virtuality.

The descent was ultra-quick this time and along with Dearden, Oscar, Jules and Trent Jackson, Tomahawk was there too, undisturbed by the ride down. They came to a gentle stop and the door of the elevator slid open on Level Four Hundred and Seventy.

"The Vastron is in the Upload room," said Lan-Si-Nu, pointing to one of the doorways in the perimeter of the circular wall. "That's where he goes to upload the data he has digested into the Vastron Cohort and from there it is uploaded into the Great Annals."

"How on Earth can he analyse an entire Reality and describe it?" Jules asked, as they reached the door.

Lan-Si-Nu faced the others. "The Data collected is summarised by statistical trends which are picked up by bio-mechanical sensors. The Information stream is very detailed but it's math is universal . . . let's go." Lan-Si-Nu entered the Upload Room and they headed to the odd sea-anemone type guy whose tentacles were waving energetically. It shifted anticlockwise until its protuberant eyes were pointing in their direction. The Tentacles ceased their wild motion, twisted into a helix and it slithered toward them.

Oscar, being the most mathematically minded of the whole bunch, marvelled at the scientific potential of the Vastron. He felt a tinge of sadness for it, in that the enormous potential of taking in the information representing a universe was locked within such an ugly body. Its formidable intellect should be encapsulated in a body shining with beauty. Oscar approached it, and they both stopped about three feet apart. He studied the life-form briefly and realised that the only way to tell which was its front was because of its eyes, which were set on the end of stalks that moved independently in a similar fashion to the eyes of a slug.

"I'm Oscar Stanway." Speaking through the Poly-linguistic Translator Oscar started off conversation

"I'm Chka," the ugly guy said.

"Pleased to meet you," said Oscar. It was a very formal meeting of minds at this point, a mutual respect type-of-thing.

"And I'm pleased to meet you," replied Chka.

"I'm thinking that the answer about what precisely happened to Harry and Esma lies hidden within the information you have assimilated," Oscar blurted out.

"You may well be correct. The problem is that with the great deal of information we have to cope with, some of the detail is overlooked in our summary that is uploaded into the Great Annals. I know it shouldn't be, but we are not perfect and we do our best. It is unfortunate that, on this occasion it was probably the most important piece of information that we might have overlooked. There could be catastrophic consequences due to the Earth people who have breached the Toraddon Buffer."

"Well between us let's try to put it right. Where do I go to analyse the data you have downloaded?"

"Come and squat by me," the ugly guy invited. Oscar was oblivious to the others who had descended to Four-seventy with him. At a slow pace he followed the Four-Seventy Vastron to where it had been stationed. One of its tentacles gathered a cable which had a tiny plug on the end and it connected the plug to an orifice in the opposite side of its body from its eye-Stalks.

"What now?" Oscar asked as the others gathered around. Tomahawk got close to the Vastron, sniffed it and when Dearden tugged the leash the wolf backed off.

"So, this is Tomahawk," the Vastron said, its eye-stalks curling close to the wolf's head.

"You've heard of him?" Jules asked.

"His fame goes before him, but more of that at some future time. For now, Oscar Stanway, and after you, Julia, place your hands on these pads, the left hand on the left pad and the right on the other. You will feel a slight tingling sensation in your hands. This is a data language download which will enable you to decrypt the aural signal you will hear when you listen to the recorded signal of our download. For this, you must go into the room over there where you will connect to the Great Annals. Lan will accompany you and help with your connections."

Oscar and Jules did as they were instructed with the pads and then Lan-Si-Nu indicated for them to follow him. They entered a room about twelve feet square.

29

Harry was surprised to see Esma in the distance. She was walking confidently toward him and a good distance behind her two other figures were trying to keep up. He chucked down the length of hard material he had been using to hit the giant growth and he started to run toward her.

As he ran, his mind worked overtime on the potential of his effort of communication. That he had heard the same harmonic sounds he was hearing now when he and Esma were in Ubertu's Oak gave him the idea that a cross-dimensional communicative network existed that he could tap into. The fact that it was non-human and that it was using a network entirely different from any form of communication he had previously conceived, didn't matter a damn.

His experiences with the Grid and the aliens from Wasiri-Chanchiya had radicalised Harry's understanding of the universe. He had long thought that any process originating in the mind could be translated into physical reality. If the originating mind of the communication process was non-human, and the body form of the intelligence was not bio-pedal, but it got them back home, so damn what.

This was his thinking as he ran to Esma.

"Am I glad to see you," he said. They were simple words he said to her. They were together. That was all that mattered and, even if she never returned to her familiar home, she felt that her home was in his arms. "I missed you," she said. And the look in Harry's eyes conveyed a love that would never grow cold or die.

* * *

Villiers and Martell arrived out of breath. By that time Harry and Esma had finished saying the personal things.

"What the hell have you been doing," Villiers challenged, looking at the heavy stick Harry was still holding. There was no reason for Villiers' bombastic attitude and Harry had wised-up to the superficial superiority the Prof sometimes assumed, so he didn't react.

"Morse-code," he said. "I'm using the Mycorrhizal network to transmit Morse."

"Do you *really* think that will work?" Villiers sniggered.

"Another of his hair brained schemes," Martell threw in. His cynicism was taxing but Harry kept his cool. Kept silent.

Call it intuition, a hunch, but Harry often went along with his gut feelings about obscure issues and more often than not the answers were positive. It was more an innate feel he had for situations. Same applied this time, that what his gut was telling him would work out. "I'm setting up camp over there," he pointed. "In the shelter of that thing." He indicated the megalithic tree-like form he had been hitting with his coded message. He hefted the stick he had been using. Swung it like a club.

"You carry on with that, young man," Villiers said. "We'll go back and man the camp near the gate we came through. Maybe it'll open up to good old Earth again. I would suggest that you keep in touch regularly. Send the young woman as a runner." Harry didn't like the older man's arrogance. Villiers turned and began to trudge back the way he and Martell came from, following the footprints left in the soft, dusty soil, which lazily settled back to the ground in the slowness of the physics in the alien reality. Martell called Villiers to wait for him. As he caught up with his colleague Martell put his arm around the other man's shoulders and began conversing. He looked back at Harry, who picked up the cynicism. He shrugged it off.

"We need to build a shelter," Harry said, getting a machete out of his tote-bag.

* * *

They gathered fallen vegetation and started to make a shelter near the immense structure Harry had been hitting with his Morse-code. "This place will be OK as a camp, unless the noise from these things gets too much," he said, hoping for a spell of peace and quiet.

In the jungle-like outcrop that extended as far as they could see, long streamers hanging from the succulent-like formations far above added to the sense of alien wilderness. The vegetative matter moved slowly in the cloying breeze and it was tough to cut, but having done so, what they cut down was ideal for tying their rough structure together to strengthen it.

It was when Esma was dragging some of the foliage over to the pile of material ready to use, that she was distracted by a movement. It had not been in her direct line of sight and, at first, she thought she imagined it. Then it occurred again. The quick passage of something disturbing the ground left a track of footprints which circled around them as if examining them. And then the dust settled back to the ground around the footprints in slow motion.

The event was eerie. Harry's pulse notched up after Esma nudged him and pointed to the rapidly moving footprints.

He was briefly triggered back to the Jack and the beanstalk pantomime he went to with his folks. They were in the Gods at the theatre, looking a long way down to the stage, which was illuminated in magical colours. Jack had climbed up the

201

beanstalk. At the time, Harry imagined he was with Jack. He was under the kitchen table, hiding from the ogres, who were sleeping and Harry was willing them not to wake up.

Back in the present something happened that took the fear of the unknown away. Whatever it was, the invisible alien, whose presence was made manifest by its footprints, nudged him the same as Esma had done. It nudged him on the shoulder and then it nudged Esma. It was a lightweight touch, nothing offensive or painful. It was more . . . playful, as if the thing was playing a game, and then it chuckled and was gone.

Harry looked at Esma and grinned. She was more uncertain than him and her grip tightened on his arm but her experiences in Leofwin's Hundred had opened up her mind to experiences that were way out of the ordinary. So, she grinned back at him, understanding, by the comedy of the situation, that whatever had rushed by was not a threat.

Harry selected the broadest fronds, hoisted them aloft and spread them out to cover branches he had cut for roof supports, then they rested underneath what they had built.

A few Earth hours passed and Esma awoke. A shuffling noise intruded on the dream where she was back in Earl Leofwin's time playing blind man's buff with Rowan. She grasped Harry's hand gently so as not to startle him.

She was scared. Said nothing, but indicated there was something outside their shelter. She pointed to the cleaver Harry used to chop down the framework for their shelter. Harry grabbed the weapon while Esma edged around the aperture left in one of the walls as a doorway, and pointed to the ground a few yards away.

"There. Look it's there again."

A track appeared again. Not a continuous trail such as may

be left by a snake, but a series of rapidly formed depressions, footprints with a ribbed tread, one after the other left in the soft ground. The movement appeared frenzied for a few seconds and then it stopped. The marks shuffled round, as if to face them. Harry looked up at the same time. The great bracts of the growth high above them were directed downwards, as if watching, as if in a state of awareness.

"I think we're being assessed," Harry whispered.

"Assessed . . . what is being assessed?" Esma asked.

*   *   *

The Entity was interested in the ones creating a shelter from the materials to hand. It was pleasing to watch the activity. They were so different to the local life-forms on this planet because they were quick in their movements. Not as quick as the Entity's own movements, maybe a twentieth as quick, but whoever had built the shelter was refreshing. Different to the stasis of this dimension.

It had been time to move on. But then some events away, only a short distance back in time, the Entity had seen two bipedal life-forms use the Gate into this dimension and they had remained. The way back to their home dimension was restricted by the technology that was out of harmony and creating danger. It was so simple to engage the transfer, dimension-to-dimension if one knew how to engage the correct technology. Now this younger pair came through the gate, making four in total.

30

In a quiet area of Leofwin's Hundred, sunlight shining through the leaf canopy created dappled shade on the forest floor. Tomahawk ambled toward the rapidly moving imprints in the leaf mold. Gil Heskin saw them too and so did Frieda. When she saw the oval shaped footprints forming from an invisible source, she wished herself miles away from Leofwin's Hundred. She gripped Gil's hand and held back.

It was different for Tomahawk, the make-up of his eyes being of a different nature to that of humans. The receptors in the wolf's eyes picked up objects on wavelengths which were sometimes impossible to see for humans. This was a genetic quirk inherited by Tomahawk, a unique visual ability in his species which, in time would prove very useful.

Tomahawk saw an unusual creature, who looked somewhat similar to the Food-beast he associated with the *Dearden* sound. The creature had bright eyes and it was larger than the Dearden food-beast. Tomahawk thought of his mother again. Unbidden thoughts occurred to the Black Alaskan wolf that were counter to his primal drivers of food, sleep and the growth of his species. The creature drew him forward, encouraged him with a gentle wave of the hand, and forward Tomahawk of Offchurch went, ears erect, as an equal, sharing a new and exciting freedom.

"At least Tom's moving now," Gil said. Frieda nodded and reached for Gil's hand again. Gripped it tight. Got close. They followed the Wolf, who sniffed the ground and carried on past Uberatu's Oak, following a narrow path, maybe it was a badger trail, going deeper into the forest. This time the wolf tugged Gil Heskin, urgently.

The way they went was dark and silent. Unusually so. Usually there was the sound of forest-life, the rustling of leaves and birds . . . sometimes the call of a fox. Dearden had told Gil that, on one occasion, he was sure he had heard the squeal of a wild boar somewhere far off, deep in the forest.

"Are you sure about this," Frieda asked.

"About what?"

"We haven't been this far into the forest before." Gil tugged the leash and Tomahawk drew closer, like a guardian.

"Jem said this is *old forest*, Gil."

"What did he mean by that?"

"That it's unspoiled, right through history, since long ago. Old things may still be in the forest here . . . this deep in." She looked at the footprints going on before them in the leaf-litter as they walked, and she shivered. Tomahawk seemed unperturbed. Gil cleared his throat. Sometimes he did that when he was nervous. They walked on for a while and then heard the distant sound of water echoing amongst the stout tree-trunks.

They came to where the ground fell away sharply and saw, some distance below, a clear pool which was fed by a cascading waterfall.

"Look at that, Frie." She looked to where he indicated, to a dark patch behind the tumbling sheet of water."

"Looks like a cave," she said.

The active trail of prints in front of them paused at the edge, where there was a steady slope downwards, and then they saw movement down a steep path between moss-covered boulders. Tomahawk tugged on the leash again, stronger this time than before, and he made his way cautiously down the slope, leading the Heskins, who were now intensely curious.

The elevator door opened when it returned to the first level below ground at the Hub. Dearden glanced around the room, which was packed with complex equipment, and he quickly made his way up the spiral stairs and entered the familiar ground-level room. Dearden indicated for the team to gather round.

"What do you make of it? Let's have some feedback,"

"At the moment, I've got information overload. But when our alien friend gives us the pack of information from the Vastrons, and we analyse it, we might make progress," Jules said.

"It is strange how our alien friend implies that we have more original thought processes than they have, considering how far in advance of us they are with their science," Red Cloud observed.

"No doubt that is a hereditary genetic feature we have to our advantage," said Oscar.

"How shall we use our genetic advantage?" Clive asked.

"That remains to be seen after we give it some serious thought," Roberts said.

"We need to go back to the great hall, chill out a bit and then brainstorm our ideas," Doughty suggested,

"Sounds sensible. While you do that, me and Possum Chaser will try and follow things up around Uberatu's Oak. It is an interesting place, my friends. Maybe it has more to reveal." Red Cloud indicated for Possum Chaser to come with him, and they went out of the Hub, across the clearing to the ancient oak.

Red spotted the recently trodden leaf mold. "Three people passed this way. One of them was considerably larger than the other two," he said to Possum Chaser. "And large paw prints are here too. If I am not mistaken they belong to Tomahawk."

"I know. Do you think I have no eyes? They are lupine footprints. In this place it has to be Tomahawk, and there is something else . . ."

"What?"

She had left her statement in mid-air. Purposely. To wind Red Cloud up. He looked puzzled. "What have you seen, Possy?"

She waited a few seconds more than she needed, then, "There are three sets of footprints, one is a man's, another set is a woman's and there is Tomahawk's paw-prints, but there are other footprints that I do not recognise."

Red went forward to where the footprints were visible in the rotten leafage. He got down on his knees to examine the ground closely because his eyes were not as good as they used to be, and then he spotted them, an incised tread left by some sort of shoe; the shape, oval, bigger than his own size eleven footprints, but light and toe-down on the ground, as if moving quickly. "Your eyes are better than mine now, Possy. I used to be able to see hairs dropped on the ground but not now." He sighed. Possum Chaser reached her hand down to him. He grasped it and stood.

"Thank you," he said. "What we have seen is unusual."

"You bet it is. I think we must follow, but mind these puffballs. We should not damage them . . . I think they are something special."

"Might taste good fried up," Red Cloud said.

They followed the trail and eventually they came to where the ground fell away and the waterfall cascaded down from Shadow Brook.

Lan-Si-Nu watched the group of Earths ascend the stairs out of the Virtuality. Three of them, the older ones, found the stairs more difficult than the others did because of the height of the treads.

"We will await their analysis," Lan-Si-Nu said to Thal-Nar and Fen-Nu as the door at the top of the stairs closed behind Templestone. "But this will help them." He clasped a summation of the Vastrons' latest research in his right hand. In his left was a device on which to play the results. He raced up the steps to ground level, and shouted, "Here is the information you needed from the Vastrons." His voice boomed.

Dearden went back and took the metallic-looking box from the alien. "Thank you, Lan, we appreciate your help."

The alien commander responded in an unexpected way. "And we yours," he said. "We are entering what you Earths might call a minefield of information. Keep in touch with us, Jem. We will be available here if you need us, but before you go, here's how to operate this data-player." Dearden was handed a phial of highly viscous fluid that was deep purple in colour. "This is a data-storage bank. It is derived from the Super-quantum. Insert it here, into this orifice."

The tall alien stuck out his thumb and three-fingered hand. Dearden grasped it and they shook.

Dearden got back to the great hall and switched on the device. It came as a surprise that the information on the data bank was in English. Lan-Si-Nu thought of everything. The information was in aural and visual form; the visual being on a screen with perfect definition. The information playback began with a view of one of the underground levels of the Hub.

The same sound came from the speaker that they heard in Matt Roberts' recording when he and Storm Petrel had been inside Uberatu's Oak. An undulating musical sound for a while, which was then overlaid with Morse-code.

"I recognise the symbol on the wall," Trent Jackson said, bending closer to the screen. "It's the gate to Level Four Hundred and Seventy." He seemed puzzled. "Look at that mud on the floor, and the direction of the skid-mark. Someone came out of that gate fast and almost lost their balance."

"Who on earth would that have been?" Clive Fraser's brow puckered. He pushed Trent gently to the side so he could see the screen better.

"It's certainly not Harry . . . or Esma," Templestone said. "If it was them, Lan-Si-Nu and his team would have got them back to us double-quick."

"I hope it's not any of those guys from Nibiru," Wynter said.

"No worries there," Dearden reassured him. "Nibiru and its rebels have been thoroughly dealt with. But whatever came through that gate was definitely in a hurry. It made its escape from the gate even though the security in the Hub is second to none." Dearden strolled away from the table. He stooped down to the prepared fire, lit the paper. The kindling Gil Heskin had laid began to burn and crackle. He placed three thin logs onto the flames and they started to burn. A few larger logs were at the hearth-side so Dearden called Heskin on the two-way to get him to bring more logs from the store.

"What?" was Heskin's response. He was usually formally polite . . . one of *The Old School.* Dearden heard an echoing noise in the background, and Heskin's voice was distant.

"Where are you?" Dearden asked.

"Sorry Jem . . . didn't mean to be abrupt. We're in the forest. Deep in. Things have taken an unusual twist."

There was a brief explanation, after which, there being safety in numbers when there could be trouble, Cell One piled into two vehicles and made for the forest. Twenty minutes after talking to Heskin they were parked up at Uberatu's Oak. Dearden thumbed the transmit button on the two-way and Gil Heskin picked up.

"Gil, we're at Uberatu's Oak. Guide us in from here, will you?"

"OK. With the Hub at your back, there's a badger trail to the right of Uberatu's Oak. Follow that. After a while the path splits to right and left around a very large coppiced hazel with an immense trunk, you can't miss it. Take the path to its right."

*　*　*

As Red Cloud reached the edge of the depression he indicated to Possum Chaser to be quiet, and he held his arm out to stop her going any further. They could see Tomahawk heading down, nearly at the bottom. Gil Heskin was holding him with the studded leash. Frieda was at the rear, slipping sometimes on the steep moss-covered slope. The wide, cascading waterfall feeding the pool hid the large dark patch of the cave and mist from the waterfall hung over the area.

"Look," Red cloud whispered. "See it there, through the mist?"

Possum Chaser squinted against the sunlight, saw the cave, and saw silhouetted against the dark entrance, a tall figure, made manifest by the water vapour. It was standing still as if enjoying being drenched by the cascade.

"It is invisible to our eyes," she said, "But the waterfall and the mist is making it visible. What shall we do?"

He decided, "Hey, you down there," He called, which startled possum Chaser and those down at the bottom, apart from Tomahawk, who was gazing at the Entity.

Gil and Frieda had seen it too, in the mist, before they reached the bottom. It didn't cause them alarm, even though it was obviously alien. What did frighten them was the shout from above, the "Hey, you down there." The person drifting in and out of visibility shifted quickly and looked up at Red Cloud.

"Hi, Red Cloud . . . Possum Chaser. Come on down," Gil shouted. "It's safe. He doesn't wish us any harm."

"You sure about that?" Red's voice echoed as he shouted into the steep dell.

"Dead sure. Things feel safe." More echo.

Possum Chaser gave Red a shove in the back, not too hard because she didn't want him to fall down the slope but sure as hell she wasn't going down first.

"Don't push like that. I'm going as fast as I can," Red Cloud said. "If it's too steep for you, slide down on your arse."

*   *   *

Dearden cautioned the others to keep their voices down as they approached the place where the ground fell away. Gil Heskin had told him about the sound of the waterfall and directed him so he could find the path leading to it. *And then*, Heskin had said, *when you reach the edge, make your way slightly left and take the path down to the waterfall. You should see us, and maybe you'll see the thing we've been following.*

It was the first time Dearden had seen this place in the forest. It had a touch of the orient about it, with sharp-angled rocks and stunted, full-leafed trees. There was something else that Dearden picked up. Mist from the waterfall seemed to create an air of mystery that hung over the place. He indicated for Cell One to stop, put his finger to his lips for silence and then he walked cautiously along the edge of the steep decline.

What he could see at the bottom was bizarre. Made obvious by the waterfall and the rising mist was a tall being that was making its way to a cave at the back of the waterfall through the considerable force of the falling water.

Dearden led the way down. As they struggled downwards, the Entity heard them approaching above the sound of the waterfall. It turned to face them, looked for a second or two and then carried on toward the rear of the deluge.

"What the hell is it?" Matt Roberts asked. He could see vague features on the creature's face . . . It looked human.

Five minutes later, after a careful descent, they reached the bottom. They headed over to where the Heskins, Red Cloud and Possum Chaser were standing close to the action, and getting drenched from the outlying spray. It was pleasant and unseasonably warm in the microclimate of the valley. Wynter kept his eyes on the humanoid shape in the mist caused by the falling water. Parts of its form came in and out of visibility.

"What brings you here?" Dearden asked the Heskins.

"We were hunting puffballs," Frieda said, keeping her eyes on the Entity. "We got diverted."

"What about you, Red . . . Possy?" Dearden asked, with a sidelong glance at the partially revealed manifestation, unsure whether it could be trusted.

"That thing's footprints caught our Lakota Sioux eyes," Possum Chaser pointed to her eyes and then to the activity as, further ahead, the creature made its way through the waterfall.

Matt Roberts grasped Storm Petrel's arm, steadied her as they stood on a flat boulder close to where the water from Shadow Brook cascaded into the pool. Rowan got near to Dearden and he put his arm around her shoulders. She could see the creature's shape being made more visible by the water it was walking through.

It was Oscar Stanway who made the connection. The skidmarks through the mud on the floor by the gate to the Reality on Level Four Hundred and Seventy. The way this could have occurred without being noticed by those populating the Virtuality was the invisibility element of the unusual being getting drenched by the waterfall. It all tied in.

Oscar got as close as he could to the pool without getting drenched and the others followed, feeling the water vapour on their skin. Tomahawk pulled on the lead, wanting to get to Dearden, who was standing near the track leading to the cave behind the waterfall. Heskin handed Tomahawk's leash to Dearden and the wolf pulled hard to get to the creature up ahead.

"You stay there," Dearden said to the group as he went down the slope with Tomahawk. Typically, Jules disregarded Dearden's command to *stay there*, and she followed, a few paces behind. Her consummate Shotokan skill was lethal. She didn't intend Dearden to get into trouble and watch it happening She was loyal that way, so she followed him.

Dearden understood from the wolf's action that it was safe to approach the creature. He had seen Tomahawk display aggression driven by his wilderness genes. The wolf always picked up when there was a threat before Dearden did because his genes took over, aggression kicked in and people round-about would be very, very cautious. But there was no aggression evident as the wolf meandered down along the path toward the creature, who was now in the cave behind the waterfall.

The track leading to the cave was tricky, strewn with stones and boulders worn smooth and slippery by years of water-erosion and the growth of algae. But Tomahawk had got the curious-smelling, but attractive scent of the creature in his nostrils and he picked out a trail between the rocks to get to it. His eyes, so different to human eyes, could easily see the creature's body and he hankered to get close to it. There was an attraction about the creature the other side of the waterfall, like the Dearden food-beast was attractive when it offered food.

Dearden had an occasional glimpse of the creature's features as the flowing water outlined them and, while it was still dripping water, and therefore visible to his eyes, he was able to see most of its body and could see that it looked human.

Dearden didn't hear Jules approach because of the noise of the waterfall, She startled him when she shouted "Thought you might need help."

"Why, do you think you could take that thing on?"

"Two onto one in some circumstances is best," Julia said. She never backed down from a challenge. Just then Doughty and Roberts turned up and stood next to them, one each side. And then the others were there, spread out and ready.

The being went further into the cave, away from the descending water. He had moved quickly, like a character might in one of the old, silent films before being synced to look natural.

"You alright, my man?" Lee Wynter shouted at it. They both stood still, about eight feet apart. The alien uttered a noise that Wynter took to be conversation because of its cadences and intonations. Wynter saw humour in the situation when Trent Jackson, the language guy, mimicked the unusual language and the alien's jaw dropped in surprise.

"Didn't know you could speak that kind of shit," Wynter shouted at Jackson, who was at his side.

"I can't, but I've got a good ear for spoken language, and I can easily mimic it." Jackson went closer to the alien, who had started to be less visible as the moisture dripped off it. Jackson did some sign language. Must have practised that sort of thing a lot too, because the individual seemed to understand and did some sign language back.

"What did it say?" Pierpoint asked. Jackson looked perplexed.

"I'm unsure," he said. "I'm trying to form some sort of common ground to start with." There was movement at Jackson's side. It was Red Cloud. He moved up to confront the alien; got close up to it and spoke loud to Jackson out of the left corner of his mouth.

"Mister Jackson, with all due respect, I am going to give you a lesson in Hand-talk."

Red looked into the eyes of the Entity, who had slipped unseen out of the deepest level of the Virtuality. The eyes were so bright, set in a wise-looking visage which, being quite wet, was still visible. And conversation, of a sort, started.

31

Way down the Virtuality Column, in the Level of Latest Defining, Lan-Si-Nu studied the skid marks through the patch of mud.

"He has shown up again," the commander said to his two crew members, Fen-Nu and Thal-Nar. He knelt on the floor, dipped a finger into the mud, which was still fluid, and he smelt the purple substance. "Smell this," he said.

The other two did the same. Knelt down, finger in, sniffed. "I think you are right," Thal-Nar said. "This is evidence of someone's passage through level Four Hundred and Seventy but the person was not seen throughout the whole of the Virtuality." Thal-Nar wiped the mud on his clothing. He didn't care because the smell was good, like a fine perfume. The unique physics binding each Reality into its own unity sometimes held surprises that tested the imagination.

"What shall we do?" Fen-Nu remembered the last encounter with fondness. She wanted it to be repeated. Whether events could be steered remained to be seen in the coming mission. It was obvious there *would* be a mission, there was after every awakening.

"It broke through the sensors and is loose on this world. Its voice sometimes resonates through the tree the Earths call Uberatu's Oak. Also, when you were on the surface yesterday you said that the evidence of its network-presence in the forest floor has grown quickly this time."

"The Entity is maturing rapidly, that is why. The evidence grows more quickly as it matures. Also, it doesn't really need to use the Virtuality, but it has an inbuilt curiosity and probably it was trying the Virtuality out as a means of transport."

"It may have got some sort of thrill out of the experience. Did you know that some of the Earths are eating the growths?"

"Are they? What will it do to them. Is there a precedent?"

"That I do not know. Time will tell." Lan-Si-Nu stood to his full height and beckoned the others to get close. "This is what we will do," he whispered. "We must consult the Great Annals for information about the Entity's network. The fungal evidence may help us find the Entity."

"Also, seeing how the Mycelia has bridged the Realities we have proof of how widespread is the Entity's Network."

*   *   *

The cave behind the waterfall was smaller at the entrance than it was inside, so there was plenty of room for Cell One to spread out in the cavernous interior.

They were soaked to the skin. Jules slipped away from the group to what she thought was the back of the cave to get away from the chill of the entrance. It was black as night so she used a small flash light which she had on a keyring to light her way. There was a bend in the cave, and beyond the bend a dark passage led further away from the entrance. She walked on, shining the torch onto the surrounding rock. Its appearance showed it had been worn smooth an archaeological age ago, eroded by an underground river.

Jules was startled by Rowan and Storm Petrel coming up behind her. They had seen her disappear into the darkness and they followed the torchlight.

"Don't worry, we're curious too," Storm said. She was speaking a fraction above a whisper. The sound of the waterfall had dwindled to almost nothing this far into the cave. Jules nodded her head and shone her torch in front to illuminate the way forward. There was illumination further on in the cave, and as they rounded another bend they saw a large patch of light on the right-hand wall a short distance ahead. They walked toward it cautiously, with the beam of Jules' torch picking out the well-worn path, and when they got near the source of light they saw an illuminated panel displaying a picture, that was set into the wall.

"What's this doing here?" Storm muttered as she reached the panel, which must have stood eight feet high, with its base starting at the junction of the floor and the wall.

"I have no idea," Jules said, getting close to the image to examine the technique and the pigment used. She touched it and the surface of the image shimmered, as if it was liquid. "Would you believe the detail in this? It looks as though it's a live scene." The image of the strangest landscape she had ever seen re-formed after she touched it.

There were trees of a sort, a wild jungle of them, most with bulbous appendages at the top of towering trunks. There was thickly growing scrub below, that almost obliterated any vestige of soil but under one of the growths was a patch of purple looking ground on which there was a rough shelter. It looked hastily put together, and the gigantic growths put the shelter in proportion because it was miniscule by comparison.

"Those trees are moving," Rowan said. "See how slow they all move." She touched the appendages high up on the image, which shimmered in expanding circles from where her finger touched and she stepped back in surprise.

Storm Petrel saw another movement, faster than the way the tree-growths were moving. "What's that . . . look there, by the shelter?" Captivated by the unravelling scene, they moved closer to the wall but what they saw was too small to make out any detail.

* * *

The Entity saw three of the Earths, female ones, leaving the Sanctuary and going into the darkness at the back of the cavern. Wherever the Entity travelled seeking new experience there was a Sanctuary, but this particular one was home. He returned to this Sanctuary when he felt the inner need for the comfort of being close to Beginnings, close to the Purpose. Here he could rest awhile particularly in a new awakening. And once again he could look for the love he had lost.

The falling element outside the entrance was always refreshing to his body and mind after the heat caused by the energy used to traverse the laminae of existences. There had been no rush to follow the inhabitants of this planet into the back of the cavern, for speed was not one of the Entity's needs. He could soon catch up with any movement, anywhere.

The Earths are an interesting people, he thought. They are curious by nature. Adventurous to the extreme considering the strict physical boundaries of *their* Reality. The humans sometimes risked far too much for their own safety. The Entity, invisible to the Earths' eyes once again because it was dry, followed the three into the deep region of the Sanctuary.

* * *

Tomahawk, off the leash and quite able to see all that was happening, plodded after the Entity. He had not had this sort of experience before; this urge, where he was drawn on . . . where his imperatives of food, sleep and the growth of his species was, in some unfathomable way to him, subservient to

219

a new and powerful force that pulled him onward.

Tomahawk was an adventurer *par excellence*. Had the guts to face any foe. His instinct helped the Food-beast, and his brain was pliant, so he followed the interesting beast as it went toward the place where light was dim.

32

Commander Lan-Si-Nu and his two close companions, settled down in their level above ground. At the back of the museum level they had their private space. The door to it was invisible to all but those with microscopic eyesight.

"This is what I propose," the Commander said. "If you do not agree, give me your alternatives. We know the Entity is roaming this planet, close to us, in Leofwin's Hundred. We will enter the Room of Quietness and investigate the Great Annals to learn more about the Entity because his presence may be more than coincidence." He felt that events were twisting in upon themselves to create uncertainty. Action was needed. He stood, and stretched.

Life is interesting, he thought. *With the Entity active once again there is no telling what lies ahead.* Lan-Si-Nu and his crew entered the Room of Quietness, which lay at the rear of their private quarters.

The room was full of the scent of home. Fen-Nu donned a headset. Pressed the button when she was invited to link to the Knowledge-bank. She aimed her thoughts into the deeper recesses of mind and, in Wasar, the universal language of the planet Wasiri-Poya, she thought-spoke the word, *Entity.*

The response via the quantum was immediate. Each event relating to the Entity was spoken into Fen-Nu's mind, last event first. An easy-to-listen-to voice told of the Entity's exploits when it arrived on monitored destinations. Loss of contact was reported regularly. The mind download extended for thirty-two beats and it was tiring.

"Are you hearing the reports?" Fen-Nu asked the other

221

two. Lan-Si-Nu was sitting to her left and Thal-Nar to her right. Lan-Si-Nu removed his headset and slowly stood up.

"I hear them." His features condensed. "What do you make of the Entity's performance?" As usual when he was deep in thought his face had gone a deeper green. He wondered if the other two had arrived at the same conclusion.

"The disappearances are interesting. Why are they happening?" Thal-Nar was intrigued with why the Entity sometimes went missing. After a presence prominent by its effect on the surroundings, *why would he disappear*, he thought.

Fen-Nu stood up too. She was gathering her thoughts as she gracefully moved to the centre of the room, composing how she would describe her conclusion. What had become clear to her, after listening to the reports made by the Vastrons, going back many years, was the constant feature of contact being made by the Entity with particular beings who are hunters, across a multitude of dimensions.

"It is lonely," she said. Lan-Si-Nu nodded. He recognised Fen-Nu's awareness, the incisive grasp of situations where her intuitiveness led to correct answers.

"What do you suggest we do?" he asked.

"Track it down . . . but there is something else." Fen-Nu was briefly silent, and she fidgeted. She fidgeted when things were tense, which was rarely. "Usually the Entity's visits to its chosen realities are fleeting. The Vastrons tell us that, typically, the Entity remains in a particular reality for no more than 530 beats. It has stayed here on Planet Earth far longer than its typical stay. *Why?*"

The others stayed quiet. The question was rhetorical and they waited for the answer.

"He has found a helper. That could be the major reason he

is remaining. But what else is going on around here that is unusual?" Thal-Nar withdrew into his mind momentarily and sought out the loose ends from events occurring, drawing them together to form a tight knot of explanation.

"Hnirath Harry Stanway and Esma are lost in the Four-hundred and seventieth Reality. We conclude that is so from the Vastron's report about an unregulated intrusion into the Four Hundred and Seventieth reality. Harry's contact attempts are breaking through Uberatu's Oak into our Reality. Maybe the Entity is aware of Harry's attempts to contact the Earths, and that is another reason for him to remain on this planet, maybe he is seeking a way to assist."

"He is sympathetic to Harry's problem, you mean?"

"That is so and I am aware that here on Earth the Entity can be assisted in its personal search."

"What is it formulating?"

"I am unsure about that. The Entity's mind is distant from mine. I can only pick up the outer fringes of its consciousness. It protects its privacy intensely."

"Therefore, we need to communicate with it directly," Lan-Si-Nu suggested

"That will be difficult because the Entity is very elusive," Thal-Nar said.

"That is true but direct contact has to be attempted. Our ancestors sometimes succeeded in their contact with those of the Entity's kind. We must try anew. The Entity is a multi-reality life-form. It's ability to access the Realities has no boundary. Because of that, the Entity could help us locate Hnirath Harry Stanway and Esma in Four-hundred and Seventy, and get them back to Earth."

"Which will also prevent the ultimate paradox of a clash of Realities."

Lan-Si-Nu nodded. "Something is telling me that the Entity already knows about Hnirath Harry and the impending Reality paradox. Its activity is very much out of character. Could be it intends to contact us."

"I do hope you are correct," said Fen-Nu. In her mind she tried to picture how the Reality paradox would unfold and she shivered as the thought of non-existence loomed large.

33

Since the second passage of Nibiru, folks in general felt as though they had escaped the outcome of the Doomsday Clock of nuclear holocaust which, since its inception, had hovered close to the midnight hour. Most people wanted to live up to the new rules in which, after an exchange of vows between the Wasiri-Chanchiyans and Lars Knudsen, Earth's representative, a future without the carnage of war was more or less guaranteed.

The morning after Lan-Si-Nu and the other two Wasiri aliens introduced Dearden to the subterranean levels of the Hub, the outer doors of Dearden Hall rattled open and then shut with a resounding clunk. Heavy footfalls could be heard coming through the entrance-hall toward the door of the great hall.

Templestone was still jumpy. He was getting on in years now, and slowing up a bit. He walked slower, and sometimes used a stick when he was unsure of his footing because of his worsening eyesight, but his mind was still youthful and if push really came to shove he could still summon up the old rage and hit fast and hard, so he hadn't slowed-up in that way.

He still packed his Smith and Wesson 38. It was a habit borne from the old troubled times. So, when the front doors thumped open. Templestone went for his 38. The new rules prevented him from taking it from his pocket but he grasped its cold, reassuring shape, flicked the safety off in the dark of his pocket and aimed it at the door into the great hall.

Jules saw what he had done and signalled with her eyes for him to relax. She recognised the sounds, the footfalls, the slight drag as each foot was lifted. She went to the door and opened it before Commander Lan-Si-Nu and his crew reached the door.

"We may have information that will help get Hnirath Harry Stanway and Esma back here to Earth," he said, by way of introduction.

There were short greetings and Dearden pulled out a chair, the biggest one, and indicated for Lan-Si-Nu to sit. He waved the offer off.

"Is Oscar Stanway still here?" he asked. An affirmative nod from Dearden. "And Trent Jackson?" Another nod.

"A bunch of them are upstairs in Harry's lab," Dearden said. "They're trying to decipher the sounds coming from Uberatu's Oak . . . but they're not making much progress."

"They may not, Jem. What you are hearing is not from this dimension. But I have to tell you, there is an invisible presence in Leofwin's Hundred who may be able to help get back Hnirath Harry, and Esma."

"You mean the fast-moving being our eyesight doesn't pick up? The way it rushed out from the rear of the cave after Rowan came back with Jules and Storm caused some consternation. It disturbed the air by its velocity."

"I'm sure he did . . . he is most unusual. We have not given him a name, we just call him the Entity. We have Vastron records of it that go back many generations. It is a trans-dimensional being that shows up once in a while. We have had no real contact with it, but we believe it to be friendly. It is interested in what is going on in Leofwin's Hundred."

"Most interesting, tell us more," Oscar called from the other side the hall as he came in from Harry's pad with Trent Jackson.

Lan-Si-Nu indicated the table. "This may take a while to

explain," he said. "Sit and relax will you Oscar. Take it easy. It is imperative that you help us contact the Entity."

There were fourteen of them who sat around the table. They were the old hands of SHaFT. They were used to the unusual, which often took place around Leofwin's Hundred.

Jem, at the head of the table, with Rowan sitting next to him, noticed the burn mark scorched into the table's surface from Leofwin's beeswax candle The area of charred wood always triggered Jem back to when he met Rowan of Maldon. He fingered the scorch-mark, remembering the time so long ago and yet, paradoxically, through the House of the West Wind, a time so recent. Rowan saw him touching the candle burn and she reached under the table secretly for his other hand. She knew how his mind worked. He looked at her and they smiled, which was when Lan-Si-Nu began his explanation.

"The Vastron's records of the Entity go back into the pre-history of your human race, to the early times of the Virtuality. When level eight was first opened an anomaly was noticed."

"What was it?" Oscar asked.

"The details are sketchy. Because of the nature of the anomaly, and its occurrence being in the early years of our experience with the Virtuality, it was only possible to record the barest summary of information. The anomaly that occurred was a life-form that is strange, to say the least. It is a chimera. People of Earth, when you travelled to our planet, Wasiri-Poya and entered the Hnioss to meet the Council of Worlds, you saw many different life-forms. Many of them that you saw are carbon-based, even though their outward appearance shows a great variety of genetic design. The variety of life-forms across the Virtuality is wider still in their differences because each Reality has its own hierarchy of physical laws in which the life-forms were created."

"Please, will you get back to the anomaly," Storm Petrel interjected. Matt Roberts nudged Storm. She glanced at him and he mouthed to *shut it*.

"The Entity flits about from Reality to Reality with impunity. It is elusive and it has no boundaries that we are aware of and because of that it will be useful in helping us locate Harry and Esma. There is also a severe dis-harmony in the Realities associated with Harry and Esma's transfer that will be addressed on their return to planet Earth. We also think that the Entity is looking for a lost companion."

"We have encountered the being that you are talking about, Red Cloud said. "We have followed it as best we can when it moves about in the forest. There is a cave that it seems to use as a base. Tell me, my friend, what makes you think it is looking for a companion?"

"Because it has stayed here longer than ever it has stayed in any of the other Realities it has visited. It has formed brief associations in the past, but we have sensed an aura of loneliness associated with it. A major problem, of course, is that the Entity is sometimes invisible to our eyes, much the same as it is to yours."

"That doesn't help, does it?" Dearden said.

Dearden's Great Hall, occupied with people who were normally quite verbal, was silent as each individual mulled over what Lan-Si-Nu revealed.

Trent Jackson questioned, "Are you suggesting that the Entity's metabolism is able to change?"

"I am. He is somewhat chameleon-like. And there is something else that you may recognise which shifts the focus onto this planet of yours. You have a folk-tale called the Pied Piper of Hamelin . . . there is evidence that the Entity was associated with that event. In the year 1284, the Piper became aware that he was needed to deal with an overwhelming infestation of rats in the town of Hamelin.

"Bear in mind that this event occurred in your medieval past. In all of the Virtuality, inharmonious events in any of the Realities are dealt with using methods available at the time in that Reality's hierarchy of physics. A paradoxical situation must not be created.

"At the time of the event in Hamelin the Piper played his pipe. Because of the hypnotic sound of the instrument, the infestation of rats followed him. They were drowned in the nearby River Weser. There was nothing high-tech about the removal of the problem. A problem that did arise afterwards was that the townspeople backed out of their promise to pay the Piper for ridding Hamelin of the rats. The money did not really matter. What did matter was the morality of the situation. A promise was made, a severe problem was eliminated and then the promise was broken."

"A *so-called* fairy-story. Did you know that the follow-up to the Piper's visit to get Hamelin rid of the rats is really sinister?" Templestone said, in a suitably quiet voice.

"What is the follow-up?" Lee Wynter asked. Templestone's word, *sinister* had caused the hairs to rise on the back of Wynter's neck. As usual, Templestone didn't answer the question straight away. He went for effect; but it was Storm Petrel who explained,

"There was a piece of poetry by Robert Browning; he brought the legend up to date. It was part of the prospectus when I majored in English and American Lit. I remember it well, guys. It's like, stuck in my mind."

"Can you recite it?" Jules said. Storm thought for a couple of minutes, summoning the metre of the poetry to mind from her collegiate days. She took advantage of the situation, sort of sucked-up the atmosphere much like Templestone did. With the lights down low in the great hall, and the fire casting flickering shadows that danced on the walls, she moved to Dearden's usual position in front of the great Norman fireplace and began to recite, slowly, in a southern US drawl.

When, lo! as they reached the mountain-side,
A wondrous portal opened wide,
As if a cavern was suddenly hollowed;
And the Piper advanced and the children followed,
And when all were in to the very last,
The door in the mountain-side shut fast.

"There's no smoke without fire," Mitch Doughty said.

"What means that, *no smoke without fire?*" Rowan asked. Waiting for the answer she felt a sudden chill in the room, maybe it was the cold from outside . . . maybe the words of the legend. She went to the basket of logs by the side of the fireplace, chucked another couple of logs onto those settling down in the immense hearth and then she sat on the floor close to the fire.

Doughty explained, "*No smoke without fire* is a saying we have that is sometimes associated with legends. In reality, if you see smoke, it is evidence of a fire. There is often truth at the root of a legend. The smoke tells us that we need to examine the legend to find the truth. The fire is the original truth that has become distorted over the years."

"Are you *really* suggestin' that the invisible guy runnin'

around in the forest could be the Pied Piper of Hamelin?" Wynter challenged.

"I'm not saying that the Entity *definitely* is the Piper, but there are indications that he may well be associated with your legend," Lan-Si-Nu affirmed.

"You mean the musical sound coming from Uberatu's Oak could be the Piper of Hamelin doin' his ancient music?"

"Well, the Entity has been around for a long, long time" It was unusual for Lan-Si-Nu and the other two Wasiri Chanchiyans not to be direct. The other two aliens looked at their Commander and Lee Wynter saw avoidance in their eyes.

"Well, I hope that the Entity you Wasiri's seem so fond of doesn't get real with the legend in Browning's re-write," Storm Petrel said.

"Are you sayin' we're goin' to get led off by the Piper?"

Matt Roberts, always ready for a wind-up, saw Wynter was unsettled. He sidled over to him. Got close. "Yep. You've got it," Matt said. "The weirdo likes caves. He led us into the cave at the back of the waterfall . . . he'll seal us in next time."

231

34

Penitentiaries were the bastions which ensured the survival of the old, pre-Nibiru morality. The mentality of *dog-eat-dog* was still nurtured by the majority of the penitentiary inmates. The strongest thrived in a hierarchy of the survival of the fittest. The new morality of universal peace was unacceptable to the majority of the inmates so they were kept inside by the heavy, steel-faced outer gates because they would be a danger to the population outside. It was in this rarefied atmosphere that Uberatu's twisted hatred of most things grew to full bloom.

Raegenhere was dying of cancer and weakening by the hour. He gasped a request to the guards standing by his hospital bed. He wanted to see his old buddy, Theodore Uberatu.

Theo had to get close to him to hear what he said.

"I'm going, Theo," Raegenhere whispered.

"Where to?" Uberatu was not very intuitive.

"I'm bloody dying. Anyway, I'm leaving you the lot. The house, Dracasfeld, everything in it . . . the business—here," Raegenhere managed to lift a newly drafted will and he placed it gently into Theo's hand. "Enjoy," Raegenhere said, like a waiter handing over a meal.

Uberatu suddenly twigged what was happening. "Thanks Reg."

"Why do you never bloody listen, Theo. I'm not Reg . . . I'm bloody Raegenhere," he whispered . . . and then his eyes closed and his breath left his body.

The doctor felt for a pulse. There was none. "He's gone."

"Fat lot of good that'll do you, Lifer," The guard at

Uberatu's side said, nodding at the last will and testament. He had been a witness to its signing.

Uberatu stared at the guard. "That's what you think, Chump." The guard lifted his baton but didn't use it. He caught the expression in the prisoner's eyes; it was cold, dark, and menacing and it unnerved him.

* * *

Theodore Uberatu was a thoroughly shifty character. He, along with Raegenhere, had created nuclear mayhem in Manhattan when they tried to steal the priceless 1933 Gold Double Eagle coin. They had been imprisoned when their attempt failed. In effect, the jailers, by order of the Supreme Court, had thrown away the key.

After finding out that he was the sole beneficiary in Raegenhere's will, Uberatu, over a number of months, winkled his way into the good books of the prison governor. He put on a posh English accent, a fairly simple thing for a character who was a fairly good actor. Uberatu's charade of bonhomie duped the man in charge and he got a job in the services department where, amongst other thankless tasks, they gathered dirty laundry to send to a contractor for washing.

Uberatu stole a passably clean civilian suit of clothes put in for dry cleaning and, wearing this, he made his exit from the prison by the old dodge of a laundry trolley. One of the six that were going to the laundry contained Uberatu on his outward journey from jail. He was glad there was always a lot of washing needed for the bed-sheets and the clothes of a determinedly filthy set of inmates.

A mile away from the gates of the prison the flat-bed truck carrying the stuff for washing stopped at traffic lights and

Uberatu clawed to the surface of the stinking laundry. He poked his head out into the daylight, blinked, saw no-one was about and eased his way quickly from the mess of clothes to the deck of the truck. He leaped to the tarmac just before the lights turned green.

Uberatu sauntered onto the side walk and turned to look at the concrete edifice where he had been imprisoned. He recalled the Alexander Korda film where a genie, let out of a bottle, shouted repeatedly *I'm free . . . I'm free*, and then, heading in the direction signposted to the airport, Uberatu breathed in the invigorating air of freedom.

One of Raegenhere's contacts in the States, Stet Burford, who was a good organiser, lived near the airport.

"What the hell are you doing here?" Burford asked, when Uberatu knocked his door. Without a word, the heavily built, black bearded Uberatu forced his way past Burford into the house.

"Shut your mouth," Uberatu said, soft and sinister-like to Burford's wife as she opened her mouth to scream. Burford came into the room quick, dodged to a side-cupboard drawer for the Colt he kept for emergencies, but he wasn't quick enough. Uberatu got to the drawer quicker, shoved Burford aside and had the pistol level and steady when Burford recovered his footing.

"What are you doing here, Theo?" Burford asked. His wife, Helen, slowly moved to her husband's side. She tried to grasp his hand but Burford's mind was elsewhere and he gently shoved his wife to one side, out of the field of play.

"I got out. By a clever ruse, I might add . . . but hardly original. Let's relax, Stet. I want out of the States. Are you still at Westchester Airport?" Burford nodded he was.

"Get me on a plane to the UK and no harm will come to you or your wife."

"How the hell can I do that. Westchester's more tightly controlled than ever since Raegenhere and you made idiots out of the security there."

"No plane . . . you get pain," Uberatu parodied in a cartoon character voice. Helen Burford flinched as he waved the gun in the air. He refrained from firing it into the ceiling because somebody might hear.

"There aren't many flights out to anywhere, since Nibiru. That includes the UK," Burford said. Normally he was not shy of throwing his weight around but he thought better of it because of the gun and the wild, out-of-control look in Uberatu's eyes. Burford decided to try delaying tactics to get himself time to work out what to do.

"I'll see what I can do," he said. He immediately thought of a favour he could call in. Burford was ground crew. Last year a flight attendant had approached him.

"Want to earn a bit of cash on the side?" the man had asked in a low voice. Burford had no need for the money. His operation was growing in line with the increase in yield from a hidden plot of Marijuana, but another source of income was always useful. Last year, what the flight attendant had wanted was related to a flight from Amsterdam to Westchester and it concerned a package of diamonds. Burford fitted out a safe place to stash the loot after the flight into the States. The operation worked like a dream.

"Give me two hours," Burford said to Uberatu.

"You've got two hours; and Stet . . . it had better work."

Burford held out his hand for his wife to get up.

"What do you think you're doing," Uberatu got out of the chair and when he swung the Beretta to within six inches of

Burford's face the man backed away.

"She stays here while you get the trip settled," Uberatu snarled.

Burford's eyes narrowed, "You harm her and it will be the last thing you do on God's Earth." He normally didn't go in for religion but he thought he would bring the Almighty into things to carry more weight.

Uberatu grinned. "Just go and get it done Stet, there's a good chap." Uberatu elaborated his English accent. Burford's jaw clenched. He saw Helen's brief nod that it would be OK, and her lips moved in a blown kiss. Stet walked out the door to his car and he sped away on the five mile trip to where Barry O'Toole shacked up with his latest girl.

"Let's make sure Stet plays ball, shall we, Helen?" Uberatu moved closer to her and she flinched away. "Oh, don't worry, the only harm that'll come to you will be if your loving husband doesn't get my trip home sorted. No, I see you have a car of your own in the drive." It was coloured pink. "Where are the keys?"

"Over there." She pointed to a dish on the sideboard. Her hand was shaking.

"Good girl. We're going for a little ride. You're driving"

"Where are we going?"

"You'll see." He didn't know where they would go, just that they wouldn't be at home when Burford came back. It would add spice to the drama, and leverage to getting the flight finalised.

On the way to O'Toole's home Stet Burford tried to conceive a way of getting Uberatu on a flight and of getting him dead. He was worried about his wife and found it difficult to concentrate on the road while he worked on the problem.

To get Uberatu onto an aircraft, customs would have to be avoided, as would any other flight-side security, which made things very difficult.

To stow him away in warm clothes in one of the landing-wheel bays could work on short-haul, but not on a transatlantic flight. At Heathrow, Uberatu's body would be found and an investigation would point to the guys involved with the aircraft's ground checks. Then Stet Burford hit on the idea of a packing case with false labelling. The plan would need authentic looking paperwork and, with air-holes in the base of the packing case, it could work. It would need someone the other end to open the case. Some of Raegenhere's ex-workers were still about in the UK, they would help with the operation UK-side.

At Westchester, a packing and transit company produced cases to order and Burford was on golfing terms with the CEO. The golfing buddies at *the club* were a tight knit fraternity who made sure the brotherhood was OK. A phone call would set the plan in motion.

O'Toole was surprised to see Burford on his doorstep. They didn't socialise outside of work, but the visitor was invited in and they discussed the transit problem. O'Toole agreed to help. *One good turn deserves another,* he said. In reality he was scared that Burford would blow the can on the diamond racket.

"I'm like this with one of the loading crew." O'Toole crossed his fingers to show just *how-in* he was with the ground crew. "You can count on me, Stet. When do you need it done?"

Burford was dismayed to see that Helen's car was missing when he got home. The oil-patch was there but no car. The front door was unlocked and he shouted her name as he rushed into the house. His mind was in turmoil as he raced through room after room, calling her. He got back to the living room and swore as he went to her chair. No note on the occasional table by her chair. Nothing slipped between the moulding and the glass of the antique clock, where she normally left a note telling him where she was if she had to go out.

He was frantic with worry. Uberatu on the loose with a gun, holding his wife hostage, was his worst nightmare. It was then that he noticed the corner of a business card tucked between the seat squab and the arm of the easy chair where she had been sitting. He grabbed at it and in his rush to get it, it slipped further down the narrow gap. He forced his fingers in and managed to get hold of a corner of the card. He pulled it out and stared at it.

Maisie's Bar and Diner
Boston Post Road.
Call for bookings.

Uberatu must have asked her where they could go, so she suggested Maisie's and then secreted the card where he would find it.

He and Helen went there occasionally, maybe once every six weeks. Burford rushed upstairs, now in attack mode because of Uberatu taking Helen. In the drawer of his wife's vanity unit there was a North American Arms 22 calibre short mini-revolver. It was small and compact but deadly at the right distance. By this time Burford's heart was pumping at 160 and he felt the pressure building in his chest. He sat on the bed to let it pass. The doctor told him to take things easy because he sometimes had these warnings. He looked at his watch, gave himself five minutes and then opened his wife's drawer. There it was, walnut handles, stainless steel and it was loaded. The gun fitted easily into his pocket.

He went down the stairs two at a time. Drove off leaving a cloud of burned rubber from his tyres as they screeched to get a grip.

When he got close to the Diner his anger was ominous. He parked the car at a general store out of sight of Maisie's and crept along the frontage. He felt for the pistol, grasped the handle but kept it hidden in his pocket. He inched up to the window and there they were. Uberatu had a beer and Helen a white wine. She looked cowed.

Uberatu was talking and then he smirked. There was a mirror behind the bar and another one at the far end of the diner. The angle of the mirrors coincided to pick up Burford's reflection. Uberatu stood and went to the chair next to Helen, pulled it from under the table, then returned to the chair opposite her.

Burford sauntered in through the door, fingering the gun. Got to the table and stood at the side of Uberatu. He felt cold rage inside, ready to lash out, but like him Uberatu had a gun in his pocket and Burford could see its shape pointing at his wife's head.

"I thought you'd never get here, Stet. Pray, sit down. Make yourself comfortable." Burford glowered at him. "How did you get on, flight all arranged, is it?"

"Nearly." Burford's anger settled to a throbbing vein in his temple. At least his wife was safe. He looked at her, swallowed hard and stared at Uberatu. He calmed his remaining rage. "Here's the plan." He described his meeting with Barry

O'Toole and the idea of the packing case.

"Sounds feasible. When'll it be?"

Just then three police vehicles rushed by, sirens blaring. Uberatu looked outside casually. Turned back to Burford.

"The flight will be easy to arrange. We'll arrange paperwork for the freight and get the case made, but a week should see you on your way."

*   *   *

It had been stifling in the packing case, but there was food, water, a bottle of whiskey and a large can with a stopper. There were straps to hold to save being rolled around when the loading and unloading took place. The ruse had worked well enough right through from the States, to a back way out of Heathrow avoiding the Customs, which was pretty much defunct after Nibiru.

Uberatu cursed under his breath when the fork-lift let him down as if the case contained junk. Reagenhere's Dracasfeld estate manager, Dec Settle directed transfer of the packing case onto a flat-back truck. A few miles down the road he pulled into a lay-by and Dec Settle's oppo jemmied the lid off the case.

Uberatu stood shakily, blinking in the bright sunlight. He stretched to ease his muscles, looked down at his rescuers and clambered stiffly off the truck.

"Welcome to England, you ugly old bastard." Dec Settle grinned at Uberatu. "You've lost some weight,"

"Put that down to the hotel," Uberatu smirked.

"Where to now?" the guy with the jemmy asked, as he stepped up into the cab.

"Raegenhere's old place. What's it like there?"

"Derelict. Trees collapsed through the roof during the

cyclone. No-one's about to repair it now."

"Dracasfeld will do fine even if it is ruined. It's mine now. I'll get to repair it. Anyway, on the way back stop by the garage in Wyverne Hardewicke. I want to collect the dog from Ozzie."

"OK, you're the boss now."

"I am. Don't you forget it."

Theo bought some Schmackos at the local store. He had no idea if Snarl would still be with Ozzie. It was over two years since he left the dog with the mechanic but Uberatu wanted to be safe. The dog would ensure Uberatu's safety at Dracasfeld and food would ensure Uberatu wouldn't get attacked by the dog.

They pulled up at the garage and Uberatu went to the workshop door. It was as if nothing had changed inside since he saw it last. The mechanic was sitting in the same chair. The same car was on the ramp. Snarl was there at Ozzie's side, but at a respectable distance. The dog growled the same deep I-don't-like-you growl as it did over two years ago, when it saw Uberatu.

Uberatu anticipated the reaction and had opened the Schmackos as he stood outside the garage door. He took one out and approached Snarl, who looked menacingly at Uberatu, and then hungrily at the Schmacko. There was a slight wag of the tail as Snarl stood and ambled over for the treat. It had been a love-hate relationship for both of them before and it looked as if it wasn't going to change, but food was the key. Snarl grabbed the Schmacko quickly and ambled into a corner with it.

"I've come for the dog."

"You can have it with pleasure."

"Been OK with it?"

"So-so." Ozzie's hand, which had a scar on the back, moved as if to say fifty-fiftyish.

"Come here," Uberatu growled, facing Snarl head-on, staring him in the eyes. The dog moved toward him cautiously. It was more thick-set than it had been before he left it. Now it was full of muscle.

"Got the lead, Ozzie?" The mechanic chucked over the lead without a word. Snarl growled as Uberatu caught it.

"Get here!" The dog shambled over and sat at Uberatu's feet, avoiding the man's eyes. Uberatu attached the lead.

"What do I owe you?"

"A settee."

"A what?"

"*A settee*," Ozzie said, more loudly than necessary.

"How come?"

"That dog tore it to shreds."

This is the way the conversation went for another twenty minutes. Short and snappy, to the point, no wasted words. Ending with a promise of money for a settee.

Uberatu got Dec Settle to tie Snarl up on the back of the truck. "But he'll be cold," the man argued. Uberatu grinned.

Dracasfeld looked forlorn. They drove through the busted wrought-iron gates, wrecked by SHaFT when they raided the mansion before the Manhattan mission.

"There's a few rooms surviving on the left of the building. That's where I live," Settle said. The mansion was facing them full on. Blue cedars that had once stood majestically at the rear of the building now rested with their mass penetrating the roof. Their foliage, which was still alive, was blowing in the strong breeze. Settle tooled the truck toward the building which, Uberatu could see as they neared it, was in worse condition than it looked from afar. The mansion's lawns and shrubbery were overgrown. The whole place was in a state of disrepair.

"Not a bad place for free, eh?" Settle chortled. Uberatu snapped a look at him.

"That's what you think," Uberatu said.

"What do you mean, Theo?"

"You're paying rent from now on . . . and by the way, it's not Theo, it's Sir."

They pulled up on the circular arrival area at the top end of the drive. The white-gravelled area was smothered with two years of weeds and algae.

"This way," Settle said, making off to the left along a path trodden through the overgrown grass.

"Get the dog," Uberatu said. Settle swung around. For over two years now he had the run of Dracasfeld with no-one telling him what to do. Uberatu had Burford's gun out. It was by his side, to enforce the ground-rules.

"OK . . . OK. I'll get the dog. No need for the gun."

They went inside and Uberatu began a walk-through of his new possession. Apart from dust, the rooms on the left of the building were top quality. One of the rooms had been Raegenhere's dining-room. Most of the furniture had gone now and the paintings too, but the rooms were as Theo remembered them from when he and Raegenhere sat and planned the Manhattan steal, and other more successful jobs.

Now he was back and the mansion was his. He got up from the single remaining arm-chair and looked at Snarl, who was gazing suspiciously at him from the opposite end of the large room. As Uberatu strutted up and down the room

243

Snarl's gaze followed him like an audience follows a game of tennis. It was an oversize room compared to the average, but it was a cavernous space to Uberatu because of his recent incarceration in an eight by twelve-foot cell.

He opened one of the windows. Thrust it wide. It happened to be in the direction of Dearden Hall, some miles away in Hampton in Arden.

"I'm back, Dearden," he yelled. His voice echoed into the countryside. "Oh, Jeremiah Dearden, I'm coming to get you."

This went on for half an hour. Dec Settle heard it all from the window above where he was standing on the overgrown lawn, and he wondered what the hell he had let himself in for.

Uberatu called down to Settle. "Any of the lads still about?"

"What lads?" Settle shouted back.

"Raegenhere's lads. Who do you think I meant?"

"Could scrape some together, maybe."

"Then do it. I want them here by five tonight."

By the time five o'clock came around seven rough looking types had shown up at Dracasfeld. One of them who came in was a giant of a guy with a squashed nose and a scar down his left cheek. Uberatu stood at the head of the stairs holding a side-by-side shotgun he found in what used to be Raegenhere's bedroom. He knew how to hold the gun. Broken, but loaded to enforce his authority. His dark looks inherited from his Brazilian tribal mother disquieted the new guys . . . his team.

They stood in front of him in a vague semi-circle . . . shuffling because of the shotgun. Even the guy with the squashed nose and the scar was shuffling. Uberatu was pleased with his role at the top of the chain of command and even though his headquarters was a mansion that was half-wrecked . . . it was still a mansion in impressive acreage.

"Get this," was his opening gambit. "I want a guy that lives a few miles away dead." Uberatu went into some emotional stuff about Raegenhere's being his amanuensis. It was meant to be a homage to his dead boss but it was unconnected drivel that left his team puzzled. Anyway, money looked plentiful so *what the hell*, the team thought. The mad guy with the shotgun and the dark eyes had the money and he wanted someone named Dearden dead . . . so what the hell?

"What's the plan?" Squashed Nose asked. He had assumed leadership of the other six.

"Dearden lives at this place." Uberatu grabbed a large Ordnance-Survey map off a nearby table. Pointed out Hampton-in-Arden and Dearden Hall. "Go down this road," his finger traced the route to Hampton in Arden. "There's electronic gates and the place is bristling with security. Once you get near the place, park the vehicles and approach Dearden's place on foot from the forest, here." His finger stabbed the large green patch on the map.

"Guns?" It was Squashed Nose again.

"What you got?" Uberatu asked.

"A few pieces in the cars."

"I've got a Bren gun," a mousey guy at the back said. Uberatu looked gratified with this.

"How about you . . . what you got?" he asked a man to the left of the group. He looked like Anton Beggs with some weight-loss. Uberatu hadn't seen Beggs since the Manhattan mission went wrong but . . . "Are you Beggsy?" Uberatu asked, coming down a few stairs and squinting at the man.

"Here again boss, ready and willing," Beggs said.

"What stone have you crawled from?" Uberatu asked.

"Whatever stone a turncoat *can* crawl from. I've come from a village down the road," Beggs explained. He had an agenda with Uberatu that he kept quiet about. Like Uberatu's agenda with Dearden, it was revenge stuff.

"OK. We go in at three o'clock in the morning . . . when they're at their lowest. Dearden doesn't know I'm back on his doorstep, and he doesn't know I've got an army. Uberatu looked at his army. Felt proud of it. He went down the stairs and walked down the ragged line of them, like he was the monarch on Trooping the Colour day.

"One grand each. That's what you got if Dearden ends up in my hands or dead," he said, when he got to the end of the line. He closed and locked the shotgun. Lifted it and blasted both barrels into the ceiling.

35

"The Entity homes in on the cave at the back of the waterfall," Oscar Stanway said. "You three experienced that when we went to the cave," he said to Jules, Storm and Rowan. "It followed you to where the device is set into the wall further in the cave. The question is, who put it there and what's it for?"

"I couldn't even hazard a guess," Jules said.

"We could go back to the cave and investigate, see if we can contact the Entity," Clive suggested.

"We would need detection gear," said Oscar.

"OK, back to the cave it is." Dearden said. "Oscar, Jules, you're into the science stuff . . . what equipment will we need?"

"Got to be infrared heat detection," Oscar said. "That guy's invisible most of the time. We need infrared . . . the best computer enhanced gear we can get. There has to be body heat coming from the Entity. Whatever the life-form, some measure of heat will be radiated."

"What equipment do you suggest?" Will Pierpoint asked.

"I can help with that. I have some residual gear from Ranstad Nanotech. Amongst other projects, we were working on a high definition multi-spectral surveillance system. It is adaptable for short or long range use, whatever's needed, and it is extremely portable."

"Where is this equipment?" asked Will Pierpoint."

"It's in Southampton . . . if my place survived."

"Is it likely to have survived? I mean, is it worth trekking there to retrieve it?" Sir Will asked.

"It's a fifty-fifty chance. From what I heard the area where

I lived was inundated but I did store the equipment in a place away from the damp . . . electronics, you know."

"Away from the damp is one thing. Away from the tsunami is another, Mitch Doughty said."

"I know. I can't guarantee it survived, but it's worth looking."

"OK, I'm with you on that, it would be a great asset," Dearden said. "Who's up for going?"

*   *   *

Four of Cell One were in Jules' Jeep Grand Cherokee, on their way to Southampton with Oscar. Jules shared time at the wheel with Clive Fraser. Oscar was in the back, with Storm Petrel in the middle and Matt Roberts the other side.

Old currency, after a near-fatal dip in confidence, was becoming marginally acceptable again and petrol, although limited in supply, was readily available to those on official business. Jules had flashed her pass in one of the few service stations open and the fuel gurgled into the tank right up to the neck.

Clive Fraser was back driving. "Take the next turn to the right," Oscar said. Silt and waterborne debris lined the road. A tide-line from the tsunami was visible on the house frontages. Front garden walls were smashed. A large motor cruiser with its bows crushed had made a front room open to the elements. A settee was on its back in the garden of the house and what was once a flower border now contained broken dining chairs and flattened shrubs.

Oscar pointed further up the road to a large detached place with a once-landscaped garden. "That's my place," he said. The tide-line was showing above the large downstairs windows, some of the sealed units were cracked but surviving, and there was a bent double-garage door with a loft above it.

"We may be in luck," Oscar said, as they drove into the silted-up drive. He went to the larger of the windows, waited a second or so while he looked in. He shook his head and got out a bunch of keys.

He snicked the lock in the front door. It was stiff but it opened. There was a scene of ruination inside. Months of water saturation in the enclosed space made it stink of decay. Oscar led the way over once-expensive Persian rugs into the right side of the house. The door leading to stairs into the loft room was jammed in its frame.

"Let me try." Roberts backed off a couple of feet and launched himself at the door . . . once . . . twice. On the third smack the door flew open. He stood aside and let Oscar through.

The stair carpet was stained where the damp had penetrated. Oscar muttered under his breath and took the steps two at a time. At the end of a short landing he thrust a key into the lock of a heavy-looking door.

"It's a fire-door," he said. "Wood effect over steel." The door opened easily and they trailed into the room which was brightly lit by the sun shining through a window to the right.

Shelves were hung on the wall opposite the window and racking filled the wall in front of them. Steel boxes, some with combination locks lay on the racking.

"That's the one," Oscar pointed to a box on the top shelf. He reached up, took the box to a desk below the window, fiddled with the lock and took the object out. The instrument was wrapped in a strong polythene vacuum sack with the air sucked out. He pulled open a drawer and unclasped a large penknife which he used to cut the polythene. He reached into his pocket for some AA batteries. "These are re-chargeable, should be OK," he said. After loading them into the base of the instrument. He switched it on.

"This is the best there is. Absolutely no false positive rate. Size and aspect ratio are truly represented on screen, and multi resolution localisation of—"

"—Does the thing work?" Matt Roberts cut in.

"This is not a thing. It has a pre-production name," Oscar said.

"So sorry. What is its name?"

"Nosey Wilfred."

Roberts sniggered.

"You may laugh," Oscar said. "The name's a homage to Wilf Janson. He was my co-designer of this . . . instrument. Wilf died shortly after its first test." Oscar focussed the instrument on Storm Petrel. She was at the far side of the room looking at a poster on the wall. Storm's profile being resolved on screen was very obviously female. There was a readout at the side of the screen.

99% certainty of image:
Human female.
Posterior view.
Age, by comparison with standard model of 10,000 subjects:
27 years and 3.9 months

The detail on screen began to morph from the usual colours, the blues, greens and reds of an off-the-shelf thermal imager. It resolved into a standard video image. On-screen, Storm Petrel, in full detail and colour, turned to face them. "Hi guys," she said, giving them a theatrical wave.

36

Dearden was restless. Sometimes he had nights where sleep was distant. Rowan was asleep, the sheets off her shapely form, highlighted by the moonlight coming through the window. It was a full moon . . . Jem called moons like this an Anglo-Saxon moon. He looked out the window. The moon was shining brightly over the forest and it reminded him of the nights they spent in Leofwin's Hundred back in Rowan's time.

Although he had a tough edge that he could draw on when needed, Jem Dearden was a romantic at heart. He turned from the moon and looked at Rowan, how perfect she looked in the silvery light. And then he thought of the distance they had travelled through time to be together. He turned to the forest again, where it all began. The myriad stars, the fluorescent band of the Milky Way vibrant against the black velvet of infinity coalesced in Jem's mind and bound all of time and space together into the present.

A movement below caught his eye. It was a fast, indefinable movement. Something like a mirage when it disturbs the normality of vision.

"Rowan . . . Rowan."

"Mmm?"

"Wake up."

"What is it?"

"Here . . . look at this."

She slid off the bed, grabbed a robe and put it on. Pulled the belt tight and looked to where he pointed. There it was, the miraged patch, flitting about in the moonlight.

"The Entity's here," Rowan said. "What shall we do?"

"Go down . . . see what's going on."

"No Jem. Leave it. I am frightened."

"It means us no harm. It's . . . it's investigating." Dearden put on jeans and a shirt. Kissed Rowan. "Look out of the window, watch what happens." Dearden ran along the passage and down the stairs into the great hall. He looked behind as he heard a door open and footsteps running behind him. It was Mitch Doughty.

In the great hall, illuminated by the glowing remnants of the evening's logs burning in the Norman fireplace, Tomahawk Shahn of Offchurch was standing by the floor to ceiling window, looking out into the night. Dearden went to the wolf, who seemed to be transfixed on the scene outside. Unusually, he took no notice as Dearden touched the top of his head and slid his hand onto the studded collar and pulled gently.

"Come on, Tom." Dearden pulled again, harder this time and clipped the heavy leash to the collar. "Let's go."

It was then that vehicle lights came hurtling down the drive toward the electronic gates. They stopped and a number of men with guns got out, and were silhouetted black in the bright vehicle-lights.

"Warn those upstairs Mitch," Dearden shouted. "I'll head that lot off." Dearden ran to the Jacobean sideboard, unlocked the drawer and got out his Beretta. He checked it was loaded and ran to the entrance door as Gil Heskin came into the hall. A commotion occurred upstairs after Doughty raised the alarm. Jules was down in a few seconds, and then Oscar and Bill Templestone, with his Smith and Wesson 38.

Dearden, with Tomahawk close by, opened the front door wide. The others crowded round. Matt pushed to the front, ready for action.

It was then that something very strange happened. The Entity, only seen by the distortion of the objects behind it, rushed to the electronic gate and was up and over it in a split second. The metalwork of the gate clattered and moved violently as the life-form leaped over it, and then there were yells from the group with guns as they panicked wildly in all directions.

But one of them shouted and Dearden recognised the voice. "Remember me? I'll get you, Dearden," and Dearden saw Uberatu turn to face the miraged Entity. He recoiled, shouted something unintelligible and ran toward the forest.

"Man, did you see that?" Wynter yelled. "The invisible Woojie's on our side." The steel gate was still rattling after the Entity's body had been on it.

Just then, another person, whose profile Dearden also recognised, scrambled over the gate and came running toward them.

"It's me," the man called. "It's Beggs . . . I want to help."

Anton Beggs had lost a lot of weight since Dearden last saw him. He looked athletic.

"How come you think we need your help, you gave us the run-around back in Heanton," Jules asked.

"I was taken for a mug by Uberatu . . . cost me hundreds of pounds. Now it's my turn. Did you know that Reagenhere's dead?"

"No. But I can't say I'm sorry," Dearden said.

"Nor me. He left the house, money, the lot to Uberatu."

"That might be so," Pierpoint called as he came into the great hall from upstairs. "But if you're with us you play by the rules."

* * *

253

A ground sweep of the forest began, Cell One were out in pairs, each pair armed and with some of the old Motorola two-ways for communication. The Heskin's, Bill Templestone and Rowan stayed back. Templestone with his 38 and Gil Heskin with a Miroku MK70 over and under shotgun. "This is adequate for me," Templestone said, checking the chamber of his 38 as Dearden was about to leave with Mitch Doughty.

By now, all sign of the Entity had gone. Coincidence or not, it had been around at the right time and it weighed-in single-handed to help those in Dearden Hall against Uberatu's mob.

Dearden and Doughty, with Tomahawk leading, set off in pursuit of Uberatu by the light of his torch, following the track they saw him take into the forest. Uberatu had taken the main track, the one leading to the Hub and Uberatu's Oak.

Right from the start Tomahawk tugged hard on the leash, which divided at the top into two handles, so Doughty grasped the leather as well as Dearden. Tomahawk was pulling with frantic energy when they entered the forest, as if hunting prey. Doughty kept the torch switched off where he could to keep their presence hidden and with the bright moonlight and Tomahawk's unerring sense of direction, they made quick progress.

After a while they heard the sound of Shadow Brook up ahead as it gurgled over the old stepping-stones used before a bridge was installed. The watercourse was more a small river than a stream at the point where the bridge crossed over it, and as they reached the watercourse the moonlight shone on its rippling surface, highlighting the position of the bridge.

Turning left after crossing Shadow Brook, they soon passed Old Jack, the mighty oak that they had seen when it was a young sapling almost a thousand years in the past.

"Listen," Doughty said, after they had walked on for a while and the background noise of Shadow Brook had quietened to a murmur. Dearden stopped. Said, in a loud authoritative whisper, *Stay, Tom*, and he jerked hard on the leash. The three halted and all was quiet.

The sound of an owl pierced the night and then Dearden heard what Doughty had picked up. The sound was unmistakable and the source was now familiar, the melodious background sound overlaid by tapping, coming from Uberatu's Oak, a short distance ahead.

37

The drive back to Dearden Hall from Southampton, other than for another show of the card authorising no limit on petrol, was uneventful. They were about half way home when, after a long spell of silence, Matt looked at Oscar, who was asleep. Matt nudged him. Oscar awoke with a start and held up his hand defensively. Matt laughed. "Sorry, take it easy . . . it's just that I've got a question." He blew away a loose strand of long hair that got loose from his bandana.

"Fire away."

"I might be naïve but why have we gone to the trouble of going to your place in Southampton for this high-tech gear," he tapped the metal instrument case on Oscar's lap, "When we could have sprayed the Invisible Runner with water."

Jules, driving, answered, "You've got no sense as usual Matt. Just think it through. You're on an alien planet, exploring the place, maybe. Some inhabitants confront you and you get sprayed. What would *you* do?"

Roberts fingered the Bowie in a sheath on his belt. "I'd probably use Mavis." He unclipped the fastener holding the knife he called Mavis in its sheath and then took out the weapon. He fingered the edge he kept honed in his spare time. "Yep. I wouldn't know what they sprayed me with. I would consider it an attack."

"That's it in one, Matt," Oscar said. "So far the Invisible Runner has done nothing offensive. Just the opposite, in fact. So, we choose a benign method to try to identify him . . . my gadget, Nosey Wilfred." He tapped it again. "And as you saw back in the loft room it is a good gadget. Cutting edge. There's nothing else like it. We get a body-heat trace, a chemical analysis and a computer enhanced real-time image of the subject, or subjects, if there's more than one."

Jules said, "Remember when Lan-Si-Nu likened the Entity to the Pied Piper of Hamelin, Lee asked him if the Entity *is* the Pied Piper. For all his knowledge and his science, our alien didn't give us a definite answer."

What Storm said next brought silence again. "What if it is . . . I mean, what if the Invisible Runner really *is* the Pied Piper, it means that guy has been around for nigh-on nine-hundred years."

"A multi-reality life-form, Lan-Si-Nu called it. This gets weirder by the day, Jules," Clive said.

"You'll get used to it Clive. Takes a while, but your mind will get more flexible so you can accept the strange crap without flinching. Just stick with it."

Jules and Clive had got close over the months since they first met. Different in temperament they were, but that is what forged the link. She, feisty. Useful to have around in a rough and tumble . . . trustworthy, loyal. Him, gentlemanly, courteous in an old-fashioned way. But they blended. Each of them valued what the other added to the relationship. He made Jules feel valued. She made him feel needed. She reached her hand to his for a second or so. With a quick sideways glance and an impish smile, she put her hand back on the steering wheel.

In their private time together at Moat-Field Cottage near Kenilworth Castle she was teaching him karate. Together, in the garage, on some nights, a regular thumping noise could be heard as they took turns hitting the Makiwara. Clive was getting good. Getting confident. His knuckles were toughening-up and he could smash a chunk of tight-grained wood with his bare hands.

They pulled into the long, winding drive leading to Dearden Hall. It ended at some electronic gates where there was an intercom visitors could use to announce their arrival.

Jules pulled up at the gate, glad to be back after the Southampton trip. She pressed the button on the intercom, waited for a few seconds but the gate remained shut. She pressed again, and still there was no response. The gates were usually opened by Gil Heskin who responded to the intercom by pressing a button situated by a window overlooking the gate. Access to the grounds was never usually a problem. Jules got out to open the gate manually and Roberts went to help.

"Jem checked the system out last week and it was working fine," Jules frowned. "This is odd, Jem's on the ball with security."

"Let me get to it," Matt said. He tried the intercom and then pulled the gate vigorously but it didn't budge.

It was unusually silent around the house and grounds.

"OK, up and over," Roberts said. "But be quiet about it." Clive indicated to get close and clasped his hands together . . . Jules stepped in and a second later she was over, The others followed, and Clive scrambled over last.

They crept to the archway between the house and the outbuildings, hugging the wall of the house as they headed to the medieval front door, which was unlocked.

38

"Where did you shelter when Nibiru got close?" Sir Will Pierpoint asked Beggs.

"On the bank of the River Avon outside Warwick. In the cave near Guys Cliffe where Earl Guy of Warwick lived when he came back from the Crusades. I thought I would be safe there. It was high up. Isolated and strong."

"Did the Avon back-up around Warwick? The tornado was torrential here in the Midlands." The conversation went this way between the pair. An unlikely pair to team up but Sir Willoughby wanted some responsibility again. The former head of SHaFT craved responsibility. It was in his genes, so he chose to have Anton Beggs, the former rebel, as his partner.

"The Avon did back up, but it stopped rising a couple of feet short of the floor of the cave. My lucky day, or what?"

"You were close to the gate at Dearden Hall when the Entity climbed over it. What did you make of that?"

"I don't know, but it put the fear of God into Uberatu. His brain doesn't work normally at the best of times. Whatever climbed over the gate targeted the guys with the weapons. It was too quick for them to cope with . . . disarmed all of them in seconds."

"We've had brief contact with that creature too, it comes across as peaceful."

* * *

On a far-off planet, in a reality where time was slow and some of the physics was totally alien to him, Harry Stanway was contemplating Esma. He was very attached to her, but he didn't blame himself for the predicament they were in. He had no feeling of guilt for involving Esma in the escapade. He had a blind spot that kicked in sometimes and on more than one occasion this had been the saviour of him and those close to him because the blind spot made him totally focussed. Not that he was without emotion. So, he was contemplating Esma's beauty as she was leisurely spit-roasting one of the long vegetables that Professor Villiers said was tasty.

True to form, in this alien reality, flames licked around the vegetable in a slow-motion fashion, and smoke from the fire arose in a hypnotically slow and lazy way. Harry went from their shelter to where Esma was slowly rotating the food over the flames and he slipped his arm around her shoulders. She turned to him, smiled and leant in close.

Although they were further from their true home than Esma could contemplate, she felt no need for things to be any different. She had her man close by, and she knew that she was loved and that he would never leave her. True, she did not have her other friends close-by . . . Rowan of Maldon, Jem and Jules, but maybe, just maybe, someday, she would return to that other life.

Harry went with his club to the giant growth and he began to knock out the interminable Morse message on the soft bark. As he started, so did the other tones commence, sometimes harmonic, at other times vaguely dissonant, repeated from the life-forms close-by and far distant, as if the performance was being enacted by a mighty orchestra.

"They are talking to each-other again," Esma said.

"They are. I feel sure they are intelligent. I can detect familiar tones when I knock out the letters. The growths recognise the rhythm of the sounds. And another thing, I've heard similar sounds coming from Uberatu's Oak. I'm convinced the network is universal, trans-dimensional."

Harry, for quite some time, had communicated his inner thoughts to Esma. She was adept at listening to these way-out ideas without forming preconceived conclusions and she was learning how to visualise his ideas. She also remembered the singing tree from her own time, before she came with Rowan and the others to the twenty-first century.

"I heard it as well . . . back in Leofwin's time."

"Did you really?"

She nodded yes. She had refrained from telling him about this previously.

"This is most odd," Harry said, suddenly glancing over Esma's right shoulder to a movement that attracted his attention.

"What is odd?"

"It's back again — look," Harry pointed and Esma turned to see where he was looking. The depressions were forming in the soft ground nearby. The accompanying undercurrent of sound was melodious to the ear and reached deep inside.

"Do you think we can attract it?" he asked her. "It seems that whenever I try to contact those at home on Earth this life-form arrives."

Esma looked uneasy. "I do not know if I want to attract it."

Harry stood and walked toward the depressions, which, as he approached them, ceased their restless movement. A vague shimmering delineated the life-form as Harry got closer to it. It could be vaguely seen because of a mist, caused by the heat of the day meeting the cool of evening. He could see that the life-form was taller than him by about a foot.

The unexpected thing was when it appeared to sit down on the ground, because its apparent height, judged by its effect on the background, was diminished by half, and an area of ground sank beneath its weight. Harry noticed that the indentations took the form of buttocks.

"Who are you?" Harry asked, as Esma came cautiously to his side. She felt for his hand and grasped it, held on tight. There was no vocal response to his question, just a feint shadowy movement from the place where its hands might be.

Harry felt that the life-form was regarding them . . . that it was curious, and then it reached out and touched Harry and Esma's clasped hands, held on gently and uttered a plaintive sound, a sound of longing that Harry felt deep inside. He recalled the word *hiraeth*, a deep-down longing for home, from when he studied the Welsh language. And then the Entity let go, stood and was gone.

* * *

Dearden and Doughty reached Uberatu's Oak. Tomahawk was with them on the leash. No free roaming for the wolf now with the odd stuff going on. The whole forest was strangely silent and no sounds were issuing from the oak. "See this?" Dearden shone the torch on the ground around the tree. Large footprints were embedded in the forest floor around the oak and a miniature forest of fungus had grown in the area.

"It's certainly interested in this tree," Doughty observed as he moved around the tree to the doorway leading into its hollow centre.

"Shine the torch here, Jem." The footprints were most dense around the entrance. "He's tried to get in, see how the bark's been removed near the catch? And look, the fungal growths are germinating again where it's trod." Doughty lifted the padlock on the door. "Still locked, but it looks as though it wanted to get inside the tree."

Tomahawk sniffed the track near the oak. He tugged the leash and pressed on remorselessly.

"He's heading in the direction of Uberatu's cottage on the border of Leofwin's Hundred," Dearden said. He remembered the direction to the old granite-built place.

"Tom sure is on the hunt." Doughty said, switching on his torch briefly to light the way after a cloud covered the moon. He could see Dearden trying to hold the wolf back as best he could as the way ahead became illuminated once more in the moonlight. Doughty switched off his torch. Other than the occasional whispered comment, the two of them made no noise . . . nor did the wolf, as if a spell of silence had been cast over the place.

At length they reached the far border of the forest and saw the slate roof of the herdsman's shelter shining in the moonlight. The granite bulk of the cottage was still in darkness as they approached it through a gap in the hedge.

It was then that Tomahawk became really active. As a full-grown Black Alaskan wolf, he was real big and muscular. His eyes glowed a golden yellow in the light of the moon. To wolf lovers, and other wolves, he was attractive. Menacing to those who got on the wrong side of him.

Uberatu, from the darkness the other side the cottage, saw the wolf's eyes. The incident in the storm-drain under Manhattan flashed through his mind; how the wolf and Julia Linden-Barthorpe came hurtling out of a side-tunnel like a pair of demented banshees to rescue Dearden and Doughty.

And then, as if Leofwin's Hundred was transferred to the great Alaskan wilderness, Tomahawk raised his head to the moon and howled. The sound echoed amongst the trees and

Dearden felt the hairs rise on the back of his neck as the sound from the wilderness echoed again and again.

Uberatu ran when he saw the wolf's shining eyes and Dearden and Doughty approaching. He ran like the wind. Never had he ran so fast before, until he saw those shining wolf-eyes and heard the wolf's dreadful howl.

What the three humans didn't see, that the wolf did see because of the structure of his eyes, was the interesting-looking alien. Tomahawk didn't care about the fleeing Uberatu, he was not worth biting because the wolf saw only the other creature. He struggled and slipped his collar, and ran off into the darkness, following his new companion.

Two and a half hours later Tomahawk returned to Dearden Hall. Dearden heard him scratching at the door. He had been concerned that Tomahawk would roam off into the countryside and come into harm's way by creating havoc in the neighbourhood.

After Tomahawk had slipped the leash and went off into the forest night, unusual events took place. One might say, and it would be truthful to say this, that out-of-this-world events occurred, events to do with Tomahawk and the Piper.

Jem Dearden and Mitch Doughty were only involved on the periphery, at the start of things. After the wolf howled, the echoes pulsated again and again through the dark forest, and the sound of the wild reached deep inside Dearden. But obviously, not being a wolf, nor being cognizant of wolf language and wolf-lore, Dearden had no *inward* awareness of the way wolf minds worked for him to really understand Tomahawk's reaction.

Tomahawk felt he had *come home*.

Oh, how they roamed that night, Tomahawk and the Piper. They went quadrillions of miles over the Transdimensional network. They visited places undreamed of in the mind of man. Little wonder Tomahawk's eyes were bright on his return, for his eyes had been opened to far, far more than stench and food and procreation.

39

"Spray me with liquid," the Entity said. Harry was startled. Neither he nor Esma had seen the Entity return and Harry was thrown into a state of fearful confusion when it spoke. There was no warning. apart from a minor precursor in the form of musical sounds emanating from the gigantic tree-like life-forms that spread for miles around. The invisible guy spoke with the normal cadences of speech and the melodious background sound ceased while it spoke.

"You speak English?" was all Harry could think of saying.

"Of course. Everyone speaks English," it chuckled. "English has been adopted as a universal language and, let me tell you, it is a very colourful amalgam of thought patterns that translate into the audible tones of communication."

Harry thought that explanation was rather comical but subdued the rising chuckle himself. This was bizarre. So, he asked "Where are you from?" His throat felt a touch constricted as he spoke.

"I come from anywhere and everywhere, and why am I here, in this place?" If Harry and Esma had been able to see him they would have seen the Entity indicating the surroundings. "I am in this place because there is imbalance here due to you and the others of your kind transferring to this reality. *You shouldn't be here.* This imbalance is in danger of causing a dimensional fracture, a paradox, because your transfer hasn't been handled correctly. Anyway, first things first . . . have you got some liquid handy? If you spray me with liquid I will become visible to your eyes. It would be better if you could see me."

"Hold on," Harry said, quickly standing. He went into the

shelter and got the container of Fumble he had secreted from Villiers' store. "This is alcoholic, does it matter?"

"Not one bit."

"Do you want to drink some?" Esma asked.

"Better not, while I'm travelling."

"I haven't got a spray . . . shall I just pour it over you?" Harry stood next to the mirage-like shape with the stopper off the container.

"Go ahead. Between us we may figure out a way you can see me without this palaver of getting me soaked. I understand that you are a Wasiri-Chanchiyan Hnirath of Science. You are held in high regard by the People from the Beginning of Time."

"I have helped the Wasiri Chanchiyans," Harry said, as he poured where he thought the Entity's head was. The liquid splashed onto its shoulder and it looked as though it had been decapitated. He splashed the Fumble a bit higher and the Entity looked more complete.

"I thought you sounded upset a minute back," Harry said, thinking of the Entity's sound of longing, and the Welsh *hiraeth* word. He looked at the Entity now it was fully visible. He saw that it had human form. It was perfect in form and its eyes radiated wisdom and, Harry thought, understanding, and maybe, just maybe, there was a touch of humour.

"I am searching." The Entity's voice became serious.

"What do you want to find?" Esma asked.

"Someone who I have lost, so I am incomplete. There is also a major Reality imbalance that must be corrected."

"Is that your responsibility?" Harry asked.

"That is partly what I am for. I re-awaken when imbalances occur that could have a catastrophic outcome."

Harry thought for a beat, and then, "I think Esma and me

are in a different reality to the one where we were born . . . how come you are here . . . how is it that you know about us?" Harry thought about what he just said. "Let me rephrase that. This place is a different dimension to that of our origin." Harry indicated the landscape with a sweep of his hand. "Are you really capable of moving across dimensions?"

"I am."

"To put right imbalances?"

"That is correct. And you four Earth people on this planet have caused the major imbalance."

Harry looked dismayed. "What will be the outcome?" He felt chilled inside.

"Well I am hoping you will return to your home planet."

"Can you get us back home?"

"I am hoping so."

"Why only hoping so? Surely, if you can traverse dimensions you should be capable of getting us home."

"Wait, I am needed elsewhere." The Entity suddenly stood. It looked to one side, as if it was listening. A background susurrating noise came from one of the nearby tree-like growths. The Entity's visage took on a serious demeanour. By this time, it had begun to dry off. Parts of it looking solid and parts were looking mirage-like. It saw Harry gazing at its two piece clothing, which had been woven in bright coloured fabric.

"Yes . . . the Pied Piper of Hamelin; clothing as per legend." the Entity stated. "Don't believe the bad bits that have come down to you over the years." And then it left them, rapidly, amongst a scattering of purple soil and leaf debris. Harry and Esma attempted to follow it, and as they did, a hauntingly beautiful melody echoed across the landscape.

40

"We need to go back to R1," Oscar said to Dearden.

"Why's that?"

"I've been thinking about the metal door frame. I reckon it was slightly warmer than the ambient temperature of the lab. I knew when we were there last that there's active electronics inside it. Problem is, Jem, that there's been so much going on here. You're used to it but I'm not."

Dearden smiled and nodded in agreement.

"If I can get back into Villiers' lab I may get to grips with the physics behind Harry's disappearance."

"That place hides a multitude of secrets, Oscar," Dearden said, "We can go straight into R1 without special permission now. But we'll contact Mike Ramsay, he'll want to be in on it." The others in the great hall were attentive as Dearden rang Ramsay at Kineton Base.

When the call was done Dearden spoke to Beggs. "I want you to stay here, Beggsy. Team up with Gil Heskin . . . Gil," Heskin stepped forward. "You and Beggsy make sure Dearden Hall stays secure while the rest of us go into R1."

*   *   *

"Feel this," Oscar said, removing his hand from the stainless steel door frame. Jules reached out and touched it.

"There's electronic activity behind this panel," she was close to the right side of the door frame and she picked up a slight buzzing sound from inside the fabrication. She stood to one side as Oscar moved close to the fabricated frame with a flat-bladed screwdriver. A series of stainless steel set-screws held a panel onto the front face of both the right and left side of the door frame. The right side of the frame was slightly warmer than the left, so Oscar undid the screws on the right and removed the panel. He handed it to Doughty, who laid it on the floor.

Oscar got close to the frame and peered inside. There were the usual components one would expect with electronic circuitry of the nineteen-fifties, and there was something unexpected too.

"Where the hell did Villiers get those from?" Jules questioned. Placed vertically in the circuitry were a number of crystals, which looked like a miniature version of the two great crystals in the Hub. The crystals were active, coruscating violently from within with swirling random shapes of a scarlet colour amidst the deepest black. Each of the crystals had a metallic ring fixed horizontally around its centre. Attached to each ring was a flying lead which had its other end attached to the stainless steel door-frame.

"Magnetron arrangement again," Templestone observed.

"And there's only one place Villiers could have got those crystals. The Hub," Dearden said. He changed the wolf's leash into his left hand and felt the metalwork with his right. Dearden looked at Tomahawk, who was surprisingly quiet and he saw the fiery activity within the crystals reflected in the creature's eyes.

Jules stepped back from the others grouped around the door frame. She had recalled the Wiltshire dig she had been involved with a few years back, where she found another, although smaller, version of the Hub. She had kept quiet about it at the time. It would have been a complication too far to bring that other place into open knowledge. Anyway, it had been buried again . . . out of sight out of mind. But how many more such machines could there be dotted around the country in obscure places. Nodes in an ancient alien network. She shrugged-off the memories. "Villiers was years ahead of his time with this stuff," She said. "And this construction is over sixty years old." Jules analysed the components. "This circuitry is not sub-miniature, but for the nineteen-fifties it's in a different league to the electronics of the time."

"Those crystals in the circuitry . . . where did the knowledge come from to tell Villiers to use them, particularly in a magnetron configuration, it was decidedly odd all those years back," Oscar mused in a quiet voice. And then louder, addressing Templestone, "When you were telling me about the Hub and its function, you mentioned harmonics."

"Yeah, Harry and I back-engineered and built a miniature version of the Hub. It worked in harmony with the big one in the forest. Harry said he thought the process was a form of quantum entanglement."

Oscar nodded. "I wonder if that's what Villiers has stumbled across. It looks as though he got hold of some of the components from the Hub like you did."

Dearden looked thoughtful. "That does seem likely," he said. "Villiers was experimenting here during the nineteen-fifties, which was when my grandfather, Josiah Dearden lived in Dearden Hall Farm. It looks as though he and Villiers knew each-other and found a way into the Hub back then."

"Have you ever heard anything about your grand-daddy getting' into the Hub?" Wynter asked.

"Not a thing, but nothing surprises me around here."

"Where did Max get his knowledge about the Hub?" Will Pierpoint asked. Willoughby Pierpoint had been a friend of Jem's father, Maxwell Dearden . . . as had Bill Templestone.

"Maybe Joss Dearden took my dad into the forest on his shoulders the same as my dad did with me. Dad showed me the Hub and said it was an engine-house. I was probably about two or three years old but I remember the event as if it was yesterday. Dad's diaries show he had a good knowledge of the Hub . . . looks as though my grandfather knew about it too."

"OK, let's get back to the point," Oscar said. "The evidence is that your grandfather knew Charles Villiers and they found a way into the Hub."

"And they found the cupboards where the spare components for the Hub are stored," Jules said.

"Which indicates that Villiers tried to back-engineer the mechanics that make the Hub function. Point is that he got a totally unexpected result," Jules said. "His result isn't the same as what the Hub achieves."

"It looks as if the components we see in Professor Villiers' set-up enables his structure to connect to the Grid, but in a multidimensional mode," concluded Oscar.

"I understand your thinking so far but the question is, how the hell does this information help us rescue Harry and Esma?" Pierpoint challenged.

There was no rational explanation for what happened next. At least, no rational explanation according to Earth-type rationale. There was a sudden movement and the sound of heavy footsteps behind the group standing around the stainless-steel door frame in R1. They all reacted quickly, but in a variety of ways. It was like one of those *'look behind you'* pantomime moments when something frightened the kids and they grasped their dad's hand.

There was the sound of running footsteps and then Villiers' old oak desk moved as if it was made of balsa wood. The footsteps sound stopped a short distance away from Cell

One, standing near the door frame. Tomahawk stood bolt upright, faced the sound and loped forward. Ordinarily, upon any form of intrusion, Tomahawk reacted with a teeth-bared snarl, but this time the intruder was greeted as an equal. Red Cloud, who was amongst the group with Possum Chaser, afterwards said that the wolf welcomed the intruder like a trusted member of the pack.

Oscar reached into his tote bag for the infrared heat detector, switched it on and pointed it in the direction the sound came from. There was still a background noise . . . slight movement, and the sound of breathing.

"What happens now, my man?" Wynter asked, to no-one in particular. He got no answer, until . . .

"Can you see me, Oscar?" The voice came from about four yards away and startled them all. The old-fashioned overhead lighting of Villiers' lab picked out a mirage-like interference with the furniture behind where the Entity was standing.

Oscar looked in the direction of the voice, which sounded cultured and friendly. He could see, on the screen of the infrared camera, the image of the Entity resolving itself from infrared data to a standard spectrographic image. Red Cloud was standing behind Oscar's shoulder and was able to see the Entity morphing to a visible person.

"We can see you well now," the Lakota Sioux Chieftain said. The Entity's clothing came as a surprise. "It is good to see you . . . what is your name?"

Dearden thought how strange it was, under the present surreal conditions, how Red Cloud could communicate so easily with the alien; asking questions as if it were an everyday experience. He was glad of Red's presence right now.

"My name is of little consequence. It is what I *do* that

counts. The nearest you will get to understanding my name is the phrase, *Longing for what might be achieved.* What I do, my purpose, is *to put things right.*"

"Like we do in SHaFT," Pierpoint said, assuming that the Entity had heard of SHaFT. It seemed it had.

"The motives are just the same, but my sphere of operations is far wider than yours."

"How wide?"

"You entered the Virtuality, didn't you?"

"We did; and we went down to the deepest level."

"Level Four Hundred and Seventy, the newest Reality they have revealed. It is an interesting Reality. I came out of it rather fast."

"I know," Oscar said. "We saw the skid-marks through the mud when we were in that Level of the Virtuality. I have since wondered if it was you who caused it."

Wynter needed an answer to something that had been puzzling him. "Are you the Pied Piper?" he asked.

The Entity shot him a glance. "Ah . . . Hamelin, all those years ago. Yes, I got rid of the rats. The problem was that a great many children were being educated in a school near an open sewer. The plague of rats lived off the waste. All of Hamelin's waste from the population and its tanning industry flowed into the River Weser, and typhus and cholera were rampant. Something had to be done. I stepped in and helped."

"What happened?" Clive Fraser asked.

"For a start, they needed isolating from the source of the problem and the rest of the population. I went back at night and burned the school down."

"How about the children?" Storm Petrel asked.

"I transferred them to a different planet in the Reality

where we are now, the Prime dimension. It was a very advanced planet I transferred them to. It seemed like Paradise compared to ancient Hamelin. The children were cured and they soon settled in."

"What, all of them?"

"Every last one. Afterwards they lived a long life and after many generations their descendants are still alive. They have a legend about their arrival from a distant world. But listen. I must go to my origin. I have a task to do . . . one that has to do with my metabolism. You need to be able see me without dousing me with liquid."

The Entity went out of Villiers' Lab as quick as it entered. The old desk was knocked aside the same as when it came in.

"Looks as though it's clumsy; moves before it gets its brain into gear," Wynter remarked.

"It moves so quick. See how it barged into the old desk? It moved like it was made of Balsa wood and the Entity wasn't fazed by it." Clive was working out what would occur if he collided with Villiers' oak desk in a similar way.

"We have just seen evidence that its metabolism is totally different to ours," Jules said. She didn't yet want to draw conclusions because there was no empirical evidence provided by experiment. She had intended to ask the Entity the purpose of the screen set into the wall of the cave, and why the Entity's passage through the forest was marked by a trail of fungus, but the invisible guy vanished before she had chance to question him.

"Shall we give him name?" Rowan asked.

"Piper," Jules suggested . . . and then, "I wish the sod didn't keep disappearing."

Mitch Doughty thought invisibility would have been an

advantage in some of SHaFT's missions. "Invisibility gives it the edge where security is involved, Jules," he said.

Dearden was trying to think through how to rein Piper in. "Tell you what, guys," he said. "It looks as though we've got Piper onside. Remember how he dealt with Uberatu and his mob when they came calling. They were disarmed and scared witless. So maybe, when Piper appears again, we should just be straight and tell him to sit down and take things easy for a while so we can discuss the situation about Harry and Esma."

"Did you take in what he said last, that he was going to do something about his metabolism?" Red Cloud said.

"Probably gets sick of getting wet," Storm Petrel suggested, thinking what it would be like having to get soaked so the others could see her.

Oscar and Jules were apart from the others, analysing the interior of the door frame, discussing the circuitry. "I think we need to get Lan-Si-Nu here," Oscar concluded. "If Villiers has stumbled on a way to create a harmonic reaction with the Grid he's found a way to bypass all of the Virtuality gateways the Wasiri created under the Hub."

"Thing is, his method of doing it is way out of control," Jules added.

*　*　*

Dearden, Jules and Oscar were in the Hub, in the room of the exhibits, off which Lan-Si-Nu and his two crew members had their private quarters. Usually, when the Wasiri-Chanchiyans went missing, they were in their living space having some down-time.

Dearden had a rubber mallet with him and he was using it to tap the wall, trying to discover where it was hollow, which would reveal where the doorway was to the aliens' hideaway.

Suddenly, to the left of where he was tapping, a partition eased backward and then sideways, revealing a brightly lit interior.

"I thought I heard some knocking. Come in," Fen-Nu said.

The three Earth people crossed the threshold into yet another part of the Hub that was new to them. They were in a circular entrance area, where there were nine other doorways apart from the entrance leading off the room. Fen-Nu beckoned them to follow her and she touched the centre of the middle door. It slid sideways and she walked through.

The interior of this room was laid out for relaxation. There were couches, tables and chairs, all ergonomically shaped to fit the physique of the Wasiri. Some of the seats were lower. Fen-Nu pointed to these seats and indicated for them to sit.

"We have been expecting you," she said.

"How come?" Dearden asked.

"Events occurring to do with the Entity point toward the need for collaboration between you Earth people and we Wasiri."

"He is an elusive character," Thal-Nar interjected.

"But he is on our side," Dearden said.

"Definitely. He supports the Prime Directive of universal peace," Fen-Nu added.

"Are you sure he can be trusted?" Oscar asked.

"Implicitly."

"Then we'll do our best to communicate with him. By the way, we've called him Piper because of his historical context, remember?"

"Hamelin?"

"Yes. Piper told us the events of the legend are fact."

277

"Our ancestors who were involved with the Grid at the time of the Pied Piper were intrigued with the events that went on in Hamelin," Fen-Nu said.

"I'm not surprised . . . but thinking about the current situation, Piper's interest in us could be used to our advantage. And there's an obvious link between Piper and Tomahawk that could be helpful."

"Seems so Oscar. There's definitely a strong connection," Dearden said. "How about this. Tomahawk is an instinctive hunter. He has superbly sensitive ears, and his wolf sense of smell is a hundred times more efficient than we human's. Maybe Piper needs Tomahawk to hunt something down."

"Whenever Piper shows up Tom gets cosied up to him."

"Sits on his foot," Jules grinned."

"I saw you sitting on Clive's foot the other day, Jules," it was Oscar's turn to grin.

"What is this custom of sitting on the foot that different species of you Earth beings find so special?" Fen-Nu was interested in the customs and traditions of life alien to her.

Jules batted-off the embarrassment and got Fen-Nu thinking. "We often sit on the foot of those we are close to," she said.

Fen-Nu wrinkled up her nose, "That is disgusting."

"Everyone to their own customs," Jules smirked. "Anyway, Tomahawk sat on Piper's foot, so that suggests they're close. Do you agree, Jem?"

"Seems so, but how do we use that to get Harry and Esma back?" Dearden threw the question open to all in the room and waited for a response.

It was Oscar who answered. "I have an idea," he said. "It may be a long shot but it's worth a try."

"Any suggestion is worth a try. We've got nothing at

present, just a few coded hints and some very weird technology."

"OK, Jem . . . think this through. What *do* we have? First, with the lower levels of the Hub we have the use of technology that links to alternative Realities. That technology gives us an advantage when there's convincing evidence Harry and Esma have transferred to an alternative reality. Because of the information suggesting Level Four-seventy has a severe dis-harmony problem it is assumed that is where Harry and Esma have transferred too.

"Next point, the Piper can access Realities at will . . . and at speed; that will be useful in the search. Point three, Piper is compelled to return to Earth regularly to search for the one he has lost. He *won't* abscond. Now, I think we have a very powerful tool at our disposal. A tool that works in a highly instinctive mode, Tomahawk Shahn of Offchurch."

"And Tom has an affinity with Piper," said Dearden.

"There are other things to consider," Jules said. "The Piper centres his visits on Leofwin's Hundred. With the choice of all the world's continents he returns to our neck of the woods. And there's the footprints and fungal growths which concentrate around Uberatu's Oak. Piper keeps going back there. At the back of the waterfall there's the cave with the hi-tech screen in the wall. So, our part of the Earth is special to Piper. A focus. We must get to know him better and maybe help him. That could help us get Harry and Esma back."

Commander Lan-Si-Nu and his two compatriots had followed the reasoning. "What will you do now," he asked.

Oscar stood. "What we will do is this . . ." and he explained the plan he had devised.

41

It was impossible to tell when the Piper would return. But Oscar reasoned that he would return because of his apparent link with Tomahawk and his desire to be in Leofwin's Hundred. "It would be good to know why the Piper needs Tomahawk's company," he said.

Dearden looked around to see if anyone else would hear what he was going to say to Oscar. Rowan was the only other one close enough to hear. Rowan and Jem always shared how they felt, held nothing back.

"To me, Tomahawk is special. Got me out of a time when I was at my lowest. I was very close to a girl before I met Rowan." Jem caught Rowan's glance and she understood. "Jackie Mason was killed and shortly afterward I bought Tomahawk. He filled a void." Rowan reached for Jem's hand, held it tight.

Dearden was quiet, locked in thought.

"Jem!" Oscar prodded.

"Yeah . . . yeah, the void was filled, but it's in the past now." Dearden briefly thought of how the past of a thousand years ago had come up trumps for him with Rowan. And then he felt a sharp pang of jealousy. "How anyone so alien as the Piper can get close to Tomahawk beggars belief."

"Who knows why? The point is, I'm certain Piper will head back here to Leofwin's Hundred, and when he does we'll try to enlist his help," Oscar said.

* * *

Gil and Frieda Heskin were back in the forest, near Uberatu's Oak, foraging for more fungus. It seemed to be prolific there. The knocking came again from the tree. It was as if it was in surround-sound, coming from all around. And this time the knocking was distinctly slower. Gil recognised the sounds and the gaps between them, and he automatically went into the mindset he used to adopt in Portsmouth when he was helping John Partington practice for his forthcoming Morse-test. Gil closed his eyes, thinking back. Listening intently.

Dit-dit-dit-dit, **H.** Dit-dah, **A.** Dit-dah-dit, **R.** Dit-dah-dit, **R.** Dah-dit-dah-dah, **Y.**

"Hear that knocking, Frie?" She cocked her head on one side and heard it. "It's code," he said. "And you'd never guess what it's saying."

Just then, before Frieda could answer, a blurred shape came hurtling toward her out of the clearing in front of the Hub. Gil was startled when Frieda let out a scream like he'd never heard before. Playful screams there had been at times, but never a wild scream like this one. The hairs on the back of Gil's neck prickled.

It was getting toward dusk, which didn't help. Being in the primeval forest in broad daylight was OK, but at dusk . . . no, and after Frieda's scream he wished he was far away from this place of shadows and creeping things.

He turned cautiously to face whatever it was that so upset his wife, and there, three feet in front of him was a figure he recognised dressed in the most brightly coloured clothes, a jacket, quartered across the chest in two colours. Trousers, quartered in the same style.

"It would be better if you came to us more slowly." Gil said, curtly. "Don't frighten Frie like that again."

"I am sorry, I must put some restraint on my speed here on the Earth. It is difficult for me, you see, because I was created for trans-dimensional travel, where speed is of little consequence."

The apparition seemed friendly, just as it was at the cave behind Shadow Brook's waterfall.

"Where is Tomahawk?" The question took the Heskins by surprise. It was a normal sort of question, but an unusual question from someone who, demonstrably was so alien.

He was holding a flute-type instrument. "Do you want me to play?" he asked. Which was also unusual, an alien offering to play an instrument in the ancient forest.

"Play away," Gil said. He thought it best to go along with what the alien wanted. The three of them sat. Gil and Frieda were into Country and Western Dolly Parton sort of stuff but they didn't expect music of that ilk from the Alien.

He put the instrument to his lips.

The most beautiful and haunting melody Gil and Frieda had ever heard came forth. It drifted into the forest and, as it did so, it seemed as though the world stood still. Even the creatures of the forest ceased their busy chatter. The notes from the Piper eased their melodious way into the greenery of Leofwin's Hundred.

Gil Heskin felt the music deep inside, It touched a chord, as the saying goes, and he glanced at Frieda. He handed her a handkerchief to help with the tears, that he also felt.

It was a short melody, but one that both Gil and Frieda could have listened to for hours on end. When the Piper stopped Gil felt a touch lost. He wanted to just sit there and continue to listen.

The birds began their song again.

"Come on, Frie, we'll have to get back," Gil said.

"Do we have to?"

"I think so. Mister Dearden will wonder where we've got

to." He stood and looked around. Wondered what this strange place was all about. He held out his hand to Frieda. She grasped it and he helped her stand. He looked at the Entity. He was putting the flute away in a large pocket inside his jacket.

"I've got something to tell you," the Entity said.

"What is it?"

"Tell Jem Dearden that I know about Harry and Esma."

It was when they were on the way back through the forest track that Gil made his decision. "Frie, You know Bill Templestone and Harry were close?"

She nodded.

"I have a plan," he said. "I'm going to let Templestone know we've heard the Morse Code coming from the tree. Then I'll suggest to him that we send a message back."

"How will we do that?"

42

"There's something we need to tell you." Gil Heskin said. On the way back to Dearden Hall, he and Frieda had talked about the weird stuff they had experienced. They decided that they would only tell Dearden *some* of what happened.

Gil shifted about uncomfortably. Frieda grasped his hand.

Dearden noticed.

"Don't worry, spill it out," he said.

"We went into the forest to collect some of that fungus—"

"Did you . . . what happened?"

"Something was there."

"What was it?" Dearden became attentive.

"The creature we saw at the cave. It's come back."

"It spoke English," Frieda added.

Heskin was obviously nervous, "And there's more . . . this time it was visible," he said.

"OK . . . don't worry Gil. Odd things are happening here. Tell me what you know."

Heskin thought for a beat before he carried on. "It told us to tell you that it knows about Harry and Esma."

Dearden looked Heskin in the eye. "OK Gil, this is important, did it say anything else?" The Heskins looked more uncomfortable."

Frieda blurted out, "It said Harry and Esma are OK, and it asked about Tomahawk." Her husband looked first at her and then uncertainly at Dearden. Dearden was very protective with the wolf. Any sort of threat against it was taken seriously, so Heskin was surprised at the calm response.

"What did it say about Tom?" Dearden asked. He felt a nudge of unease.

"It asked where Tomahawk was. Tomahawk was with us when we first saw the alien near the cave." Dearden remembered looking down into the dell at the waterfall and seeing Tomahawk, almost all the way down the incline, fiercely pulling on the leash Gil Heskin was holding."

"Did Piper say anything else?"

"No."

*   *   *

"I think we need to take Tomahawk to the cave and wait until Piper turns up," Oscar said to Dearden.

"And when he does show up, what then?"

"Ask him straight out to help us."

"Problem is that he's elusive. Always seems to be on the move, as though his concentration gets diverted easily."

"I think that communication takes place on multiple levels, subliminally, even, so that he scoots off to undertake whatever he perceives as an imperative."

"He needs to understand that Harry and Esma are an imperative for us."

Oscar and Dearden, with Tomahawk on the leash, arrived at the edge of the deep hollow where Shadow Brook spilled some fifty feet over rocks into the pool. Dearden noted how idyllic was the scene. But he also felt uncertainty, as if he was once again entering unknown territory. Piper was going to be difficult to deal with. There seemed to be no rationale for his behaviour. No Earth-like logic was associated with his manifestation, other than an apparent affinity to Tomahawk and Leofwin's Hundred.

It was a hot day, at the end of May and after the trek through the forest the coolness of the dell as they descended,

285

was welcome. Particularly refreshing was the spray from Shadow Brook that drenched them as they walked behind the waterfall to get to the cave.

"This is different," Dearden said, looking around as they entered the cave. A warm light exuded from the walls.

"Looks more lived in now," Oscar said. "He's done some housework." The floor had been cleared of forest debris. He glanced to the back of the cave when he heard a movement. Dearden heard it too and they cautiously stepped along to the bend in the cave. As before, in the place where the cave became larger, the panel set into the wall was illuminated. This time a tall figure was standing in front of it. He glanced in their direction. Saw Tomahawk, who pulled strongly on the leash.

"Let him come to me, please," the Piper said. Dearden undid the leash and Tomahawk went to the alien's side.

"We need to talk," Oscar said.

"I thought you might, that's why I'm here. You are concerned about Harry and Esma, aren't you?" The question was unexpected.

"How do you know that?"

"Let's just say that an imbalance across the realities has been created by some of you people. I sense imbalance . . . not only to do with Harry and Esma, but with any major cause. I address imbalance and correct it . . . that is my purpose."

"We need some sort of constructive plan to tackle the imbalance caused by Harry," Dearden stated. "We think you can help us but we don't even know your name, or where you are from. And we don't know if we can trust you." Dearden always talked straight from the hip.

"Of course. Let us sit for a while and become acquainted."

Further on in the cavern were some chairs and a table, all of sleek design. They followed the Piper and sat.

"You have changed," Dearden said. "We can see you now. It was disturbing for us to only see your footprints on the ground."

"It was weird," Oscar added.

"I know. Harry and Esma had the same problem with me. I have had my metabolism altered so that you can see me."

Oscar was handling the situation well considering that his introduction to the alien nature of Leofwin's Hundred was only a few days back. "You have seen Harry?" he asked.

"I have."

"Is he alright?" Dearden asked. "And Esma . . . is she OK?"

"They are both managing to live as near to a stable life as they can, considering they are on a world that is totally alien to them.

Oscar nodded, and then Dearden asked, "A friend of ours from the planet Wasiri-Poya told us that you are the Pied Piper of Hamelin; is that right?"

"I was. In a previous awakening a long time ago, I was in that role. Not now, of course. But oh, how I danced . . . fast out of Old Hamelin with the children because their lives were at stake. The elders and the more learned knew the effects of Bubonic plague and the threat it was causing the town and its children."

Oscar frowned, picking up on the Entity's apparent purpose, that of addressing conflict.

"Why didn't you do something about the Great Plague in London town?"

"I did. I set the fire."

"But that killed thousands of people."

"Far less than would have died had the plague continued. My action was for the greater good. you see, I am only able to use the science and resources currently available within the areas where conflict exists, otherwise my actions themselves would cause imbalance."

"How about the problem with the imbalance caused by Harry and Esma?"

"There are far more resources available where they are than there were back in old London Town or Hamelin. But their return will not be easy."

"OK. Answer me this." Dearden looked the Piper in the eye. There is conflict all over the place," he thought for a second, "Well, I should say that there *has* been conflict on the Earth, for thousands of years." He remembered the Prime Directive of Peace that the Earth was now subject to. "World Wars One and Two. All of the wars over the centuries . . . why haven't you intervened with those?"

"Things got out of hand. There has only been so much I and the others can do." There is a force about that creates disharmony. It is my purpose to hunt it down and destroy it."

"Has that force made itself apparent on Nibiru?" Dearden asked.

"It has. Evil does seem to be centred on that planet. It is a dark place."

Dearden thought of SHaFT, the Shock and Force Team for justice and wondered if it could be raised to address issues on a cosmic level. *Nos Successio Procul Totus Sumptus. We Succeed At All Costs.*

"When can we get started with Harry and Esma?" He asked the Piper.

"Now. But first, in order to validate your use of this method of transfer across the Realities, we must visit the

Innermost Hall of Toraddon. If your validation is successful, you will be able to travel the Hypergrid in much the same way that I do. Of necessity, there will be some minor changes to your metabolism. There is a Buffer, an interface between Realities, that will prevent you going any further in your quest than Toraddon's Innermost Hall until your metabolism is revised. We must ensure your passage through the Buffer will be safe for you. Also, for all concerned, your trustworthiness to keep within strict guidelines needs to be guaranteed before general Reality Transfer is allowed.

Leave all that to me. We are talking about trans-dimensional travel. It is far from straightforward and for you Human Beings and our friend Tomahawk, the transfer to a different dimension is almost unheard of at present. Please stay seated." Piper stood quickly, went to the screen set into the wall of the cavern and stood in front of it.

A series of events then occurred over a period of ten hours or so, that Dearden was destined to remember for a long while afterwards.

*   *   *

Dearden was exhausted after his excursion with Oscar when they went into the cavern deep in Leofwin's Hundred. Unusually, he slept for over twelve hours. The Cell One team recognised Jem and Rowan needed time together, and there was no urgent reason for them to remain at Dearden Hall, so they dispersed to their homes. When he awoke, he and Rowan were enjoying some quiet time in the great hall and Dearden explained, with some incredulity, what occurred after they went into the cavern.

"The Piper went to the panel set in the wall of the cave

and touched it in some way. He touched a control and then the cave changed." Rowan glanced at him disbelievingly.

"How did it change?"

"The entrance was sealed from the forest outside. It was as if the cave became a capsule. The Piper said the name of the place we were going to, *Toraddon* and then the three of us stepped into the panel in the wall."

"Tell me more," Rowan said, snuggling up close.

43

They stepped through the screen in the cavern. There appeared to be no surroundings to the space they were in apart from the blackness of infinity studded with myriads of stars and galaxies. Dearden and Oscar felt disoriented but they focussed on Piper, who walked ahead six paces to a transparent shutter with markings on it to make it manifest. It shifted aside as they approached it and Piper led the way through.

The interior of the place where they emerged was brightly lit and there was a lot of activity going on. The different types of life-forms going about their business must have been commonplace because, apart from the occasional glance, the presence of the people from Earth went unnoticed.

Most of the inhabitants busying around were humanoid, although with multitudinous variations of size, shape and colour. Their voices came in various cadences, from rich and beautiful, to harsh and grunting. Dearden concluded that the humanoid type must be widely spread throughout the universe.

Dearden caught up with Oscar, who was walking normally despite the leg repaired with titanium.

Dearden nudged Oscar's arm. "Do feel OK?"

"Great. How about You?"

"I seem OK." They caught up with Piper. "Is this Toraddon?" Dearden asked.

"It is. And you have just experienced your first dimensional transfer. Toraddon equates to near normality for all of its visitors. And its access from nodes like the one in the cave behind the waterfall is designed to provide access for the carbon-based species of life inhabiting the Realities. That is its special quality. Onward through the Toraddon Portal other Realities are accessed in a different way. The Reality-transfer needs of life-forms that are silicon-based, for example, have to be addressed in a different manner."

Oscar looked at Piper quizzically. Piper saw the look and responded. "The innermost workings of this planet create an equalizing for all of its visitors from different realities. Our metabolism is morphed by means of our DNA being slightly re-structured to achieve a standardisation that allows onward Trans-dimensional travel without injury."

"Do these folks look different in their own Reality to how we are perceiving them?" Oscar asked.

"Maybe they do slightly. But the minor change that occurs to everyone who visits Toraddon to prepare for Trans-dimensional travel is on a molecular level."

They walked onward in silence as Dearden and Oscar took in what Piper told them. Oscar tried to understand the complexity of how a planet could alter the metabolism of its visitors. He shook his head and changed on to a less complicated subject. "What should we call you? You must have a name," he said.

"Of course I have a name. And Piper reeled off a series of unintelligible sounds. "But you have been calling me *Piper*, so that will do. It will be easier on your tongue."

Piper led them forward inside the building, which had towering architecture and light radiating from its walls, similar to the illumination in the cave in Leofwin's Hundred. "This place is the seat of High-learning and Science. It is the Innermost Hall of Toraddon," Piper said. "I came here to have my metabolism changed so I would be visible to you.

Now you have undergone a minor metabolic change."

"Is it a permanent change?" Oscar asked. He was a touch fearful and wondered how he would have been changed to function trans-dimensionally, and thought of the titanium in his leg.

"It can be either temporary or permanent, it is the choice of the individual, or whatever gives best functionality, within reason."

Oscar felt his previously injured leg and smiled with relief.

"Your leg is as good as new, Oscar. The titanium was converted to calcium in the blink of an eye. My metabolism has been changed for as long as my state of visibility is needed to fulfil the task in hand, that of correcting the disharmony created by your Earth people. They have crossed a dimensional boundary in a way that could spike a trend of chaos and destruction. You have to understand that dimensional transfer has to be rigidly controlled at its interfaces. The physical laws of one reality may conflict with another and be irreconcilable if transfer is not accomplished in a way that has been proven safe."

"So, the situation Harry caused is *really* serious?" Dearden asked.

"It is. We have to find your people and ensure that the physics of the gateway they have created is fully understood and then either disposed of or its physics assimilated into the transfer system that has been proved safe over millennia. The disharmony has to be smoothed out because it is on a path leading to destruction.

"However, follow me, and do as I do," Piper said. "I must tell you that a major source of disharmony are the inhabitants of Nibiru. There is a possibility that they could cause a volatile situation. Something dark drives them. They must never be allowed to gain entry to the Grid, let alone the force-field involved with the Hyper Grid that connects the Realities . . . But enough. There is urgency involved in the situation, we must go."

Piper stepped up the pace down a wide roadway where there was a lot of activity. He pointed to a narrower lane leading off to the right with an ornate sign above it, and he turned into it. They eventually came to a room that appeared to be a waiting area. Seats were arranged around three-quarters of the perimeter. A large, constantly fluctuating veil-like area, that had the appearance of a holograph was in front of the seats. "Until I join you again take utmost precautions about how you proceed. You have to be on your own for the Consolidation, the next part of your Trans-dimensional travel preparation," Piper warned. He rapidly punched some keys at the side of the panel . . . first a key that, had Dearden and Oscar been able to translate the numeral, they would have seen represented the figure *1*, followed by a symbol that represented the function *JOIN* followed by the symbols representing *470*, and then he was gone.

44

"We ought to go and see how they are," Villiers said to Martell.

"Why?

"That young man shows a great deal of promise. He may have a point with the Mycorrhizal network he was telling us about."

"Do you really think so?"

"I do. Apart from which, we don't have many choices, so it's best to try any method we can to get us back home."

Martell considered this. He had lost touch with the reasoning capacity he used to have and generally gave only cursory thought to events that occurred these days. The whole situation, after he and Villiers passed through the Switch had forced his mind to abscond from reality. These days, Dick Martell was often driven by primal fears and anger, and tended to live his life on an instinctive level.

"OK Charlie, let's go and see what they're doing." He went into the shelter and looked behind to see if Villiers was watching. He wasn't. Martell slipped a sharp object into the pocket of his tattered jacket. He had spent a long while shaping the object. Whittling it down by rubbing it continually with a rough, carborundum-like stone when Villiers was asleep.

* * *

When Villiers and Martell arrived at Harry and Esma's camp the introductory talk was brief and to the point. Harry indicated for Villiers and Martell to go into the shelter, where they sat on the ground, softened by piles of wispy foliage.

Harry was a sensitive sort of guy. During his teens he had gone through a phase when he was uncomfortably shy. In town once he went into a shop doorway to escape, as he thought, the attention of those around him. A couple of years after that his self-confidence had grown to the point where he spoke his mind with a *what the hell* sort of attitude to others, but his sensitive side left him with the ability to pick up other's feelings and sometimes Harry even picked-up Oscar's thinking with a sort of uncanny *awareness*.

Both of them, being of a scientific frame of mind, researched this level of communication and came to the conclusion that they sometimes did pick up each-others' thoughts in a way that was extraordinary . . . way outside the accepted normality of communication. It would be good, Harry contemplated in a lonely moment on his far-away planet, if this communication could take place in a more constructive way.

When they settled down inside the hut, he mentioned his efforts of communication to Villiers and Martell. "I've kept up a constant schedule with the Morse but so far there hasn't been a response. I'm convinced this will work because of what Esma heard coming from the oak near the Hub, the Scop Ac, as she calls it. She is sure the sound was identical to what we hear coming from that thing," Harry pointed to the megalithic growth they could see through the open doorway. He recalled the noises he had heard in the great hollow oak when he had been with Templestone. There was no doubting the similarity and that convinced him that he was right to use the tree to try communicating with those back on Earth.

The conversation with Villiers was suddenly interrupted by Esma. She rushed to the open door, startling the others.

"What is happening?" Harry quickly followed her, and what he saw in the alien sky frightened him.

Harry and Esma were used to seeing the sky local to Leofwin's Hundred very quickly darken and turn stormy when the Hub became active. What they saw on this horizon was different to anything they had experienced in Leofwin's Hundred. This was huge and menacing.

Above the distant hills on the far horizon, a dark region interspersed with tendrils of fiery light was amassing, growing in size as the four stood watching.

"That is not good'" Harry said, as he saw that the phenomenon was moving quickly in their direction. "Have you seen this before?" he asked Villiers.

"Never anything like that," the professor said. Martell shook his head and stayed silent. Harry saw Martell's eyes widen with fear as he saw a great mass of debris in the distance, being carried on a fierce wind.

"Hear that?" Harry now had to shout to make himself heard above the growing tempest.

"What can you hear?" Villiers shouted, trying to identify what Harry heard. Harry ignored Villiers, grasped Esma's arm and pulled. She ran with Harry, who indicated for the others to follow, as he headed for the nearby giant growth, which was hardly moving even with the increasing violence of the wind. Harry heard the noise again as he ran. It was unmistakable, and Esma and the others heard it too, the knocking sound coming from the growth they were heading to.

"Know what that knocking is?" Harry shouted. The sound was repeating. He geared up like he used to when nearing the finishing line in the school cross country race.

Dit-dit-dit-dit, the noise went. And then, **dit-dah, dit-**

dah-dit, dit-dah-dit, dah-dit-dah-dah.

"SHaFT's on the case. They've heard us," Harry shouted. And then the noise came again, louder still this time because they had reached the growth. Harry felt the bark, felt the vibration as the sounds repeated.

Dit-dit-dit-dit, dit-dah, dit-dah-dit, dit-dah-dit, dah-dit-dah-dah. There was a brief pause. And then,

"Know what it's saying?" Harry grinned as he shouted above the tempestuous wind. He could feel heat as the maelstrom neared them. "It's my name . . . **HARRY** . . . in Morse code. And there's something else." Harry listened intently. Guys, they're saying, **Are you OK.**

Which was when an aperture appeared in the trunk of the mighty structure and a voice shouted, "In, quickly." It didn't take more than a second for them to react. Harry shoved Esma in, then indicated for Villiers and Martell to get in, then he followed. As soon as they got inside, the wall sealed behind them and the noise of the tempest outside couldn't be heard.

Harry looked around for the source of the familiar voice but no-one was there. "Did you hear the voice?" Harry asked.

Martell nodded.

"Is it familiar to you?"

"Are you Joking?" Martell grinned.

"No . . . have you heard that voice before, Prof?"

"I heard it here. The only voices I have heard in this God-forsaken place are Dick's, yours and Esma's. Why, have you heard it before?

"Yes, I have, and so has Esma. Here's another question. Have either of you seen footprints appearing in the soil by someone invisible to your eyes."

Martell sniggered and Professor Villiers, who was normally impressed with Harry's reasoning smiled broadly.

Esma came to Harry's defence. "There is person who we not see who walks here. His voice we heard now."

"Esma's right." Harry thought it was pointless elaborating. If he was presented with the same information he too would find it incredible. But he added, "There is an alien on this planet with a friendly disposition who is likely to help us."

*   *   *

The interior of the giant organism was roughly circular, and made rugged by slowly writhing tendrils. There was a downward sloping path at the far side of the circular space and a few hundred paces further on, the tunnel opened into a sizeable cavern where there was a centrally placed crystal. In many ways, other than the tendrils, the surroundings were similar to the Hub in Leofwin's Hundred. Villiers had seen the great crystal in the building deep in the forest when he was with Joss Dearden way in the past. His memory of its detail was blurred, damaged, because of the trauma of their marooning.

"What the hell is all this moving stuff?" Villiers said, looking around. "Is it what I think you are going to tell us?"

"Hyphae of the Mycorrhizal network . . ."

"So you were right," Martell said.

"And it's on a macro scale," said Harry. Grasping Esma's hand he led the way through the white-coloured tendrils. As they proceeded, the Hyphae shifted out of their way, allowing them free passage through the winding cavern which was lit by a gentle, glowing light. They reached a downward sloping path where Harry stopped, assessing the situation in front of them. He was disconcerted with the light . . . whether or not he could trust it, because it reminded him of a time some years back when he was holidaying with his folks. He went

299

strolling on the beach one night because he couldn't sleep. There had been no moon that night, but a phosphorescent glow bathed the near reaches of the sea in an ethereal light.

The reason for the sleepless night was that he had met a girl, a dark-haired Cypriot beauty who held out so much promise, and the forces of youthful love had consumed him during the hours after she left the coffee shop with the promise that she would be back at seven that evening.

She stood him up. His nerves were shattered and he walked alone on the beach surrounded by an ethereal light that reached deep inside and calmed the romance down.

A similar phosphorescent light exuding from within the majestic alien growth allowed them to see their way forward. It also had a calming effect, just as had the oceanic phosphorescence that helped Harry get over being jilted. "It's the Mycorrhizal network that I thought exists here," Harry was exuberant.

Villiers looked intensely at Harry, sizing him up. He had a growing respect for the young man. He had met scores of clever young men and women in his tenure in the Old Cav, but Harry was different. For a start Harry was not full of himself, like so many of the other students had been.

Villiers was forced to concede that Harry was quietly brilliant. "I didn't really expect this," Villiers said, in a voice that had none of his old academic pride.

"Nor me, at least not on this scale," Harry admitted. "I've seen and experienced a lot of strange things in the past couple of years, but this wins first prize."

"It's exquisite," Martell said, addressing Harry directly.

"I've seen Mycelium in Leofwin's Hundred, particularly around Uberatu's Oak," Harry said. "But in my wildest dreams I never thought I would be exploring it from inside."

The knocking began again, Morse code for a certainty. Harry's heart notched up a beat with the thought that Jem, or maybe Bill Templestone, who he was particularly fond of, had picked up his signal and were responding. **Harry are you OK**, came the message.

They moved on downward, tentatively at first, but then with growing confidence. What they all detected early on, as they realised when they stopped and rested for a short while, was that they felt distinctly welcome in the surreal place.

"There's a feeling of being at home here," Martell said.

Of the four of them, Esma was the least phased by the surroundings. She quickly had to get used to twenty-first century life after her transference, with Rowan, from Anglo-Saxon England. There were mind-bending changes she had already got used to. This underground situation, with its writhing tendrils and cobweb-like structures, was no big deal compared to what she had already got used to.

They rounded a bend in the cavernous passageway and were surprised to see, some distance ahead, a dark figure silhouetted against the light.

The sight gave Harry an adrenaline rush which posed two choices, turn tail and run, or walk on and face whatever may happen. He walked on, trying to look cool as Esma trailed behind him.

"I'm surprised it took you so long to find the way in," the figure said, turning to facing Harry.

"You have the knack of finding your way into all sorts of places," Harry said, relieved it was the Piper up ahead. Harry got to within four feet of the colourful individual.

"It was me who let you into this place. What is occurring out there should not be happening. I hope it passes over."

"So, what do we do now?" Harry asked.

"Who is this person?" Villiers butted in. He could tell that the person standing a few feet in front of them was not the usual type of human. Decidedly not, in fact because it *exuded* force. An aura. Villiers had no idea how to deal with such a being, unlike Harry.

"This is the Pied Piper of Hamelin," Harry said.

Martell laughed the high sort of laugh that had no origin in humour.

"Harry," Villiers said, "I assume you are joking."

Martell wiped his eyes with a rag he pulled from his pocket and sniffed. He laughed uncontrollably again.

"Shut up, Dick," commanded Villiers.

*   *   *

"We can see you now," Esma said, as she gazed at the peaceful countenance of the stranger, and its unusual garb.

"I had some deep-level adjustments made to my molecular structure."

"Did it hurt?" she asked.

"Not at all . . . in fact the experience was exhilarating."

"What is this . . . exhilarating?"

"He means it felt good," Harry clarified. He repeated his earlier question to the Piper about what they should do now. The answer surprised him.

"We are going into the Mycorrhizal network, follow me."

"But why? Harry asked. The strands of Hyphae moved aside as they walked close to them.

"I am going to introduce you to the catalytic place from where you will begin your journey home."

"We need a catalyst?"

"In a different sense to how you presently understand the

word, catalyst." Villiers looked puzzled.

"Explain," Harry said.

"A catalyst can be a set of circumstances that produce a desired result. Could be a set of events, a place or a situation, any of which could be the factors that produce a particular outcome." What Harry understood from Piper's explanation was that a set of circumstances were going to be manipulated which would cause the outcome of a homeward trip.

"You have worked out correctly that the Mycorrhizal network is trans-dimensional," said Piper. "One of its functions is that it can be used as a transmitter of information throughout the whole of creation. In your Earth radio-wave terms, a minor function of The Mycorrhizal network is that it can act as a carrier wave."

"And it also links to what we call The Grid," Harry added.

"Exactly so. Now, other than finding how to reverse the function of your Switch in R1 at Kineton, Professor Villiers, the Mycorrhizal network *should* be able to get you back home. The problem with using your device in the laboratory under Edge Hill is that its function occurred by accident so there is no obvious information about how to control its operation."

"Both Esma and me have heard identical sounds to the ones coming both from the growths on this planet and an ancient tree in Leofwin's Hundred called Uberatu's Oak—proof they are connected across the realities, presumably by the Mycorrhizal network. Piper, I've used the network to communicate with our friends on Earth. It's a basic method I'm using, a code called Morse. I hit the outside of the giant tree we entered. They've picked up my transmissions and have responded. They are on the case."

"I know about Uberatu's Oak," Piper said. "Harry . . . the giant entities on this planet are chimeras. They are organisms that were created with two distinct, but interconnected types of cell structure, biological and vegetable. Like trees, they are rooted to the ground, but they possess a truly amazing biological function too. They have an intellectual capacity that surprises us at times. They are the fruiting bodies on this planet that grow from the Mycorrhizal Network, which will hopefully work in your favour."

Piper began to walk down the slope. "I have a similar metabolism, I am a chimera too, and sometimes after an awakening I leave traces of where I walk in the form of fungus." The Mycorrhizal Network is one of my distant relatives."

Harry nodded as he assimilated the information. What the Piper revealed made sense, while Villiers, with his strictly scientific outlook, was having difficulty to accept what the Piper told them.

Follow me," the Piper said.

"Where are we going?" Villiers asked.

"We are going to a place that gets you a step closer to returning to your home."

Martell grinned as he asked, "And where exactly is that?"

"To the Innermost Hall of Toraddon."

45

Piper was walking uncomfortably quick for the four people marooned in the Alien Reality. They were heading down a winding pathway amongst multitudinous tendrils, some of which were wrist-thick and some as fine as a webwork of spider's gossamer. Piper slowed down so that they could catch up. A few yards further on Piper stopped where the path widened into a room.

Harry surveyed the area. The Mycorrhizal network was minimised in this place. There was a screen, possibly eight feet tall, set into the wall of the room. Harry locked eyes with Piper, "Is this a portal that will take us to the place you mentioned"?

"To the Innermost Hall of Toraddon . . . yes, it is."

"Who manages all this stuff . . . the growths on this planet and the Mycorrhizal Network; presumably the network connects all the Realities?"

"The Ultimate Reality cares for it. And you are correct, the growths on this planet are part of a Mycorrhizal relationship that is universal. Your Uberatu's Oak and the arboreal and vegetable species in all of the Realities are part of a unifying factor linking the whole of creation together. We might find out more about the Ultimate Reality at some point in the future. You, and your colleagues back on Earth are experiencing a link to that network when you connect with the life-forms on this planet and Uberatu's Oak."

Villiers walked across the room to Piper in a challenging manner. Stood in front of him, "A short time back you said, 'The intellect the tree-like life-forms on this planet possess surprises US.' So how many are there of your kind?"

"I may tell you at some point, but until then just be satisfied that I am here and we are trying to get you home." A distant look came into Piper's eyes.

"Where did your band of brothers originate?" Martell pressed for an answer. Harry picked up a sarcastic tone in the man's voice.

"There are things that you do not need to know, Mister Martell; but come, we are delaying."

Harry re-focussed as Piper beckoned for them to approach the screen. He touched the wall. The screen illuminated and a scene, that initially possessed a certain amount of fluidity, became apparent. After some seconds the scene consolidated into a view of the interior of a building.

"Be prepared to be amazed," Piper said. "Remember the designation of this portal," he pointed to some characters on the wall. "Follow me." He stepped over some delicate tracery into the screen. Harry and the other three followed into a room where, in front of them, was a flat, mirage-like phenomenon stretching to the left and right, disappearing, as it seemed, into the wall each side of the room.

Harry looked behind him and saw an ornate wall in which there were many portals. He noted the characters above the portal they came through, and remembered its position.

*　*　*

Dearden, also in the Innermost Hall of Toraddon, but on the other side of the Buffer, was thrown by Piper's disappearance but his senses rallied and he quickly assessed the situation they were in, he, Oscar Stanway and Tomahawk.

"From now on take utmost precaution about how you proceed," Piper warned before he vanished. It was as if Piper wanted them take responsibility for the quest on their own.

Dearden took a quick glance at Oscar, who seemed more interested in the surroundings than he was concerned about the curious nature of their situation. In his missions with SHaFT, Dearden had developed the tenacity to adapt to whatever situation he was in. Where they were now, on Toraddon was no exception, but he wondered about Oscar's ability to cope. "Piper said we should be cautious how we proceed. Do you want to carry on?" Dearden asked.

"I can't imagine that guy would leave us if we were in any great danger, so let's carry on. But where we will carry on *to* is the question." Oscar said. He sat on one of the chairs. It was supremely comfortable. Dearden sat beside him and gazed at the surroundings. Tomahawk lay down at his side.

Oscar noticed that the Buffer disappeared into the wall each side the room. "What principle is used to achieve this?" he pointed to the buffer's extremities, disappearing into the wall to the left and right.

"What you see in front of us is a planetary effect," the Piper said. "The Buffer encircles the planet and going off into the infinity of interstellar space. The Innermost Hall of Toraddon, where we are now, is the node which allows the interface between Realities to be opened. The Buffer can be programmed according to the Realities to be traversed."

"But it seems you have the advantage of total freedom to travel the Realities."

"Yes, I don't need to use the Buffer."

The layout of the room reminded Dearden of a university lecture theatre. In front of them the wall had a fluctuating, liquid look about it and there was a dais near the right-hand wall. Dearden pulled on Tomahawk's leash and went to examine the wall. Oscar gazed at Dearden and Tomahawk.

On their way back from Portland Julia Linden-Barthorpe had told Oscar about the SHaFT guys he was going to meet at Dearden Hall. He had a vision of Dearden being somewhat of a chancer . . . a guy who would even put his life on the line to achieve justice. And there Dearden was, with a wolf, on this world, Toraddon, facing an indistinct object in a room that had a distinctly alien feel about it.

Yes, Dearden had guts, no doubt about that. He crouched in front of a moving object, examining it closely, and he nearly fell backwards when it moved quickly. Oscar went to help and Dearden nodded his thanks as he stood, his one hand on Oscar's arm and the other hand still grasping the wolf's leash. The object in front of them gradually solidified and standing in front of them, as if only a couple of meters away, but viewed as through a mist, were Harry and Esma. Two more people were behind them, and a fifth figure, standing at the back of the group, was Piper.

"How the hell did you get there so quick?" was all Dearden could say to the Piper. He glanced at his watch. He couldn't understand the situation because Piper left them half an hour back. There was obvious excitement in the group on the other side. Harry cupped his hand to his best ear, the left one, and turned toward the screen to hear better what Dearden said.

46

All of them, standing each side the Buffer, apart from Piper, were in a state of disbelief. They were all talking at once but none of them could understand what was being said. After a minute of chaos, an excited peace descended, where Harry on the one side, and Dearden on the other side, stepped close to the Buffer.

Dearden was trying to work out why there were two other people with Harry and Esma. Harry could see him scrutinising Villiers and Martell and he mouthed their names, "Charles Villiers and Richard Martell," to Dearden. Dearden looked at him quizzically and Harry pointed to each of them in turn and repeated their names. And then Dearden managed to read Harry's lips when he said, "This is Professor Charles Villiers, and this is Dick Martell." Dearden nodded, turned to Oscar, who had developed a broad grin on his face at the sight of his brother.

"That's Professor Charles Villiers, on the right and the other is Dick Martell. He was Keeper of The Knight's Sanctuary in Temple Balsall and he disappeared back in the fifties," Dearden explained. "He must have teamed up with Villiers back then."

Oscar got closer to the Buffer and gave Harry a thumbs-up. Harry did the same back and then held his hand out to Oscar who tried to clasp it. He felt, as did Harry, a repulsive force, that was keeping them apart, as would the like poles of two magnets repel each-other when placed close together.

Strangely enough, as they found out later, both Harry and Oscar had a similar thought at that time when they were facing each-other. They both thought of quantum entanglement . . . it was as if their thoughts had interacted. It was not an imaginary occurrence. Nor was it coincidental because the subject was too abstruse and well timed for coincidence. The brothers had always been close, and sometimes had these *rapport* moments, but never before, until they faced each other across the void separating them between the Realities had they felt so *intensely* close.

At that moment both of them realised that by using quantum entanglement there was a possibility of creating a means for the four people marooned to return to Earth. How to convert those ideas into realities was the almost impossible challenge that faced them.

What did occur to Harry was that Piper could also be using the laws of quantum entanglement to transfer from Reality to Reality. Probably, he thought, the technology used on the planet Toraddon had also enhanced the sometimes-present intermingling of thoughts between himself and Oscar.

Maybe, Harry reasoned to himself, this capability went a stage further with Piper, in that he may have an inbuilt structure in his genetic makeup enabling him to *entangle himself* with the quantum between whatever Realities he needed to visit, and travel using that entanglement.

Dearden glanced at Tomahawk who was still at his side, going along in his Lupine way of dealing with things, shifting, observing, trying to *fit-in*. Oscar had gone exceptionally quiet. If, at that point, Dearden had been able to delve into Oscar's mind, he would have been surprised at what was occurring.

It was a trip back in time to when Oscar and Harry were walking with their father. It was during a summer holiday and the lads were going with their father to his place of work.

Their father had no car at the time. Those years were simple, frugal, but thoroughly enjoyable. They were walking the mile or so that took them to the bus-stop where they would catch the Midland Red to Leamington Spa. "Don't call it *Royal,*" their father said, as they trudged along. Their father hated the pomposity of calling the place *Royal Leamington* Spa.

It was still dark, six thirty in the morning, and the early December sky was inky black, studded with the bright beauty of the Milky Way. "What's up there dad, beyond the stars?" Oscar remembered his younger brother Harry asking. The brothers' relationship with their father was strong. Friendlier than was usual for father and son, and it would be more-so as the years progressed.

"That's a difficult question. But as far as we know it goes on forever. Maybe, as the years progress we'll find out more to satisfy our curiosity." Oscar remembered that the morning was cold, with a touch of frost, and their breath hung on the air. It would be good when they were on the bus and they felt the warmth.

"But what do you think, dad?" Oscar took the conversation a stage further. There was a pause before the answer came, and the answer stayed with Oscar through the years . . . served him well, as it did Harry.

That walk was a pivotal time in their mental and intellectual growth because their father said, "Whatever mankind can imagine . . . what *we* can imagine . . . will become reality. It may take a long while for it to happen but it'll happen. Imagination is where reality begins, you mark my words," their father said.

Oscar's mind had ruminated on this thought on numerous occasions and he had concluded that, from somewhere out in the bright beyond, came thoughts that entered the human mind that, given the right opportunities, would gain flight and ascend to unprecedented heights of imagination, eventually solidifying into physical realities.

Dearden gazed again at Oscar, who was regarding Harry standing the other side the Buffer in the Innermost Hall of Toraddon.

Going over and over in Oscar's mind was his father's words. *Even if a concept seems very obscure, given time it can become reality*, and then Oscar's mind picked up what Harry was thinking, it was identical. There was no doubt about it, the communication was positive. They gazed at each-other, united in mind despite the physical separation caused by the Buffer. Their combined intellect was working on the given premise that quantum entanglement *could* enable a return to Earth, thus enabling the journey from one realm of Reality to another. Exactly how, was as yet, very obscure.

47

Inside the Innermost Hall of Toraddon, Tomahawk, waiting with unusual patience at Dearden's side, had seen the Piper at the rear of the group facing them. He recognised Harry and Esma and wanted to get to them because they were associated with the Food-beast, Dearden, who was standing at his side. More so did he need to get close to the One at the back of the group, the One that brought Home and Mother-thoughts, and desire for the warmth of company.

Tomahawk moved forward, felt at first the restraining thing around his neck that the Food-beast applied. And then he was unable to move toward the warm beast because his nose touched an impenetrable object, similar to the thing in the Food-beast's big den that stopped him from going out to where the air was fresh and vibrant. Oh . . . how he longed to sit at the feet of the warm being not far away.

*   *   *

"Tom, come here," Dearden said, and he tugged on the leash, gently at first. Usually Tomahawk responded obediently, but this time the wolf was obstinate and gave a deep growl that warned Dearden to be careful because he was treading on wolf-lore, which would sometimes turn vicious. Only occasionally, these days, did Tomahawk's Black Alaskan wolf-genes surface. Prompted by some primeval trigger . . . just occasionally Dearden sensed that the wolf still had a wild side deep within him.

At those times Dearden exercised extreme caution and uttered soothing noises. This was the method the Lakota Sioux chief, Red Cloud, told him would work. *Soothe him when he gets the wilderness back inside, Jem, otherwise he might go for your throat.*

"Shhhhh, Tom. Shhhhhh." Dearden slowly reached into his pocket. No quick moves. He pulled out a small lump of dried meat on a bone. He always had this stuff with him when he was with Tomahawk . . . just in case. He offered it, slowly moved his hand, and held the treat in front of Tom's nose. Dearden felt the object in front of them that was stopping Tomahawk moving forward. It was like a pane of glass, but more pliant, as if a resistive force was pushing his hand away. Then Tomahawk, who couldn't resist the offering, startled him by snatching it quick.

Dearden looked up at the group the other side of the Buffer and saw that the Piper had gone.

*   *   *

Dearden and Oscar were startled by the voice behind them which, although unexpected, had a gentle quality. In his surprise, Dearden let go Tomahawk's leash and the wolf loped to Piper's side. Piper bent down for the leash. He grasped it firmly and before handing it back to Dearden he crouched down and looked Tomahawk in the eye.

"I wouldn't do that if I were you," Dearden said, and he warned Piper about the wolf's wild streak.

"It doesn't matter," Piper said, "Now we must leave."

Oscar looked at the mirage-like Buffer in front of them, gave Harry a wave and then the Buffer became blank. He had a mix of emotions. Sadness that the link concluded, and elation that Harry was OK. It took a force of will to shake off the sadness but it was time to move onward.

"How does the Virtuality column below Leofwin's Hundred fit into this?" Oscar asked Piper. "Are there two methods of Reality-transfer, the Virtuality and the Buffer?"

"No, the gateway in every level of the Virtuality leads here to the Buffer. Toraddon is the node from where all trans-dimensional voyaging occurs. Now, Jem, Oscar and Tomahawk, you must go home and wait until I contact you. Remember, your colleagues are marooned in a very obscure Reality that is going through a major ecological upheaval due to their intrusion.

"There is a problem. Being the latest Reality to be discovered there is a steep learning curve involved with its physics. The Wasiri are trying to get to grips with it. Rest assured, with a combined effort we will hopefully get back to a balance between the Realities and your friends will return home."

"Then get us back to Dearden Hall," Oscar said.

*   *   *

Before he left them, the Piper reminded Harry, "Once you leave the Innermost Hall of Toraddon through the portal, re-trace your steps through the Mycorrhizal Network on the planet of your marooning. The atmospheric disturbance should have calmed but be on your guard and remain near the entrance to the network. At present, the planet is unstable. By the way, the world where you are marooned is designated as planet KV280 63482/5."

"Presumably the figure five represents the planet's position in its solar system," Harry assessed.

"That is so." And then the Piper left. Harry and the others went to the portal they used to get to the Innermost Hall of Toraddon, and stepped back through the screen.

Harry had hold of Esma's hand during the transfer back to planet KV280 63482/5. "At least Jem Dearden knows we are

315

alive, Esma," Harry said, trying to reassure her as the four of them neared the surface.

"Oscar looks like you," Esma said.

"My brother's a good guy, wouldn't let you down in a crisis. He's got a good brain too . . . we're a good team together, he and I."

"Then let's hope you and he can get us out of this mess," Villiers said. Martell nodded his acquiescence. None of the others saw him finger the sharp object in the ragged pocket of his jacket. The trauma of his isolation hit hard away from the place he loved, Temple Balsall, with its wooded beauty.

Harry waited for Villiers and Martell to catch up. "Here's a thought, Prof. Cast your mind back, if you can. I know this stuff I'm going to tell you may be a few years after your time in the Old Cav and your lab at MoD Kineton, but listen. This stuff might help out.

"Over recent years Physicists have been studying the Quantum. Its existence has been proved by observation and experimentation."

Villiers was attentive to Harry's reasoning when he briefly explained the latest findings about quantum entanglement of distant particles.

"So where is this taking us, young man?" Villiers asked. He was intrigued by what Harry was telling him.

Harry thought for a minute before replying. "I think that there is a strong connection between the Quantum and the Grid, the lines of energy we connect to from the Hub in Leofwin's Hundred. I'm convinced that the common factor with the Grid's ability to enable transit, temporal, spatial and inter-dimensional, are the crystalline objects . . . they are a constant factor. In some way we don't understand yet, the crystals must organise quantum entanglement"

"You think they possess *uncanny power?*" Martell ventured, raising both arms and trying to look spooky.

"There's nothing spooky about it . . . obscure, yes, but not spooky. The crystals possess a power enabling results that wouldn't have been thought possible a few years back. We just don't fully understand it yet." He pointed to his digital watch. "Consider this; inside this watch is the proof that crystals sometimes possess unique powers, The pulsation of the quartz crystal enables us to tap into an exquisitely precise method of logging the passage of time."

"How is this going to help us out of our predicament?" Villiers asked.

"I think that the force the crystalline substance possesses enables it to connect with *all* matter. This connectivity enables remarkable events to take place. The question is, how to enable the connectivity?" Harry recalled his unusual experiences of the past few years which had their beginning in Leofwin's Hundred. He remembered Jem Dearden's words, *Leofwin's Hundred is the strangest place on Earth.*

48

Things were relatively peaceful on the surface of the planet. Apart from debris strewn around the place there was nothing to show how violent had been the recent atmospheric disturbance. The four were heartened by the possibility of a return to Earth and when they got back to Harry and Esma's shelter they involved themselves in some needed repair work to its structure. Afterwards, they talked over their experience within the Mycorrhizal Network.

Harry stood and went outside, surveying the horizon to make sure things were calm. He heard Villiers coming behind him.

"Life is a glorious conundrum, and it does seem to be rather contrived at times, don't you think?" Harry said to Villiers.

"It is. I remember you saying that the creation we are experiencing, with all of its intricacies and inbuilt mathematics *has* to be the product of mind. Harry, that makes sense. The mathematics and the physics we scientists observe is so precise that it implies a designer. It's as if something . . . someone, worked the whole lot out."

"And cares about our place in the scheme of things, because what has been created isn't chaotic," Harry added.

"It becomes chaotic if we humans make it so, like I did with my invention that got us here," Villiers acknowledged his responsibility and shook his head.

"Yeah but we have freedom to make choices, hence, with our freedom to choose and your chaos we ended up in this place. But if we really do understand and obey the laws of physics around us all should go well. We ended up in this place because we didn't foresee the consequences of what our freedom allowed us to do."

"*And* we shouldn't do anything impetuous. When I opened the Switch and stepped into this Reality with Dick Martell, I acted on impulse. I had told the other chaps in the lab not to go through the Switch, but I did just that."

"Prof, I did the same as you, I was too curious and when the Switch in your lab under Edge Hill opened onto an alien world I stepped into it. Anyway, let's get down to working with what we know and do no spur-of-the-moment stuff."

"What do you suggest we do?"

Harry had an idea in mind that had gradually formed since their exit from the Mycorrhizal Network. "Remember when we entered the cavern where the hyphae were, the tendrils, we came to a crystal? Did it's being there suggest anything to you?"

"Familiarity, I guess. When I was with Joss Dearden we looked around the weird out-of-context building in the forest and found some of the crystals, small ones, in what looked like a storage room. They were strange things. It was as if they were alive, pulsating with energy, so I took some back to the lab."

"You conducted experiments with them," Harry said.

"Yes, and was thrilled with what they did, They stepped up the power in any electrical circuit we made. And then, when a flask of experimental matter was accidentally placed near a large coil and we detected a miniscule vortex in the centre of the coil, we wanted to see what would occur to the vortex if we increased the power—"

"—And you introduced some of the crystals into the circuitry to increase the power. We know that because we took off your stainless steel panel at the side of the door frame and saw the crystals."

"You are almost right Harry."

" Thought so. Prof, *the crystals* . . . the common link with all of these alien transport systems are—"

"—The crystals."

"Exactly. I think that the makeup of the crystals in the alien building in Leofwin's Hundred enables them to link to the Grid and opened up the gate enabling you to go through it onto a world in an alternative Reality."

Villiers appeared subdued. "Are you OK?" Harry asked, wondering why the sudden change in the professor's demeanour. Villiers took a deep breath, and then, "I'll tell you sometime. What I will say for now is that it would be useful to have a crystal to experiment with," said Villiers.

"There's one in the Hyphae Cave but we can't take that. It would wreck the transfer node on this planet."

"But I think we ought to go back and take another look."

* * *

They decided to sleep on the idea of going back to the Cave of the Hyphae and maybe go back next day. Harry took advantage of having a few hours to himself. An idea about the gateway they came through onto the alien world had been nagging him for a while, so he set off to examine it. He told Esma what he planned to do. He needed to concentrate on the task ahead and didn't want company so he told her to keep quiet about it and he set off on his own with the tote-bag of tools on his shoulder.

He passed the shelter built by Professor Villiers and Dick Martell. Some of the roof covering had been dislodged and lay strewn over the ground. The damage was minimal and   it looked to Harry that the recent atmospheric disturbance had almost petered out by the time it reached the shelter.

A short while later he stood in front of the sealed entry in the cliff face that he and Esma came through. Villiers had marked the position by driving in two stakes, one each side the door. Harry examined the door, concluding that it would be metallic. He also reasoned that, just as Villiers had used non-magnetic metal for his Switch in R1, so too would the builders of this device use similar materials to achieve the result of trans-dimensional shift. Studying it, he wondered how long this device had been in place, who built it and who, in its history, had passed through it.

Harry got close to the frame, camouflaged like the surrounding rock, maybe, he thought, as protection against interference. He reflected on Villiers' setup in R1 that shifted them into this other dimension. By accident, or by an, as yet, inexplicable method of communication from an alien source, Professor Villiers had duplicated the electronics of the alien Switch. Therefore, in this door frame, Harry reasoned, there should be a similar setup of electronics enclosed by panels but if panels existed here, they were not obvious.

Harry took a screwdriver from his bag, held the blade and systematically began to tap the area around the door. The material sounded solid low down so gradually Harry tapped higher, and higher until he was standing. There was a sudden hollow sound when he tapped the frame on the left side of the door just above waist-level. He touched the hollow surface, which felt cold.

Ambient temperature is low, but at least it's hollow, Harry observed. Being hollow, like the stainless steel door-frame was in Villiers' lab, implied there were electronics inside the frame of this door to activate the trans-dimensional transport system. He slowly scraped the area disguised as rock with his thumb nail and after a few seconds his nail clicked on the surface, revealing a fine crack running upwards, then at ninety degrees to the left and then downwards. He felt a thrill of excitement, stepped back and contemplated the outline of a rectangular panel.

At the base of the panel there was a wider crack, as there may be with Earth-type technology, into which a lever could be inserted to remove a cover.

Whilst working on the Hub in Leofwin's Hundred, it had crossed Harry's mind that there appeared to be a crossover between Earth technology and alien technology, implying interaction in times past. Here it was again. In something as high-tech as a gizmo enabling connection to the Grid, there was a similar-to-Earth way of levering off the outer cover to get to the circuitry.

Harry flipped the screwdriver round and inserted the blade into the slot at the bottom of the cover. He levered, and the bottom edge clicked open. He inserted his fingers into the gap and pulled the cover completely away from its housing. He laid it on the ground and contemplated the electronics in the revealed space.

The circuitry looked similar to that in Villiers' Lab but there was no internal life in the crystals in this circuit. No pulsing energy or fiery movement. He placed the cover up to the aperture, hit around its perimeter with the heel of his hand. It snapped back into place and he began his trek back to the camp.

49

When Harry was approaching their camp Esma saw him in the distance and she ran to meet him. "I was . . . afyrhte," she said, struggling for the modern English. Harry recognised what she was saying.

"No need to worry, I'm back now." He held her tight, kissed her and then they strolled to the camp.

"Where have you been?" Villiers asked. Esma had told him Harry had to go somewhere. She wouldn't say where he had gone and Villiers curiosity went into overdrive.

"I went to the Switch we came through . . . and I found a panel covering the circuitry."

"Did you, by George."

"And I opened it up to see what's inside."

Villiers was taken aback. He and Martell had been to the Switch no end of times hoping they would open it to a familiar scene of Earth. Occasionally, when they opened the door, they had seen a different world, but never Earth. More often than not it opened onto a vision of stars and galaxies.

"It never occurred to me to try and view the circuitry," the Prof said. He felt a touch of inadequacy.

"We were too tied up with surviving, Charlie," Martell interjected.

Villiers agreed. "Just surviving in this place has been a continual marathon." He felt a touch humbled as he glanced at Harry. He re-focussed his thoughts. "What did you find inside the panel?"

"More or less as we discussed. There are crystals in the circuitry. But there's a problem . . . they're inactive."

"I had noticed recently when I checked the Switch here

that I couldn't open the door. Maybe the crystals have degraded."

"There was a similar problem with the crystal in the Hub back in Leofwin's Hundred."

"But you said the Hub is active."

"It is now. I re-energised it with an electro-generator."

"Well, that's an impossibility."

"Yeah . . . but I have another idea."

*   *   *

Harry was preparing his tote bag for the hike to the giant organism they entered when the atmospheric disturbance occurred. After the escapade inside the Mycorrhizal Network, Harry noticed that Dick Martell's attitude had mellowed. "I feel there may be a way out of this place before long," Martell said when Harry asked him how he was doing. "Thanks for your help, Harry, I do appreciate it." Martell reached into his pocket, took out the knife he had been carving and gave it to Harry. "With my compliments," he said. "I've got nothing else to give you."

Harry took the knife that Martell made out of hard organic material. it had no intricate embellishments. Without many tools to carve it, Harry knew that it took many hours of work to make. He looked Martell in the eye, and they did a firm hand-shake. Not long after that, the four were on their way back to the Mycorrhizal Network.

*   *   *

"I do hope we can get into it again," Villiers said as they got to the massive organism. "Where's the entrance?"

"let's see," Martell began to walk around the trunk, looking for the opening. Harry and Villiers followed him.

Esma looked up the massive trunk to the appendages high above. What she saw startled her. She stepped away from the trunk and looked again.

"Harry," she called.

He heard her apprehension and rushed to help. She pointed to the top of the structure. "Trees know we are here. They looking at us."

As Harry gazed upwards he remembered what the Piper said about the giant organisms. *They are chimeras with two distinct but interconnected types of cell structure, biological and vegetable and that they have an intellectual capacity that at times is surprising.*

"Esma, when we were in the underground network with the Piper he told us that these things are a form of life that is surprisingly intellectual at times." Harry reached out and touched it. He kept his hand on the surface.

"What is this . . . you say, intellectual?"

He thought how best to answer. "We humans are intellectual, We can understand ideas and work things out and . . . here's the point . . . we can *communicate* our ideas to other people."

"These trees are more than trees." Esma approached the organism and touched it, almost reverently, with both hands. She looked up at its great height, spreading her fingers wide on the surface. She felt a sensation in her fingertips.

"Fingers tingle," she said. He got close to her and was about to do the same, to feel the surface to test what she felt, when a portion of the surface opened, as if the chimera knew they wanted to get inside.

"Prof, Dick . . . here, now," he shouted. Villiers' jaw dropped when he saw the open portal and the familiar illuminated interior.

"Why wait?" Martell said, stepping into the entrance with new-found confidence. The others cautiously followed and then the opening to the outside closed. Harry had been last in, ushering Esma in before him and he was facing the entrance when it closed, or rather blended into the background.

"Wait," Harry said. The other three stopped. Including Harry, they were edgy, attentive. "It's what we wondered about." He echoed what Esma realised, "These organisms know we are here."

"This thing has opened up twice for us. And the first time we were in desperate need, so it seems they're working with us." stated Villiers.

"Either this one or the whole group knew we wanted to get in just now," Harry said, and he led the way forward.

"I hope they carry on helping us," muttered Martell.

As before, the hyphae made way for them as they walked along the downward slope. "This world is full of surprises," Martell added and Harry wondered how he and Villiers would have coped with the unusual events in Leofwin's Hundred in recent years.

They approached the cavernous space where the great crystal was active. It was an exact copy of the arrangement in the Hub in Leofwin's Hundred. There was a metallic band around the crystal about half way up its height. Four thick cables arched away from the metal band and were coupled to the wall of the cave. A fiery red coruscation flashed and erupted deep within the crystal, which indicated to Harry that the system was in standby mode.

It was Esma who figured out the next step. Back in Anglo-Saxon times, a gathering was held by Earl Leofric of Mercia and Countess Godgyfu at Castle Coufaentree. A traveller with very dark skin had brought jewellery from one of the far lands of Byzantium and the Earl showed his guests an exquisite raw crystal. It was the beautiful purple colour of a dye from lichen that clung to some of the trees deep in Leofwin's Hundred.

"This jewel has a child," said the dark-skinned traveller," and he pointed out a smaller crystal joined to the base of its parent. And that is what Esma saw. Hidden at the lowest part of the great active crystal in the middle of the cavern. A small crystal was lying in the deep shadow created by the cradle holding its parent.

"Harry, look . . . crystal has child," she pointed to the base of the cradle. Harry squinted and then he saw it.

"Well spotted, Esma."

"My eyes good," she said, as Harry stepped over some of the hyphae to get to the crystals. He guessed the small one was about thirty centimetres high, 12 wide at the base, and it tapered to a point which was sharp at the top when he touched it. He took hold of it and pulled but its lower third was fixed solidly to the large crystal. Harry examined it as Villiers and Martell came close. He shifted slightly and looking at the illumination flashing deep within both crystals, detected a cleavage plane between them.

"I think we're in luck," he said, reaching into his tote-bag for Martell's knife. "Anyone see a stone that'll do as a hammer?"

"I see one," Esma said. She gave it to Harry and he inserted the knife in the slight gap between the two crystals.

"Are you sure about this?" the Prof asked.

"Pretty sure but this is the first time I've tried cleaving a precious stone. The plane between the crystals is obvious, so they should separate OK. As long as what I'm about to do doesn't affect the Mycorrhizal link to Toraddon we should be alright. Look at the two crystals . . . see how they are coruscating differently? That means each one's action is independent of the other, which proves that it is safe to separate them." The reasoning made sense to Villiers. He bent down and took hold of the small crystal at its base, preparing himself to take the weight when it separated.

Martell was worried. "Why not let the Piper get us back?" he challenged.

"Things can always go wrong, Dick. The Piper's an elusive character. I'd prefer to have a second option, just in case we need it." Martell didn't look convinced and flinched when Harry struck his knife with the stone.

It separated successfully and Villiers grunted with the sudden weight. Harry assisted. "OK, let it go, I've got it. He stood and stepped away from the large crystal and, with a sigh of relief he saw both crystals were still active and felt calmness, as tension eased from his body.

"I suggest we go back to your camp with this and see if we can work out a way of introducing it into the alien circuitry," Harry said to Villiers.

"And we'll take turns to carry it," Martell said. Stepping forward he grasped the crystal and took it from Harry.

50

Oscar shivered. He looked pale and, although there was only a mild chill in the air, he sat in the winged chair close to the fire. Templestone was elated after Oscar told him Harry and Esma were OK.

"Tell me about it," Templestone wanted to know what happened in the cave. Oscar thought tangentially about how to answer him.

"Remember a while back we talked about the crystals in the circuitry Villiers built into the Switch at the back of his lab in R1?"

"I remember it well."

"And you mentioned harmonics."

"I did. Harry and I back-engineered the apparatus in the Hub and made a small duplicate. Jules found some spare crystals in the Hub and we used one of them in the circuitry. It harmonised with the large crystal in the Hub and enabled us to do some physical transfers from one location to another."

"So the transfer of the physical objects was via the Grid and your experiment used the internal force and the harmonics between the crystals to accomplish the transfer?"

"That's right . . . there's no other explanation."

And that is how the conversation went, with Oscar, musing on the potential of the force within the crystals to connect with the Grid and enable physical objects to shift from one place to another. *"We're going to do it,"* There it was again, sibling communication, and he fancied he heard Harry talking to him. At the same time, he felt an urge, a compulsion, to return to Villiers' laboratory.

"The answer lies in quantum entanglement of superior mass," he said loudly, startling Templestone who was drifting off to sleep. Oscar recalled the posters explaining quantum theory on Harry's wall in his pad upstairs. His kid brother must have had the same idea.

"What of it, this quantum stuff?"

"That's what it's all about, Bill. That's what happens when the Grid and the crystals are active. The crystals create quantum entanglement via the controls in the Hub. They assimilate physical objects for transfer from one node to another and use the lines of force of the Grid as a conduit."

"How does that help us get Harry and Esma back?"

"And Professor Villiers and Richard Martell. I forgot to say, Villiers and Martell are there too, with Harry and Esma."

"Really? This is getting too complex to handle. I'm told that Dick disappeared back in the fifties."

"Maybe so but he's alive and kicking still in some obscure place."

"How's that possible? He was in his sixties when he disappeared and that was over sixty years ago."

"Which would make him at least a hundred and twenty now." Oscar was thoughtful. "Bill, they were both very active, moving quickly. Not affected by the years that have gone by."

"As if time's stood still you mean? I wish time would damn well stand still for me." Templestone grinned and rubbed his knee, which had stiffened. The arthritis played up at times. He looked up as Dearden came over to speak to him.

"Oscar's filled you in on the detail?"

"He has. I'm so relieved Harry and Esma are OK." Templestone missed his conversations, sometimes into the early hours with Harry, often about obscure but interesting things. "What can I do to help get them back, Jem?"

"At present nothing, but thanks for your concern. It's good to have you about, Bill. You're helpful riding shotgun . . . apart from that I like your company." Templestone glanced at Dearden with a look of affection. "Anyway, sorry to cut this short, something's cropped up that could put a spanner in the works."

"Why, what's happened?"

"I'm going to explain."

Dearden went over to Leofwin's table, glanced at its familiar wear-marks and touched the scorch left by the Earl's beeswax candle all those years ago. He wondered how long this would go on with the uncertainty that had arisen. His life here at Dearden Hall with Rowan, the Golden Maid of Maldon could be coming to an end. How he loved her . . . but she might have to return to her Anglo-Saxon time.

"Gather round folks," he commanded, as leader of SHaFT, his emotion set aside. They were all there, all of Cell One, more friends than work colleagues, fourteen of them including Anton Beggs who was now determined to help Dearden and the others. Some of them were in a relaxed frame of mind, resting and others were chatting, whiling away the time. Dearden hadn't dismissed Cell One. He had sensed they may be needed, now they were.

Cell One settled down in silence, waiting.

"We were depending on the Piper to help us get Harry and Esma back but we have a problem, Piper's gone missing. Lan-Si Nu told me it does happen sometimes. The disappearances have to do with the Piper's missing companion. Apparently, there are times when he finds it almost impossible to cope with the loss and whatever the wider consequences he goes on the hunt for her."

"That may be so, but what happens now with Harry and

Esma, Jem?" Pierpoint wondered. "I remember Lan-Si-Nu telling us that the incursion of our youngsters into another reality has created an instability that could have catastrophic consequences. The Piper was going to help directly, as he did in Hamelin."

"Will, the Piper has no magical powers. According to what Lan-Si-Nu says, he is a form of life that can traverse the Realities at will, and he has knowledge of how the whole thing works. Apart from that, which could have been *very* useful to us, he still has his foibles and is susceptible to emotional stress, just as we are. I haven't a clue what happens now . . . that's the reason I suggested all of Cell One stays here, there's safety in numbers, particularly with SHaFT's expertise, and we can brainstorm our ideas."

"I think we should get back to Vastron Chka and Lan-Si-Nu," Jules said. "They have probably experienced this sort of situation before."

" Could be there's a clue about where Piper goes to so we can find him," suggested Storm Petrel. Matt Roberts, sitting very close to Storm, nodded his agreement.

"He's certainly homing in on Leofwin's Hundred," he ventured.

"Has the forest ever been thoroughly mapped?" Clive Fraser was into history and in his short time staying at Dearden Hall he had chatted to Dearden about the history of the ancient forest.

"No, it never has been mapped in detail. Ordnance Survey shows the area and the nearby hamlets, but Leofwin's Hundred itself is shown as a mass of green. The forest's internal detail isn't shown and no outsiders have been allowed access to it . . . there's secrecy involved because of the unusual events that have taken place here over thousands of years."

"But how about you, Jem. Have you explored the forest?"

"Haven't had time to do that . . . I wish I had. It's an interesting place and there's no telling what might be found."

"My friends, listen to me," Chief Red Cloud drew attention, "For all we know the Piper could be somewhere in the forest, seeding down obscure regions with fungus as he walks about,"

"Looking for love he has lost," Rowan whispered, loud enough for Jem to hear.

"You could well be right," he whispered back.

"Lan-Si-Nu told us how urgent this situation is because of the instability caused by our people accessing another Reality in an uncontrolled way. I suggest that we approach the problem in a controlled way, scientifically. Apart from that. Harry's my brother, I want him back alive."

"What do you recommend Oscar?" Jules asked.

"OK, first, the Switch in Villiers' Lab needs to be manned all the time in case action occurs that we need to work on. Being scientists, it needs to be Jules and me that do that."

"And me," Clive Fraser chipped in. He didn't intend Oscar Stanway to be shacked-up with Jules. He could trust her and he knew she was quite able to fight off any importune advances but he was just plain jealous.

"I'll go too," Templestone added. "I'm a good engineer. You might need something knocking-up quickly and there's a well-equipped machine-shop there."

"Good thinking, Bill. Next, the forest needs to be explored and mapped systematically. Like you say Red, the Piper may be hunkered down somewhere trying to sort his mind out."

"And we have no idea how that person's mind works," Trent Jackson added. "He might look human but when we were in the Virtuality we were told he is a chimera." Jackson

333

recalled the bizarre conversation. "Part biological, part vegetable. So the nature of the beast is totally alien compared to our physiology."

"OK. Thanks Trent, point taken . . . Oscar, your plan sounds good. We'll grid the Ordnance Survey map of the forest and do a systematic search. There are regions we haven't been into yet, so I hope there aren't any big surprises. We've got to sort this out, and quick . . . otherwise, if I correctly understand Lan-Si-Nu's warning about how catastrophic the Reality imbalance could be, it could lead to the annihilation of both our Reality and Four Hundred and Seventy. Talk the situation through amongst yourselves for an hour." Dearden looked at his watch. "Let's get organised." He laid the large map on Leofwin's table and using a three foot rule and a biro, he began to mark off the forest area in an accurate grid system.

Oscar, Clive Fraser, Jules and Bill Templestone got together away from the others and chatted through the equipment and essentials they would need for a stay in Villiers' old lab

Dearden finished gridding the map. He looked around the room and was heartened to see the team getting organised. Once again SHaFT was stepping up to the mark, this time confronted with what could be their most important task. He went to Will Pierpoint and shook his hand. Then he grasped Tomahawks heavy leash and spoke out in a commanding tone of voice. "Nos Successio Procul Totus Sumptus, guys. We Succeed At All Costs, and let's hope we do, this time."

51

Harry took the crystal off Martell. It was still coruscating wildly and upon handling it, Harry felt a mild sensation in his fingertips, as if there was a passage of electricity from the crystal into his body. At the same time, he felt a gradual easing of the tension that had been building in his mind.

"At least there's a bonus carrying this thing."

"You can feel it as well?" Martell asked. "I could feel it all the time I was carrying the crystal." Harry had been counting Martell's paces, eight-hundred of them. In Earth terms, roughly half a mile.

"We have a lot to learn about this type of element." Harry tapped the crystal and the coruscation fluctuated. Ever since his first introduction to the Hub in Leofwin's Hundred and the great crystal extending through the upper two floors, Harry had been enthralled with the hidden forces within crystals. He glanced at his digital watch . . . a pictorial display of the hidden force present within a quartz crystal that evidenced itself in the temporal dimension.

Harry counted out eight-hundred steps. "Your turn," he said to Villiers who, being a large and muscular man, took the weight of the crystal easily. "I see what you mean," he smiled as he felt the same ease of mind.

Harry was taking note of the inner movement within the crystal as each of them, in turn, took hold of it. There was an inner surge of energy, which settled after some ten seconds.

Esma wanted to take her turn. To the protestations of Villiers and Martell, born in a supposedly more 'gentlemanly' age, Esma hefted the crystal into both arms. The influence it had on her made her feel able to bear its weight for five-hundred and twenty-seven paces, then she grimaced and handed it to Martell.

* * *

The cliff-face loomed above them, its lower half cast in shadow, making it difficult to pick out the exact position of the doorway and then Martell picked out the stakes marking its position.

Martell placed the crystal carefully on the ground and stretched his arms to relieve his aching muscles. Harry approached the door, Located the disguised panel to its left and removing the screwdriver from his tote-bag, he inserted it into the slot at the base of the panel. He levered and the panel snicked open at the base.

Villiers, full of curiosity, pushed Harry aside, muttered an apology and inserted his fingers into the gap. He jerked the panel out of its surround, chucked it aside and contemplated the workings inside. "Looks similar to our circuitry in R1."

"How can it be? This gear is in a different Reality to our own. It was built by . . . who knows." Harry was unable to reason on the similarities.

"I owe you an explanation. It won't take long." He sat on the ground, resting his back against the cliff-face. He patted the ground next to him. Harry and Esma sat on one side and Dick Martell on the other.

"When my tenure at the Cavendish Laboratory finished I needed to find a suitable place to continue my work. The work was revolutionary, to say the least. As you are well aware, I constructed the weapon to see off the threat from the planet Nibiru, so I had to have a place that was well away from prying eyes. A high-ranking army colleague of mine was in command of the ammunition storage depot at Kineton and he told me about one of the storage buildings that hadn't been used for many years.

"He said that there were records of the place going back centuries, that the period of its construction was lost in the mists of time." Harry was intrigued.

"Of course, being as this place was underground, in an area heavily controlled by the military, and accessed through a tunnel almost five miles long, it couldn't be more secure. I jumped at the chance of using it as a place for my laboratory.

"The end of the tunnel opened out into a spacious area where we installed the machine-shop and up some spiral medieval steps at the far end of the machine-shop was another area that fired the imagination. The door had been sealed-up. I was curious about it . . . wondered what was beyond it, so my team and I broke through it. The air in the room beyond smelt musty. Dust was thick on the floor but I could see a mosaic shining through the dust and there were wall paintings too, showing oddly shaped people. Being, at best an amateur historian, I took the artwork to be Romano-Celtic in origin. We put a false wall over the paintings and a false floor over the mosaic in order to preserve them.

"There was another set of steps and another door—"

"—Around which there was electronic gear," intervened Harry. Villiers nodded and looked a touch disturbed.

"I wish we had left the damn thing alone, because that, and my curiosity was the cause of all our present woes."

"What's gone is gone . . . what happened next?" Harry's curiosity was in overdrive.

"For a while, nothing. We couldn't understand its purpose and it wasn't active. It was curious . . . electronic equipment mixed in with pre-medieval architecture doesn't add up."

"Too right it doesn't. Neither does an alien building in ancient wildwood," Harry added.

"It surely doesn't."

"And then?"

"I noticed that one of the crystals in the circuitry surrounding the door was shattered. By sheer coincidence, one of my colleagues was Josiah Dearden, of Dearden Hall Farm and he had shown me the old building in the forest. I remembered the large crystal in the top two levels. I contacted Jos and, in the store-room of the Hub we found a crystal, which was exactly the right size, to replace the one that was damaged. The circuitry came alive and you know the events that followed."

"What was the power source for the Switch in your lab?"

"I wish I knew. There is no generator connected to it. The power source for the machine-shop comes from the mains supply for MoD Kineton. That was laid in when I took on the laboratory."

"OK, I have an idea." Harry stood and looked up the cliff-face. Then he got close to the electronics and assessed the layout, looked at the top of the enclosure and found what he was looking for. He stepped back from the cliff and again looked up it. It wasn't too high, maybe fifty feet and it sloped away from the base. He looked for hand and footholds, saw a route that should be negotiable without too much effort.

"I'm going up."

"What, up there?" Dick Martell had no head for heights.

"Yep, up there." Harry walked along the rock-face to the right of the door and came to the place where his upward climb started. The other three followed.

"What's your idea?" Villiers asked.

"Nikola Tesla and free electricity. The principle Tesla discovered is universal. That's what powers the Hub in Leofwin's Hundred. Electricity drawn from the atmosphere is the principle that powers this system." He pointed back to the door. "I'm going to check it out."

"Are you saying that we don't need the crystal we brought from the Mycorrhizal Network all because of one of Tesla's hair-brained schemes?"

"I'm thinking we *might* not need it, but it's best to have it here. By the way, since you left the planet Tesla has become recognised as an absolute genius who was years before his time." He slung the tote-bag with his tools across his shoulders, like he used to with his school satchel.

"Anyway, here goes." Harry had noted the widest projections for his route up the cliff. His focus was to examine what appeared from ground level to be the flat top of an escarpment similar to that in Leofwin's Hundred into which was built the Hub.

The forward slope made the ascent easily managed and the projections were solid. Not that Harry was a natural climber but escape from where they were marooned made the climb less of a challenge. He looked down and wished he hadn't. His heart was pounding and he breathed deeply to relax.

"Are you well Harry?" Esma called, noticing that he had stopped. "OK. Needed a rest," he called down. She could see he was nearly at the top. He started climbing again and was soon scrambling onto level ground where there were giant growths and alien jungle-like outcrops of undergrowth and scrub.

Harry viewed the others, gave them a wave and began to look for signs of artificial equipment amongst the undergrowth. As with the Hub in Leofwin's Hundred, he was looking for an antenna, it purpose being to draw down into the electronics of the Switch, radiant energy in the form of positively charged particles held in the atmosphere of this negatively charged planet.

Harry hunted around the area directly above the doorway below, looking for a tower which had been used as an antenna.

There was no such evidence. His mind searched the possibilities. Would the antenna have to be a tower? Maybe not. What if it were a flat array? He bent down and scrabbled his hands amongst the low-lying undergrowth. Luckily it was soft vegetative material. No thorns and thistles. It was then that he noticed a straight, unnatural-looking item. With a cry of excitement, he pulled more of the undergrowth away, exposing a large-diameter cable.

Harry shielded his eyes and gazed toward the horizon in the direction the cable was laid and there, almost hidden in the mist of distance, was an immensely tall tower.

He traced the cable to the area above the Switch at ground level, searching for where it connected to a cable supplying radiant energy to the circuitry below. Scraping away more debris, he found a broken connection. Harry noticed a rock lying close by that had caused the damage. Maybe, he thought, the recent cyclone was responsible.

Harry wondered how he could safely join them again. Looking at the vicinity of the two cables he could see the occasional spark flashing between the two parts of the joint. As they were separated by a distance of about eighteen inches it proved high tension current was still present, so he had to be extra careful. He had no tools to lever the cable back into place so he stood and looked around. A dead branch would suffice to insulate him from the current.

Harry walked away from the cliff edge, making careful note of the topography of the land in relation to the position of the sun to make sure he remembered where the cables were. Much of the tree and plant-like life on the plateau over which he walked appeared to have suffered storm-damage, *A good sign,* he thought, *There should be what I need here,* and five minutes later he found a roughly formed, but fairly straight rod-like branch. The material appeared to be hard to the touch and would be robust enough to stand a good amount of leverage.

Harry retraced his steps and was soon back at the place where he needed to repair the cable. He peered over the edge of the cliff and shouted to those below.

He saw Villiers hold his hand to his ear so he shouted again, "I'm going to reconnect the Switch, stand back," and he saw them move away. Villiers indicated for the other two to move back further, away from the lethal potential of high tension current.

Harry stuck the roughly shaped pole behind the fractured joint and, with both hands, used it to drag the twisted cable straight. It sparked violently as it neared the other part of the joint until, when it was in contact, it ceased flashing and crackling.

It was then that Harry noticed, on the underside of the joint he had shifted, that the was a round projection, and a hole on the other part of the joint that corresponded. They were obviously intended to fit together securely. He attempted to poke the pole under the cable he moved and, with some careful lifting and positioning, he managed to drop the one part of the joint into the other.

He heard faint shouting from below and went to the edge to hear what was they were saying. Villiers and Martell were jumping up and down as if they had scored a championship goal. Esma was standing clear of them, laughing at the sight.

Harry levered the heavy rock that had caused the damage over the joint to secure it in position, went to the cliff edge and cautiously began to make his way down. He knew that the climb down would be more difficult than the upward one, and being extra careful with his footing he made it safely to the bottom.

Esma hugged him and the others, vigorously pumped his hands,

"Look," Villiers said, pointing to the electronics. "The crystals have come alive." Harry glanced at the circuitry, where the crystals were vibrant with the inner fire, now so familiar. Harry picked up the cover and snapped it back into place.

52

Camp-beds and other gear had been transported into Villiers' laboratory and set up with screens for privacy. Oscar, Clive Fraser, Jules and Bill Templestone settled in for an indeterminate but, they hoped, a short wait.

* * *

Dearden paired up with Mitch Doughty, and with Tomahawk they headed into Leofwin's Hundred to search the unexplored region beyond Shadow Brook waterfall. Cell One had split into groups of two, each pair having a portion of unexplored forest to search. Will Pierpoint, feeling his age, had remained at Dearden Hall, along with Rowan and Anton Beggs.

"I'll ride shotgun this time," Pierpoint called to Bill Templestone as he headed off to MoD Kineton with Oscar, Jules and Clive Fraser. Jules' Grand Cherokee was packed with gear they needed for the stay in Villiers' lab.

Doughty led the way down into the valley, taking the path between the Shadow Brook waterfall, and the cave behind it. The path continued on up the other side of the valley. It was steep, strewn with boulders which made the going hard and when they reached the top, they stood for a few minutes to catch their breath.

The path split in two. "I suggest we stick together," Dearden said. "Could be a good idea to take the most used path. Who knows, it could be more than a badger-trail."

They walked on along the path, which narrowed at times forcing Doughty, in the lead, to use his machete. Some half hour later, they came to a sunlit glade surrounded by trees which were festooned with lichen. Moss was growing on the trunks and branches and, most noticeably, in this place there was no birdsong. The occasional breeze teased the lichen, making it move gently, as if in slow motion.

Doughty looked around. He had the strangest feeling that in this place time stood still. He couldn't explain it when they were back at Dearden Hall afterwards. It was one of those events that occurred occasionally, once maybe, in a long span of years, when his senses were heightened, more receptive to outside influence than they were normally.

"Feel that, Jem?" he asked.

"This place, you mean?"

"Yeah . . . it's different."

"I know what you mean. It's older . . . maybe it's the heart of the forest, do you think?

"I don't know. But it's special. And look at the shape of that outcrop of rock in the middle. I looks . . . structured."

Tomahawk began to inch forward stealthily, his ears erect. He made a low sound in his throat, not an angry wolfish sound, more like a sound of curiosity. He pulled gently, insistently on the leash. Dearden unhooked it and the wolf crept slowly toward the great mass of rock and when he reached it he disappeared behind it.

Doughty glanced at Dearden. "Looks as though Tom's been here before," he whispered, as if not to disturb the quiet of the place.

"I don't let him roam the forest. The only time he could have come here was when he went missing a few weeks back, remember?"

They hurried to catch up with Tomahawk. Reaching the back of the outcrop they saw the wolf going down some stone steps. Dearden, at that point recalled the conversation he had with Lan-Si-Nu where he was told of the dire threat that could be looming ahead. *There could be catastrophic consequences due to the Earth people who have breached the Toraddon Buffer,* the alien told them.

The enormity of the situation struck home. For Dearden, the threat to existence disturbed the peace of the woodland glade. And now here they were following a wolf in the forest. It didn't make sense . . . or did it? For Tomahawk the Hunter was doing what he did best, seek and find. He was on the trail. Dearden looked down the steps. Doughty came up behind, gazed down too.

The eight steps led into a subterranean room. It was spacious, the floor grassy, the walls faintly illuminated. Dearden followed Tomahawk, stepped onto the grass, felt the room was pleasantly warm. Doughty placed his hand near the wall and realised that the wall was the source of heat and light. "This place is temperature controlled," he said.

Tomahawk's attention focussed on the grassy floor to the left and he crept cautiously over to it. Sniffed it. The wolf's action was unlike any previous performance, so Dearden was curious and he stepped across to see what the attraction was. He saw a long indentation, where the grass was crushed flat and moving rhythmically. "Mitch, get this," he whispered to Doughty, who was studying the wall closely.

Dearden pointed to the area and Doughty frowned, bent down and attempted to touch the grass at one end of the indentation but his hand touched something warm and solid a few inches above the grass.

"Jem, feel this, just here . . . be careful."

Dearden gently touched where Mitch Doughty pointed. What he felt was unmistakable. It was hair and the top of someone's head. "We've done it Mitch. Tomahawk's led us to the person Piper's been grieving over."

"And she's alive."

"And invisible. Let's dampen the air so we can see her."

"Maybe later"

The grassy indentation moved and became half as long. Dearden and Doughty moved back to give the individual some space but Tomahawk got closer to the source of movement. His head moved slightly and then his ears, as the invisible Luminant made a fuss of him.

"Are you OK?" Dearden didn't know what to say, but he thought that was a good start. The individual stood up, which was obvious because the only indentations that remained in the grass were the impressions of two feet. Not large ones. He was familiar with the size of shoe that Rowan wore . . . size 6 and the indents in the grass looked a similar size. The foot shapes turned to face him and the person spoke.

*   *   *

Tomahawk knew the trail through the forest. It was imprinted onto his memory from the time he ran like the wind through the forest, chasing the one similar to the Dearden Food-beast. As he entered the sun-warm space, strong Home and Mother thoughts returned and so too did the desire for the company of the One who was nearby.

The Dearden Food-beast released the restraint around his neck and he moved forward . . . once again he was free. Up ahead the smell pulled him. And then he was close to the beast and he savoured her company. She gently touched his head and his ears in a way that gave him warmth and comfort.

*   *   *

346

When Dearden asked the Luminant if she was OK she was still drowsy. It had been a shallow sleep this time, not like some of the sleeps of yesteryear when peace and tranquillity reigned throughout the Realities. She was needed more often these days with the advancement of technical expertise achieved by many of the races yet created. And this was so particularly since the people from planet Earth found a way to circumvent the Toraddon buffer and cross the Reality barrier freely.

Oh, how she longed to re-join her soul-mate. She missed his closeness. He was the one who had brought great meaning to her life . . . made it complete.

"Are you OK?" He had asked. She enjoyed his language because it was full of finest nuances of meaning, so she responded in his tongue.

"Thank you, I am OK," she said. Dearden detected a familiarity in the sound of her voice. It was strange, hearing words spoken from a person that appeared, on the face of things, to be non-existent.

"Is there anything we can do to help?"

"I just need time for my mind to awake fully, then I'll be ready for action." Dearden thought she seemed a bit like Julia Linden-Barthorpe. Full of fight when it was needed.

"What's your name?" Mitch Doughty asked. He too had recognised her voice.

"Can you help us to see you?" Dearden interrupted.

"Tomahawk the Hunter can see me. His eyes are different to yours—but moisture will make me visible to your eyes. It's a temporary fix."

"There is a pool and waterfall in the forest. Would that be any good?" Dearden and Doughty weren't aware of her smile . . . but the pool and the waterfall suggestion brought back delicious memories . . . of the time when two of them swam together on a summer's day. "Yes, we'll go there," she sounded enthusiastic.

"How about your name . . . and there's something about your voice, I recognise it."

"My name? You will be surprised. I am the Guardian of the Forest, and the Guardian of places much further afield too," she said. "Places that would surprise your imagination, Jem."

"You know my name?"

"I do. You knew me in a different time. I am Guennean . . . remember? I am from the dark hills of Ceredigion, and I became Countess Aelfryth of Mercia."

"I don't get this. You were Leofwin's wife, over a thousand years back." Doughty tried to rationalise what she was telling them. It made no sense, but he recognised her voice for sure.

"Our lives touched for a little while and I loved Leofwin so much. My occasional presence on the Earth is part of the greater scheme of things."

"But your children . . . what were their names?" Dearden tried to remember.

"Ingwulf and Blythe. They were not my children. Human and our Luminant genes will not intermingle."

"So, you are the one the Piper is looking for?" Mitch Doughty asked.

"I am. I must go to him. We have been apart far too long. Show me the way to the pool." Dearden felt her brush by him as she made for the exit with Tomahawk following.

"Wait," he said to her. "What shall we call you?"

"The same as before, Aelfryth, but not Countess."

* * *

348

When she stepped, soaking wet from the pool Aelfryth was visible to Dearden and Doughty. They recognised her features. Her clothing was radically different from the attire of the eleventh century noblewoman, as she was when they saw her previously. Tomahawk went to her and she touched his head, fondled his ears.

"We call the person you are very close to Piper. He helped the children from—"

"—Hamelin," she interrupted Dearden. "That was a difficult time."

"You were with him?"

"No, I was on a different mission at the time, but all we Luminants know about that rescue mission. But please, we must go."

"Wait . . . we are desperate for Piper's help . . . and yours of course," Dearden called.

"I know there's a problem. You'll have our help as soon as we're together. We work well as a team."

"Some of our friends are missing. The Wasiri-Chanchiya told us they have caused a severe Reality imbalance. Things are getting desperate." Aelfryth stopped and turned to face Dearden.

"A minor imbalance did occur some sixty of your years ago. What have the Wasiri told you?" The water was drying off and parts of her were becoming invisible again.

"I'll do my best to explain, but look, you're disappearing again. You'll have to do the same as Piper," Dearden said. "He had his metabolism changed so we can see him."

"Alright, I'll do that." Dearden and Doughty felt a rushing breeze go by them and all evidence of Aelfryth's presence vanished. They looked at each other and walked on. Dearden noticed, behind them from where they had walked, that fungus was quickly growing from the forest soil, as if on a time-lapse video.

"I really hope she'll get back quick," Dearden looked worried.

"Me too. If what Lan-Si-Nu and Aelfryth told us is true, once she and the Piper get together rescue out of this situation might be possible." A great bolt of lightning flashed out of the darkness and struck a nearby elm tree.

"This is getting too close for comfort," Dearden was partially deafened and he had to shout to make himself heard above the tempestuous wind. "I don't like this darkness, Mitch, it's unnatural."

" I know. It's not of this Dimension, I'm thinking."

53

It was when Harry had replaced the panel covering the electronics in the cliff-face that Esma's acute hearing picked up a faint noise. It startled her because she recognised the sound. She turned to look, wishing she was mistaken. Filling the distant sky, a great swathe of darkness, blacker than night, was gathering on the horizon.

"Harry," Esma gasped and when he turned to see if she was OK he saw the threat. Immense sheets of lightning were piercing the wild darkness.

"Oh hell," Dick Martell looked too. Was going to say more than *Oh hell,* but his throat felt constricted. He looked at the door that led into . . . into, "Where the hell does this go?" he managed to say, and then he shoved the door fiercely. It opened again onto blackness this time. No myriad of stars now, just blackness which matched the encroaching doom.

"It's too far to get to the place we sheltered before, Harry," Villiers was trying to think the horizon-event through, to get a solution but his thinking faculties wouldn't work. "This damn place," was all he could get out. He kept repeating those same three words.

Esma ran up to Harry, her eyes wide with fear and he held her tight. He loved her so much and he was the cause of this . . . his inquisitiveness had got them into this mess. If only he could peel back time.

Harry's compulsive mode kicked in. Strange how it did this. It always happened in the hour of need. For some reason he never got stressed out. He would start counting his paces. It was as if his mind would slip into another dimension where his faculties became heightened and he could work things out with ultimate precision. It was how he got the Hub in Leofwin's Hundred working again . . . and was awarded the accolade of Hnirath of Science by the Wasiri-Chanchiyans.

"Harry," he heard the unmistakable voice of Oscar deep inside himself.

"What is it Oscar, I'm busy right now." he said the words out loud and the others looked at him. Dick Martell thought Harry had flipped but he had no idea about sibling communication. Never even heard of it. And Esma hadn't noticed what Harry said. She was looking elsewhere.

"Feldswamas, look," she said, pointing to the ground, where fungus was forming by the door into the cliff-face.

*　*　*

In Professor Charles Villiers' lab Oscar, Clive, Jules and Bill Templestone settled in for an indeterminate stay. They had camp beds arranged with screens between them and had organised themselves into a six-hour shift system to observe the Switch and to open its door every hour to see what was visible. They had no idea how soon things would warm up.

It was Oscar's turn for a shift. "How long will it be before we see daylight again?" he said to Templestone.

"No idea. Maybe we ought to organise a shift system to o we can get some daylight," Templestone suggested.

Oscar was comfortable in the padded chair transported from Dearden Hall. He opened his book and by torchlight he began to read. After a while he looked up, turned around, thinking he felt Harry's presence. It was as if his kid brother was in the same room as him. It was odd, this sibling awareness thing that occurred at unexpected moments. It was never predictable but when it did occur it seemed so natural and it was almost a physical occurrence this time.

They had talked about this of course. During one winter's evening when the moon was full and the stars were bright they discussed this unique form of communication at length. Harry had put the cover over his telescope, the Newtonian reflector, after a couple of hours surveying the cosmos. Their minds were still focussed on the immensity of distance and the magnificence of The Double Cluster and they were cold. Frost was forming on the grass, and the fire in the living-room, and the red wine beckoned.

* * *

Here it was again, that wonderfully intense sibling connection feeling. Oscar wondered how it actually occurred. What could be the physics that enabled the link to happen. Of necessity he shrugged it off. It was fifteen hundred hours. Time to check the Switch. He bookmarked his page, stood and unlatched the door. Pushed it open . . . onto a world almost of make-believe.

He reeled back in surprise. It was one of those moments when the totally unexpected occurs. What he expected to see on opening the Switch door was the usual view of the cosmos, beautiful but in a way austere in its loneliness. Here was a place in total opposition to loneliness because there were creatures of many different species obviously at play in a setting that looked paradisaic.

Oscar let out a yell for the others to *Get here quick*. They did. The Switch door was still open and the four of them gazed in wonder, enthralled at what they were seeing.

Jules' mobile rang. It was Jem. He sounded stressed.

"Things are bad Jules,"

"How come?"

Take a look outside. We think it's what La-Si-Nu warned us about. The Reality imbalance is causing mayhem. This is really bad," he emphasised. "Get back to Dearden Hall, things are getting dangerous outside. Jules, get back here quick and be prepared for a surprise." He rang off.

When they got outside R1 they saw what Dearden warned them about. Head of MoD Kineton, Mike Ramsay had met them coming out of the tunnel to Villiers' lab and when they exited R1 they saw why Dearden called them urgently. It was evening, seven forty-five, and the surroundings were unnaturally dark for the time of day, lightning was rampant.

"Not much anyone can do about this," Ramsay said, and he told them that the weather conditions were wild and unusual worldwide. "Global warming's got nothing on this." He tugged his coat around him as the fierce wind pummelled them. "I've sent the lads home, it's pointless them staying here," he shouted to be heard. "The weaponry that was here has been destroyed. This place is historic now."

"Could be a sensible idea to come to Dearden Hall with us," Jules suggested to Ramsay.

"I might as well."

"Find a girl and get hitched," Templestone advised,

"While there's still time, you mean? Obviously, you haven't heard the news over the past twenty-four hours. The climate pundits don't know what's going on. They're talking about the Doomsday Clock, that it's half a second to midnight."

Clive Fraser grabbed Jules' hand. The five of them piled into her Jeep Grand Cherokee and she floored the pedal.

54

"So, what's the surprise," Jules asked, as the five from R1 came into the great hall. The rest of Cell One were seated around Leofwin's banqueting table in serious discussion. And then the surprise became obvious. Seated next to Rowan was a dark-haired woman who Jules thought she recognised. For a few seconds she was lost for words as she tried to recall who the woman was and then she remembered.

"What the hell are you doing here?" she asked.

Aelfryth raised a hand in acknowledgment. "Hello Julia, you will find out why I'm here shortly." Dearden, at the head of the table, introduced Mike Ramsay to the group and indicated the empty chairs for him and the others from MoD Kineton. Dearden briefly explained to Cell One how Tomahawk had led him and Mitch Doughty to where Aelfryth had been sleeping.

Aelfryth, dressed in Jeans and a colourful top belonging to Rowan, stood. Cell One focussed on her. "It was Tomahawk the Hunter who brought me out of sleep," she said. "He is attuned to we Luminants." Tomahawk was sitting close by her side. Her hand was resting on him.

"My friends," Red Cloud, looking resplendent in the war bonnet of a Lakota Sioux chief, stood. He wore his regalia when events were likely to warm up. He walked around the table to Aelfryth. stood close-by. "Tomahawk Shahn of Offchurch is special. He senses things we can only faintly perceive. He could see you, Aelfryth, with his wolf eyes."

"I was invisible to your Earth-eyes," Aelfryth explained to Cell One. "I took Jem's advice and had my metabolism changed. Under the present circumstances it's best you can see me." Aelfryth moved around the table, stopping by each of Cell One to ask their name. She greeted those she had met previously in Anglo-Saxon times with a smile.

"I must go with Tomahawk the Hunter," she said. "This mission is vitally important. Two realities depend on our actions. If we fail, our own Prime Reality and Reality Four Hundred and Seventy face extinction. I need to go to where all of this problem started . . . to Professor Charles Villiers' laboratory. Some of the famous SHaFT organisation must come with me as back-up."

They all wanted to go, every one of them. It was soon determined that the ones to help Aelfryth would be Oscar and Jules, the scientists, accompanied by Jem Dearden and Mitch Doughty, considered the most suitable SHaFT operatives, and Trent Jackson the linguist.

"This is it. Darkness descends." Jackson murmured. "Carpe Diem, Seize the Day." He walked to the floor to ceiling window facing the ancient forest, Leofwin's Hundred, which was lit constantly by lightning.

"We must do that, buddy, seize the day tight and hold on with a grip as strong as steel, otherwise it's finito," said Lee Wynter, looking at the others. The atmosphere in the great hall was serious, the weather outside furious, with wind howling through the gargoyles in the eaves and great claps of thunder rattling the doors and windows.

"We have to go now,' Aelfryth headed for the door out the great hall just as Lan-Si-Nu and his two crew members were heading in. They stooped through the door-frame.

"We're here to help if we can," Temporal Engineer, Thal-Nar said. "Our own Reality and Reality Four Hundred and Seventy are under severe stress. The chaos going on outside this building is occurring throughout the two realities and it is getting progressively worse. There is a great harmony that binds all of the Realities together and it has been distorted. Every world and every life-force in these two dimensions will implode if the balance between them isn't restored."

There was silence as the words sunk in.

"It is good you are here" Lan-Si-Nu addressed Aelfryth using her real name, which Trent Jackson tried, with difficulty, to analyse.

"Your trans Reality expertise will help," Fen-Nu interjected. "We are trying to locate your Other Self for you to work together. We have no idea where he is."

"Tomahawk the Hunter will help find him." She looked the wolf straight in the eye and they connected on a subliminal level. Then she got close to Dearden and spoke quietly. "We will see you in R1. Don't worry, Jem. Tomahawk will be fine with me."

Sir Will Pierpoint went to Aelfryth as she was heading out the door with the wolf. "We ought to bring all Cell One along. There's more brain-power in numbers and between them these guys have many skills. They could be useful."

"Do it," said Aelfryth, and then she and Tomahawk Shahn of Offchurch left the great hall.

"And we others will use the Hub in Spatial Transfer mode to get to Villiers' Laboratory. It is instant and time is critical," said Temporal Engineer Thal-Nar. "Have a few minutes to get suitable clothing. The Hub is waiting and locked-on to the lab's position."

Gil Heskin opened the door for them and, with grim determination, the Cell One SHaFT team and Lan-Si-Nu and his crew stepped into the maelstrom of weather. The three aliens ran into the forest faster than Dearden had seen previously and then, when Cell One were halfway to the vehicles Dearden stopped, told Rowan to get in the vehicle with Jules, and ran back to the house. In the entrance hall he called for Gil and Frieda Heskin. They looked pale and agitated. "The news is bad Jem. There's no television now and the only radio station I can get says it'll shut down in an hour. What's happening?"

" You've got to come with us, I'll explain on the way."

"I'll get my bag." Frieda rushed through to their rooms and Gil followed. "Hurry," Dearden called after them. "Get coats and waterproof shoes."

*   *   *

"Get prepared for transfer," Thal-Nar's voice came over the speakers to Cell One, gathered in the topmost room of the Hub, known as the Portal.

"Don't worry about the transfer . . . it's straightforward," Dearden reassured those new to the alien technology. The sound of a relay cut in with a heavy clunking sound and a cushioned feeling surrounded each of the them when the transfer began.

"I wonder if they are still using the Co-Orditrax?" Oscar recalled how he designed the equipment at Ranstad-Nanotech, enabling the extremely accurate determination in three dimensions of a homing target for spatial transfer.

And then they were in a different location, Villiers' laboratory. The electric lights were still on, and the camp beds still arranged just as Oscar and the three with him had left them when Jem told them to get back to Dearden Hall.

Only a few seconds after their arrival in the lab Lan-Si-Nu arrived over the Spatial Transfer System. It was strange for the others in the laboratory to see him arrive. A light appeared in an area away from the Cell One group, as if the transfer system's spatial awareness mathematics determined a position where there would be no collision between the one arriving and those already there. Lan was on his own.

"It is getting really bad on the surface," he said. "Darkness has come upon the Earth and it is planet-wide. There is great disturbance of the atmosphere. No stars can be seen and the wind is cyclonic."

Oscar and Jules had been discussing the situation. Analysing the possibilities. They devised a plan to get near the Switch. At least they could be ready to act at a moment's notice if needed. Then all of them in the subterranean laboratory felt the ground tremble.

"I fear the end is close," Lan-Si-Nu said, as the whole place trembled.

There was a noise from the room at the far end of the laboratory in which lay the Switch and the Gothic shaped door swung open, revealing Aelfryth and Tomahawk Shahn of Offchurch.

55

It had quickly grown so dark that Harry could hardly see the door into the cliff and the atmospheric disturbance had become almost overpowering in its intensity. The ground shook again under his feet.

"Harry!" Oscar's voice was there again. "Can you hear that, Esma?" he asked her. She was standing close to him, feeling safe . . . Harry would protect her, after all, he was a Hnirath of Science.

"What is you hear?" Her modern English was slightly askew again, but he loved her for it.

"I'm hearing Oscar's voice, Esma." The Prof and Dick Martell had come close and they heard what Harry said about his brother. Villiers had started to have doubts about Harry. The young man for whom he had the highest respect was now losing it.

"Harry. Get ready." It was unmistakably Oscar's voice he could hear. "The Switch is cyclic again."

A tremendous thunderclap startled Harry and caused Martell to utter Anglo-Saxon profanities that Esma said she recognised. Harry grinned. He knelt down. Felt the fungus . . . even felt it growing. He thought it was significant that the fruiting bodies of the mycelial network were growing so rapidly, that there could only be one reason for it, when a voice spoke out of the darkness a few feet behind them.

"I'm back," the voice said. To which there were more profanities from Martell, and Villiers this time, because both of them were really rattled by the voice coming out of the darkness.

"See that crystal over there," Piper said. "Give it to me quickly, the Mycorrhizal Network beckons." The crystal Harry had pared from the larger one was lying on the ground and it was alive with fiery internal movement. Harry stepped cautiously over to it, feeling his way because of the darkness. The Piper was visible and Harry saw his vague shape in the light coming from the crystal. Harry picked it up and took it to him.

Harry, Esma, Professor Villiers and Richard Martell saw the Piper clearly. He looked radiant as he linked to the force within the crystal. He carried it to the door into the cliff-face and, as he got close to it, the door swung open. Piper placed the crystal by the door to keep it open. The light inside the cliff was bright and welcoming and coming toward them silhouetted by the brightness were two figures. One of them was tall and beautiful and the other was half the height of the other but he was attractive in his own wild way.

Tomahawk Shahn of Offchurch howled in a fashion that caused the hairs to rise on the back of Harry's neck. Esma ran to Aelfryth, recognising her from Leofwin's time and they held each other tight for a second or so. Aelfryth glanced up and saw the features of the Luminant she would love throughout all of time flowing into eternity, and she ran into his arms.

Their greeting was brief.

The ground shook once again and some of the cliff-face sheered, a great mass of it falling some twenty yards away.

"Be quick, get through the door now," Piper shouted, and they ran like the wind that shrieked fiercely around them. Piper was last through the door and as he slammed it shut they looked ahead to see where they were going.

The normally stern and academic Professor Charles Villiers recognised it all. The Romano-Celtic mosaic on the floor and the Gothic door ahead. There were people about. He was used to people being about because he was a teacher. He didn't recognise them, but what the hell, for beyond the people and beyond the door, he could see his old desk. He let out a wild whoop of joy as he ran into his laboratory.

He went to his desk and, tentatively opened the bottom right-hand drawer. He shifted some papers and lying under them, just where he had left them, were two bar magnets. The bar magnets were painted an exciting bright red, apart from a quarter-inch of shiny metal at the north ends, which were stamped with a capital N. The red was a hot colour, not a dull nondescript red, but a brilliant flame-red, appropriate for the hidden forces lying within. *Like poles repel, unlike poles attract*, he remembered reading, all those years ago, in the Encyclopaedia Britannica. He let out a great sigh and closed the drawer.

Harry and Esma, Charles Villiers and Dick Martell and all the others underground in Repository One couldn't see the events taking place throughout the Prime Reality and Reality Four Hundred and Seventy.

What was happening up above and throughout the Cosmos they had accessed using the Grid, was a new day dawning. The darkness rolled away and the Realities faced a bright, fresh beginning.

56

With the return of Harry, Esma, Villiers and Martell to the Earth the harmony between the Realities was restored. The threat of an Inter-reality implosion was averted and there was great rejoicing at Dearden Hall. In other places both near, in galactic terms, and in the other affected Reality, far beyond the mind of humankind, there was great rejoicing too.

No-one else on Earth, apart from SHaFT and the denizens of the Hub was aware how close the two Realities, the Prime and Four Hundred and Seventy, came to annihilation. And not many knew who the people were who had saved the day.

All of SHaFT were at Dearden Hall, all the cells, and the old place was big enough to accommodate the revellers. New friends were made and old friendships restored. Bill Templestone had returned the guardianship of the Knight's Sanctuary to Richard Martell and he moved back into the apartment above the stained glass studio in the courtyard at Dearden Hall.

It was remarkable how Professor Charles Villiers and Dick Martell hadn't aged during their long marooning on planet KV280 63482/5. "One of the few positive things that have happened, or should I say, haven't happened on that planet, is our ageing," Villiers said to Sir Willoughby Pierpoint. They had soon become friends and were sitting in a small group away from the others. Oscar and Harry were there too, in the small group, which was inclined toward science. Julia Linden-Barthorpe was there too, along with Clive Fraser.

"What will you do now, Charles?" Jules asked the professor.

"Go to the seaside for a spell, maybe to Weymouth."

"Weymouth has changed since Nibiru, Prof. The sea has gone inland there by about half a mile. A lot of the sea front buildings have gone and Radipole Lake is part of the sea now." Jules recalled the trip to Portland, looking for Oscar.

"How about your laboratory, Professor Villiers, will you continue your research?" Oscar Stanway asked. Villiers looked embarrassed.

"It was me who caused that awful situation, I may close the damn place down. It's too much of a liability."

"How would it be if you put the place in mothballs for a while, give yourself some space." Jules suggested. She realised her choice of words, *Give yourself some space* were not the best. Villiers was heartily sick of *space*. She added, "We scientists could probably work together and there is so much potential. Think of the places we could visit and, by all accounts, the mode of Trans-Reality transport you stumbled upon does away with the Toraddon Buffer."

"I don't know, Jules. I'll take the holiday first . . . but, I must admit, we together," his hand indicated the others in their small group, "Could achieve a great deal."

"But we must take a lesson from our recent experience and avoid impetuous action," Harry warned. "I was partly to blame for what happened. I went through your Switch without thinking of the possible consequences."

* * *

The old house had returned to a measure of normality. The SHaFT Cells had left and quiet had descended upon the ancient building and the two people whose house it was for the duration of their tenure.

Rowan of Maldon stood up from the sofa, stepped back a

couple of paces and appraised Dearden. She saw the same man that she had fallen in love with at first sight back in Anglo-Saxon times.

"I love you, Jeremiah de Arden," she said, recalling the Norman-French pronunciation of his family name.

"And I love you, Lady Rowan of Maldon . . . more than you love me." She knelt in front of him, and playfully punched him on the shoulder.

"No, I love you more," she said, and climbed up close to him. "I love you . . . more than all the stars in heaven, Jem Dearden." She stood and walked over to the floor-to-ceiling window facing the forest, Leofwin's Hundred, where it all began, and she lifted her eyes to the sky. Dusk was falling and the stars of the Milky Way were glowing brightly. She felt a movement at her side, touching her thigh. She looked down at Tomahawk, who had seen movement amongst the trees.

Where will we go next, Jem?" she asked.

He put his arm around her. "Where would you like to go? You choose."

The End

J.J. Overton,
Coventry,
England.

Well, readers, is this the end of The Grid Saga? Will Jem Dearden and Rowan of Maldon slip quietly into their twilight years? I wonder, after their experiences so far, brought about by that wild forest called Leofwin's Hundred, if they would really allow that to happen.

The wolf, Tomahawk pesters them regularly for an outing into the forest . . . and they feel compelled to go. On the odd occasion that they detect movement up ahead their curiosity is tweaked as to what it may be. They rarely see Lan-Si-Nu or any of the inhabitants of The Hub, or the travellers who use it these days, and when the movement amongst the trees does occur, it makes Tomahawk restless and attentive.

The forest is such an old place. So much has occured in its confines and so many people we have become acquainted with have trod its ancient pathways. Bill Templestone, Mitch Doughty, Julia Linden-Barthorpe, Harry Stanway and his girl, Esma. Sir Willoughby Pierpoint as well . . . in fact the whole of the SHaFT team.

Something tells me that they may show up again. We'll see. In the meantime, I'm just going for a walk in the forest, Come on, Tomahawk, your leash awaits . . .

John James Overton

Printed in Great Britain
by Amazon